I0621949

NEVER SAY JUST

By

KATIE HARPER

ᚼ

Decadent Publishing Company
www.decadentpublishing.com

This book is a work of fiction. Names, characters, places, and incidents are the products of the author's imagination or used fictitiously. Any resemblance to actual events, locales or persons, living or dead, is entirely coincidental.

Never Say Just
Copyright 2012 by Katie Harper
ISBN: 978-1-61333-409-6
Cover design by Fantasia Frog and Cribley Designs

All rights reserved. Except for use in any review, the reproduction or utilization of this work, in whole or in part, in any form by any electronic, mechanical or other means now known or hereafter invented, is forbidden without the written permission of the publisher.

Published by Decadent Publishing Company
www.decadentpublishing.com

Printed in the United States of America

Chapter One

I am a cow. Just paint block spots on me and teach me to moo because it's official. I'm a Holstein. There were at least five hundred head of cattle crammed into a pen decorated with vomit-colored industrial carpet and covered in Tag Heuer and Kay Jewelers advertisements. Just as I felt a long, melodious, and forlorn *moo* creep up my throat, the screen above the cattle yard changed from "On Time" to "Arrived." Halle-freaking-lujah! My brother's plane had landed and my barnyard hell would be over.

After eighteen months he would finally be home. Any moment he would ride down the escalator and I'd be able to hug him and make sure he'd returned home, healthy, and in one piece. Bouncing on the balls of my feet, I tried to see over the head of the Andre the Giant wannabe in front of me. I threw an elbow when a man with questionable fashion sense and way too much aftershave got too close. When I felt the unmistakable piercing of a cheap kitten-heel pump on the top of my foot, I very nearly spit cud at a woman who'd clearly eaten New Orleans's share of fried Twinkies while waiting for her Internet love match to arrive.

The TSA sponsored bestial torture could be worse. Remember when you could practically walk right up to the plane, shake the pilot's hand, and ask the flight attendants for a rum and Coke? When people crowded in front of the arrivals terminal as if they were the oldest group of single bridesmaids on the planet and the bride was about to throw the bouquet? After 9/11 they expected the family members, friends, and would-be terrorists to stand in the baggage area and wait for their passengers like civilized people.

I waited in the cattle chute from hell for my older brother, Tyler Wallace. Tyler was my hero. When the call to war resonated throughout our country, he left behind a full ride scholarship to Stanford to join the Marine Corps. Everyone thought he had gone nuts. In my opinion, he was definitely somewhere between a macadamia and a pecan, but he didn't care. He wanted to serve his country as our father and grandfather and great-grandfather and great-great.... Well, you get the idea. My brother was probably the smartest person to be accepted to every Ivy League university in the country. If he ever went on "Who Wants to be a Millionaire," he could answer all the questions correctly, use zero life lines, and walk off with the million dollar novelty check before the first commercial break.

Middle Eastern languages had been a hobby of his since the first Gulf War. He spoke fluent Arabic, Hebrew, Farsi, and Dari. He took his hobbies seriously. Staff Sergeant Wallace could have been an officer stationed in a nice, safe office with a view of a golf course or yacht club. To no one's astonishment he turned a life of leisure down and demanded his constitutional right to make stupid decisions and became a grunt.

He wanted to be in the trenches, or dunes, or whatever they're called in this war. And that is why I saw him roll toward me in a wheel chair instead of on two healthy legs. *Wait! A wheelchair? What is he doing in a wheel chair?* Yes, he'd been injured in an explosion, but I had no idea he wasn't ambulatory. I shouldered my way past the Jerseys, Guernseys, and Holsteins to get to him. Just as a TSA officer tried to rugby-tackle me to the ground and drag me off to some secret underground prison in the Louis Armstrong Airport, Tyler stood up, as if he'd been faith-healed, and walked toward me. As you can imagine, I was extremely relieved. I expressed how happy I felt to see him whole and healthy by throwing a punch aimed at his jaw, which he expertly blocked. After that nothing-but-love-hey-how-are-ya, I gripped Tyler in a fierce hug.

"What the hell?" I pointed to the empty wheel chair.

He pulled away from me. "What kind of big brother would I be if I didn't tease my little sister?"

Son of a bitch.

He pressed a light kiss to my forehead. "How've you been, kitten?"

Emotion didn't scare me. I didn't consider tears a sign of weakness or anything. They're just a waste of the Earth's finite water resources. But hearing the one and only person left on the planet who could call me kitten without getting five fisted digits to the solar plexus whisper in my ear almost made me tear up. As the storms cleared, I saw five lethal Marines behind my brother. They just stood there, obviously uncomfortable, waiting for something.

I wanted to find the inconsiderate jerks who'd leave their country's warriors to fend for themselves when Tyler released me and turned to face his brothers in khaki. He kept an arm around my shoulders and said, "Martinez, Switch, Doc, Horndog, Shooter, this is my little sister, Kat Boudreaux."

They all nodded their heads slightly and said, "Ma'am," in unison.

"We were all in the same unit. I told them they could stay with us." He paused and cleared his throat. "For the summer."

Tyler tightened his grip on my shoulder, firmly rooting me to the vomit-colored industrial carpet. I didn't know what my face said, but it didn't say, "I'm so glad! Please come and stay in my home. You're always welcome." In fact, I'm almost positive it said, "WTF!"

My darling brother stood his ground under the intense heat of my glare. The laws of physiology stopped. Daggers, real live actual daggers shot from my eyes and embedded into my brother's neck. Okay, maybe that had been a hallucination, but my anger must have been tangible because my six-foot-four, two-hundred-eighty pound, big brother cowered under the stare of his five-foot-six, one-hundred-twenty pound little sister. His face resembled a lobster's after it had been pulled from the safety of the tank at the local Tail n' Claw. He knew he was about to be boiled alive and devoured.

"It's okay, isn't it?" As I'm about to say *hell no*, he hits me with, "They have nowhere else to go."

Great! Just freaking great! Tyler and I had been orphans for a while and even though our parents died when we were both technically adults, we were still a little lost. Tyler knew I couldn't turn someone away who had no family to go home to. He knew my weak spots and he'd exploited them. Bastard. It's not that I didn't have the room, I had acres of room. I didn't like strange people in my house. I didn't take in stray dogs or run an orphanage for abandoned kittens. I just wasn't that kind of girl.

They have nowhere else to go. The second those words crossed Tyler's lips they sent electricity into my cold, dead heart. I glared at him and then at Martinez, Switch, Doc, Horndog, and Shooter. Though their builds and stances resembled Spartan warriors that would have made Leonidas proud, they had matching expressions on their faces that looked like Cindy Lou Who asking the Grinch for a glass of milk. Not even the Grinch escaped the effects of Cindy Lou, so I didn't feel too badly when I slumped from my brother's grasp and pulled my cell phone from my bag.

"You better get down on your knees and thank God for the massive thunderstorm last night that forced me to bring the Escalade." I pushed buttons on my phone with the same force required to slam a hot rivet through iron. "We're on our way out, Gregory. All seven of us. Don't ask. You don't want to know."

My new contingent of Marines followed me to the baggage carousel. As we watched the luggage, I observed my little group of the few, the proud. The one Tyler had called Switch helped a blue-haired lady maneuver a suitcase the size of a steamer trunk onto a Handi-Cart. Doc sat on his haunches while he thumb-wrestled a young boy whose mother pulled a Buzz Lightyear suitcase from the parade of black Samsonite. Martinez gave directions to an Asian couple. Obviously the self-appointed guardian of the group, Shooter stood back with his arms folded over his huge chest. Horndog flirted with a group of sorority sisters. Guess that explained the name. While their actions didn't endear them to me, they did cause the permafrost that encased my heart to break a sweat. They reminded me of Tyler and myself, the lost boys. No family, except each other.

The big khaki duffels wormed their way up and out of the ejection ramp and on to the carousel. My Marines picked up their bags and hefted them onto their shoulders. As we walked to the curb, I saw them shoot each other wary glances. They most certainly didn't feel welcomed to the great city of New Orleans. And they definitely would not receive the red carpet treatment when we arrived at my home in Bayou Boudreaux. It wasn't my responsibility to make life any easier for them. They could blame Tyler for my less than Southern hospitality.

We emerged on the other side of the sliding doors and were instantly hit in the face by the trademark humidity of the Crescent City. My Marines staggered as if they'd received a physical blow. It took all the powers of heaven and hell to not turn around, point, and laugh. I guess going from an arid desert to a climate that allowed you to skinny dip in the open air could be a shock to the system. I led them to the curb where a black Escalade with dark tinted windows waited. Gregory had driven and maintained the Boudreaux family cars for years. He was part chauffer, part father figure. He got out of the driver's seat, rounded the car, opened the back, and offered the interlopers help with their bags. They all declined.

My home was sixty-three minutes from the New Orleans airport, and the entire sixty-three minutes were spent in absolute silence. The Escalade had been tricked out with DVD players, TVs, satellite, game consoles, and a mini fridge. Was that why they held their tongues? Nope, the lack of chatter could be attributed to the hostility rolling off my body. I turned to see the six Marines wedged into the back two benches. They reminded me of too many pickles crammed into a jar. That gave me a bit too much joy. It was wrong to be happy about their discomfort. But I was.

You must understand. I didn't hate these men. My gratitude for the sacrifices they'd made for their country ran deep, and at any other time it would have been an honor to be in their presence. But the fact was, I did not handle strangers well. Not very long ago, if a stranger knocked on my front door, I would have had a full blown panic attack. My vision would tunnel, my hands would sweat and tingle, I would hyperventilate and have a stab of fear not unlike what I imagine every big-breasted blonde in every horror movie ever made had when she ran up the stairs instead of out the front door. I didn't blame them for throwing me into a panic-induced tailspin. How could they have known what their presence would do? No, the fault rested squarely on the well-muscled shoulders of my brother. The man I had been absolutely beside myself with worry over was the one responsible for my level of stress. He knew my fears. He knew *why* I had these fears. He knew what his guests would do to me. But did he take five seconds to consider me before he invited Private Gump and his band of Bubbas to stay at my house? No, no he did not. And for that he would pay. Dearly.

Strangers and visitors hadn't always frightened me. Once upon a time my job required me to be cool and controlled at all times. Blending in literally meant life or death. I could have been an old woman in a bazaar or a young man on a dirt bike. Rolling with the punches and anticipating my opponents every move had been second nature. I had to know their thoughts before they did. My life literally depended on my ability to think on my feet and never let anyone know how terrified I was, not even myself. Over the years my skills had obviously cankered.

The sixty-three minute drive to my house took us through

the city, on the freeway, across highways, down country roads filled with potholes, and through bayou country until we reached my driveway. *My side dish to accompany my entrée of fear tonight will be a lovely steamed portion of apprehension on a bed of extreme anxiety.* My apprehension wasn't because my Marines would be forced to sleep in pup tents on my front lawn and battle gators for empty yard space. I was nervous because these Marines with nowhere else to go would be staying in the Boudreaux Plantation House, the largest private home in the South. Boudreaux House ranked number ten in the list of largest homes in the country—smaller than Whitehall in Palm Beach and larger than the White House in DC. These men, who had lived out of the back of a Humvee for the past eighteen months, would judge me based on the opulence of my home.

Boudreaux House wasn't the home I'd been raised in. I grew up in a brown brick rambler with one fully functioning bathroom in Oklahoma. I married the plantation house. Three years before, it had become mine. All fifty-two thousand square feet, sixteen bedrooms, twenty-two bathrooms, two gourmet kitchens, theater, ballroom, library, music room, conservatory, six galleries, seven staircases, eighteen other rooms that could be used for anything from a book club meeting to a state dinner, and staff quarters complete with the workforce necessary to clean all the previously mentioned space. The grounds were home to a natural lake, formal gardens, tennis courts, stables, assorted outbuildings, and a natatorium—which is just rich speak for a building that housed a swimming pool. My daughter and I lived there with seventeen staff members: maids, cooks, gardeners, guards, and a driver. Yup, seventeen people to take care of two. If I wasn't comfortable there, how were my "guests" supposed to feel at home?

As we pulled up to the gate and guard house, Jake, my head of security, craned his neck to peer into the Escalade. "Looks like you caught yourself 'bout half a dozen there, Ms. Kat. Five more than ya went out for. Not a bad day's fishin' if you ask me."

Biting back my retort, I said, "Yes, I definitely went over my limit."

He chuckled and pushed the button to let us in. In the past three years the people who lived with my daughter and I had become much closer than staff. They were closer than friends. They were family. And I took care of my family. I should have closed up most of the house, but that would eliminate the need for the majority of the select people on the planet I could stand to be around for more than three hours. I kept the estate running for them. They needed it. Some of them had been with the place since they were kids, their parents cleaning the floors and pruning the bushes before them. Others were raising their own children there. Sending them all an eviction notice would be cruel.

As we drove down my driveway, I pulled the visor down. Through the mirror I could see the expressions on my Marines' faces. Their reaction to my home would help me determine if the summer would be the Dante levels of hell I expected or the Rob Zombie horror fest I'd prepared for. The moment Boudreaux House came into view, I cataloged and analyzed their responses. Martinez raised an eyebrow and glanced at Switch who rolled his eyes. Doc's jaw disengaged and hit the floor of the Escalade. Horndog calculated how many bikini clad Southern belles he could keep in a place that big. Shooter had no expression. He kept his arms crossed over his chest, staring straight ahead. Tyler had spent a lot of time in my home and was no longer impressed. He sat directly behind me, asleep, drooling on my leather interior. The sweetness of payback warmed my soul.

As we stopped in front of the two sweeping sets of front steps that led into the antebellum palace, I placed my hand on Gregory's forearm and turned my gaze to my sweet, sleeping brother. Gregory knew me well enough to understand what my intentions were. I opened the front door, turned on the ball of my foot to face the back passenger door, and without warning, opened it, spilling my darling brother onto the pavement.

"Son of a—!" he yelled.

He jumped up, determined to kill the person who'd so rudely interrupted his Z's. He'd forgotten he no longer had to battle immature Marines for bed space and when he righted himself, he threw a punch. At me. His fist never made contact. Big Joe, my enormous gardener with a heart the size of Texas, appeared and caught Tyler's fist in the palm of his hand. Big Joe's mahogany paw tightened on my brother's clenched fist.

"I don' really care who ya be, Mr. Tyler. You throw a punch at my Miss Kat, and we's gonna have a problem."

I placed a calming hand on the big man's shoulder. "It's all right Joe. He'd never hurt me. I startled him is all."

He turned his molasses-colored eyes on me, read my face. Once he realized I had never been in any danger, he released my brother's injured hand. Big Joe had been born in the staff quarters of the house thirty-seven years before. His mother had been let go from a more "respectable" home in New Orleans when her employers discovered she was pregnant with the chauffer's baby. My mother-in-law took her in as a maid. Etienne and Madeleine Boudreaux insisted she stop working until six weeks after the birth. The baby came early. He had been so large that he got caught in the birth canal, deprived of oxygen. His mother lost a lot of blood bringing him into the world. She died during childbirth.

Etienne and Madeleine didn't send him to child services or pawn him off on a relative. They took care of him and raised him with their own son. When it came time to put him in school, a very uncompassionate school counselor told them Joe had severe learning disabilities. Etienne and Madeleine fought tooth and nail to keep him in school. Finally, they decided to hire a tutor and educate him at home. He never learned to read or write. But he loved the outdoors and became very close with the gardener. He taught Big Joe how to grow flowers and mow a lawn and how to prune a pecan tree and how to get rid of kudzu. He grew to be the best gardener in all of Louisiana. And years ago he had been ordered to look after me by someone who once meant everything to me. He took that job very seriously.

Five Marines peeled out of the Escalade. A smile crossed my face when I saw them practically fall on their asses. It looked like a herd of hippos crashing out of a clown car. Grace must not be part of military training. I left them to get their bags. They were big boys; they could handle themselves. Besides, if I didn't inform Edna Mae, my ancient housekeeper, about the impending horde, she'd kick my ass up one side and down the other.

I rushed through the big, white double doors and ran to the kitchen. Edna would be there. You could always find her in the kitchen even if she never had been, technically, the cook. I ran around two corners, down one set of stairs, through a long hallway, and crashed through swinging kitchen doors. When I skidded across the black-and-white tile floor, I caught myself on one of the free-standing stainless steel counters. The mansion had a gym, but the treadmills and stationary bikes were rarely used. Running the place gave me enough cardio, thank you very much. Edna jumped to her feet. Her steel grey hair didn't move from its bun even though she had been thrown into an obvious state of distress.

"Where's Lilly?" I asked.

"She's out back pickin' some herbs from the garden. Land sakes, child, what is goin' on? Is Derek fishing with dynamite again?" Edna always got to the point.

"My brother," I said through gritted teeth, "invited five of his Marine buddies to stay with us for the summer. I need five more rooms made up on the second floor, and I need to tell Lilly to make, like, ten times the amount of food then she normally makes. These guys must make the manager at the Golden Corral weep when they walk in. Tell her not to worry about the *etouffee*. We don't have time. Tell her to just boil the shrimp and crawfish. But we'll need lots of jambalaya. And don't worry about serving in the dining room. We'll eat in the back yard."

Edna nodded and went to work. I knew she'd have the

rooms ready before Hurricane *Semper Fi* made landfall upstairs. If that woman had been in charge of the Normandy invasion, we would have made it up the beach and into Germany in under a month. With washed and pressed uniforms.

I trekked back to the front of the house, the whole time thinking of ways to punish Tyler. He didn't know it yet, but it was so on. Where in that beautiful, brilliant brain of his did he come up with the idea that it would be super great to invite five strangers to stay in my house for the summer? Not for a week, for the summer. That's like, a fourth of the year!

I found all my Marines, except my brother, standing outside the door. I denied myself the pleasure of slamming the ten-foot tall, double white-washed door on their faces and waved them in. Why hadn't Tyler invited them in? Maybe he had let them know I wasn't too thrilled to have their company so they waited for me. Maybe they suspected my house had been set with booby traps. At this thought a wry smile moved across my lips. *Note to self, install booby traps to impale, blow up, fry, and/or electrocute Tyler.*

They followed me through the house, up the stairs, and to their rooms. I showed them their bathrooms and pointed out the cupboards with towels and washcloths. Edna could work miracles. All the curtains were drawn, fresh linens were on the beds, and the showers were stocked with soap and shampoo. No doubt the medicine cabinets had been filled with spare toothbrushes, toothpaste, deodorant, band aids, Tylenol, combs, and other stuff people tend to forget when traveling. Based on where these guys had come from, I guessed they'd need all of it. After they put their duffels down, I rounded them up in the hall.

"Follow me," I said and, being good little soldiers used to taking orders, they did. We walked in silence to the end of the corridor. Edna had placed them in this wing of the house for a reason.

At the end of their hall was, what I to refer to as the

Gentleman's Club at Boudreaux House. It was a gentleman's club in the most traditional sense. It wasn't a place where naked tweakers danced around poles waiting for the random perv to slip a five dollar bill in their g-strings. My Club had a fully stocked bar, pool table, fireplace, humidor, 103" flat screen TV, every sports package known to man, card table, leather club chairs, and a variety of dead heads and skins from Africa hanging on the wall. All cherry wood and dark green, it was a big boys' playroom. It hadn't been used in years, but I kept things updated. I'd installed the bigger TV six months ago and made sure the room was ready to use. I had intended on giving the man cave to Tyler as a gift, but I didn't know if he really deserved it any more.

When my Marines saw the haven of all things testosterone, a jolt of pride surged through me. They clearly liked it. *Good, maybe they'll stay in here all summer, and I won't have to worry about them.*

"Wait here. I'll find Tyler. He can give you the tour. You're welcome to use anything in my home but consider this area your base. It's kind of the guys' room in the house."

"Mrs. Boudreaux."

I had started to leave but stopped when the deep, slow, surprisingly quiet voice began to speak. I turned back.

Shooter had the dark, thick-as-cold-honey voice. "Thank you for letting us stay here. Thank you for taking care of my men."

I nodded and said much quieter than I wanted, "If you're going to live here, I think you best call me Kat." *No, no, no! Absolutely not! They are not allowed to be nice to me. They are imposing. They should be arrogant, lazy, and disrespectful.* Their gratitude made it harder for me to be mad at my brother. Harder, but not impossible.

As I walked down the hall, I heard what could only be Horndog's voice say, "Is it just me, or is Tongue's sister really hot?"

I spun on my heel ready to give Horndog a piece of my mind

and possibly a black eye when the unmistakable sound of an antique ivory pool ball hitting a human target rang through the corridor. I paused, waiting to hear which Marine had bean-balled Horndog. My stomach clenched when I heard Shooter say, "We're not here for that, Dog. Get your head on straight. And I mean your big head, not the one below your waist you tend to think with."

A smile crept onto my face. Shooter had earned three gold stars. The rest were still on my no-fly list. Normally I would never let someone else fight my battles, but I wanted to be around the tall, quiet, and deadly crowd as little as possible, so I let Shooter handle Horndog. It truly was a sacrifice. I hadn't hit something with the intent to harm in a long damn time. But I had more important things to take care of. Finding and executing my brother was on the top of that list.

I searched all his usual haunts in the house but didn't turn up so much as a toenail. I checked his room, the theater, the kitchen, and the library. Nothing. I ran into Jason, the young man in charge of the indoor plants. He told me he saw Tyler going up to the third floor. There would be only one reason for Tyler to go to the third floor and that reason is about three feet tall, has long blond hair, and two missing front teeth. I ran the stairs stopping on the landing of the top floor of the house. I paused outside a pink door and took a deep breath. I opened it and found Tyler.

He sat on the pink carpet wearing a tutu, boa, and tiara drinking a cup of imaginary tea. He even had his pinky extended, as no doubt Sam had insisted. Across from Tyler sat the only person in the world that made me truly happy, my five-year-old daughter Samantha. Samantha was an absolute joy. She never complained, never whined, and never caused trouble. She always had a warm hug and an *I love you* waiting for me. She saw me and ran at me, catching me around the waist.

"Hey, girlie, what have you done to Uncle Tyler?"

"Nothing, Mom, he wanted some tea and I had to make sure he dressed for it." Sam was a Southern girl to her core.

"Well that's very nice of you. How about you let me and Uncle Tyler talk? He needs to do something for me, but when he's done he can come back and finish his tea."

"The tea party's over. So he can go. I have to move Barbie's furniture to her new house and then I have to make sure all my bears are comfortable."

Oh, how I wanted her concerns.

Tyler stood up and followed me out the door. "What's scratchin', kitten?"

I hated it when he'd say that. It reminded me of cat scratch fever and that was just disgusting. I didn't say anything until we reached my suite of rooms. I didn't want Sam to hear me give her beloved uncle a tongue lashing. I closed the door behind him, sufficiently trapping him, a rat in cage. He sat in an overstuffed white chair in my sitting room.

Sitting across from him, I said, "You know you're going to die right?"

"I figured." He said it like a man on death row who had exhausted all his appeals and was just waiting for the priest and the executioner to show.

"Of course, I won't kill you right away. I need you to do some things for me first. Your friends are down in the Club. They need a tour. Show them the entire house and grounds. After that, set up tables and chairs on the back lawn for dinner." Then I had a spark of brilliance. "And I trust you guys only have your khakis to wear. They'll be too hot through the summer and they are absolutely dreadful. So you're going shopping. Go to Lakeside in Metarie. They have J. Crew, Banana Republic, Eddie Bauer—you can get everything in one stop. Make them get casual clothes and shoes. I'll arrange for Christopher to come in and fit all six of you for a tux. You'll be here for the Founder's Day Celebration. You know what that means." I hadn't asked him to break Mt. Everest into gravel, but the look he gave me said I might as well have. "I'm assuming the Corps doesn't provide you with any of those things."

He pushed himself off the chair to stand in front of me. "Is this how the entire summer is going to be? You're going to torture me."

I stood and stared him in the eye. "Torture? No, honey, this isn't torture. This is hospitality. The torture starts tomorrow."

Chapter Two

I was naturally an inquisitive person. But I wouldn't say I was inappropriate or rude. I felt the need to know and protect those under my care. Their safety and happiness were my number one priority. And those were the only reasons I stood in the wall of the Club eavesdropping on my Marines. It wasn't because I had a sick need to know all gossip first or to collect information that may be used against someone in the future. Nope, not at all. Whatever, old habits die hard.

About a century ago the Boudreaux living in the mammoth house grew extremely paranoid. Stashing four mistresses in the same house as your wife and relying on prayer to make sure they didn't find out about each other will do that to a man. He was the reason the original servants' passageways had been closed in, creating hidden passages, secret staircases, clandestine rooms, and unseen portals perfect for spying. He was also the reason the house had been busier than the local temperance hall during the country's failed attempt at prohibition. According to legend, only the actual owner of the house is to know of the passages. So when the previous owner kicked the bucket the new owner was presented with keys, the deed, and a really cool treasure map of secrets within the house. I hadn't told the staff about them, though I knew they had discovered some secrets while carrying out their duties. I didn't acknowledge it, and neither did they. They seemed to know that it wasn't something you talked about.

I watched them play pool, drink, watch TV, and read the newspapers. Tyler hadn't shown up yet to tell them what they were in for tomorrow. Their reaction would be priceless. I had to see it. *Damn, where's a camera when you really need one?* Despite the glee in my heart at witnessing their pain, something felt off. It was in the way they were standing. I'd been born with the ability to read people. I'd been trained to analyze minute changes in body language. They tried to look like they were relaxed, but they weren't. It was almost like they were about to go out on a mission. They didn't want to think about it, and they tried everything to not think about it, but they couldn't not think about it. It was written all over their faces. With every crack of a pool ball, every flip of the TV channel, they waited for go time.

Shooter paced the Club with his arms crossed over his chest. He'd stop at every window, pull the curtains aside, look across the lawn, and move on to the next. *Someone had a hard time leaving the job at the office.* Just as Shooter reached the fifth window for the sixth time, Tyler decided to make an appearance. He had several rolled up scrolls of paper under his arms. He came in, closed and locked the door. As if it had been choreographed, my Marines cleared the pool table and took their places around its periphery.

What the hell was going on? Tyler was not playing tour guide like he'd been ordered to. They weren't studying a map to the mall in Metairie, creating a plan of attack. They all stared down at what appeared to be blueprints. I stood too far away to get any idea of what held their attention. But anyone with a semi-functional pair of eyes could recognize the Boudreaux family crest on the blue prints, which meant they were studying a property the family owned. Why would Tyler have those blueprints? And where the hell had he gotten them?

My brother may have brought the intel, but Shooter chaired

the meeting. "I want armed look-out posts here, here, and here. Horndog, we'll need demo placed here and here. I want cameras all over the place. If it breathes, moves, eats, sleeps or shits, I want a time and date stamp on it. I'll scout around and find the best place for me. Tongue, you're on evac. We'll go over several different scenarios later. Doc, I need you to man one of the guns, but your primary duty is to offer medical help. We don't know what to expect, and I really hope your skills aren't needed, but it's always good to be prepared."

Ok, seriously, what the hell?

"Getting our gear will be easier than we thought," Tyler said. "My sister wants me to take you all into Metairie in the morning to get kitted out so we don't embarrass her. She expects us to buy a new wardrobe so we fit in with all her fancy-ass friends. Don't worry. It won't be so bad. We can grab a few things to make her happy, then stop by the docks. I've got the info on the container and the authorities have been taken care of, so it should be easy in and out. I'll tell Gregory to stay behind. He's her driver, not mine. Smooth sailing."

He couldn't be more wrong. He just made his life far more complicated than it needed to be. Until I found out what they were up to, I would be all over them like ticks in July.

Shooter nodded. "I'm supposed to give you all a tour of the house," Tyler continued. "But you can familiarize yourself with your new surroundings with these." He pointed to the rolls of papers. Those were blueprints of my house. He had classified Boudreaux family documents! Tyler was going to die over a period of several days.

That son of a bitch! If keeping the passageways secret wasn't so damn high on my list of priorities, I would have chewed my way through plaster and paint just to rip Tyler's trachea out with my teeth. I could hear the blood pumping in my ears. My lungs rubbed up against my ribcage like a couple teenagers in the backseat of Dad's Pontiac. The room shrank to the size of a shoebox. Air caught in my throat, trapped from entering my bloodstream by an iron door that had been slammed shut. Control. I needed to get myself under control. The next step was hyperventilation and after that loomed a gaping pit of terror. I willed myself to calm down. No dice. I ran through my passageway, up a set of hidden stairs, and into my bedroom. I lay down on the bed, praying to the Lord in heaven that I didn't black out.

Safe in my room, I gulped fresh, clean air into my lungs. Slowly I gained a bit of control over my autonomic nervous system. I had to plan. I had to strategize. How should I handle something like this? Did I break down the Club door and kick all my Marines out? Did I confront Tyler? Did I not worry about it?

Definitely, no to not worrying about it. For one, I was a girl and a trait attached to every XX chromosome coupling compelled all of my gender to stick their noses in where they may or may not belong. And for two, they'd said demo, and for some reason I didn't think they were talking about showing me how to take full advantage of my Kirby vacuum. People I loved and cared about lived in this house. If one of them lost a leg because of a misplaced brick of C4, it would be replaced with one of my Marines' appendages.

I couldn't ignore them, and confronting Tyler would be completely useless. If he wanted to tell me, he would have. He wouldn't have made up the story that they had nowhere else to go. He would lie to me. They would all lie to me. Breaking down the Club's door wasn't smart either. The doors were original to the house and I really didn't want to face the shrews on the historical board when they found out what I'd done. That, and I didn't think I would be able to resist shanking a few Marines once the double oaks were breached.

So what did that leave me with? My only options were sneaky and shady. Two things I was very, very good at. It had to do with the whole being a girl thing and a past life. Determined to put a leash on the situation, I left my bedroom for my private office. On a piece of Boudreaux stationary I wrote, *Operation Me vs. The Marines.*

Yes, I wrote it down. I was a list person, and I get a warm fuzzy in my stomach whenever I created one. Neurotic, yes. Stupid, no. Next to the number one I wrote, "Find out everything about them."

I went on to two and nearly puked. "Be nice to them." I would not be nice out of social courtesy or because I was a good person. Being nice would make them comfortable and entice them into telling me why they were in my house and what their plans were for it.

Number three, "Be involved." From then on they would never have a moment's peace from me. They turn around in the yard, and I'd be there. They walk one step backward, and they'd bump into me. They sneeze, I'd hand them a hanky. They need to pee...okay, maybe they could handle that on their own. But, anything short of private bodily functions, and I would be there.

Number four.... As I wrote number four, I couldn't believe my brain had told my hand to print it on a piece of paper. It was absolutely humiliating. No way was I going to do it. "Seduce one." That's what my idiot of a hand wrote. I tasted a little throw up in the back of my mouth and moved to cross the item out until a little annoying voice in the back of my head spoke up. The voice came from a girl I went to school with named Carrie.

Carrie had been known at John Taylor High School as having slept her way through three principals, the math department, the football teams—both varsity and JV—and the school district superintendent. These weren't the rumors of a small town. She had video evidence and a web site. For $10.99, anyone could see her do the nasty with Mr. Willis right before he changed her grade from a D to an A. She went to Harvard on an academic scholarship and practiced corporate law.

The Carrie voice said, "Sex is the most powerful tool in the female's repertoire. You can get any man to do anything if you make them think they'll get a little nooky. Actually give it to them, and you won't even have to ask." I noticed how she spoke in plurals. She didn't say him, she said them.

So maybe I shouldn't be taking advice from the Whore of Babylon, but she did have a point. There were five strapping, youthful, sex-starved men in my house. One of them had the name Horndog for crying out loud! And Carrie had said I didn't have to have sex with them to get what I wanted. I just had to make them *think* I would. *Great, now I'm speaking in plurals!* Completely disgusted with myself, I left number four alone.

Number five: "You are Bond, Jane Bond. Don't forget it." I had no idea why I put that on the list, but a little pep talk never hurt anybody. I slipped the paper into my desk drawer and left my office, walking into my dressing area. We would all gather to eat dinner outside. Casual, unassuming, innocent, the perfect time to pounce. If I planned on accomplishing number four, I had to start right away.

I had no idea how to seduce a man. I'd never really even seduced my husband. We met at the gym and ended up being sparring partners. He refused to hit a girl so I knocked him unconscious, and he took me to breakfast. I never had to try to be sexy for him. He took me as I came, rough edges and all. And that had been enough. Yes, I was definitely in uncharted waters. I turned around in my closet.

I should tell you that, though I was not girly in any way, I loved clothes. I loved to have the perfect outfit for any occasion. My twenty-five-hundred-square-foot closet housed more clothes than a Neiman Marcus. I had the dreaded day dresses for garden parties, the uncomfortable gowns for more formal affairs, sweet dresses for church, take-me-serious suits for work, swimsuits for the pool, lake, and beach, jeans and T-shirts, slacks and blouses, clothes for staying in, clothes for going out, Pilates clothes, yoga clothes, cardio clothes, and the ever important training clothes. These were my favorite. When I put them on, I felt powerful. I had been fighting my entire life. In high school, I had been known as the girl no one wanted to mess with. Some did and paid dearly for it.

But I wouldn't get to put on my training clothes that night. Nope, I had to be alluring. *Eck, I hate that word!* I rummaged through the racks until I found the perfect dress. I took off the cream slacks and blue blouse I had worn to the airport and pulled the dress over my head. I caught my image in the mirror and felt as if I'd just walked into homeroom naked. The white halter sun dress with a pleated skirt was covered in little red flowers. I looked like Mrs. Cleaver, if Mrs. Cleaver had ever had the goal to seduce five Marines.

Walking past a bank of mirrors, I paused and scowled. My hair was pulled up into a ponytail. A ponytail said either *innocent* or *lazy* and I couldn't appear be either. I pulled the elastic out and my long auburn waves hung down to the middle of my back. I could do a ponytail, French twist, I could even roll my hair up so it formed a wreath around my head, but making it cooperate down was always a trial. It reminded me of an auburn lion's mane. It didn't matter. I had an objective. Thick and all over the place would have to do.

My relationship with makeup was worse than my relationship with hair. I was really only comfortable with mascara and lip gloss so I stuck with what I knew. If I went much further, my face would look like a showgirl and a circus clown had a demonic baby whose evil powers were fed by Lancôme and Estee Lauder. I inspected myself in the mirror. I'd hoped to see courage in my green eyes. Nope, no courage. Plenty of fear and anxiety though. I stood up and started toward my bedroom door. The soft plush of carpet under my feet stopped me in my tracks. *Dammit!* I needed shoes. I went back to the closet, inspired by the dimensions of the Sistine Chapel, and searched wall after wall of shoes. Shoes and I didn't get along either. Usually I would call Edna Mae or Sissy to help me choose. They had an unnatural fondness for footwear. But I didn't want them to even suspect I would be whoring myself out for information. I stared at the wall, at my feet, at the wall, at my feet. This went on for several minutes until it was perfectly clear that shoes and I had reached an impasse. I went into my bathroom, painted my ten little piggies bright red, and called it good.

I ran down the back stairs hoping to avoid as many people as possible and sneaked into the kitchen. Samantha helped Edna put miniature loaves of cornbread into baskets. I could smell the dirty spice of jambalaya, and I felt home. The amount of food that filled the kitchen could have fed all the people trapped in the Superdome during Katrina or six Marines, seventeen friends, a five year old, and one unwilling hostess.

The racket of my Marines setting up chairs and tables in the yard rang through the kitchen door. Edna turned on her stool. Damn, she saw me. Her eyebrows disappeared into her steel grey hair and her sharp brown eyes widened to the size of hub caps. I shook my head. She would not say anything, but I knew what she thought. A twinge of guilt shot through my stomach when I thought how happy she would be to see me "getting myself out there." I didn't have the heart to tell her I only looked that way to discover what treacherous things my brother and his buddies were up to.

Just then, caught completely off guard, I saw Shooter stroll through the kitchen door.

"The tables and chairs are set up. The men are putting on the linens and the plates and stuff. I just wanted to know...." He lifted his stare from his hands, and we caught each other's gaze dead in the eye. He turned the same color as a ripe strawberry and quickly lowered his head again. "I just wondered if you needed any help taking the food out."

"That would be lovely," Edna said. "There's a lot here. It'll take several trips. But I don't want any of the others carrying it. With the way they were slamming those chairs together, we'd end up eating like pigs from a trough."

"It's all right, ma'am. I'll take care of it." He grabbed a giant bowl of potato salad and carried it to the door. Just as he reached it, Horndog stepped up into the kitchen. Shooter sent a glare through him that, I'm sure if it hadn't been summer in Louisiana, would have frozen him into a block of ice. The Marine backed out into the yard. Shooter came back in at least ten more times to carry all the food out to the tables.

"You know, there are a lot of people that could have helped him," I said to Edna.

She patted my arm and said, "But then he wouldn't have an excuse to look at ya, *cher.*"

Great, just great. Edna had slipped into matchmaker mode, and my plan was in serious jeopardy of becoming a tragic, embarrassing, horrifying story told to warn other women away from manipulating men with a bit of leg and a lot of cleavage.

Once the tables were set and the food scattered over them, Samantha, Edna, and I took our seats. Oh, and imagine that. The only chair available sat across from Shooter. When it came to spreading gossip amongst the staff, Edna was faster than a BellSouth party line. The staff and my Marines stared at me. I was that girl in all those stupid teen movies. You know the ones where the ugly girl gets popularity, the captain of the football team, and the respect of her peers when her fairy godmothers, Maybelline and Wonderbra, wave their magic wands. All that was missing was a pink taffeta prom dress, punch spiked with rotgut, and a slow, nauseating scene where the dream boy tells the now non-ugly girl he wanted her even when she wore overalls covered in paint. The music slows, the camera closes in and they share a soft, passionless kiss. Yeah, that was me.

The situation needed an injection of liquor, STAT. A pitcher of Lilly's famous mint juleps sat right in front of me. Thank you, Lord! Lilly wouldn't reveal the ingredients, but after years of drinking it, I was convinced it was made with moonshine, a sprig of mint, and a splash of antifreeze for color. Since I didn't see a straw or funnel on the table, I decided to be civilized and pour it into my glass rather than chugging it straight from the pitcher. My glass was empty in two seconds flat. The second glass was gone at one-point-five.

As I started to pour the third, Tyler covered my glass with his hand. "How about we put some food on that stomach before you end up on the table singing *Barracuda* in nothing but your underwear."

He would never let me forget one stupid night in Panama

City. But, I recognized his plan as a solid idea and agreed to it.

He loaded my plate with crawfish, shrimp, jambalaya, cornbread, and potato salad. I could have fed an entire refugee camp with what had been heaped on my dish. I ate my food with all the dignity and manners of a backhoe. Cut me a break. I was nervous, okay?

For the first time I really looked at my Marines. At the airport and in the house earlier I hadn't really cared what they looked like, but in my inebriated state I'd become suddenly curious. They were a very proud group who would do anything for the men next to them. Oh yeah, and they were all hotter than a solar flare. It had been an extra good day when God created these men. Seriously, no single man had the right to walk around so damn sexy. And there were five of them. They had a dangerous air about them that rocketed their fine factor off the charts. They were positively lickable. Every muscle in their bodies had been honed for one purpose. That one purpose was to kill. Damn if that wasn't the single sexiest thing about them. Behind the five gorgeous sets of eyes sat turmoil. It was as if they'd seen every horrible thing the world had to offer and survived.

Doc had dark skin, hair and eyes. He seemed to be more refined than the rest of the group. He could fit in on the battlefield or at tea with the Queen of England. That kind of class couldn't be learned. You had to be born with it. It was the reason why I didn't get invited to the ladies card games in New Orleans. Doc's eyes were empty. He didn't see anyone at the table. If I had to make a guess, I'd say he was somewhere else, somewhere a lot louder and a whole lot bloodier.

Anyone with a set of working eyeballs could see that Horndog was a notorious lady killer. He had beautiful multicolored hair that hung to his jaw. It looked like those tweed jackets stuffy professors wear to lecture in. A rainbow of blondes and browns. His eyes were the color of ice cold Coke on a summer day. He had a look to him that said, "I forgot my homework but I'm super cute so you'll forgive me."

I hated men with that look.

At over six-feet-two-inches and weighing, at most, one hundred eighty pounds, Switch had the slimmest build of the group. This wasn't my first trip through the warrior showroom. I knew from experience that strength came in all shapes and sizes. He had short, manicured black hair and mean black eyes. Switch looked as if he could fillet all the meat off your bones and enjoy it.

Martinez had to be the most difficult to figure out. He sat farthest from the head of the table. His dark black hair hung down into his face hiding his purple eyes. They weren't violet like Elizabeth Taylor's. They were purple, like amethysts. He never said a word. He ate in silence, not even asking for the salt. Martinez was young, very young. He should have been worried about Pledge Week, not hunting down terrorists.

I left Shooter for the last. He had the body of a rhinoceros and could probably bench press a Mini Cooper. He had chocolate brown, wavy hair that skimmed his shoulders. His eyes were as blue as the Mediterranean, and he kept his uniform clean and crisp. Anyone who saw him knew he would chew enemy's heart out with his own teeth and relish the taste of it. But, in a weird way, a person could trust him to watch over a senile granny. He gave off a menacing yet protective aura. If Tyler was the brains, Horndog the looks, Doc the savior, Switch the bad attitude, and Martinez the cannon fodder, Shooter was the guardian angel.

"What's the deal with all the long, flowy hair? I thought the Corps had standards?" Normally I wasn't quite so direct. Damn Lilly and her demon drink!

"We're a Marine Force Recon unit. We grow our hair and beards out to blend in." Tyler acted as mouth piece for the group.

Thankfully they had shaved before they'd landed on my door step. To me, only men with something to hide grew facial hair. Everyone on my staff knew that. Unless they wanted me to rip their chin pubes out by their roots, they shaved every day.

I needed to start the information gathering but didn't really know how to go about doing it. What did people do when they met someone new? I knew they asked questions but the only one that came to my pickled mind was, how do you keep sand out of your crotch in the desert? Somehow I didn't think Miss Manners would be impressed.

Okay, what did I know about them? Their names and that they were in the Marines. Martinez, Shooter, Doc, Switch, Horndog, and Tongue. Wait, I didn't know their names. I knew their stupid handles. Without thinking, I said, "So what's with the names? I can't imagine your mother gave you the name Horndog."

"Actually she did. She said it came to her in a dream."

So Horndog's the joker.

"Just kidding. A nun gave it to me." He didn't elaborate, and I wasn't sure if I wanted him to.

It took everything within me not to throw my now-empty glass at him. I had to gather all my niceness together just to give a token chuckle. "I know Tyler is called Tongue, and I'm guessing it's because he's the translator. Doc is easy. You're the medic. Horndog, self-explanatory. What about the rest of you?"

I turned my attention to Switch. "What about you? Are you a mechanic or do you cross dress on the weekends?"

The man didn't appreciate my well thought out question. He growled, literally. He growled at me. He must be the testy one. Good to know.

"Relax, honey we're a progressive group of people. What you do on your own time is your business," I said as I reached for the pitcher of electric green hooch. It may be the blood of demons, but it sure took the edge off.

He rose from his chair, producing a switchblade from nowhere. "It's for my favorite weapon," he growled.

Shooter put a hand on Switch's shoulder and forced him back into his seat. Change that—Switch wasn't the testy one, he was the mean one.

"He's also our communications guy," said Horndog.

"Martinez, why don't you have a cute name? Have you not earned yours yet?" I said in a mocking tone.

Horndog laughed. "Nope he's got one. It's Martinez. His real name is something Italian I don't care to remember. He replaced an awesome Marine named Martinez who caught a piece of shrapnel in the head that took half his skull off. Until he earns the right to be called something else, that's his name."

Martinez didn't appear to be happy but didn't say anything. I could only imagine that catching all the shit was part of his trial by fire.

Why was it that when you really wanted the fates to work in your favor, they sat back on their crusty, bitchy asses and kept their freaking hands off? Why couldn't someone have volunteered Shooter's information? I knew they were waiting for me to ask. He just had something about him, something that made me feel like he could see into my soul through my eyeballs. And my soul wasn't exactly pristine white. Something inside me didn't want him to see it. That thought alone made him dangerous. Very, very dangerous. Well, there's really only one thing to do. I had to pull up my big girl panties and slay the soul-reading dragon.

"Shooter, I'll bet you were the best watermelon seed spitter in three counties. I'm right, huh?"

"No, ma'am," he said leaning back in his chair with his arms folded tight across his chest. And of course he wasn't going to make it easy on me.

"All right, then you must be the worst or the best shot in your platoon. I'm going with the best. You aren't the kind of guy that breaks under pressure." That sounded casual, right? I didn't reveal that I knew his super power, did I?

"Shooter's our sniper." Tyler beamed with pride and admiration. "He's got more kills than anyone in our battalion. He's racked up...."

Shooter shook his head.

Hmm, he didn't enjoy the kill. But he did it because he had a job to do, a duty. That was something I could totally get behind. Despite his ability to see into my soul, Shooter had quickly become my favorite. Of course, that meant I had to crush him like a fallen cornflake, but life sucks. Especially if you're a cornflake.

No one said anything for several seconds. The toll of socializing with people outside my household weighed on my shoulders. I desperately needed to go to bed. Not that I would be able to sleep, but I needed to be alone. Amanda, my daughter's nanny, had already taken Sam up to bed. I excused myself from the table with the intention of joining Samantha and Amanda for our nightly ritual and the hardest part of my day.

Chapter Three

Some nights the long staircase to the third floor was just too damn long. I should move mine and Samantha's rooms to the first floor. But then I wouldn't have the best bathroom in the house, and I'd miss my closet too much. It was worth climbing the freaking stairs.

I dreaded putting my daughter to bed. It's not that I didn't love her more than life itself. It's that every night I take a rusty blade and rip open old wounds. Figuratively speaking. The mint juleps made my head spin, and I felt guilty going to my daughter a bit sauced. But, it had to be done. I had an obligation to her. Her pink door loomed in front of me. I smoothed my hands over my dress, took a deep breath, and opened the door.

Entering her room was like walking into a Pepto Bismol nightmare. She loved pink. Samantha was very, very girly. I think she dreamed of pink princesses riding pink unicorns through a field of pink grass full of pink fairies. She usually got everything she asked for. I didn't know if I gave into her to assuage my own guilt or if it was my attempt to fill a very obvious, vacant hole in her life.

Amanda had put Sam in her pretty pink pajamas and helped her into bed. The nanny smiled at me and left the room.

She was a sweetheart. She was a combination of Mary Poppins, Mother Earth, and Sister Maria from *The Sound of Music*. The day I gave birth to Sam, I swore I would raise her myself. But, Amanda had been my husband's nanny, and she was family. When Stephan outgrew her, she had been permitted to live at the house to help out here and there. When she found out I was pregnant, she cried and cried, grateful to have a child to care for again. I think she felt a little lost without a ward, so I consented to her caring for Sam. It was one of the best decisions I ever made.

I took my seat next to Sam's bed and grabbed the small, red scrapbook off the shelf. The book was only three years old, but it was extremely worn. I opened the cover and on the first page was a picture of a young man with blond hair holding a three-month-old Sam. The man was her father, Stephan Boudreaux. I flipped through the pages one by one. Each page held a photo of Stephan and Sam. On the last page was a head shot of my husband. I held the book up so Sam could kiss her daddy goodnight, and I leaned down kissing the top of her head. I told her I loved her, and she snuggled down into her covers.

When I left her room, the all too familiar frigid ache in my chest returned. It was like someone had removed my heart, cryogenically frozen it, and put it back in my rib cage. For some reason, it was worse than normal. A hand had gripped the organ, squeezing the life out of it. I clutched at my chest, barely making it to my room.

Though it was summer in Louisiana, I was cold, freezing from the inside out. My source of warmth had gone. He'd left me alone with a big empty house and a completely vacant bed. I changed into a white cotton nightgown and crawled under my covers. With my sleep patterns, my nightly routine should involve a handful of Ambien and a bottle of Jack. I didn't like to feel out of control so I had to settle for a heavy down comforter and a book. Confession time. I was a Jane Austaniac. Most people who knew me would expect me to be into Stephen King. But those books were way too close to what I actually dreamed every night so I tended to stay away from them. No sense feeding the beast. *Emma* wasn't my favorite Austen, but it was still a classic, and I'd read it at least fifty times. If I actually tried, I could probably recite the novel verbatim. I read for a while, turned out my light, closed my eyes, and waited for the demented images my brain had in store for me.

I had always had bad dreams, but over the previous two years they had grown worse. It wasn't some big mystery why they'd gone from mildly disturbing to a horror so depraved John Carpenter would scream like a little girl and pee himself. My twisted, fried brain just refused to accept or acknowledge that one night of violence in a lifetime of nights could have so much control. My brain had never recovered from the battle damage it had received. Every time I'd fall asleep, I'd jolt from my slumber, forced awake, unable to go back to sleep for at least two hours, then fall asleep only to wake up in a cold sweat two hours later. This was my version of a sleep cycle.

My brain flooded my unconsciousness with horrifying images after I'd closed my eyes. As though someone set an air horn off next to my ear, I was ripped from sleep. Ugh, my first trip through the terror park had been a doozy. I looked around my room and saw my nightmare come to life in the shadows. I lay in bed hoping the fear would release me. I focused on filling my lungs with oxygen and releasing carbon dioxide. The rise and fall of my ribcage was normally enough to send the demons back to hell. *Shit! It wasn't enough.* When it got that bad, I couldn't stay in my room. I had to get up, do something else for a while, then make a second attempt at sleep. Most people got all bent out of shape when a full bladder woke them up in the middle of the night. I'd much rather have to pee than look for the nearest weapon to fight off an unseen monster.

I threw the duvet off and climbed out of bed. Just once I'd like to have a good night's sleep. I slipped down the stairs to the first floor. And yes, I turned every light on along the way. The shadows tried to coalesce into the solid form of the villain in my dream. One more gallery was all that separated me from my sanctuary. The library was my refuge from the world. So when I saw a sliver of light shooting through the half closed door, I didn't feel too bad when I reached for a gun. Damn! I should never have stopped sleeping armed. The absence of a firearm on my hip sent me into a tailspin for the slightest of moments. I didn't need a gun to defend myself. I didn't need a weapon. Hell, I didn't need anything to dispatch someone to the great beyond. Even so, the weighty comfort of a.45 would have been reassuring in this situation. Normally, I was alone in my night wanderings. I could only guess the room was occupied by at least one of my Marines. I approached cautiously, because while logically I knew the person in the room was indeed a person and not a reject from a house of horrors, I wasn't taking any chances. Especially when I wasn't packing. I got to the door and pulled it open quickly, hoping to scare the invader back to hell where it belonged.

On the other side of the door, Shooter stood in front of a floor to ceiling bookcase. He turned to see who had interrupted his solace and when he saw me, his eyes darted to anywhere in the room other than to me. He shifted his weight from one foot to other and rubbed the back of his neck. Great, he was completely uncomfortable around me. How the hell was I supposed to seduce him? I guess I'd just have to switch targets. He turned to leave, and I stopped him. "You don't have to go. There's plenty of room in here for both of us."

I might want to rip his face off and wear it as a hat for invading my library, but I wouldn't miss an opportunity to put a check mark next to a task on my list. Even though I knew Shooter was not the spawn of Satan, and therefore, not a participant in my dreams, my heart still pounded and my stomach twisted in knots. What was happening to me? I must be coming down with something.

He turned back to his bookshelf to search for a book. The library was my domain. I didn't need to browse. I pulled *Sense and Sensibility* off the shelf before Shooter scanned one row. I sat on one of the big, leather, overstuffed chairs, curling my legs underneath me, and opened the novel. Just as Miss Austen told me John Dashwood was amply provided for by the fortune of his mother, I felt a pair of eyes bore into my soul from the chair across the priceless Persian carpet. I tried to ignore them, but failed, miserably. I snapped my head up, ready to ask what problem Shooter had with me. When my eyes met his, I was struck dumb. No, more than dumb. I couldn't even form a thought in my head much less words with my mouth. His stare was complex. In one look he asked a million questions. Questions I did not want to answer. I was so not comfortable with the ocular interrogation, and since I lacked the ability to speak, I slammed my book closed. My outburst did not bring an end to the world's worst staring contest.

His gaze persisted. He didn't even blink when he asked, "Why can't you sleep?"

The sound of his voice pulled me from the realm of the tongue tied. "Who says I can't sleep?"

He cocked his head and sent me one of those "are you kidding me" looks. I hated those looks. "Oh, I'm sorry. It's totally normal for someone to have a two-thirty a.m. Austen craving. I'm here because I just couldn't continue on if I didn't at least start *Pride and Prejudice.*"

Was he mocking Miss Jane? I wouldn't stand for that shit. Austen was a member of the literary Pantheon and deserved the respect of mere mortals. "Why aren't you sleeping?"

He shrugged. "Jet lag."

"Then where are your fellow brothers in arms? I'm willing to bet you all stayed awake on the flight so you would be so exhausted you'd collapse the second your eyes received the external visual light cues that send your brain into sleep mode."

"Maybe I slept on the plane."

"Nope, you didn't. If you had slept, you would be leaving your men unprotected, and you are all about protecting your men." I enjoyed watching him squirm in his seat. I had hit the nail on the head.

He ran his hand through his hair. "You tell me yours, and

I'll tell you mine."

Bingo! Exactly what I wanted.

"I have nightmares," I answered honestly.

"So do I."

Great, a soldier with PTSD. Oops. Pot, meet kettle.

"What was yours about?"

"Just so I'm clear, this is tit for tat. I tell you. You tell me. Got it?"

He nodded.

I settled deeper into my chair. Up until that moment I had never shared my nightmares with anyone. Psychologists did not possess the skill to unravel all my crazy. Dream journals were never going to happen. If anyone got their hands on my dreams, I would be forcibly committed. But I wanted to know more about the enigmatic sniper, so I really had no choice. The ugliest part of my corroded brain was about to be put on display.

"I left a bar in the middle of nowhere. Someone grabbed me from behind and forced me into a trunk. I must have been drugged because I regained consciousness in an underground dungeon. I looked around me, and there were three other women in various states of torture, each one worse than the last. One had her belly cut open with her guts on the table next to her. They were still attached to her body. It was like someone had taken them out and planned on putting them back. Someone else had her forearm cut open and her flexor muscles lay on the table. The last one had a shaved head and nails through her skull. The man who took me branded something into her chest. I can still smell the burning flesh. Over a three week period I was tortured over and over. In my dream, I never lost consciousness. I was awake for every painful moment.

"I learned that every Friday the man kidnapped another victim. He held the woman captive for twenty-one days. The torture progressed day by day. On the twenty-first day he branded them with a '21' and released them. None of them retained their sanity. None of them were able to send for help.

Except me. I kept my mind and when I was released, rather than calling the police, I went back to the bar he had abducted me from. When I saw him take another girl, I followed him to his torture chamber."

I took a deep breath. "When he was gone, I snuck in and, rather than helping the victims escape, I gave them medical attention. I wrapped one girl's stomach with plastic wrap to hold her guts in. I replaced the missing muscles in another girl's forearm with rubber bands. I woke up when I used a nail gun to reattach the top half of another girl's skull."

I stared at my book. Looking at Shooter would make it harder. He would know. He could read my mind and find out why I have nightmares. I wouldn't be able to handle that. I didn't want pity. I wanted a life. He would offer pity. But at some point I had to look at him. He would be in the house for three freaking months. I couldn't spend the entire summer inspecting the tops of my feet.

It took more courage than jumping out of a plane at seventy-five thousand feet into a mine field. I looked up. I expected him to have a look of complete horror on his face. Imagine my surprise when his eyes read compassion and understanding. That was scary. What does he dream if he was compelled to comfort me from mine?

"Is this a recurring nightmare?"

"Nope. I'm not answering that until you tell me yours. Fair's fair. You made the rules, remember."

I could tell he hoped to get out of sharing his dream. Not gonna happen. I told him mine, and that was not easy. I don't tell my deepest darkest secrets to total strangers. I could see his mind search for a loophole in his rules. "Spill it," I said.

Unlike me, he didn't stare at his lap. He looked me dead in the eye. I had no choice but to hold his gaze. It was as if his eyes were magnetic and I was iron ferrite. "Mine isn't as involved or as detailed as yours. It is simple. I get orders to take out a high ranking member of Hussein's Republican Guard. Just like every other assignment, I gather my gear, and me and my spotter head out. We set up a nest on the fourth floor of an abandoned school about eighteen hundred meters from the target's front door and wait. We know the target leaves his house every morning at oh-seven-hundred for a run, and we wait through the dawn anticipating his arrival. As the time gets closer, I lie on my belly and look through my scope. At oh-seven-hundred on the dot, he opens his door. I take aim, and just as I squeeze the trigger his seven-year-old daughter steps in front of him. The bullet goes through her skull, making it explode like a melon, and through the target's heart, killing them both."

I didn't know what to say. In so many ways his dream was much worse than mine. I felt compelled to rush over and hug him, something completely foreign to me. What the hell was wrong with me? I didn't do shit like that. I had to force myself to stay in my seat. But it seemed to be a night full of not-usually-what-I-dos. I had threatened my brother, spied on guests, wore a dress to dinner, interrogated my Marines, drank too much, and spilled my guts about a dream. I slammed a lid on all that out of character crap.

After a long silence he said, "So, do you have your dream all the time?"

"No, it's a different one every night."

"So when you go to bed, you don't know what to expect?"

"No," I answered. "What about you? Do you dream the same thing over and over?"

"Every single night," he said quietly.

"But while mine is a dream, yours is a memory." I couldn't believe that came out of my mouth. Way to make a guy comfortable.

He stood. "I'm going to try to go to sleep."

As he left the library, my fear returned. I hadn't noticed before, but I had been calm when he was near me. You'd think I'd welcome him and the Xanax that seemed to ooze from his pores. Nope, vulnerability was never a good thing. I didn't like that I had found someone that could make me feel safe. No one could be trusted with emotional safety. My staff provided the physical protection and stability I needed but, my emotional security was all mine. I was going to stay away from Shooter like he was gonorrhea and I was a virgin.

Damn. There was no way I would be able to read my book. Shit, I'd read the same page five freaking times. My powers of concentration were zilch. My mind craved the safety of Shooter's presence. I slammed the book down on the mahogany table next to my chair. Yes, that is what a fit looked like on me. Take a picture. They don't happen all that often.

I made my way up the stairs, walked right down the hall, and around the corner to peer down Shooter's hall. All the lights were off but his. Of course he had lied. He had about as much chance of falling asleep as a kid on Christmas Eve tanked up on sugar and caffeine. I crept down the hall, stopping at his cracked door. Did I mention it was in my DNA to stick my nose in where it didn't belong?

He sat on his bed staring at a photo. Who was in that photo? Why did he lovingly brush his thumb over the picture? Why did he have a tortured look on his face? It had better be a picture of the young girl he'd killed in Iraq! If it was a picture of an ex-girlfriend he pined over, it was so on! For like five one hundredths of a second I thought about breaking in and grabbing the picture. Thankfully, I came to my senses before I could react. Could I be any more pathetic and desperate? No, no I could not. I turned around and went to my room.

Lying in bed, I tried to decipher the foreign sensations swirling through my body. My stomach had somehow been taken over by an entire family of foot-long earthworms, and spiders had started building cobwebs in my brain. Both the earthworms and spiders were poisonous. They spewed an odd toxin into my bloodstream that made me feel all...gooey. Gooey was not an emotion I was comfortable with. Gooey and I didn't get along.

I had developed a completely inappropriate claim on Shooter. I wouldn't say I had romantic feelings for him. It was more like when we were in preschool and Jamie Pearson hogged the Strawberry Shortcake doll. I wasn't in love with the doll, but it was mine. Jamie ended up with five stitches in her eyebrow when I whacked her with a roller skate to assert my claim on the strawberry scented toy. I couldn't stop my thoughts from turning to Shooter, the calm that surrounded him, and my claim. So I watched the sun rise, wondering if Shooter was doing the same. Pathetic, pathetic, pathetic.

I knew Tyler would be in the gym. He and I had an arrangement. I didn't give him crap for being a total ass ninety-nine percent of the time, and he let me "work out" with him. Our workouts didn't involve weights or elliptical machines. We preferred a more hands on approach to fitness. I changed into my all-powerful training clothes, pulled my hair up in a braid, and ran downstairs to the basement. I know, you're thinking you can't have a basement in Louisiana. Well, you can. Most plantations had them and used them to punish slaves who were belligerent enough to want freedom.

Yes, I said the "S" word. That may be a taboo subject among most established respectable families but, while I married into an established family, I had never been respectable so I could talk about it all I wanted.

The sound of someone beating the crap out of a bag rang through the corridor outside the gym and a smile crossed my lips. I hadn't sparred in days, and I loved sparring with Tyler. He was the only person I'd ever fought that didn't hold back because I was a girl. He'd crack my jaw or bust my lip open without hesitation, and I loved him for it.

I entered the state–of-the-art gym, Tyler stopped hitting the bag and smiled. "I wondered when you were going to show up."

I smiled, inserted my mouth guard, and headed to a row of posts nailed to the wall that held boxing gloves. I pulled a pair of Velcro gloves on. I preferred the lace up variety, but with no one around to assist, getting them on was a challenge. My brother and I climbed the ropes and squared off in front of each other.

Our grandfather had taught us how to fight. In his youth

he'd made a pretty good living as an illegal street fighter. Think UFC minus the rules.

I balanced on the balls of my feet, waiting for Tyler to throw the first punch. It was our version of the bell. Our fights didn't have rounds or refs. They ended when one of us gave up. He threw a right cross that never made contact. I saw the punch coming and swung my body out of the way. I countered with a jab that landed squarely on his nose, making it bleed. To my brother's credit he didn't wince or blink his eyes. He knew better than to show weakness with me. He clocked me with a hit to the body, and I got him with a jab cross combo. He faked another right cross and caught me in the lip. The metallic flavor of blood welled in my mouth. I smiled, no doubt showing him a row of bloody teeth through my clear mouth guard.

I threw my arm around his neck, holding him tight in a headlock and pounded his face. He broke free and danced around a bit to clear his vision. I wiped my right glove on my shirt, staining it with his blood. I smiled another gory smile. And then the fight got dirty.

He came at me with a kick to the gut, forcing all the air out of my body. I caught my breath and jumped up, spinning in mid-air, landing a kick to the side of his head and bruising the little bones in my feet. As he stumbled around trying to regain his balance, I flipped him onto his back. My knees pinned his arms to the floor. Blow after blow turned his face into a lumpy, bruised mass of flesh and bone. He flipped me over and slammed his fist into my cheek. Stars clouded my vision, but I wasn't stupid enough to let him know that. The most important part of fighting was making your opponent think they couldn't get to you.

I kicked him off of me and allowed him a moment to find his feet. I gave him two seconds then attacked with the ferocity of a rabid tiger. I pummeled his head from all sides. When I knew he'd be too dazed to fight back, I switched to body shots. I worked his kidneys like a baker works dough. I stopped just short of making him piss blood for two days. Then, I faltered. I fell prey to overconfidence. I got sloppy. I turned to kick my brother and finish the match, but he beat me to it. I flew across the ring, slamming into the ropes. He was done playing. Tyler threw me to the mat and sat on my pelvis ready to give my face a good tenderizing when all of a sudden he flew off of me. No joke. For a split second I thought he'd sprouted fairy wings until I saw Shooter standing over me.

"What the hell do you think you're doing?" His hands were in tight fists at his sides. He gritted his teeth, and he stood as if he wanted to kill something.

Though he stared at me, it was Tyler who answered. "Sparring. What the hell did it look like? And thank you very much. Now, I have to forfeit."

Shooter gripped me under my arms, pulled me completely off the mat, and slammed me to my feet. "It looked like you were trying to kill each other!"

"It looked like the beginning of the coolest fight ever!"

I turned when I heard Horndog's voice. Every one of my Marines leaned against the ropes. They acted like someone had cancelled their birthdays. It seemed as though Shooter was the only one worried about our safety.

"Doc, get up here and look her over."

"He's worse off than I am. Doc. Check Tyler first," I said as I stripped my gloves.

Tyler's eyes had started to swell, and I'm pretty sure I'd broken his nose...again.

"No!" Shooter ordered. "You take care of Kat. I have something to say to Tongue."

He'd never said my name before. My stomach filled with a warm goo that reminded me of hot chocolate chip cookies. For a moment I softened toward him, then I remembered how he'd just interrupted my workout and I had to hate him again.

As Doc climbed through the ropes, Shooter went over to "talk" to Tyler. Just before Doc blocked my vision I saw Shooter bare knuckle my brother in the face. A volcano went off inside my body. I shoved Doc to the ground and went after Shooter. I knocked him onto his back and got one good hit in before I was pulled off by Martinez and Switch. Instinct took over. I slammed my head into Switch's nose and kicked Martinez in the solar plexus. To their credit, they managed to hang on to me while I tried to kill them.

"What the hell are you doing? That was totally uncalled for!" To say I was upset would be the understatement of the century.

Tyler stood in front of me, blood pouring down his face. "It's okay. Rat Bastard rules. We don't hit girls. I just never really thought of you as a girl."

How dumb was that? I agree that in most cases boys shouldn't hit girls, but Tyler and I were sparring. "It was consensual! You big freaking...." I couldn't think of a name bad enough for Shooter. As far as I was concerned, he was the one out of line. You don't bare knuckle someone unless you planned on doing some serious damage. I stalked toward Shooter, who was back on his feet. I wrapped my hand around his throat. "You're lucky your balls don't resemble cooked oatmeal. You pull that shit again, and I will personally hang you from the ceiling and beat you till you bleed to death on my kitchen floor. Feel me?" I turned on my heel and climbed out of the ring. I didn't say anything to the rest of my Marines. I didn't make eye contact. I completely ignored them. At that moment, they weren't worthy of my attention.

As I left the gym, I heard Horndog say, "That is the baddest ass chick I've ever met."

And then I heard the slap of fist hitting face.

Chapter Four

I didn't really care who'd hit Horndog or why. What I did care about was that someone hit him for paying me what I viewed as a compliment. Of course, if they knew the truth, they wouldn't think I was so badass. None of that really mattered. Shooter had pissed me right the hell off. Only an idiot interrupted a death match between me and Tyler.

"Miss Kat! What is wrong with your face? You've got blood pouring from your mouth and nose!"

Shit. I hadn't realized I'd walked right through the main part of the house. Sissy, one of my maids, had caught me. The floor was spotted with a trail of my blood. Great, now I had to deal with Edna. She'd fry me up and serve me for breakfast.

Sissy grabbed the sides of my face gently with her palms. "Who's done this to you, ma'am? You tell me who and I'll make sure they pay for this. *Big Joe!*" she screeched.

This was not going to end well. The only person in my household that knew I liked to fight was my usual sparring partner and head of security, Jake. Big Joe, on the other hand, saw me as a delicate magnolia, and he would take my current state as a personal challenge.

I tried to calm Sissy, but she just kept hollering for Big Joe. I tried to explain that I'd chosen to have the shit kicked out of me and that it was a workout, but she just didn't catch on. She wailed like a banshee that someone had attacked me and that, of course, brought the entire house running to my rescue. Maids, cooks, Edna, Gregory, Amanda, my Marines, Tyler, and Sam all ran into the front foyer to see what Sissy was carrying on about. When they saw my face, the staff all had looks that could kill. They believed someone had tried to hurt me. Then they saw Tyler's face and connected the dots; they knew they had front row tickets to the biggest ass whooping in history. The impending bout between Tyler and Big Joe was worthy of pay per view.

As if called out by Michael Buffer, Big Joe stepped through the double front doors. *Llllet's get ready to rumblllle!* He looked at me and surveyed the crowd. His gaze landed on Tyler. I knew no one could stop Big Joe, but like an idiot, I stood in front of the Goliath of a man in a lame effort to protect my bigger idiot brother. A fight between Big Joe and Tyler would be like a war between the United States and Sardinia. Sardinia would be ravaged, burned, bombed, and thoroughly beaten into submission. The only advantage Tyler had over Big Joe was speed.

"Tyler," I said as calmly as possible, "run."

Tyler didn't hesitate. He took off like a demon just let out of hell. Big Joe followed, and behind trailed the gawkers. Some of us were worried about the safety of one fighter or the other. Others followed to see who would bleed more. And there were a few that had no idea why they ran but followed the crowd like lemmings off a cliff. I was in the first group, but secretly a small part of me, probably the part that was still profusely bleeding, was in the second. Tyler led us on a truly epic chase. If my Marines hadn't had a formal tour earlier, they were getting one now. Granted it was on fast forward but a tour none the less. He led us through galleries with priceless paintings on the wall, through large rooms packed with antiques, up and down staircases, and all the way I left a trail of blood drops.

Tyler zoomed through the kitchen and out the door to the

yard. He ran past the gardener's shed, around the horse stables, across the lawn, through a stand of trees, and into the lake. It was probably the best decision Tyler had ever made. Open water terrified Big Joe. He couldn't swim, and he thought fish would nibble on his toes. He stopped at the edge of the lake. Conflict raged in his mind. Should he jump in and drown Tyler, or should he wait till he came out and kill him on dry land? Thankfully dry land won the day.

He paced up and down the beach with a menacing glare that never left Tyler. Only I could bring the battle to a peaceful conclusion, but it was just too much fun, and I didn't want it to end. Unfortunately I had stuff to do, so I could spend the next decade and a half waiting for Tyler to leave the lake, or I could force an armistice. I cautiously stepped in front of Big Joe. Shooter and the rest of my Marines quickly came to my flanks. Big Joe didn't notice. I placed my hand on his massive forearm. Out of reaction, he raised his other fist to me. Shooter grabbed Joe's arm but he didn't need to. Recognition flashed through his eyes. He had broken his promise. He'd threatened me. He hung his head. Shame covered his entire being.

I held his giant face in my hands and spoke so softly only Shooter, Big Joe, and I could hear. "Listen to me, Joe. Tyler might have hurt me, but I hurt him too. We were boxing, not fighting. If you're going to punish him, you have to punish me too."

He shook his head and said, "He shouldn't be layin' his hands on you in any way, ma'am. He shouldn't never hurt you. You don't deserve to get hurt."

"You're right," I said. "No one deserves to get hurt. And if you hurt Tyler, you'll be hurting me. Do you want to hurt me?"

He shook his head.

"Then you have to let him go. If you hurt my brother, you'll hurt me real, real bad. Inside, you know. You'd make me cry for days. I know you don't want to make me cry."

Joe stepped away from my grasp and surrendered. I turned to Tyler and motioned for him to come out of the lake. He very cautiously waded out of the water, never taking his eyes off Big Joe. When he got to the edge, all my Marines, except Shooter who stayed next to me, surrounded my brother.

Big Joe pointed his over large finger at Tyler. "You best consider yourself lucky that I don't never hurt Ms. Kat. I ain't gonna beat you bloody, but I see her like this again, and no one will be able to stop me."

I knew he just wanted to strike the fear of God into Tyler. He would never do anything to hurt me, and as long as hurting Tyler hurt me, Joe wouldn't touch him. I looked around at the crowd that had formed around us. Some of them looked relieved. Others looked like they had just paid $54.99 to watch the Tyson v. Spinks fight only to have it end in ninety-one seconds. Whether happy or bummed, they all left and returned to their duties. Big Joe shot Tyler one last I-really-would-like-to-set-you-on-fire glare and left to tend to his garden.

Just as I was about to return to the house to clean the gore off my face, I felt a hand as strong as Darth Vader's death grip clamp around my wrist. I looked back at Shooter, who handed out orders.

"Doc, look over Tongue. Make sure he doesn't have a concussion. The rest of you get back in the house. We have shit to do. You come with me."

I was not used to being ordered around, and I really wanted to tell Shooter where he could stick his demands. Before I could say anything, he dragged me off in the direction of the house. I dug in my heels, but he was not a man who allowed people to disobey his orders. He dragged me tripping and fighting the entire way, then yanked me up the stairs to the third floor and into my room. He threw me on the bed, which thanks to Sissy had already been made, and ordered me to stay there. He waltzed into my bathroom like he freaking owned the place. I followed his orders for about half a second before following him.

"Get your ass back on that bed!" he demanded as he pulled a washcloth from my cabinet.

Why did men have to act that way? They think they can fix any situation by hitching up their pants and telling you exactly what you're going to do. In my experience, that's a total shit plan. Most of the time their "help" ended in something being set on fire and a trip to the emergency room. Still, part of me liked that he wanted to look me over. A man hadn't shown care and concern for me in years. Yeah, I had Tyler, but he knew I could take care of myself and that I didn't like people fussing over me. With Shooter, it was different. I wanted him to see that I was okay. Of course, because I have more relationship hang-ups than the Kardashian sisters, that meant I'd have to make him completely miserable.

I freaked out. "This is my room! You don't get to give orders in my room!"

He wet the washcloth, frog marched me back to my bed, and threw me down onto it again.

I tried to stand up. It didn't matter if I sat or stood, I just knew I didn't want to be where he wanted me. He pushed me back down and stood in front of me, clamping my legs between his so I couldn't move. He tried to press the washcloth to my bleeding lip, but I knocked it away. He went at me again and again, but I swatted it away every time. He didn't get to play Florence Nightingale with me.

Like an idiot he just wouldn't give up. There really was no other option. I unleashed the same tactics employed by a five-year-old little girl trying to swat a bee away. I closed my eyes and waved both my hands in front of my face, blocking any attempt Shooter made with the wet rag. He laughed, and that just pissed me off. My eyes flew open and my fist buried itself in his gut.

I have no idea how that happened. I didn't tell my brain to knock the stuffing out of Shooter. My fist reacted all on its own. I got a little too much pleasure when he doubled over in pain. I tried to push him out of the way, but he recovered too quickly. He threw the washcloth onto the bed and trapped both my wrists in one of his hands. He stepped inside my personal bubble. I could feel the heat radiating from his body, hear every breath he took, and he smelled fantastic. I couldn't pinpoint one single thing about him that made my insides twitch. Everything about him screamed alpha. I had to screw my head on straight or I'd do something I would most definitely regret. He picked up the rag and dabbed at my face. I tried to evade him by moving my head out of the way but it took way too much effort. I had to give in or risk being hogtied, and that would not happen.

"You know," he said, "when I first saw you, I knew you'd be trouble."

I didn't respond. He had no idea how much trouble I could be, but I seriously wanted to show him.

"Then I saw you with Joe when Tongue nearly hit you, and I knew you were protective." He continued to wipe my face clean with surprisingly gentle strokes. "Last night in the library, I added complicated to your list of traits. This morning you proved you're strong."

I relaxed a little. I couldn't tell where he was going, but I liked being called strong.

"At the lake with Big Joe you were caring. There was one constant attribute from the airport until now. You are the single most stubborn human being on the planet. Now strip."

Huh! So not going to happen. "Oh, I don't think so."

"I need to see if you have internal bleeding. I saw Tongue kick you, and you could bleed to death without knowing it. Now strip."

"Not happening, cowboy."

"Dammit! I have no desire to see you naked. I need to medically assess your injuries!"

I wasn't sure if I should be comforted or insulted by Shooter's statement. I pulled my top off to reveal a skin-tight black tank top. "This is all you get. You can check my stomach and that's it. My heart and lungs are protected by my rib cage, and I don't have any vital organs below my waist." Shooter cocked an eyebrow. It took me a minute to realize what I'd just said but when I did, I wanted to kick my own ass.

"Lie down."

I did as he asked and moved my tank up out of the way so he could see my abdomen. He palpated my belly. Okay, he was right, I need to be looked after. There were more sore spots than I'd initially thought.

"So, do you have training as a medic or something?" I needed conversation. The situation was already more uncomfortable than getting a pelvic exam with a pine tree. Something needed to ease the tension.

"The Corps doesn't have medical staff. Doc is technically a Navy corpsman. So no, I don't have training as a medic." He spoke as he worked, but I didn't get the feeling that he was distracted by my need to fill the empty space with words.

"Then how do you know what you're doing?" Had it really taken me that long to ascertain his credentials.

"What I am is a Marine Force Recon sniper. I cost a lot of money to train so the military wants to keep me alive as long as possible. I took a class on how to not die." He smiled when I laughed. Then I groaned as the pain of my injuries settled in.

"My turn," he said. "Who taught you to fight?"

That was none of his damn business. "Your mother."

He paused in his examination to insult me. "Here's the deal, princess. You can either tell me, or I'll go ask Tongue."

Dammit! My brother wouldn't hesitate to brag that I can kick anyone's ass six times before they had a chance to cry for their mommies. He thought my single best attribute was my ability to kick someone's teeth in. *Crap*! "My grandfather taught me." Shooter hadn't earned any other explanation.

He continued to palpate my body. "And why are you such a tiger? Anyone can learn to fight. To take a punch like you did, that takes purpose. Why do you fight?"

No, absolutely not! I was not about to tell that story. What did I know about him? I knew he was a Marine with bad dreams because he accidentally killed a young girl. Shit. That sentence actually told me a lot about Shooter. I knew more about him than I thought I did. Dammit. Big effing deal! That did not mean I had to go all Sally Jesse Raphael with Shooter. But did my mouth get that message? No. And for its sedition, I would have to cut my tongue out.

"I've always been able to fight. I've never been afraid to really hit someone. In sixth grade there was this girl, Penny. She wasn't well liked. She had really bad acne and this horrible bronze hair. Her mom made her wear homemade dresses to school every day that looked like sacks with sleeves. All the girls teased her like crazy. But she always took it, kept her head held high, never let them see her cry. She had real courage. I always felt bad for her, but I never said anything. I never spoke up for her.

"One day I found out that this group of really mean girls wanted to hurt her. I couldn't let that happen. I finally had the balls to stand up. I ran across the school to the girls' restroom where the bitches waited. But I was too late. They had her pinned to the ground, shaving her head. This really big, burly girl grabbed me from behind and slammed me against the wall. I tried to throw her off me, but she was huge. Baby elephant huge. I watched as Penny's hair fell on the bathroom floor, her scalp nicked and bleeding from the dull blade they'd used. She didn't cry, didn't struggle, she just took it.

"That night, she shot herself in the head with her daddy's .357 Magnum. Every time I fight, I think of Penny and what I wish I could have done to those girls. No one deserves to be treated like that. No one." Shooter had stopped his examination. He looked at me with stupid in his eyes, "What?"

"Nothing. It's just, very few people shock me." He resumed his inspection.

I stopped myself from saying, *You're lucky. Most of them shock the hell out of me.* That would have been too *Pretty Woman.*

He moved his hands up my rib cage along my sides. He pressed his fingers up my neck and against my skull before he paused and looked me in the eye. With very little effort, he could kiss me. A rush of white hot fear surged through my body. I freaked out. I jumped up, freed myself from his grasp, hit the top of my head on the bottom of his chin.

"Dammit, woman, I'm trying to help you!"

"I don't need your help. Get out of my room!"

"That's gratitude for you! See if I ever offer my services again." He'd straightened to his full height and put his hands on his hips. I could tell he was trying to lighten the mood, but I didn't to feel comfortable around him.

"Your services are not required or wanted. Leave!"

His stance switched from teasing to hurt. "Look, the whole reason I'm here is to help you! You are the most ungrateful, prickly person I've ever met. And I've met Saddam Hussein!"

"Get. The. Hell. Out. *Now!*"

He threw his hands up in the air, "I am! I'm leaving! No wonder you have no one significant in your life! Who would want you? You push people away who only have your best interest at heart! I'm gone!" He turned and left without giving me a chance to beat him to a bloody pulp.

I fell to the floor. I couldn't be worse than Saddam Hussein. I'd never committed genocide, but I did manage to poison every relationship I'd ever had. Even with Stephan. He was the most patient, loving, compassionate man in the world. And I managed to push him away, too. But, he always came back because he loved me. Until the last time. The last time we fought he left in anger and never came back. You'd think I'd learn. But I had issues with people who were kind to me with no expectation of a return on their investment. That just didn't compute in my messed up brain.

I stood up and found my way to the bathroom, and turned the shower on. I let it get blisteringly hot, then undressed and stepped in. Normally the stream of lava acted like a tonic. It could wash away all my bad qualities, bad memories, and bad thoughts. Of course, it failed me.

Why did Shooter affect me the way he did? Why did I care about what he thought about me? Why did I want to hide my less than attractive personality traits from him? Why did he make me so freaking mad? And why did that bother me?

I turned the shower off, pissed it hadn't done its job of cleansing my soul. As I toweled off, I looked in the mirror. I don't normally look at myself naked. I could tell you it was because I'm a bit Puritanical, but that would be a lie. The real reason I didn't let Shooter see me in my panties and bra stared at me through the glass. No one but my doctor and Edna had seen the puckered pink scars that crisscrossed my abdomen and breasts. Stephan had never seen them. He was gone by the time I'd acquired them. They were gifts, little reminders, of the worst night of my life. They were the reason I worked out every day, kept my muscles strong, and why I am the way I am. You can't go through something like that without changing. At least that's what my doctor told me.

I threw the towel at the mirror and angrily got dressed. I put on a pair of skin tight black pants and a short sleeved black cashmere sweater. I pulled on my shopping boots, black leather with buttons running from heel to knee. They didn't look it, but they were really comfortable. I twisted my hair up into a French twist and applied mascara and lip gloss. Armor on, I headed downstairs for breakfast. Perhaps brunch was a more apt term.

As I entered the kitchen, I was not surprised to see Tyler and all my Marines sitting at the butcher block table shoveling food into their pie holes. I took my seat and helped myself to fruit, bacon, sausage, eggs, muffin, croissant, beignets, and coffee. The rest of the diners stopped mid-bite to take in the quantity of food on my plate. I was stress eating but I didn't care. Sometimes a girl needed a hug that started in her stomach and ended in a pair of jeans one size larger.

I ignored the stares and started the mammoth task of consuming the Mount Kilimanjaro made of breakfast on my plate. Most respectable Southern ladies wouldn't be caught dead Hoovering mass quantities of food into their mouths. But I wasn't Southern, respectable, or a lady, so I figured that social law didn't apply to me. I cleared my plate in about ten minutes.

My Marines finished eating long before I did, but none of them left. I think they wanted to see if I could finish. I wiped my mouth with a linen napkin. "So we're going shopping today. Tyler did tell you, didn't he?"

"Yeah, I told them. But we hadn't planned on company." Tyler told me in the most polite way he knew how that I wasn't welcome.

"I'm not company. I'm the wallet and the ride, so I'm coming. I want to make sure you are all kitted out for the summer." I crossed my arms over my chest, sending the table the universal signal that I wasn't about to budge.

"Don't you have something you need to do, like plan a Founder's Day Celebration?" Tyler tried everything to get rid of me.

"Nope, and you know the committee plans the celebration. I just provide the place. Are we all ready then?" No one stood up.

"Let me put this as nicely as possible," Shooter chimed in. "We don't want you with us. Stay home."

I uncrossed my arms and leaned forward on the table. "Not happening. I'm going. I need to know you'll be presentable. People will know you're staying with me, and they expect a certain level of...sophistication from my guests. Since I'm almost positive the Corps didn't issue you with a sense of fashion, I have to be the one to provide that."

They stood up and left the kitchen.

I stood to follow them when Edna grabbed my arm. "Don't you think you should go a little easy on them? They're not used to you."

"My Marines can handle it."

"Your Marines?" she said, raising an eyebrow.

"What?"

Her eyes penetrated my soul. "You just called them your Marines."

I waved her off. "No I didn't."

She hit me with a look that said *you know what you said and so do I.* When had I laid claim to a bunch of misfit

Marines? I hadn't realized it until then, but I had been referring to them as *my Marines* in my head since I picked them up. *Great. Just freaking great!*

Somehow I had become attached to them. It would really suck when I inevitably had to feed their bodies into a wood chipper.

Chapter Five

On the other side of the kitchen door, I nearly ran into Horndog with his hands against the wall and Sissy trapped between them. Sissy was an adorable, innocent, blonde haired, blue-eyed Southern girl. In other words, Horndog's kryptonite. She noticed me before Horndog did, recognized the look of shock and horror on my face, and wisely scampered off. Horndog was not so smart. I started to wonder if his mother fed him paint chips as a kid instead Wheaties. He just stood there with a silly grin on his face like Angelina Jolie had just kissed him on the mouth. I stomped toward him. It took all the discipline I possessed to not slap him across the face.

I stood on my tiptoes so I could look him in the eye. "Listen up, Horndog, because I'm only going to say this once. If I find any of my staff between your sheets, I'm going to replace your favorite appendage with a piece of cooked spaghetti. Am I clear?"

The cocky bastard actually smiled at me. "I wasn't trying to sleep with the sweet Miss Sissy. I was only trying to find out what type of detergent she uses. I love the smell of my sheets."

I leaned in, centimeters from his face. "How stupid do you think I am? Stay away from Sissy."

"How can I stay away from her when she works all over this

house?"

"Use your considerably small brain to figure it out," I said menacingly.

He took a step back. "Geez, you act like I'm trying to deflower your virgin sister."

I poked his chest with my finger. "Sissy means much more to me than a sister. Her family has been with the Boudreauxs for four generations. She didn't even go to public school. She was taught here by her mother. I don't think she's ever been on a date. So, you referring to her as my virgin sister is not far off the mark. Stay away from her, or I swear on everything that is holy, you will live to regret it." I left without giving him a chance to reply and trudged up the stairs to collect my things for our shopping trip.

With purse in hand, I walked out the front doors. The Escalade had been brought around to the front of the house and my Marines were inside. Shooter sat in the driver's seat. It didn't really bother me that he wanted to drive, but that didn't mean I couldn't give him crap. It was the principle of the thing. I circled the SUV to the driver's side door and opened it.

He glared at me, and I said, "I hope you don't expect to drive."

"I do. Get in." He didn't look at me. He just gripped the steering wheel and gritted his teeth.

I cocked an eyebrow. "Oh yeah, and how do you get there, genius?"

"That's why God invented GPS. Now get in. Look, I even made the guys sit in the back so you could have the front." He smiled and patted the seat next to him.

"How nice of you, considering it's my car." I'm big enough to say he started to annoy the shit out of me.

"Hop in, honey. Shopping won't wait." *Okay, now he's mocking me.* Little did he know, I excelled at backseat driving. I wanted to object. All right, I wanted to crush his wind pipe with a chop to the neck, but that would accomplish nothing. Well, not nothing. It would get Shooter out of my hair for a while.

There wasn't anything I could do that wouldn't end in bloodshed, so I made my way to the front passenger door, hopped in as requested, and we were off.

Before we reached the end of the driveway, I started giving Shooter driving advice. "Now when you come out of the driveway, you need to look really good because it's kind of a blind corner." Further down the road I offered, "The city never repairs this road so you kind of have to slalom through the pot holes." He hit every one. "This bridge is narrow. Make sure you're closer to it than any oncoming traffic.

"Slow down. I need to wave to Mrs. Johnson if she's out in her yard." He didn't even tap his brakes. "Now when you merge onto the highway...." I began, but then he really slammed on the brakes. If it hadn't been for the seatbelt, I would have gotten some up close and personal time with the hood of my Escalade.

"You can ride inside, or I can strap you to the grill. It's your choice." It wasn't a threat. It was a promise. I folded my arms in front of me and sat back in my seat. Shooter just didn't know how to have fun. So I didn't give him anymore driving tips. Even when the GPS sent him in circles, I didn't offer any advice. I made him ask for it.

"How the hell do you get into this mall?"

"Are you asking for my expert opinion?" I couldn't help myself. I had to needle him.

"I am asking you to point me in the right direction." The muscle in his jaw popped. I made a note to see if I could get Shooter mad enough to make it jump through his skin.

"Because it sounds like you're asking me for help. I could be wrong, but that's what it sounds like."

He gritted his teeth. "Yes, Kat, I'm asking you for help. Now tell me which way to go!"

I wanted to tell him to go straight down and keep digging till he felt his eyebrows singe off, but I restrained myself. "Left at the light, then right at the first stop sign." He did as instructed, and we pulled into an empty parking space. "I told you I should drive." I couldn't help myself. It was like word vomit. Shooter slammed the door. If I hadn't installed bullet resistant glass, it would have shattered.

My Marines and I paraded into the mall. "Should we start from the inside and work our way out," I suggested. "We can stop at Macy's to get underwear, socks, and workout clothes. Then we'll start with the fun stuff." They looked like they wanted to kill me. Oh this was going to be fun. As I headed for the department store, I noticed random shoppers giving me odd looks. I didn't quite understand the attention until I turned to see my pack of behemoths. They were an intimidating sight. If I saw them coming at me in the mountains of Afghanistan, I'd run as far and as fast as I could. I heard one woman say "I wonder who she is?" Please, as if I needed to walk around with six bodyguards.

I also heard the sound of fist hitting clothed skin and several times. Tyler and Shooter said, "Cut it out," and "Stop that." I didn't turn to see what caused all the ruckus until I heard Tyler yell, "Horndog, I swear on everything that's holy, if you don't stop staring at my sister's ass I'm going to hold you down while Doc cuts your dick off!" Well, that got my attention.

Apparently Horndog could change the object of his attentions as fast as a NASCAR driver changed gears. I thought about yelling at him then I thought about tearing off his arms and beating him to death with them. Then I thought of something far more devious.

My Marines stopped as I turned and approached Horndog. They probably expected some type of violent reaction so they were floored when I said, "You like my ass, Horndog? Well, go ahead and look. I work real hard on it, and it deserves to be noticed."

Tyler looked like he wanted to strangle me. Shooter, to my surprise, looked like he wanted to strangle Horndog.

Horndog politely said, "Yes, ma'am," and continued to ogle.

Switch, Martinez, and Doc looked uncomfortable. Making them squirm wasn't on my list, but I decided to add it. Just for fun.

They hit Macy's with all the enthusiasm of men who'd just been handed their last cigarette and a blindfold. The packages of men's underwear could have been a firing squad. I started with Shooter. "So, Shooter, do you wear boxers, briefs, or boxer briefs? And what size are you?" Shooter ignored me and grabbed a package off the rack. "Oh come now, you'll need more than that. You grabbed boxers, size large, right?" I threw two more at him. "Okay, Horndog, now you. And yes, you are required to wear underwear in my house. No commando."

Tyler grabbed my arm and dragged me off to the footwear department. "Stop it. Right now, Kat. Stop."

"What? I'm just helping your friends shop," I said innocently.

"No, you're not. You're trying to humiliate them. I won't allow that. See my foot? It's down. Show them the respect they deserve as human beings and have earned as Marines."

Well, hell. How could I deny them that? I sort of...kind of...a little bit...had been acting the bitch.

It completely went against my nature, but I stayed in the background giving them their privacy to pick their preferred undergarments and socks. When I could tell they were done, I led them to the checkout. They lined up like good little soldiers. Shooter was first, of course, because he was always first. When the cashier finished ringing him up, I assumed he would step out of the way to allow Martinez to hand over his undies. When he didn't and pulled out a debit card, I grabbed his hand.

"I'm the one demanding you get new clothes so I'm paying."

"No, you're not." He ripped his hand away.

"Yes, I am. And, before this turns into a vaudeville skit, let me get my wallet." He protested, but I ignored him and handed the guy behind the counter a Visa Black Card.

The cashier grabbed the card from my hand and said to Shooter, "I'm sorry, honey, but her card trumps yours."

"Put everything on that please." He nodded and proceeded to tally up the rest of the purchases. He passed out the bags, and I could tell by the look in their eyes I had robbed these strong warriors of some of their pride. I couldn't stand to see these proud men humbled. I had to throw them a bone.

"This isn't charity," I said. "This is payment for past and future services. I'm sure you're the five who rescued Tyler from that building, and for that I can never repay you. I'll need extra security for the Founder's Day Celebration and you're it. Also, I want you to assess my current security and offer any tips on how to improve it." All of them, except Shooter, seemed to relax a bit knowing they were earning their shopping spree.

As we left Macy's, despite my earlier convictions, I wanted to be cordial.. I linked my arm in Tyler's and led them off down the mall. With my new found respect for my Marines, I looked over at them. A girl could do worse. Switch, Doc, and Martinez were still mysteries. It was as good a time as any to get to know them.

"Switch," I began, "you're the communications guy, right?" He nodded. "So could you set up a com system that would allow all my security to communicate on little Bluetooth headset thingies rather than walkie-talkies? The current system's a little old." That was not a lie. I had grown lazy about my home security. I felt safe there. It was exactly the situation an intruder could exploit. It needed a twenty-first century upgrade.

"Yes, ma'am," he said.

"Good, because I don't want everyone and their dog to overhear what's going on. And can you modernize my intercom system in the house? The one I have was installed in the late seventies, and I think it's safe to say it's a bit outdated." That was true, too. He nodded.

Horndog jumped in. "Can I ask you a question, Kat?"

"Of course." I won't lie, I was a little afraid of Horndog's question.

"I counted at least six security personnel at your house, so it's obvious you care about your safety, but you don't have security with you now."

"There are nine security guards at my house, by the way. And well, I don't need security with me today because I'm with all of you. I don't think you'll let anything happen to me." Oh Lord, being that sweet was going to make me puke or slip into a diabetic coma.

"You were alone at the airport, too."

Thank you, Captain Horndog Obvious.

"Airports have great security. I only take a guard with me if I know I'm going to be in danger. Besides, the system at the house isn't just for me. It's for everyone who works for me too."

And I can take care of myself thank you very much.

"Are the people in your house in danger?" Doc asked.

Wow, I think that's the first time I'd heard Doc speak. He had the kind of voice that could make you feel at ease even if your guts were spilled out on the floor. I guess that was part of his job.

"My husband's business provides me with a lot of enemies." It was true. In the current, climate we're viewed on the same level as cockroaches and Hamas.

"And your husband's company would be...?" Doc continued.

"Boudreaux Oil." I expected at least a little reaction when I revealed the source of my lifestyle. Boudreaux Oil was the largest petroleum company in America. We harvested oil from the Gulf of Mexico, Alaska, Venezuela, Saudi Arabia, Kuwait, and Iran. I had been invited to attend functions at OPEC summits for crying out loud! They should react to that kind of information. The Boudreaux name had been enough to make foreign heads of state bow to me, but my Marines showed no reaction whatsoever. Maybe they'd already figured it out. My last name was Boudreaux, and they had been to Iraq several times. Maybe Boudreaux Oil and I were old news.

Just as I considered this, Horndog piped up, "Wait a minute, your last name's Boudreaux, you own Boudreaux Oil, you live in Bayou Boudreaux, and you're planning a Founder's Day Celebration. You're the Boudreauxs of Bayou Boudreaux, aren't you?"

Switch snorted. "Are you seriously that stupid, Horndog? You just figured that out? How in the hell does the Corps trust you with explosives?" Everyone laughed, including Horndog, at Switch's assessment. It was nice to know I wasn't the only one to question Horndog's brain power.

Our next stop was Banana Republic. I ordered them to choose ten pairs of shorts and/or pants. When they had made their selections, I forced them to try them on and model for me. What woman wouldn't want six smoking hot men strutting in front of her like cocks in the hen house? Surprisingly, Horndog and Doc were into it. Martinez had to model because Horndog ordered him to. Shooter refused outright, and Switch gave me a look that said he'd rather be force fed his own eyeballs than try on clothes. Working on the whole respect and dignity thing, I let him off.

While they shopped, I had found a few pieces that I had to have. And yes, I shopped at the mall. I know you probably thought I had a closet full of couture, and I did have some designer stuff, but I was comfortable in regular clothes. So that's what I bought. I didn't grab too many things, only like, ten. And of course I made my Marines give me their opinions as I tried them all on. When I got to a tight little black dress with a plunging V neckline, Horndog whooped his approval. For his exuberance Shooter smacked him in the back of the head. Shooter took the whole Marine Corp rule about respecting women seriously.

I continued my inquiry as we left the store. "Doc, Shooter tells me you're a Navy corpsman, not a real Marine. How do you handle being around these jarheads all day?"

My Marines stopped dead in their tracks and stared at me as if they were five and I just told them Santa Claus was dead.

Horndog spoke up, "First of all, he is a real Marine. He may not wear the eagle, globe, and anchor, but he is all Marine."

"Thanks, Dog." Doc put a hand on Horndog to calm him down. "A medic's job is to look after the wellbeing of his troops. I'm not just responsible for stitching them up when their injured. It's my job to make sure they're healthy and happy. I'm part doctor, part nutritionist, part therapist, part mother, and part soldier." He dropped his head to look at his hands. "My job is to serve these Marines. You can't serve someone without growing to love them."

"That is quite possibly the single most beautiful piece of bro love I've ever heard, Doc," I said.

Horndog threw an arm around Doc's shoulders and kissed him loudly on the cheek. "I love you too, man. In a total bromance, platonic, I-don't-want-to-spoon-with-you kind of way."

"When was the last time you spooned with anyone, Horndog?" Doc threw Horndog's arm off his shoulders.

"That would be never, Doc. Never have and never will. I'm not a cuddler." So Horndog was a wham-bam-thank-you-ma'am type. Didn't see that one coming. *Yeah right.*

Off to J. Crew for tops. Again Horndog, Doc, and a reluctant Martinez tried on all their button ups and polos for me. Shooter and Switch denied me my fun. And of course I had to do a fashion show of my own. This time Horndog helped me pick out a few things. He knew way more than any straight man should about women's fashion. He chose a cowl neck top that I would normally stay away from. But, it was a beautiful ruby red so I relented and tried it on.

When I walked out of the dressing room, Horndog said, "You're wearing that wrong." He stood up from his chair and approached me. Just as he was about to adjust the neckline, Shooter shoved him out of the way, grabbed the droopy collar, and pulled it down over my shoulders.

"That's how you wear that. It looks much better," he said in a whisper.

I was in total shock when he moved back to his spot behind his brothers. I didn't miss the significant looks they gave each other. Honestly, I had been shocked stupid, as well. What was that all about? And why the hell did I have that gooey reaction in my stomach again? I totally did not want to explore that can of worms. I cleared my throat to get their attention and they all agreed the blouse looked better Shooter's way.

We left J. Crew and I led them in the direction of Express. Man cannot live on khakis and polos alone. I still needed to get some info on Martinez. "What about you, Martinez? What do you do?"

"My specialty is close quarters combat. But, really, I'm just a gun." When he answered me, I realized I had never actually heard him speak either. He had a very soothing, deep voice. Not thick and rich like Shooter's, but peaceful.

His proficiency at hand-to-hand combat actually got me excited. "Do you want to spar?" I could barely contain my excitement.

Before he could answer Tyler, Shooter, Doc, Switch, and Horndog all said, "No."

"Why not? I can hold my own. Tyler and I had just gotten warmed up when you stopped us. You didn't even see my best moves," I whined. I'm not above whining.

"We may not have seen your best moves, but we have seen Martinez's, and I'm pretty sure he would kill you," Horndog said.

I leaned around Tyler and caught Martinez's eye. "Tomorrow morning, six a.m."

Shooter and Tyler grumbled. I'd never get my chance to spar with the deadly Marine. What a disappointment.

In Express we were helped by a very tall, very thin, very beautiful woman. She looked like she'd stepped out of one of the floor to ceiling advertisements. What the purposes of these advertisements are I have never been able to figure out. It's like a group of glamazons were telling you, "Look what you can buy here and look how great it will look while you're running barefoot through the woods."

The glamazon, whose name was Candy, of course, was extremely helpful. If you classify flirting and bending over to give everyone a better view of her cleavage helpful, then yeah she was very helpful. She flipped her just-climbed-out-of-bed hair over her shoulder at a rate of twenty flips per minute and laughed if one of my Marines said something hysterical like,

"Do you have this in a bigger size?" or "Does this come in black?" You'd think they'd all missed their callings as comedians. What I liked was how they seemed to be annoyed by her constant flirting, flipping, and laughing. Even Horndog, who prior to this had convinced me he would flirt with anything with a mouth, seemed to really dislike her.

While the glamazon "helped" them pick out slacks, dress shirts, and ties, I helped myself to another round of power shopping. Express was the best place in the world to buy a sexy dress. Not that I actually wore them, but I liked having them as part of my closet.

As soon as I finished with my picks, and I could see the guys were close to strangling Candy, I ushered them to the dressing rooms. To my extreme surprise, Shooter actually tried on his choices. He said it was because he hadn't worn slacks in such a long time, he didn't know which fit he liked. But I think he just needed a break from Candy. When he came out in black slacks, a black shirt, and a black tie tied in a small knot I had to ask, "Are you trying to look like the Grim Reaper?"

"I think he looks perfect. Very chic." Candy offered her unwanted opinion.

I ignored her and pulled a deep red tie off the rack. I untied the black one and tied the red one in a Prince Albert knot. "There, that's much better."

He looked in the mirror and smiled. "I like that knot. Where'd you learn to do that?"

"I used to take Tyler to church every Sunday."

He stroked the tie. "I like it. Can you show me how to do it?"

"Sure." I stood in front of him and untied his tie. I showed him step by step how to tie the Prince Albert. It was the most time I had spent up close to Shooter without wanting to punch him in the face. He smelled wonderful. Like man and cedar. Could I get that scent made into an air freshener? I would spray my whole house with it. After I knew he had the hang of the knot, I reluctantly backed away.

He changed back into his khakis and joined me in watching

the Marine fashion show. My Marines hadn't picked out most of what they tried on. I had to replace half the choices and the other half got thrown out all-together. But eventually we got through it.

Then it was my turn. Candy had taken my chair between Shooter and Horndog. I came out in my first option, a shiny red, ruched, strapless number, you'd think I'd just won the Super Bowl. Apparently they really liked the dress. When I appeared in the second, nude sleeveless with a black lace overlay, I won the Stanley Cup. The third was greeted with the same level of cheering as when the Red Sox won the World Series. Confused didn't begin to describe me. True, the dresses were great, but I didn't get nearly that much attention in the other stores. And then I saw Candy. The glamazon had turned into Godzilla in the last three dresses. She was clearly jealous of the attention I got. Maybe I didn't deserve it, but she did deserve to be brought down a few notches. So I tried on dress after dress and reveled in the attention. When I put on a strapless short, tight leopard creation, Horndog and Doc got in a mock fight over my attentions. At that point Candy turned into a harpy, sprouted wings, grew a beak, and tried to bite out my trachea. Or at least that's what she looked like she wanted to do.

We made our purchases and left with my ego stronger than it had ever been. Our last stop was at the end of the long mall corridor. Dillard's was the perfect place for men's shoes. We passed The Build-a-Bear Workshop. A very young girl stood in the middle of the mall crying with tears and snot running down her face. Obviously, she was lost. If that had been my daughter, I would want someone to help her, so I headed in her direction. Shooter beat me to her. I thought the girl would be terrified by such a large man approaching her, but it seemed, like me, she could sense the peace Shooter brought with him. Unlike me, she was able to enjoy it.

He picked her up and held her in his arm while he spoke softly to her and wiped her face with his shirt. Within seconds the girl had stopped crying and laid her head on his shoulder.

"How about we go find your mommy?" he cooed in her ear.

I had seen the leader Shooter and the tough Shooter and the Marine Force Recon Shooter. But I had never seen the child-loving Shooter. I didn't think the Corps nurtured that part of their Marines. And since I assumed all Shooter's personality traits were issued with his khaki socks, I didn't think it existed in him.

Across from the Build-a-Bear shop was an American Eagle and a Swim n' Sport. Shooter looked over the two and went into the Swim n' Sport. A very good choice in my opinion, since it was swimsuit season and nothing distracted a woman like a bulge in the wrong place while in a bikini. He ignored the racks of next to nothing spandex and aimed straight for the dressing rooms. "Are any of you ladies missing a cute little brunette with brown eyes?"

A woman shrieked as if she just noticed her spawn had gone missing and opened the door with nothing on but a Kenneth Cole tiffany-blue Brazilian bikini.

"Oooh my gooosh," she said with an accent so thick you could use it for target practice. "I can't believe she wandered off like that! McKenna, you need to stay by Momma."

Yeah, blame the three-year-old for your crappy parenting skills.

"I'd keep an eye on her, ma'am," Shooter said. "I'd hate to see anything happen to her."

Miss Brazilian bikini looked Shooter up and down like she was a USDA inspector with her Prime Cut stamp ready. "Thank you for takin' care of my little girl. How can I repay you, Mister...." She lingered on the *mister* and actually ran an obscenely long, fake fingernail in need of a fill down his chest.

Trailer park trashy bitch, get your hands off my Marine!

Whoa, where the hell had that come from?

Shooter grabbed her wrist stopping her finger as it moved farther south. "Shooter. My name is Shooter," he practically growled, "and you can start by focusing on your child instead of using your very limited brain power to land your next Mr. Right Now wearing nothing more than two postage stamps and a cork. I can guarantee that the kind of man who will have you in what you have on right now is not the kind of man you should want around your daughter. Put on some clothes, take your daughter out to lunch, and see if you can buy some dignity because it's obvious you don't have any on you."

Now that's *my* Marine.

Shooter patted McKenna on the top of the head and smiled at her before guiding me out of the store with his hand at the small of my back.

"That was impressive," I said as we exited the store.

"Why do women do that? They think they have to dress in a hankie to get a man's attention. In my humble opinion, class outranks ass any day." I could hear the aggravation in his voice.

"I meant how you treated McKenna. It was like she knew you." Okay I was actually talking about what he had said to McKenna's mom but for some reason I didn't want him to know that.

"I've always been good with kids," he said, dismissing the fact that a hysterical little girl was calmed by a man who looked like he could wrap her up in a bun and eat her for a snack.

Suddenly I felt like a war vet having a flash back. I remembered Shooter's dream/memory. It was obvious he cared about kids. Last night at dinner he had completely won Sam over by teaching her a magic trick with a napkin and a salt shaker where he made it look like he pushed the salt through the table. Killing a child, even by accident, must have destroyed him. I needed to hug him again, but that was so not happening. Shooter had gone through a hell not even I could comprehend, and he came through it a good man. True, he would be plagued with the memory and the nightmares for the rest of his life, but that experience probably shaped him more than any other single moment in his life. If it had been me, I probably would have tried to kill myself with a rusty ice pick. But that's me, and Shooter was so much stronger than me in so many different ways. I hadn't thought of anyone outside my staff and Tyler as a good man in a long time. From then on I would not fight with Shooter. I would not make him uncomfortable, and I would not disrespect him in any way. He deserved better than that. What? I can be nice!

Shooter didn't move his hand from my back when we rejoined everyone else. He guided me down the mall to Dillard's where they picked out gym shoes, casual shoes, and dress shoes. By the time we were finished, we were all heavy laden and hungry. I would like to express my thanks to the man who invented the mall food court. Variety, value, air conditioning, and a place to sit. What more could a girl need?

As we ate, my Marines talked and laughed over hideous things the others had tried on and Candy's painfully obvious attempts at getting one of them, any of them, alone in a dressing room for five minutes. It was the most comfortable and human I'd seen them. As relaxed as they were, they were still on. Their eyes never stopped scanning, never stopped looking for threats. The other diners didn't know it, but they were eating at the safest damn Panda Express in the known universe.

When we'd finished our gyros, pizzas, burgers, and Chinese food, we made our way back to the car. We could barely fit all the bags into the back of the Escalade. I love that feeling. You know, the one where your stomach warms after buying a bunch of new things? They don't even have to be for you. There's nothing better than a full trunk.

My Marines hesitated before getting back into the car. I had almost forgotten that they had a side trip to the docks planned to pick up a shipment after the shopping trip. It was the whole reason I had insisted on coming. How had I forgotten about it?

They finally climbed in and Tyler said, "We need to make a stop on our way home. Switch has some communications stuff that he can use on your house to pick up at the docks. It shouldn't take more than a minute. You good with that?"

"Sure, I've got nothing going on for the rest of the day."

They would try to keep me as far away from the action as possible. And Tyler was trying to make me think they needed to pick something up that was simply too valuable or too big to take on an airplane. I'm not stupid. That obviously wasn't the case. The cargo would be something illegal to take on the plane and, quite possibly, illegal for a civilian to have, period. They may have planned to keep whatever they were doing from me, but I intended to find out sooner rather than later what the hell they were up to.

Chapter Six

The ride to the Port of New Orleans was a quiet one. I could tell my Marines had switched into battle mode. The aura around them had gone from light and fun to dark and scary. I rode in the car with six real live actual professional killers. And I was worried about them. Fear for their safety was not the only thing that caused my stomach to turn into a pot of boiled spaghetti. A far more intense debilitating emotion gripped me. The emotion didn't really have a name. Fear was too tame and terror didn't really cut it. I guess it would resemble the emotion you'd have if you were to jump out of an airplane without a parachute, naked, covered in honey with a projected impact point of a cactus field infested with bullet ants, and somehow you knew you'd survive to experience every last little bit of pain.

This was where it had happened. This was where I woke up to find my body broken, bloodied, and violated, then kept awake to make sure the monsters could adequately show me what I had missed. My heart beat a tattoo in my chest and it seemed as if all the oxygen had been sucked out of the city of New Orleans. Why had Shooter chosen to take this route? There was a far more direct way to the port, but he chose to take the scenic route through the Lower Ninth Ward. Tyler sat behind me. He alone knew what had happened. He placed a hand on my shoulder. I grabbed it, grateful for the reassurance. My heart slowed and the band around my ribcage began to loosen.

Why were ports always in the seediest parts of town? Did ships breed vice and crime? When I thought about it, historically, yeah they kind of did. Anyone who's ever seen Pirates of the Caribbean knew that. Though, I would take a helping of vice and crime if it was served up by Johnny Depp.

We drove through the dregs of the city, through housing tenements and red light districts, past drug houses and underground casinos. I think we even drove over a couple of those chalk outlines cops trace in movies when they come across a dead body. Then it got truly pathetic. We drove through the neighborhoods destroyed by Katrina where young children played in the tall, unkempt grass in front of the condemned homes. A young woman stepped out of one of the doorways to call her kids. People had squatted in these destroyed dwellings as soon as the flood waters had receded. They just wanted a life, and they tried to create one from the wreckage.

On the outside of the house with the young woman was a strange hieroglyph. Anyone who lived on the Gulf Coast could decipher the code. It was a giant X. On the top of the X was spray painted *9-1*, to the left, *CA F8*, and to the right, *3 in attic*. It meant the house had been checked after Katrina on September first by unit CA F8, and that three dead bodies were found in the attic.

I don't care how callous you are, seeing something like that had to affect you. If it didn't, then you're as creepy and cold as Jeffrey Dahmer showing up at a bar-b-cue with a Ziploc baggie of mystery meat.

We continued through the worn streets of New Orleans. I imagine at one time this part of the city was beautiful. The beauty probably lasted about a week. I don't doubt that when the French Quarter had first been constructed, it was something to behold. But then the pimps, hookers, and opium dealers moved in and most of it went to hell. Since then it's been in a perpetual state of decay and not just the structural kind. So, unless you want to get completely wasted and end up in bed with a cross-dressing hooker, your best friend's mom, and a stray dog, stay away from Bourbon Street.

Don't get me wrong. There were parts of the city that had been maintained or rejuvenated over the years and these were truly beautiful. The Garden District was stunning. And let's not forget the history the city holds. Who wouldn't love to go on a ghost tour through the most paranormal city on the planet? Or visit all the historical buildings and vampire bars.

For me, my single favorite parts of New Orleans were the Cities of The Dead. People were "buried" above ground in stone crypts lined up in neat little rows. You could climb somebody's family tree by reading the epitaphs engraved on the sides. I wasn't some Goth chick with too much eyeliner who sat in a dark basement writing bad poetry, nor was I hoping to die. I just liked how they viewed death. The people of New Orleans commemorated death in the glaring light of day. I wanted a New Orleans funeral. I didn't care if I lived in Salt Lake City, Utah. A dirge would be played on the way to the cemetery and a jazz band would lead all my loved ones to the nearest bar where they'd get completely trashed in my honor. New Orleanians celebrated a person's life; they didn't mourn their death.

We turned onto Plauche Street, and Shooter stopped the SUV to talk to the guard at the gate to the port. He gave him a name I couldn't quite hear, and the guard waved us through. Shooter clearly knew where he was going and drove through the rows of containers and cargo ships. As we meandered through the port, I wondered where all the security was. I knew there was port police, but the part of the port we drove through was completely void of human life. The instincts I'd buried years ago came back to life. Something was wrong, very wrong. It went beyond the lack of people. The authorities had been taken care of. The pricking on the back of my neck meant something more. I'd learned to trust my instincts and right then, they screamed. My muscles tensed, jumping for a fight. I reached for my weapon. It wasn't there. I'd flashed back to a different life. A life where I went everywhere armed. In my new life, I never carried a gun. How had I gotten so careless? Shooter pulled in to, not so much an empty parking space as an empty cargo container space, and my Marines got out of the SUV. I figured what's good for the soldier is good for the civilian, so I climbed out and joined them.

Tyler quickly grabbed me by the arm and led me back to the passenger side door. "You're not coming with us. You need to get back in the car."

"I want to come." Yes, I sounded like a petulant child, but I wanted to know what was going on in my house and everything in me said they needed some backup.

"You are not coming," he said, gritting his teeth.

"Why not? If you're just picking up communications equipment from a federally regulated port, I don't see why I can't tag along." I thought that was perfectly sensible. Tyler, not so much.

"Switch is picking up some...sensitive equipment. That he wants to keep under wraps."

I crossed my arms over my chest, "Translation: illegal equipment."

"Yes, some of it is illegal if used for anything non-military." Tyler looked around as if he was afraid someone might hear him.

"And he's going to install and store this stuff at my house. I have a right to know what I could go to jail for." A completely valid point in my opinion.

"You'll be protected if you don't know what is being stored at your house." Had he caught a case of the stupids?

I raised my eyebrow. "That makes about as much sense as going to Disneyland to find strippers and score cocaine. If it's my house and illegal stuff is found there, I'm responsible. Saying 'I didn't know,' to a judge isn't going to fly."

"Look, Kat, the stuff is technically illegal, so we had to use some less then legal methods to ship it. These methods employ people who shoot first and ask questions later. I won't let you get caught in the crossfire." A look of concern filled his eyes. Sweet.

"And you think I'm prepared to allow you to put yourself in danger. No way! I'm going." I fought against his hold.

"No you're not! You're staying here!"

I broke away from him and ran to the group of men gathered at the back of the Escalade. If I thought I'd find safe harbor there, I was wrong. As soon as I reached my group of Marines, Shooter grabbed me, flung me over his shoulder like a sack of fertilizer, and hauled me to the front of the SUV. He didn't handle me as gently as Tyler had, and he didn't explain himself. He opened the car and threw me onto the passenger seat. The second my tush hit leather, I sat back up to try to escape. I knew it would ultimately prove to be ridiculous, but I had to try. Just as I expected, Shooter tried to lock me in. He held me to the seat with his palm on my chest. He pulled the seat belt around my torso and locked it into place. Seriously, did he really think that would hold me? Unfortunately, he didn't remove his hand from my chest. He held me there while he rummaged for something in one of the many pockets attached to the side of his Marine issue khakis. *What the hell? Who carries zip ties around in his pockets?* Shooter zip tied me to the damn seat belt!

"You're staying here," he said calmly and shut the door. He hit the security button on the key fob so that if I tried to open the door, the alarm would go off, and they would know I had escaped my cage. I rolled my eyes.

As I watched him walk away with the rest of my Marines, I had to laugh. Not because of the ridiculous situation I'd found myself in or because I had just been successfully beaten. No, I laughed because in a few brief moments, they had revealed most of their plan and a few weaknesses to me. I knew by Tyler's reaction they weren't there to collect communications equipment. It was a pretty safe bet they were there for weapons. If they were so worried I'd get hurt they zip tied me to the car, then the people they'd hired were probably Somali pirates and my Marines, therefore, needed backup.

The weapons they were bringing into the country were not the type used for hunting Bambi. They were used to kill people, blow up tanks, and bring down airplanes. And I totally got why they might need that kind of weaponry in Bayou Boudreaux. You know, in case the French Foreign Legion invaded the town. All joking aside, I really had no idea why they needed heavy weaponry, but it was only a matter of time before they messed up and gave me that information too. I learned they were loyal not only to each other, but that their umbrella of protection seemed to include me. So, all I really needed to do was put myself in danger, and they would change their plans to protect me. Unless their plan already included protecting me, then I was pretty much screwed. But what would they need to protect me from? True, there were parts of my past that could possibly come back to bite me in the ass, but the likelihood of that was slim.

There were a few things they didn't know about me. They didn't know I would chew my way through the seatbelt to get out of the car. But that wouldn't be necessary. They didn't know I travelled armed everywhere I go. It may just be a knife concealed in my boot, but that's all I really needed. And they didn't know I kept an extra security fob in the glove box to give to valets. So basically I just blew their entire plan of trapping me in the Escalade to hell.

I crossed my right leg over my left and pulled the seatbelt out to give me enough slack to reach the concealed three inch blade from the top of my boot. I kind of had to wrench my hand in a funny position to get at my bindings, but I eventually got it. Hands free, I took the security fob from the glove box. I didn't unlock the doors right away. I knew that if they were smart they had parked a good distance from the actual pick-up point. They would want to get in position and have a few men hidden for back up before they actually met their contact. Sitting there doing nothing killed me! What I really wanted to do was run up behind Shooter, put my hands over his eyes and yell, "guess who?" But that would probably only end in bloodshed, so I made myself wait. I waited for ten as-long-as-eternity minutes, then I left the Escalade.

When I stepped out of my car, I didn't really know where to go or what to look for. I figured I'd walk in the same general direction as my Marines and hope for the best. As I crept through the towers of cargo containers, I became familiar with what it was like to live in Louisiana in the summer surrounded by corrugated metal. It was like a furnace. And I didn't mean the kind you have to heat your house. I meant the kind they used to cremate bodies. Sweat ran down and stung my eyes and just when I thought it couldn't get worse, I ran into a dead end. *Great!* I had to trek back through the center of the sun and make an educated guess as to which turn I should make.

I was about to go back to the SUV and zip tie myself to the seatbelt when I heard an ominous sound. For any of you who don't know, calling a silencer a silencer is really just bad marketing. It's called a suppressor. It doesn't silence the gunshot, it suppresses it. You still hear a shot, and you still hear the sound of the action working in the gun. So, like any sane woman, I ran toward the gunshot. The only problem was that if I was surrounded by metal, so were my Marines. The sound I heard could have been an echo and could have come from anywhere. But thankfully, the shooting started again, and I found my way to the edge of the battle.

I peeked around a container and saw Shooter crouched firing a handgun. I actually kind of felt bad for the guys on the wrong end of his gun. I didn't know a whole lot about the man, but I knew he didn't miss. He wouldn't allow it.

At that point my brain engaged and said, "Kat, your survival instinct and I have talked, and we've decided it would be a good idea for you to stay out of the crosshairs." Since my brain and survival instinct had a point, I did as recommended and hid behind a container. I couldn't help but look out every once in a while to see if I could see anyone else besides Shooter. Who had fired the first shot, who was injured, who was dead, and, most importantly, were any of them my Marines? I knew these guys could handle themselves, but I had to repeat that over and over to myself to keep my butt safely behind the container.

What happened next either happened in the blink of an eye or over several decades. I peeked my head around the corner and saw an African man walk quietly toward Shooter. No way was that guy on our side. I didn't really think about what happened next. It was as if my body took control of itself, this was instinct. I left my brain back behind the container and quickly snuck up on the man threatening Shooter. Apparently my approach wasn't as stealthy as his had been, because just as I got up to the man, Shooter turned to see his would-be attacker and me. Startled at being caught, the man paused. That stutter was what I had been waiting for and all I needed. In a matter of moments I wrapped my left forearm around his head, anchoring my hand on his right ear. I wrapped my left leg around his, rooting him to the ground. Finally, I grabbed his chin with my right hand and in a quick up and over motion I heard the pop that meant he was dead. I dropped the unknown man to the ground.

Shooter stared at me as if he hadn't seen what he saw. "I told you I have skills," I said, wanting him to know that what I did wasn't a fluke or just a lucky mistake.

Suddenly his stare went from stunned to soldier. He raised his gun. I turned my whole body around to face the threat, ready to attack. He fired at a man who stood behind me just as a knife flew from the guy's hand. The blade sailed through the air and embedded in my abdomen. The first thing I thought after being stabbed in the belly was, *seriously, you brought a knife?* But then I remembered that's all I'd brought, so I had to give the guy a little slack. The next thing I thought was, *why is someone soaking me with warm water?* I looked down to see a wet spot on my black shirt growing in diameter. I still hadn't wrapped my brain around the idea that I'd been stabbed. Shooter reached me and laid me down on the ground.

He said something but I couldn't really hear him. I focused on his lips and was able to see him say, "Hang on, baby. You're okay. You'll get through this." And then the sound came back when he yelled, "*Doc!*" The roar that came from Shooter wasn't what I expected. It wasn't the call for help that you'd expect someone to yell in response to a fallen soldier. It was the sound of someone being ripped open and having their heart torn from their chest. I thought he'd be pissed, not concerned. Weird.

As I lay on the pavement, bleeding, there was no pain. There should be pain when you had six inches of steel rammed into your body. But there was nothing. And that made me panic. I couldn't feel my legs, my arms, my chest, or my stomach. Intellectually I knew the knife was far to the right of my spine but that didn't matter. I looked at Shooter with abject terror in my eyes. He palmed the sides of my face. His hands were sticky, coated in my blood. The scent of iron was so thick in the air I could taste it. It was not a good situation.

"You're gonna be fine, sweetheart. This is nothing. You'll be just fine." He moved one of his hands to my hand and gave it a squeeze. "You feel that? You can feel that can't you?"

Surprisingly, I could. His touch gave me more relief than I thought possible. How did he know I had been worried about losing the use of my arms and legs? He had been around a lot of wounds. Maybe he'd picked up a few things.

Shooter released my hand and face. He shoved my top up out of the way so he could get a better look at my injury. Apparently the blade was actually in my pelvis because he ripped my pants to get at the knife. He pulled his shirt over his head and used it to wipe the blood away. I knew what he would see, and I knew the moment he saw it.

"Holy Mary, mother of..." he breathed. Shooter looked me in the eye and then went to work. He used his shirt to stabilize the blade and staunch the bleeding. When he rolled me over to my side to see if the knife had gone through to my back, I was given the greatest blessing of my life. I felt the pain of the knife. Then I felt the extreme searing white-hot, excruciating agony of having a six inch blade stuck in my pelvis. And I willingly and gratefully passed out.

I flickered in and out of consciousness for the next year. At least it seemed like a year. I was out, then awake when Doc came over and shined a bright annoying light in my eye. One of my Marines picked me up, and I was out again. They put me in the SUV, and I came back from the dead. Then Shooter peeled out of the port like a bat out of hell, and I was out. I stayed out until I heard Edna shouting orders.

Was I at home? Shouldn't I be in a hospital? I came around long enough to tell them to take care of Sam, and then I went out again.

Chapter Seven

The fog was thick and dark. I couldn't find my way through it.
I needed an anchor or rope or whatever the appropriate
metaphor was. I wasn't really in a fog bank; I just felt like I was.
Only two things seemed real. One, I was in my bed. The
permanent impressions made by my body in my mattress
cradled me. And two, a deep, honey-coated voice was talking.
No, not talking, reading. Someone was reading from *Emma*, out
loud. It was weird to hear Mrs. Elton in a male voice. I couldn't
remember falling asleep. I couldn't even remember getting into
bed. And more disturbing was that I hadn't had a nightmare.
Something was seriously wrong.

Shit! Had I blacked out again? I ran through my memory
bank. I could remember violently breaking someone's neck, but
I couldn't remember who. *Oh no*! What had I done? I had killed
someone! Someone I, quite possibly, cared about? Who had it
been? I really hope it hadn't been Tyler or one of my Marines. I
searched my memory further, remembered being with them all
morning and afternoon. Who was it? Which one had I killed?
Michael Vick, on his worst day, was a better person than me.

I attempted to sit up only to find that someone had parked a
battleship in my pelvis. The pain of flexing my abs sent waves of

memory flooding back to me. I remembered an unknown man dead at my feet. *An unknown man.* So it hadn't been someone I knew. Relief poured through me like liquid gold. I remembered another, now dead, man throwing a blade through the air. And I remembered that blade buried in my pelvis. I hadn't blacked out! I hadn't blacked out! I had been in complete control when I killed. But then I focused on the most acute memory. I had been stabbed in the pelvis. I frantically moved my hands all over my stomach looking for the offending object.

Two large hands covered mine. The same voice I'd heard earlier said, "You're okay, Kat. You're home and you're fine."

I finally recognized the voice. I hadn't yet opened my eyes. They flew open. It was Shooter. Relief washed over me. I soaked up the comfort he offered. I would be okay. I was safe. Shooter was there, watching over me. He wouldn't let me hurt anyone and he wouldn't let anyone hurt me. The peace that filled me was palpable. And that whole idea just pissed me off.

Before I could tell him to back the hell off, he looked me in the eye. His penetrating gaze held me. I couldn't move. I couldn't fight. I didn't want to fight.

"You're okay. The knife is gone. Doc and Dr. Wells have patched you up." I tried, again, to sit up this time I pushed myself up with my arms. "No, no. Lay down, sweetheart. You need to rest."

Why was that the answer to everything? You have a cold, you need to rest. You stub your toe, you need to rest. You have a gaping gunshot wound, you need to rest. I didn't want to rest. But it was very difficult to move, and I didn't want Shooter to leave, so I decided to just lie there for a minute.

Shooter hadn't used the authoritative voice I had grown accustomed to. He used the same mellow one he had when he'd spoken to the little girl in the mall. It did not have the effect on me I assumed he was hoping for. Despite the calm that oozed off of him. His tone reminded me of when a tough cop in a movie has to go tell his partner's wife her husband had been killed in the line of duty. He held me down until he knew I would stay down then moved back to sit in the overstuffed white chair that had been brought in from my sitting room. My copy of *Emma* rested open on the arm of the chair. It hadn't occurred to me until then that Shooter had been the one reading aloud. Cut me a break, okay! I was stabbed like...like...how long ago had I been stabbed?

"What time is it?" I asked.

"It's oh-two-thirty."

So that would mean I had been stabbed about ten hours ago.

"And it's Saturday."

I had been stabbed ten hours and two days ago.

"They've kept you pretty doped up. Your doctor, Dr. Wells, said he knows you and suggested we keep you sedated for a while unless we wanted you to rip your stitches out. He insisted you'd try to jump out of bed and fight your way out of your room if you had to. I should tell you I'm breaking the rules. I was supposed to give you another dose about an hour ago, but I thought you'd be pissed if we kept you out too long without letting you know what happened."

I nodded my head in the universal non-verbal gesture of thanks and moved my hand against my skin to find the stitches. That's when I noticed I had no clothes on. Not a single freaking thing. No nightgown, no panties, no nothing. I slid further down into my blankets.

"We didn't undress you. Edna did, and she made Sissy and Lilly help her get you into bed. Me and Doc helped Dr. Wells with your surgery, but you were covered the whole time."

Sometime I'd have to ask Shooter if he could read minds.

I made the enormous mistake of going into panic mode when I heard the word surgery and tried to sit up again. My body thanked me by gifting me with a shot of pain that made me dry heave. It took a moment to compose myself and calm Shooter down. I asked, "What surgery? And if I had surgery, why am I not in a hospital?"

Shooter cleared his throat. There was obviously something

he didn't want to tell me. I pierced him with my best *I don't care if you have to tell me I'm packing a new set of hardware between my legs, tell me* look.

He cleared his throat again and said, "The blade pierced your ovary. When Doc saw that, he decided it was out of his area of expertise. We called Dr. Wells. Edna gave us the number. He came over and decided to remove it. Between him and Doc we had all the stuff needed to put you out and do the operation so we did it on your kitchen table."

Okay, I'm never going to feel the same about eating breakfast there again.

"And you aren't in the hospital because it's Louisiana law to report any injury that may have occurred during a criminal act to the police. We didn't want that kind of hassle so we brought you here. Dr. Wells was cool. Doc had already removed the knife by the time he got here. We told him you fell on a pitchfork in the stables. He didn't believe us, but he didn't ask any questions either. We tried to get your permission to remove the ovary, but you slipped in and out of consciousness, and we couldn't really get anything out of you."

I waved my hand as if he'd just told me he spilled milk on the floor and said, "It doesn't matter, I've got another one." I could tell Shooter had been really worried about my reaction to being forcibly separated from one of my body parts, so I threw him a smile. He relaxed, minutely, then started to shift in his chair. I nodded at the book on the arm of the chair. "Did you have a Jane Austen craving?"

"I told you I couldn't go on until I had my Austen fix."

"Yes, but at the time you were craving *Pride and Prejudice*."

"I finished P&P last night. Every time I read it I get all worried that Miss Bennett and Mr. Darcy won't end up together. But *Emma*'s good too. Miss Woodhouse is a riot." He smiled. He was teasing me. But there was something else. He shifted in his chair. What made him so uncomfortable? Stab wound situation clear, naked situation clear, why I'd been out of it for two and a half days clear, Jane Austen situation clear.

What more could be on his mind?

He leaned forward in the chair and scrubbed his hands over his face. "Kat, I don't know how to say this, so I'm just gonna say it. I'm sorry."

Huh!? "For what? If you're trying to take the blame for me getting stabbed, you can stop that right here and now. It's not your fault. It's mine. If I had listened to you, or used even a small portion of my brain, I would have been fine. But then you would be dead and that would make me feel bad. But maybe you would have heard him and turned—"

"Kat, that's not what I'm sorry about." He stopped my ramblings. "I'm sorry about what I said that morning in your room."

Was he apologizing because he said he had no interest in seeing me naked or for telling me I was pricklier than Saddam Hussein? He pulled a folded piece of paper from his back pocket and handed it to me.

I took it, and as I opened it he said, "I'm sorry about what I said about you not having anyone in your life. I had no idea. I would never have even thought that if I had known. I'm so sorry, Kat."

I looked at the unfolded piece of paper in my hands. It was a copy of my husband's obituary. I had banned all memory of Stephan's death from the house. No obituaries and no newspaper clippings. I didn't want to focus on his passing. I wanted to remember his life.

"Where did you get this?" I asked quietly, trying to keep the volcanic eruption of anger under control.

"When I saw the way you handled that guy back at the docks, I knew you were more than you appeared to be. I asked Tongue. He refused to give me any personal details. So, I asked Switch to run a background check."

My emotions battled for dominance. Rage and violation were in the UFC octagon in a fight for the heavy weight title. To my supreme disappointment, violation won. I understood rage. Violation and I had met once or twice but we didn't get along. I turned to look at Shooter. My face had to read *pissed* off and *ready to chew his head off his neck.* "And what did you find out?"

I knew the answer. My people couldn't eliminate my entire background. He had to know things I didn't want him to know.

"I learned that you have gone through more than anyone deserves. And know you're stronger than a hell hound." I liked that he thought I was strong, but that only dampened the sense of violation. "You were twenty-six when your husband died. That is so young. How did you survive?"

I was grateful he hadn't moved on to the less than attractive parts of my history. "I had to. I had no other choice. I had Sam. I still had to be a mom. So I woke up every day, and I got out of bed, and I made sure she was taken care of. I wouldn't say I handled it well, I just had to remind myself that it was important to breathe, that my blood needed oxygen to survive. Until one day I didn't have to remind myself anymore."

"What was he like?"

That shocked the hell out of me. Most people asked, "How did he die," or "How have you managed?" I really did not want to have that conversation. I had talked about his death a thousand times, but I had deliberately not talked about his life. That was still too close to the surface.

"You don't have to be afraid, Kat," Shooter said as he took my hand that lay on the bed. "I won't take anything you say and disrespect it. Everything you say will be sacred to me."

Seriously, Shooter had to read minds. I considered myself the steward of Stephan's memory. I was the keeper of his life and his legacy. It was my responsibility to keep that safe. I had planned on keeping my big fat mouth shut. I should have given Shooter the finger and gone back to sleep. I'd vowed to never speak of Stephan again. But all the best laid plans of mice and men, and all that. It seemed as though I had come down with a terrible chronic case of word vomit, and I started to talk.

"Stephan was the anti-me. He was intelligent, charming, caring, compassionate, kind, loving. Everything I'm not. Maybe that's why we loved each other so much. He used to say, 'Never say just.' You know when you walk into a room and startle someone and you say, 'It's just me.' He would say, 'Never say just.' He made people believe they really mattered.

"We met at an all night boxing gym in New Orleans. He was a professor at Tulane, and I was...I was running from one life and looking for another. He had only been a member for a few weeks. He would get up early and come in around four a.m. I got off work around the same time and needed to blow off some steam. We were always the only two people in the gym. We'd say hi and bye. Until one morning he asked me if I wanted to work the pads with him. I said sure, and after that we'd switch off with each other most nights. One night, I'd had a really, really bad time at work. I was a bartender on Bourbon Street and had fought off drunken frat boys who didn't know the meaning of the word no all night. When I walked in, he said the sweetest thing anyone has ever said to me. He asked me if I wanted to spar. I needed to hit something breathing so, of course, I said yeah. Two minutes later he was on the mat, KO'd. By the time he finally came around, I thought he'd be pissed or at least put off by the fact that a girl had knocked his lights out. But he wasn't. He was impressed."

I couldn't look at Shooter. In the past, protecting Stephan's memory meant never talking about him. I twisted the duvet between my fingers, hoping like hell I didn't say anything that might tarnish his memory.

"He kind of threw me for a loop with that. I'd always been able to fight, and it had always intimidated the right kind of man and excited the wrong kind. But he wasn't excited or intimidated. He saw me as a woman with skills. Not a badass or a tough chick. It wouldn't have mattered if I had been good at computer programming, he would have looked at me the same way—as a woman first and then as a woman with a specific skill set. I cleaned up his face and he took me to breakfast. We had beignets and coffee. We spent the morning together just talking until he had to leave to teach a class." The corners of my mouth kicked up into a smile.

"I couldn't stop thinking about him. I was positively giddy when he called. He wanted to take me to an art exhibit. I was working that night so we made a date for the next night. We still met up at the gym, though he didn't ask to spar again. He took me to the New Orleans Museum of Art. I'm not a member of the art club. I was completely out of my element. He could tell, so he suggested we blow out of there and go for a walk. We left, and as I turned to look over my shoulder, I saw the name Boudreaux over the gallery. I knew his last name but I thought it must be a coincidence.

"He showed me the museum grounds and we talked about everything and nothing. I never saw myself as the long walks on the beach at sunset type, but I absolutely enjoyed myself. He told me about his work. He had been a teacher and a chemical engineer. He'd worked on making petroleum a more efficient fuel. I told him about my 'work' in the food and beverage industry. I told him I'd held positions as a sanitation engineer, a risk assessment manager, and an alcohol dealer. He laughed. He didn't care that I lived in a different world."

Shooter interrupted me. "Risk assessment manager?"

For the first time I looked at him. He sat on the edge of the chair completely engrossed in my story. Why did he care so damn much? No one liked hearing the stupid sappy stories of young love. I sure as hell didn't.

"Bouncer," I said with a smile. "We saw each other constantly for three weeks. Then he wanted me to meet his mother. I was terrified to say the least. No one had ever introduced me to their mother before. It was going to be hell, starring the demon of judgment. When we pulled up to this house, I tried to run. And I don't mean that in a metaphorical sense. I seriously tried to run away, down the drive and to safety. But he caught me and dragged me into the house. In my mind, his mother had to be the Miss Havisham of the bayou. I expected a frigid, uncaring icicle. What I hadn't expected was a warm, kind, loving woman who welcomed me into her home with absolutely no pretense. You couldn't help but fall in love with Madeline." I paused to rub away the ache in my chest. "She died two months later." The memory of Madeline's passing brought a whole new wave of grief. She was one of those kind, special women they just don't make any more.

"My husband had to quit his research and teaching to run the company. He insisted he had to be the one in charge of Boudreaux Oil. He said a Boudreaux had sat at the head of the company since the beginning, and he wasn't about to break that tradition. Tradition had been very important to him. When he moved from New Orleans, he asked me to come with him. I couldn't do it. I didn't believe in men on white horses riding in to save me from life. Then he asked me to marry him. I couldn't do it. The world would view me as the woman he pulled up from the dregs of society and put a pretty dress on. He told me to give him a dollar. I had no idea where he was going with that, but he asked again and again. So I gave him the damn dollar. Then he said, 'Katharine Wallace, you are the proud owner of fifty percent of Boudreaux Oil. Whether you say yes or no to my proposal, you have purchased half of everything I have.'"

Shooter continued to sit in the chair. He had zero reaction to the best business deal in the history of the world.

"So I said yes. How could I not? He saw us on an even footing. We got married and settled into life. Our marriage wasn't perfect. We fought like anyone. And most of the time it was my fault, but he never claimed a victory. His philosophy was that *we* needed to win, not me or him, we. Sometimes we would really get into it, and he would leave for a drive. He'd come back, we'd make up, and life would go on. We had Sam, and I think that was when we were happiest." I paused for a moment. The next part of the story was the hard part. It's how I killed my husband.

"Then three years ago, on Christmas Eve, we were fighting again. It was stupid. I wanted to do something that he did not want me to. It was selfish. I completely understand why he was against it. But at the time, I just couldn't let it drop. So he went for a drive. I worried when he didn't come back in his usual time frame. But I was still upset, and I went to bed without him. At six o'clock on Christmas morning, Edna woke me. She said the sheriff was downstairs and needed to talk to me. I was confused at first, but when I saw his face I knew what had happened. He told me Stephan had swerved to miss another car and ran into a tree. He died instantly."

Something firm and reassuring gripped my hand. I looked down to see Shooter's giant hand wrapped around mine. I was not a crier. I didn't think I *could* cry. I must have had malfunctioning tear ducts. In fact, I couldn't remember the last time I'd cried. I didn't cry when the sheriff told me Stephan was dead or at the funeral.

When a normal, mentally healthy person gets upset, they cry. I got the hiccups. I started in with one of the worst cases ever. I tried to speak but couldn't, all I could do was hic, hic, hic. You would think it would be one of the most uncomfortable moments in history, but it wasn't. I trusted Shooter. I knew he wouldn't tell anyone or hold my ridiculous show of emotion against me. He was an honorable man. He would never do anything like that. Besides, as far as he knew, my diaphragm had just gone into a fit of spasms.

Once my hiccups were under control, he asked, "What were you fighting about?"

That brought my hiccups to a complete stop. I couldn't tell Shooter. Not because I didn't want to. It was one of those I-could-tell-you-but-then-I'd-have-to-kill-you situations, and I wanted Shooter to live for a while longer. I shook my head and said, "It doesn't matter."

He was smart enough not to push me further.

He helped me sit up and, in all my naked glory, my sheet slipped down just enough to reveal the scars on my breasts. *Shit!* I had momentarily forgotten that he had run a background check on me. The details of a sexual assault are usually something your average background check would miss. My background had been scrubbed. Of course, anyone with access to Google could find Stephan. Shooter had access to information the average human resources department could only dream of. Was it possible that he knew about the most horrifying humiliating moment of my life? Did he want to ask me about it? He probably wanted to know every gory detail. He wouldn't let it rest. He handed me a drink of water, and as I took it, I must have given him a less than grateful look.

"What?" he asked.

I wasn't going to say anything, to acknowledge that he knew anything about me. I didn't want to give him the satisfaction of him knowing that I knew he knew. "You saw my scars?"

Dammit! What was wrong with me? I didn't volunteer information or tell someone who was basically a total stranger all my darkest secrets. What the hell was wrong with me? Oh, yeah—word vomit.

He nodded, "I saw the ones on your belly when I gave you first aid from the knife wound. I didn't see the other ones until just now."

"Aren't you going to ask?"

He straightened my blanket, sat down, and shook his head. "No, ma'am. I can't imagine that's something you like to talk about. And I don't blame you. We all have battle wounds. Some outside, some in. And who we choose to share them with is our choice. No one else's. So if you want to tell me, I'll listen, but you don't have to. I have no idea how you got them. That didn't show up on your background check. You'll tell me when—if—you're ready."

About damn time the gods decide to smile down on me. I couldn't stop anyone from finding Stephan, but I'd spent considerable resources to hide the rest of my past. I had the advantage, and I would keep it.

I smiled. He just looked at me for a long time. I couldn't decide if I wanted him to know or not. A battle waged inside my head—one side wanted to spill my guts, the other wanted to cut his eyes and tongue out so he could never see my scars again and never talk about them. Finally, the ocular tractor beam disengaged, and he slumped in the chair. My word vomit was under control, and he definitely needed a break from the horror show that was my life. So I lay down and pretended to go back to sleep.

Chapter Eight

Yellow and red light seeped through my eyelids. It had to be morning, but I was really comfortable and a decent night's sleep without nightmares was something I hadn't experienced in a long time. Pain killers were gifts from God. I lay in the nest of blankets and pillows without opening my eyes. Peace was something I hadn't experienced in years. I would enjoy it for as long as my bladder would allow. I heard Shooter reading again. I couldn't place the Jane Austen he read. It's humiliating to say it took several minutes for me to realize it wasn't Austen, it was Seuss.

"Because, after all a person's a person no matter how small...."

It was *Horton Hears a Who*, Sam's favorite book. I cracked my eyes to see Sam on Shooter's knee, completely comfortable snuggled into his broad chest.

The mother bear inside me should have crawled out of my skin. I should have been compelled to jump out of bed, lift my daughter off his knee, and rip his face off with my fingernails. Seventy two hours ago that would have been my go-to reaction. Since losing Stephan, I guess you could say I was a bit protective, a bit. But I didn't need to protect Sam from Shooter. I knew she was safe with him, and I knew he would die before any harm could come to her.

I listened to his deep, honey voice read to my daughter. He had earned some serious points. He may even force me to like him.

"*From the sun in the summer. From rain when it's fallish, I'm going to protect them. No matter how smallish. The End.*"

Sam released a deep sigh. "Will you read it again?"

"Again," Shooter whined, but you could hear the smile in his voice. "Five times? Okay, again. *On the fifteenth of May, in the jungle of Nool, in the heat of the day, in the cool of the pool....*"

I threw him a bone and made my presence known. "Mommy!" Sam yelled and hopped off Shooter's lap. As she went to jump up on the bed, I clenched my body for the impending agony.

Shooter picked her up just in time and placed her on the bed next to me. "Your momma's tummy hurts so we need to be real still on the bed, okay, Sam?"

"You were asleep a looong time. I saw them carry you in the house. I thought you were hurt really bad, but Shooter said you just spilled tomato soup on your shirt. And that it made you sick so we had to be real, real quiet and let you sleep. Shooter said this morning that you're almost better."

"Yup, I'm okay." I kissed the top of her head.

"You wanna have breakfast? Me and Shooter've been eating breakfast up here. Edna brings it. And guess what, Mom?" She lowered her voice conspiratorially. "Shooter showed me how to make oatmeal taste good. You just have to put chocolate chips in it, and it is soooo good."

I smiled at her. "I'd love to eat with you."

"And Shooter, too, Mom. He's my best friend of the soldiers. We made you a card yesterday. I'll go get it." She jumped down and ran out of the room.

Shooter had gone above and beyond the call of duty. He had comforted Sam, played with her, read to her, fed her. He got her to eat oatmeal without complaining for crying out loud! He was...he was something. I ran my fingers through my hair. Mangy, homeless dogs were cleaner. "I need a shower."

He looked at me with a concerned face. I still didn't have any clothes on.

"Can you just get my robe? It's hanging on the inside of the door in my closet."

He walked over to the closet door. "Holy shit!"

"What?" What was wrong with my closet? Had I been robbed? Violated?

"This is your closet? It's three times as big as my first apartment! How many clothes does one person need?" He brought my robe to me. I didn't say anything. Most men think as long as they have at least one pair of underwear with only three holes they're good on the wardrobe front.

I sat up, and Shooter draped the thick white terry cloth cloud around my shoulders. I tied it around my waist and tried to get out of the bed. And failed. The shot of pain that ripped through my body made me feel bad for all the people I'd gut kicked over the years. He wrapped an arm around my back and one under my knees. Before I could protest, he had lifted me off the bed and carried me into the bathroom. He set me down on the cold sink. It was ridiculous. I couldn't stand without holding on to something. Who was the idiot that didn't install a railing in my shower? That would be me. But then, when doing home renovations, the majority doesn't often think about future infirmities.

"You're going to have to get in there with me."

"Oh, no, ma'am," he said without hesitation.

"Come on, Shooter. I need a shower. We're both adults."

"Not happening." An innocent boy stood in front of me. Who knew Shooter could be such a prude?

I started to get a little irritated. "Right, I forgot. You have no desire to see me naked." And the word vomit returns.

Anger flared in his eyes. Dammit! Why did that bug me so much? I should be grateful he had no interest in me. *After I'm done in here, I'm going to go on Amazon and buy a muzzle.*

"I'll go get Edna." He propped me up against the vanity.

Why did I say shit like that? Shooter had been absolutely nothing but nice, and I had to go and open my big freaking mouth. I *was* worse than Saddam Hussein. I leaned against the countertop absolutely disgusted with myself. Since my injury I hadn't seen anyone but Shooter. For all I knew the rest of my Marines could be in the middle of an amphibious assault on Bayou Boudreaux. So what do I do? I piss off the only person who seems to care enough to be there. I had to apologize to him. Ask me how much I looked forward to that? What the hell was I saying? I didn't apologize. To anyone.

Two minutes later, Edna knocked lightly on the door. I called for her to come in. She had a velour jogging suit in her hands. Bless that woman.

She gave me a warm, kind smile. "I'm happy to see you up and about. Let's get you cleaned up. Oh, and Sam was out there with a card. She left it for you on your bedside table. She's off to get her dolls dressed for the day."

I loved that little girl. Edna turned the water on hot, just like I liked it. She helped me into the shower and held my hand to steady me. I washed myself, thank you very much. There were some things a girl just needed to do on her own. After I was cleaned, shampooed, and shaved—because stab wound or no stab wound, there was no excuse to let your legs get furry—she guided me out and helped me get dressed.

She sat me on a chair and started to brush my hair. I really had no idea why I had an upholstered chair in my bathroom. It seemed kind of silly. But there's always been one in there, and who was I to mess with tradition? Lying on my back for two days had allowed two families of rats to build nests out of my hair. Or at least that's what it felt like when Edna ripped the brush through the tangles.

"That Shooter has been sitting in that chair for almost three days now."

Great, Edna was reading far too much into Shooter's affections for me.

"Sam seems to like him."

And she played the Sam card. Excellent.

"Edna." I had to break her heart. "He's only doing all this because I saved his life, and he feels guilty about me getting stabbed."

Edna belly laughed. I scowled at her. "Child, if you think he's doing all this out of some distorted sense of duty, you're dumber than a box of hair. Do you know he stood guard over you while Dr. Wells and Doc stitched you up?"

I shrugged my shoulders. "He told me he assisted."

She threw her head back, "He did not! He watched over you to make sure they kept you modest. Nearly drove Dr. Wells nuts. He must have asked a thousand questions about your care and medications and what to expect and how to get you better faster."

"He's a Marine. They're thorough."

She knelt in front of me. "You didn't see his face when he carried you into the house. He looked like someone had just ripped out his heart and served it to him for dinner. I'm telling you, that man loves you, even if neither of you want to acknowledge it."

She pulled my hair into a long braid and opened the bathroom door. "She's done, Shooter."

I heard fast footsteps across the carpet. He had showered, shaved, and changed. I guess he'd taken the Marine Corps class on speedy hygiene. I couldn't look him in the eye. After what I'd said, and especially after what Edna had said, I just couldn't do it. He picked me up off the chair and carried me back to my bed. He tucked the covers around me and placed a breakfast tray on my lap. Two tons, seriously two tons, of food had been piled onto the plate. Where on Earth did he expect me to put all this? Then I remembered the last breakfast I ate in front of him. He obviously thought that had been a regular meal for me.

I tunneled through the mountain of hash browns and destroyed most of the eggs. My plate still had a significant amount of food on it. He had an odd look on his face. For a moment I thought I would have to stop him from cramming the rest of the meal down my throat. He took the tray and placed it on the hall floor just outside my door.

"Where are your shoes and socks?"

"In my closet. If you turn right when you get inside and go past all the rows to the very back wall, there's a wall of shoes. My socks are in the first two drawers on the left just inside."

He went in to get them. Less than a minute later he came out of the closet with a pair of gym shoes and a silk nightie.

My eyes went wide as pie plates.

"This is nice, but it's not right for what we're about to do."

Shit! "I said the right side drawers!" How humiliating!

"You said left. But don't worry. I remember where I got this. I'll put it back."

If I could have jumped off the bed, I would have tackled him to the ground, ripped the piece of red silk and lace from his hand, and cut that memory out of his brain. But since I was an invalid and not within reach of a bone saw, I had to sit there and let a Marine rummage through my unmentionables.

He returned with more appropriate attire. I reached my hand out to take the shoes and socks from him, but he held them just out of my reach. It was so not the time for an impromptu game of keep away. I tried to get the damn things out of his hand, but he was taller, had longer arms, and had the ability to stand without assistance so I was pretty much screwed.

"I could do this all day, Kat."

I stopped fighting and stuck my tongue out at him. A deep laugh rumbled through his body. His laugh rolled over me like thunder. The sound made a spring coil in the pit of my stomach. What the hell was going on with me? He pulled the blankets off of my legs, moved them so they hung off the bed, and put my shoes and socks on.

"We need to get you up walking around. We should have had you walking the day after but I didn't want...." He didn't finish his sentence.

He helped me up and let me have all my weight on my feet. As I tried to put one foot in front of the other, shards of pain tore through my body. I doubled over. I willed myself not to puke every bit of the breakfast I'd just eaten all over my pretty red tennis shoes. Shooter was right there to keep my face from meeting the carpet. But he didn't tell me to stop or sit down or take a rest.

"Make it to the bathroom and back. That's all I'll make you do today." He was damn near perfect in a lot of ways. He didn't try to do the walking for me, and he didn't let me quit at the first sign of trouble. He let me have my pride.

It took ten minutes to walk twenty feet. And Shooter was as patient as Job. I was not. By the time I got back to the bed, I was so pissed at myself I could have disowned my own body. I did not deal well with being feeble. I sat on the bed, legs extended, with my arms crossed over my chest. Yes, I looked like a child. And I didn't care. Relying on people sucked!

Shooter laughed at me.

"I'm glad you find this all so funny," I said.

"The situation is not funny. You are."

I shot him a glare that told him loud and clear that I'd like to strap him to the top of the Chrysler Building in the middle of an electrical storm. "I'm so glad I amuse you."

"It's hell to heal." He didn't say *I know* or *when I was shot* or *when I took a giant piece of shrapnel to the ass*.... He knew what I was going through but didn't have to prove it.

Just then Tyler barged through my door. "Kitten, I heard you were awake. How are you? Can I get you anything? You know if you had stayed in the car like I told you to, you wouldn't have a gaping hole in your gut right now."

No, but you would be burying Shooter. "I'm fine. No. And no kidding." My brother and I had a different way of communicating. "Did you get your weapons?"

Tyler and Shooter looked at each other and turned white.

"I may not have a brainpan the size of Wisconsin, and I may not have gone to boot camp, but I'm not stupid. I know you're all here because you think I'm in danger and you need to protect me. Why else would you put gun emplacements on the roof of my house? Yes, I know about that and no, I won't tell you how. So, spill it. Why do you think I'm in danger?"

Tyler kept his mouth shut. He just looked at his feet.

"Just before we left Iraq, Switch intercepted a communication about a threat against the president of Boudreaux Oil," Shooter said. "Tongue was with Switch when he told me about the interception. He freaked out and told us the threat had been made against his sister. I called the Bastards together and convinced the powers that be that your safety was a matter of national security. The military doesn't run without petroleum. Since you own the largest reserve of domestic oil it wasn't a tough sell. We protect our own. Until this threat is neutralized, you will have a contingent of Marines with you."

Shit, my past had come back to bite me in the ass. I knew exactly who wanted me dead, but I wasn't about to tell Tyler and Shooter who or why.

"You don't seem surprised." Tyler had picked up on my lack of response.

"Why should I be scared? I have you to protect me." I hoped like hell they bought it.

"Go tell the guys to start putting Switch's security in place," Shooter ordered Tyler. I didn't like him ordering my brother around in my house, but Tyler took it like a good Marine and left.

Shooter stared at me with a look that made me feel as if he shuffled through the filing cabinet of memories in my brain. "When I asked Switch to run your background check, we couldn't find any information on where you would have learned to break a man's neck. Your background was perfect. Too perfect, like someone had created it. Where did you learn to break that guy's neck, Kat?"

Shit. Why had I killed that guy with my bare hands? I should have hit him over the head with a tire iron or something.

"At the gym. You know, you just pick stuff up here and there."

"Try again. What you did requires training and practice. The look on your face had been one of a trained killer. You've killed up close and personal before, haven't you? Where did you learn to kill, Kat?" He'd dipped his toes into some very dangerous waters.

I turned my head to look at him and paused to emphasize my point. "Don't push this, Shooter."

"No, no you don't have the option of not answering my questions. We're here to protect you. If you conceal the truth, you put your entire staff, your daughter, and my men in danger. If you know something, you tell me, now!"

I didn't say anything.

"Let me tell you what I know. Your security for your house and your company is handled by a bunch of men you probably head hunted from some private security firm. Since you're all about hiring the best, I'm going to say you stole them from Global Security Assets. You can take classes through GSA in self-defense if you have a big enough wallet. Besides providing security for companies and rich people, GSA holds more defense contracts than any other company in the US. They're a private military firm who will, with a big enough check, rain down war on anyone you want. You got involved with them and it went bad. And now we're here expected to clean up the mess."

"I didn't hire them to make war on anyone! They're security, that's all." How could he accuse me of bringing war to people? Because he was basically right.

"I didn't say you hired them to create war. I think it's more personal than that."

Shit.

He lowered his voice. "I've seen you fight, Kat. Fighting style is like a signature. You can tell where someone has trained and for what purpose. You were trained by GSA. But you didn't just take the self-defense course, did you?"

I had been trained to resist interrogation, but truthfully I didn't want to resist anymore. Telling Shooter would be the smart thing to do. It would help protect the people I love. But this secret had been kept for such a long time it had been etched onto my bones. Did I even know how to say the words? I had been sworn to secrecy, but that secret could kill me, my daughter, and my family. Telling someone what I had done for a living could be suicide, or it could be salvation. Shooter screamed trust. If anyone could handle it, it would be him.

"On my eighteenth birthday I joined an MMA gym. I was good. I was really good. One of the instructors took notice and would wait to talk to me outside the gym. Then he started popping up at the grocery store, the movies, everywhere. He asked me strange questions like did I have any family? Did I feel people must die for the greater good? I guess I answered the questions correctly because he took me to GSA's headquarters in South Carolina. I'd never been out of Oklahoma so it was a big deal for me. They had me take all these tests. Intelligence tests, physical tests, psych tests. They discovered my psyche had the ability to completely separate itself from an act of violence. I could kill and not have to deal with the nagging guilt most people have to work through later. I was perfect. In their warped little world, I was perfect." I paused for a moment to read Shooter's face.

He didn't judge, he just listened and gathered intel.

"The training that takes most people years to complete, I finished in a matter of months. I learned to kill with my hands, with a knife, with a gun, with poison, with explosives, and with anything that happened to be handy. I was really, really good at it. There is something you need to understand. GSA isn't just a mercenary factory. They have spies, assassins, small strike forces, everything the government has only on a smaller, more private scale. Sometimes the US government needs to spy on a country or take out a general or leader but make it look like they had nothing to do with it. GSA steps in, completes the mission and the US government has plausible deniability. Even if the foreign government suspected foul play, GSA would pull its operatives out before it was too late. The offended country would have to apply for extradition, which would be denied.

"My first target had been a general who wanted to build his own army and overthrow the leader of one of the few truly democratic countries in Africa. I understood why I had to kill him. I snuck into his camp, slit his throat, and got out of the country before he bled out on the floor. After two years as GSA's personal grim reaper, I was assigned to take out an Iranian sheikh. The sheikh had been rich and powerful. By that time I'd stopped asking for the whys of the job. I just did it. I trusted that GSA knew what they were doing and that all the people they sent me to eliminate needed to be killed. When I found the sheikh, something was off. I watched him for several days. He appeared to be a respected elder. No one anyone would want dead. But I had seen it before, people who looked innocent that were really ruthless killers. I gave him an injection of succinylcholine. Everyone thought he'd died of a heart attack."

Shooter didn't say anything. He sat there and let me tell my story.

"Something about the sheikh made me uneasy. I didn't see any of the usual signs of an evil person. I started digging. I found that he'd objected to a mining company mining on his people's ancestral land. His people wouldn't see a nickel from the company. The sheikh wanted to protect them and their heritage. His son didn't. He made the deal his father wouldn't and promised to grant the mining company access to the land when he was in charge. The company paid GSA to execute the sheikh and put his heir in power. I had committed murder. I killed someone for money. I took the life of someone that had done nothing wrong." I had never said those words out loud. I expected Shooter to jump up and call me horrible names. He didn't. Concern filled his eyes. Damn, that man was incredible.

"The one thing GSA and the son didn't consider was the sheikh's brother. He was a very powerful man in a neighboring village. He interrogated his nephew and discovered GSA's hand in his brother's death. He has vowed to kill the people responsible. I'm at the top of that list. As I should be."

Shooter didn't say anything. I turned my head, unable to look at him. While he had fought for honor, I had killed for money. I had thought about offering my skills to the military, but they couldn't match GSA's pay. In the end I lost everything. I lost my money, my pride, my self-respect, my humanity, everything. A gentle hand squeezed mine. I looked at it.

"Thank you," he said. "That explains a lot."

"A lot? Yeah, it explains a lot. It explains why I don't trust anyone, why I don't have any friends, why I don't let anyone near me, why I don't date, why I'm completely focused on the security of my household. Yeah, it explains how anyone who gets close to me is in danger. It explains a whole hell of a lot."

Shooter stroked the back of my hand. "Kat, I know with everything you've been through you feel broken, but that's not true...."

"Broken." My voice hitched in my throat, and I finally looked at him. "I'm not broken, Shooter. I'm ruined. Do you know what the difference is? When something's broken, you can fix it or at least send it back to the manufacturer for a refund. When something's ruined, you throw it away, or wait for it to die."

His face went hard. "You are not ruined. You hear me? You are not ruined. You are the most courageous woman on Earth. You left GSA. Once you found out why they had you kill the sheikh, you didn't stay. You left. I'd bet my left nut they didn't like losing you. I'll bet they threatened you, froze your assets. But you didn't care. You knew what they were doing was wrong, and you gave them the finger and walked away. That took some serious balls, Kat. Most people would have gone with the status quo, but you didn't."

I had to stop him. I couldn't let him go on thinking I was something I wasn't. "I left, yes. But I didn't do anything to repair what I had done. When I married Stephan and gained access to billions of dollars, did I try to buy the mineral rights from the mining company and return them to the tribe? No, I didn't. I was so happy to finally be safe that I didn't give a damn about those people. All those people forced from their homes. I'm not brave. I'm not a hero. I'm a coward. And frankly, the only reason you're nice to me is because you're a good man, and I saved your life. That's it. If we weren't in this situation, you wouldn't see me the same way."

Shooter stood up. From my vantage point he was six feet five inches of pure menace. "First of all, don't tell me what I should be thinking. And second, how dare you! How dare you call yourself a coward! You had been running for a long time and safety is something everyone wants. I don't think less of you for that. And if you still want to help those people, why can't you do it now? Their land is still there. You still have money. You can still help them."

"No, I can't. The area has been the center of an intertribal war for the past two years. I had my people look into it. They said no one really owns it. The company that holds the deed has abandoned the land. So even if I could buy it and give it back, they wouldn't want it."

"I'm going to have Switch look into that. I know tribal wars, and I know they can be settled. I won't let you carry this around anymore. You leave it to me. I'll help you." He paced the length of my bed. "So you think the people who are after you are from the sheikh's brother's tribe?"

I nodded.

"Well that's good. That means it's not organized terrorists, religious zealots, or government operatives. They won't be trained. They'll be easy to see coming and they'll be easy to kill."

I shuddered. Someone else would die because of me and the decisions I'd made a hundred years ago.

"I need you to do a favor for me, Kat. I need you to tell the rest of the team what you just told me. They need to know everything. It will make their job a lot easier. I can tell them, but I think it would be best if it came from you." He had slipped into his leadership position as if it were a second skin.

How could I do that? How could I tell relative strangers the darkest parts of me? How could I tell Tyler? He'd called me once while I was on a mission. All my numbers had been forwarded to a satellite phone I carried with me. He'd called me in the middle of cutting up a body for disposal. He told me about a fire fight he'd been in while I crammed intestines into a Glad bag. I had to put him on hold so I could deal with the ribcage. It was like bagging groceries. I told him I needed to change my laundry from the washer to the dryer. How could he forgive me for all the lies I'd told him? He thought I sold paper. He had no idea that I killed world leaders to pay the bills. He would never trust me again.

But, I had to think about the other people in my life. I had a responsibility to care for everyone under my roof. It wasn't about me; it was about them. I had to protect them. Even if it meant I'd lose my brother. I almost wished that knife would have killed me. I wouldn't have a gaping hole in my chest where someone cut my heart out. It had to be done.

I nodded to Shooter. "I need to tell Tyler first. And I need to tell him alone."

"That's fine, but I'm staying."

It wasn't a negotiation, but I needed to tell Tyler without an audience. "No, I need to do this alone. And if you don't agree, I'll have Tyler throw you out."

Shooter turned and stomped out of the room.

Tyler came in a few minutes later. I told him to sit in the chair and I took his hand. He looked scared, like I was going to tell him I was dying of Ebola and would soon bleed out of all my orifices. He had no idea that what I was about to say would be so much worse. But, I told him. I shared everything I'd told Shooter. Tyler's reaction was not as calm as Shooter's had been.

He bolted out of the chair. "How could you do this, Kat? You worked for mercenaries, for God's sake! You were a mercenary! You betrayed me, lied to me. How could you? How could you allow people like that into your life? How could you allow yourself to be used to kill people, Kat? How many missions did they send you on? How many, Kat, how many people did you kill?"

He did not need to know that. "Why does that matter? I doubt my number is as high as yours."

"I fought a war. You carried out vendettas. You evened personal scores. How. Many?"

I didn't want to answer. I could lie and say I didn't know, but Tyler was too smart for that. All assassins know their own record. Hell, most of them tracked each other like they were following pro athletes. I squared my jaw and said, "Fifty-three."

"You're wrong. You beat me by forty. You have more than Shooter. You probably have more than all of us put together!" He stopped flailing his arms and pointed at me, "But you wanna know the difference between you and us? We killed for our country and to liberate another. You killed because someone told you to. How many innocents did you kill, Kat?"

"Hang on, that's not fair! I quit the second I found out I had been used that way. I never would have done it if I had known!" That just pissed me off.

"How could you not have known? Did you honestly believe the United States government didn't have the assets to take out its enemies?" The flailing returned.

"I was that asset! I told you why the United States government used GSA, and you know that's true. I have no idea when I started working for private companies, but I know I quit the second I found out. Do you have any idea how hard that was? GSA doesn't just let their operatives go. I had to kill to stay alive. It took an entire year of being chased before GSA decided they'd lost too many operatives to me."

"And that makes everything you did okay? You killed for money!" he yelled. "You are no better than a goddamned mob hit man!"

The door flew open and Shooter ran at Tyler. He bent low like a linebacker and threw my brother across the room. Shooter picked him up by his collar and held him against the wall. "You will not talk to her that way. You will give her the respect she deserves. She's been through hell, and I won't allow you to treat her this way."

"Stay out of it, Shooter! This is none of your business."
"She is my business." He threw Tyler out of my room.

Chapter Nine

Shooter returned with the rest of my Marines at his back. I must have had a startled look on my face because they looked at me as if I had just watched my dog get run over. I had to pull myself together. So Tyler had just called me a vile, scab-covered murderess. I could deal with that. He was right. So Shooter had just said something I didn't expect or know how to react to. I could deal with that, right? Yeah, right.

My Marines stood at the foot of my bed.

"Kat has some Intel on our current situation she's going to share with us." He didn't sit on his chair next to my bed; he sat right next to me and grabbed my hand. I wasn't the only one that noticed his sudden affectionate nature. My Marines' eyes went huge. They were as confused as I was. Shooter didn't move his hand, and I didn't move mine. I had honestly been shocked by Tyler's reaction. I thought of all people he would understand. His explosion, though warranted, had been a complete surprise. I needed help if I had to go through anything like that again. Yes, I said it. I needed help.

For the third time in under an hour I told my deepest secret. No one was disgusted. They didn't hate me. They didn't judge me. The range of acceptance and respect they gave me shocked me to my core.

"I told you she's the toughest chick, ever!" Horndog was thrilled.

"Maybe we should allow you to fight Martinez. I'd pay to see something like that," Doc said.

"And you have inferior security. What kind of idiot are you?" Switch tried to pick a fight. *How sweet.*

"I've wanted to take the military advanced weapons and tactics course at GSA for years." Martinez was actually jealous.

I let out the deep breath I'd held since starting the story. I never thought I would find anyone who understood me and my past. I could have hugged every single one of them, if I wasn't as prickly as Saddam Hussein.

"So what now?" Switch asked Shooter.

"We stick to the original plan."

"What about Tongue?" Horndog asked.

"He'll calm down. We can still count on him. He'll do his duty." Shooter had a lot more faith in my brother than I did.

My Marines left. Shooter stayed on the bed next to me.

"Sooo...what's the plan?"

"I'll tell you later. You've had a big morning. You need to rest. I'll wake you for lunch."

I didn't want to sleep. But, I didn't want to be conscious either. Shooter helped me lie down. He moved back to the chair. Fear shot through me. It seemed the comfort Shooter carried around with him diminished the farther he was from me. I had started to rely on him and that was dangerous.

A little while later, I shot up in my bed and screamed. I shot up out of fear. I screamed from pain.

"Kat!" Shooter had palmed my face. "What's wrong? Are you in pain? Tell me what's wrong."

It took a second for me to realize I wasn't in a dark, dank dungeon and was, in fact, in my own bed. With Shooter standing guard. His eyebrows had pulled together, and he studied me.

I leaned my cheek into his palm. "Nothing. I just

remembered why I don't take naps." He relaxed his grip but didn't let me go. He kissed the top of my forehead. The sensation of his lips on my skin sent me to heaven. I hadn't been cared for by anyone other than my staff in years. That one simple gesture was enough to remind me that I was still a part of the human race. I let myself feel it. I let my stomach warm. I let my face relax, I sighed, and I didn't regret it.

He released my face, I nearly panicked. His touch had become vital. When he touched me, a deep down sense of peace filled me. He put his arm around my shoulders and sat next to me. I couldn't help myself; I laid my head on his chest. I was starved for affection. How had I gotten so empty? I sucked the energy right out of him. He brushed my hair with his hand, and I listened to him breathe in and out. I wrapped my arm around his waist. His breathing hitched. What the hell was that all about? I didn't really care. As long as he didn't make me move, I didn't care.

He curled around me and let me melt against him. His huge body formed a protective shell around mine. I'd never been so safe. Usually these feelings would make me want to run for the hills armed to the teeth. But, with Shooter it was different. It was okay to be safe with him. It was a different kind of safe than I'd felt with Stephan. Stephan's status and money gave me protection from my past. Shooter's skill and compassion guarded my present and my future.

Something brushed against my cheek. I shook my head. I was comfortable. Whoever or whatever it was would have to come back at a later time. But it wouldn't stop.

"Kat, Kat, you need to wake up, honey. You need to eat, and you need to take your medication." I heard and understood Shooter's voice, but he'd said I needed to wake up. I wasn't asleep. There had been no horrifying nightmare. There was always a nightmare. But my eyes were closed and my body was completely relaxed. I had, in fact, been asleep.

I opened my eyes. At some point my legs had wrapped around his. I should be humiliated. But I wasn't. I had slept, *really* slept. Shooter had given me the one thing I'd craved for years. Dreamless sleep. *This was bad. This was so, so bad.* Not only did he bring peace and safety, he also had the power to help me sleep. Great, just freaking great. In the very near future he'd probably catch me crawling out of his wall (because I would be afraid I'd get caught in the hall), climbing into his bed, curling up next to him, and getting a K-Bar to the chest. No one sneaks up on a sleeping Marine. Yup, this was just great.

Shooter eased his body from mine to collect the food tray. His clothes were wrinkled. The clock on my bedside table said it was one in the afternoon. He had let me sprawl all over him like a drunken prom queen for three hours. What if I snored? What if I drooled? Oh, it was worse than could be imagined.

"Did you sleep well?" he asked.

"You tell me," I answered cautiously.

"Dead people don't sleep that well." He smiled at me, like he knew he was responsible for my first trip to no-dream land. The corners of my mouth raised into a smile. I hoped to hell I looked casual about the whole sleeping arrangement.

He placed the tray in front of me and handed me two pills.

"What are these?" I asked.

"That one is an antibiotic and that one is a pain killer."

"I don't need this one." I handed the pain killer back to him.

He didn't take it. "Yes, you do. Your body can't heal if you're in pain."

"I don't need it." I pressed the tablet into his hand.

"You don't have to play the tough hero. That's stupid. Take it." He tried to force me to take the pill from his hand. I clenched my fists.

"I don't need it."

"Yes, you do."

"No, I don't."

"Take it, Kat."

"No."

"Kat...."

"Shooter."

He slumped his shoulders, "Kat. Take this. I won't tell anyone. I'll even tell everyone you didn't take it. You don't have to be strong for me. I already know you're stronger than Atlas."

He held his hand with the pill in it toward me. I closed my hand around his. "I'm not trying to be tough, and I'm not trying to make your life difficult. I'm not in pain, and I don't think I should take it unless I am."

He studied my eyes for several moments. "Okay, but it will be right here next to your bed in case you need it. And if you need it, take it. I'll turn my back if it makes it easier on you."

I nodded and dug into my lunch. God bless Lilly! She made the best crab salad on the planet. And she knew it was my favorite. I really shouldn't eat in front of Shooter. That was just rude. When I actually looked over at him and saw he had his own tray, I dove in with all the grace and dignity of a roughneck with a secret desire to be a ballerina. For the first time my brain had the chance to assess the Shooter situation. What must my staff be thinking? They were worse than any beauty shop or bar when it came to gossip. They had to *know* Shooter and I had been knocking boots for the past three days. That the stab wound was just a diversionary tactic so he would have an excuse to shack up in my room. And no doubt, they were positive a baby was just nine months away. Hopefully, Edna would keep them straight.

We didn't talk as we ate. It wasn't an uncomfortable silence. It was nice, natural. The pit of my stomach squirmed. I sniffed the crab. Had it turned bad? No, it smelled fine. I looked over at Shooter. He gave me a sweet smile. Someone turned up the tempo on the snakes doing the mambo in my stomach. Odd. I ignored it and focused on my food. Someone knocked on my door. Edna led Dr. Wells into my room. Dr. Wells was a good-looking man in his thirties. Everyone respected him. Even the older residents of Bayou Boudreaux, who had nearly rioted when Dr. Fontaine retired, valued his opinion.

"Dr. Wells is here to see you, ma'am," Edna announced. She took the tray from my lap.

"Thank you, Edna."

Dr. Wells stopped at my bedside. Shooter took up his post behind him. My Marine was at least five inches taller than the young doctor, so he could easily see over his shoulder. Dr. Wells sat next to me to take my vital signs. We talked casually without saying anything, really. The entire time my bodyguard stood over the good doctor with his arms folded over his chest. When Dr. Wells touched the incision on my pelvis, I jumped. It didn't really hurt. It was more of a protective reflex. Shooter's eyes flared. For a moment I thought the good doctor might be in danger of being filleted. I caught Shooter's gaze and held it, hoping to calm him. He relaxed after Dr. Wells replaced the bandage and got the hell away from the source of my pain.

"Have you gotten out of bed yet?" Dr. Wells asked.

"Yes, Edna helped me shower, and Shooter took me for a walk from there to the bathroom and back."

"Did he?" His tone made it clear that he did not like the other man. "He takes good care of you?"

"Yes." *Where the hell was this going?*

Dr. Wells turned to look at my Marine. If Shooter's reaction to him was any kind of clue, Dr. Wells did not have a nice look on his face. "Well, Mrs. Boudreaux, I know this goes against all propriety but I wanted to ask you to accompany me to the Founder's Day Carnival. But I don't think you'll be ready to be on your feet for that long in just ten days."

Shooter dropped his arms and clenched his fists. He had one seriously protective nature. I could go out for an evening without my company of Marines.

"How sweet of you." I smiled. I glanced at Shooter. He looked as if he had been kicked in the gut. "But, as you said, I don't think I'll be up to it in just ten days."

"I didn't think so," Dr. Wells said with a sad look on his face. He stood, collected his things and told me he would return in three days to check on me. He probably told me to rest, but I didn't hear him. I had been caught in Shooter's stare. The door closed and he just stared at me. The electricity between us could have powered New Orleans for a month.

"Would you have gone with him if you could have?" he asked quietly.

I shook my head. "No," I whispered.

In milliseconds he'd slid next to me and cupped my face in his hands. He bent his head and kissed me softly, sweetly. If the kiss on my forehead had revealed how empty I was, this kiss filled me to the brim. He was gentle, far more gentle than I expected. He didn't demand, he led. And I followed. He wrapped his arms around me and deepened the kiss.

BAM, BAM, BAM!

What the hell? You have got to be kidding me? Seriously? Someone wants to come in here now? *I don't care who it is, I'm going to pull their bottom lip over their head.*

Shooter broke our kiss and leaned his forehead against mine.

"Shooter," Switch yelled.

"Yeah," Shooter said, hoarsely as he pulled away from me.

"We need to talk, man."

Dear Lord, Thank you for keeping the host of Marines in the sitting room.

"I'll be back," he whispered.

After he left, I had a chance to clear my head. My brain had been pickled in a vat of Lilly's mint juleps. What had I been doing? I practically made out with a man I had known for four days. And I had been unconscious for two and a half of those days! Yes, he was kind, compassionate, loyal, honest, and a great kisser, but that was so off limits it didn't even chart. And yes, I was attracted to Shooter. What woman with a pulse wouldn't be? He was sexy as hell! But not in a boy band kind of way. He was sexy like a man should be. Shooter had a face that could make a Botticelli angel cry and his body would have thrown the Greek god of war into fits of jealous rage.

But it didn't matter how attracted to him I may have been or how perfect he seemed to be. There were too many things against him. Where was a piece of paper when I really needed one? This deserved a list, but without the necessary implements I would just have to make one up in my head. One, he's my brother's superior. I couldn't put either of them in that position. What's worse than sleeping with the boss? Your little sister sleeping with the boss. Shooter would feel obligated to treat Tyler differently, and Tyler would think he had a free pass because of me. They were both honorable men, and it would compromise them. I just couldn't do it.

Two, he would be gone at the end of the summer. He said a contingent of Marines would be with me until the threat against me was neutralized. He didn't say he would be with me the whole time. He could be called back to war at any time. He had a very rare, very valuable skill set that the Corps would not waste protecting some woman. Eventually he would have to leave. If we tried to extend anything beyond the summer, it wouldn't work. I would get all depressed pining for him. And he would probably get shot and killed because his mind wasn't on his job. He had to keep his shit tight, and I did not want to unravel it.

Three, it would hurt Sam. My daughter had become very fond of him. You'd think this would be in the plus column. It wasn't. When whatever was between me and Shooter ended, and it would end even if he didn't have to go back to Iraq, it would end. It always does. It would destroy her. She had never known what it was like to have a father figure. It would be way too cruel of me to give her a taste only to take it away. I might as well tell her Santa Claus was fake, the Easter Bunny wasn't real, and Mickey Mouse was just some overweight chick in a costume. I'd win mom of the year!

Four, he would never accept me or my past. Yes, he gave a brilliant showing when I told him I had once been a mercenary assassin, but that was just shock. Once he had time to actually think about the horrible the things I'd done, he could look at me honestly, and he wouldn't like what he saw. Even if we got married, my past would always be there, a big freakin' purple elephant in the room. Wait, how had we gone from one kiss to altar in five minutes?

Whatever. If we were ever in a relationship, my past would make him suffer. I was not the type of woman you took to movies or to meet your mom. As Tyler so eloquently put it, there was little difference between me and a mob hit man. Moms didn't like mob hit men. I would start to doubt his compassion and support and drive him away. I may have been neurotic, but I understood and accepted my neuroses. The damage they could inflict on a fellow human being was criminal.

Five, and it really killed me to admit this, he only acted sweet and compassionate because I saved his life. After the post-life-saving euphoria wore off, he'd see me for what I really was, and he'd regret taking care of me, comforting me, reading to Sam. He'd regret helping me with physical therapy and helping me sleep. He'd regret everything. Of course he was probably too honorable to actually admit that so he'd suffer with my presence for the summer only to fling himself into the nearest firefight the second he got back to Iraq. He'd probably get injured but break out of the hospital because he'd have horrible flashbacks about me and my own convalescence. He'd get an infection that would probably kill him. As he lay dying, he'd beg God to accept him into heaven because he'd already spent his time in hell. The time he spent with me. I wouldn't have his death and eternal life on my hands. I had to let him go. His life depended on it.

As I lay there gathering my courage to tell Shooter that we could never allow anything like that kiss happen again, my Marines—all of them including Tyler and Shooter—stormed my room. They stood at the end of my bed, their arms folded across their chests. They had changed out of their new clothes and back into their Marine issues. Doc threw a khaki camouflage shirt at me. I would have been less confused if they'd thrown a donkey dressed in a tutu on my bed. I held it up in front of me. In the spot where a Marine would put his nametag were the words "Hell Kat."

"Katharine Boudreaux, you are an official Rat Bastard."

My Marines snapped to attention. Horndog continued in short military cadence. "You will be known from now on as Hell Kat. The Rat Bastards expect your loyalty. You are to expect ours. We will come when you call. You will come when we call. You will never bring dishonor to the Rat Bastards. You will be bonded to the Rat Bastards for the rest of your life. Your initiation will come when you least expect it. It will be swift, it will be carried out in stealth, and it will be painful."

As a group, my Marines shouted, "Ooh-rah!"

I waited for the donkey ballerina. I had no idea what to say. What the hell was going on? Why was I a Rat Bastard? What was a Rat Bastard? What the hell was this initiation, and why would it be painful? How was I to be bonded to the Rat Bastards for life? Was a priest involved or did we just exchange friendship bracelets? *Seriously. Info, people.* I needed some info!

They turned on the balls of their feet and marched out of my room. All of them except Tyler. He relaxed his stance when the rest were gone. His confident soldier's attitude was replaced with trepidation and shame. He looked at his boots. "I'm sorry for what I said and how I acted earlier."

I held out my hand. He walked around to my side of the bed and gripped it. "I should have been honest with you from the beginning. I thought I was protecting you."

He looked up at me. "Protecting me from what?"

"From me. From my shit storm of a life. I wanted you to look at me like a sister. Not like a killer. You were the only normal thing I had. And I wanted to keep that."

He sat on the edge of my bed. "You'll always be my sister. You're just a much tougher version. I talked to the guys and they straightened me out. I'm sorry I kind of blew up in here."

"I thought about calling you Vesuvius, but I like Tyler better."

He smiled.

"So what's all this Rat Bastard stuff?"

Pride shone in his eyes. "Rat Bastards is the name of our unit. You're a member. You may not be a Marine, but like Doc, you saved a Rat Bastard's life so that makes you a Rat Bastard."

"About this whole initiation thing, why is it going to be painful? I've taken a knife for one of you. Is that not painful enough? If I have to, I'll fight, and I'm not your regular gyrene fresh from Parris Island. I'll kick every single one of your teeth in if I have to."

Tyler laughed. "Normally it would come in the form of a GI shower or a classic beat down. But I think you'd like that too much, and none of us are all that into hurting a girl, despite how tough she might be. So, you'll have a special initiation."

"GI shower?"

"We scrub you down with Brillo pads, steel wool, toilet brushes. Then pour salt water over your head. It sucks."

I could tell he spoke from experience. "So what will my special initiation be like?"

"Oh, you'll know it when you see it, little sis. I have a few ideas. I won't let you know when we solidify our plans. And don't try to beat it out of your staff. They won't be involved." He kissed me on the cheek and left.

That's how Tyler and I were. We could try to kill each other in the morning and grill steaks in the back yard by lunch. As he left, Shooter came in. I did not look forward to the impending conversation. He sat in his chair. We couldn't look each other in the eye.

"Listen," he said, "I don't think we should let what happened happen again."

I visibly sighed. *Thank you God for Shooter's obvious telepathic abilities.*

"I'm not leaving this room until you can walk out on your own. And I'm determined that will be in, at the most, seven days, so I hope you plan on getting to work tomorrow."

"I agree. Thank you. And I'm ready."

He smiled. If kissing hadn't just been outlawed, I could have kissed that man. He said what needed to be said and gave me a purpose. I had to at least meet his challenge. I would walk on my own in seven days, if not five. I could be as stubborn as a mule, but sometimes that could be a good thing.

Chapter Ten

*A*n evil witch controlled me. It was my duty to kill every mother I had ever known. How nice of them to line up for me. One by one they came into my chamber. I hit them twice in the back of the skull with the head of a hammer and used the claw to rip the back of their skull off. There was no emotion associated with it. It was a job, just like any other. My own mother was last in line. I started to get a little uneasy.

As she came in, she said, "Katharine, I don't want to die. Please don't kill me. You can save me. Please save me."

I crumpled to the ground weeping.

"Kat, Kat, wake up. It's a dream. You're just having a dream."

I opened my eyes. Shooter stroked my face. *I hate these damn nightmares!* I hated how debilitating they were, how they ruled my sleep, and how only Shooter could make them go away.

He sat next to me, wrapped an arm around my shoulders, and allowed me to curl into him. I wrapped my arm over his stomach and snaked my leg through his. Despite our earlier conversation, he didn't try to move me. He let me stay melded to his side. And I slept—better than road kill. When the sun bled through my eyelids, I feared I was in the middle of another nightmare. I thought my night of perfect sleep was a trick and at any moment I'd stand on the top of a volcano about to drop babies into it.

As I stretched, my arm hit something. Something fleshy. And I heard a harrumph. How could this not be a dream? It was morning. Only one nightmare had woken me up during night. I opened my eyes and recognized the broad chest of Shooter. My Shooter, better than Ambien and alcohol.

"Good morning to you, too," a groggy voice grumbled.

I looked up to see him rub his nose. I guess that explained the something fleshy I hit.

"Did you stay here all night?" I was shocked, but grateful, and I hoped my tone expressed that.

"You pinned me to the bed. How was I supposed to move?" He chuckled and smiled.

"Did you sleep at all? I slept great!" I shouldn't have said that.

"I slept just fine."

I could sense he held something back. But, I didn't ask what it was. We had boundaries, boundaries that allowed us to sleep together but not kiss. Suddenly I felt like a hooker.

I pushed him out of bed. It wasn't meant to be mean. I had to pee. Slowly, painfully, and with a few choice curse words, I struggled out of bed. Shooter didn't help me. And I loved him for it. He stayed next to me all the way to the bathroom and all the way back. He didn't once ask me if I was doing okay or if I needed a break, and he never offered his hand to help steady me. He would get me well the Marine Corps way. Suck it up and carry on.

Just as we reached my bed, Sissy and another maid, Ella, brought the breakfast trays. They were the youngest on my staff and like sorority sisters. They giggled and made a hasty retreat.

"So what's on the schedule for today?" I asked Shooter.

"We're going to get you to walk up and down the hall outside."

Yeah, right. "You mean we'll try." I knew that wasn't going

to happen. The hall was at least eighty feet long!

"There is no try. Only do or do not."

I laughed, nearly shooting coffee out of my nose at his gratuitous Star Wars reference. "Yes, Master Yoda," I said when I composed myself. "Can you get Edna for me? I need to take a shower."

"No."

"Oh, are you going to help me with my shower?" I hated the note of hope that crept into my voice.

He turned red. "No, you have to do it on your own."

I'll admit that scared the shit out of me. "Uh, the shower is wet and when wet mixes with tile, they combine to form slippery. Slippery equals falling and falling delays my recovery. So get Edna or get naked."

"No and no. You need to learn to trust yourself. You need to get your confidence back. You can't do that until you actually do it. So, no Edna, no me. All you." I must have looked truly terrified. "Don't worry. I'll stand outside the door and if I hear the sound of flesh hitting tile and bones breaking, I'll rescue you."

He stood up and headed into my closet. I could hear him rummaging around in there for several minutes. The thought of him elbow deep in my clothes made me cringe. I actually, physically cringed. He was a man. He'd probably pick my most frilly, lacy panties and bra and, more than likely, one of the dresses I bought at Express the other day.

"Do you need any help in there?" I yelled.

"A map would be nice," he hollered back.

I moved to extricate myself from the mound of tangled blankets when he came out of the closet. He surprised me. He had another velour track suit and completely appropriate undergarments. How could I have doubted him? He may be a man, but he was also a Marine, and they valued function over form. He handed the stack of clothes to me, and I gently, slowly stood up.

"Stand up straight," he ordered.

I glared at him. It was so not going to be a fun day. Lovely, just lovely. I pulled all my pride, dignity, and willpower together to stand fully erect. Each time I moved my right leg a stab of pain shot through me. But I wouldn't let him see it or that the pain had gotten to me. It took a while to get to the bathroom, but less time than it had taken yesterday or earlier that morning.

"Don't lock the door," he cautioned as I stepped in. When I got inside, I slumped on the counter. I nearly cried—nearly.

The boiling stream of water was heaven on my skin. It relaxed my muscles and eased my mind. Until I thought about Shooter. Despite the list I had made yesterday, I knew something I thought was dead, buried, and decayed stirred inside me. When I woke up, I was home. Like I'd been away for a long time and had finally found my way back into my own bed in my own house. Whether that was a good thing or a bad thing was still a mystery. It was dangerous to put so much trust in one person. When Shooter was around, all the ambient noise that buzzed around in my head stopped. It was nice, peaceful. It felt right. But it was wrong. No matter how good it might be, I couldn't put Shooter through the horrors of my life. They locked war criminals up in The Hague for less.

Before I wanted it to be, my shower was over. I had to face the day, no matter how painful it would definitely be. I dressed, grabbed a brush and hair tie from the vanity, and left the bathroom. Shooter sat in his chair showered, shaved, and dressed.

"I thought you said you'd wait in case I fell and broke my hip," I teased.

"Don't worry, I didn't leave you alone. I stationed Horndog by your door."

"You put Horndog in charge of coming into the bathroom to rescue me if I slipped in the shower?" I paused for a moment then added, "While I was naked! You put Horndog in charge of rescuing me in all my nakedness?"

I started the long, painful walk back to the bed.

"Stand up straight," Shooter ordered, and I righted myself. "You didn't need him, did you? Besides, he would show you, and all your nakedness, the utmost respect. You're a Rat Bastard. You're one of us."

"Yes, but none of you have all this to worry about." I drew a big circle around my torso hoping he understood what the "all this" was about. "I still can't believe you put Horndog in charge. He's...he's Horndog, for crying out loud!" I'd made it to the chair, and Shooter maneuvered me around to sit in it. "Don't ever put Horndog on guard when 'me' and 'naked' can be said in the same sentence."

He took the brush and hair tie from my hand as he pressed on my shoulder to get me to sit in the chair. I wasn't really thinking so I let him guide me.

"Okay, next time I'll ask Switch or Doc." He started to brush my hair.

Doc might be okay. Actually, no, he'd seen my scars and that created an element of weirdness between us. Switch knew that I'd basically killed my husband, and I didn't think I could take his pity. "No, not Switch or Doc either."

"Fine, Martinez or Tongue."

Tongue was my brother, and he hadn't seen me naked since he was three and I was one, and I'd really like to keep it that way, thank you very much. And Martinez had the opposite problem. I didn't know him well enough. "No, neither of them either."

He paused mid-stroke. "So are you saying I'm the only one you want to see you naked?"

Dammit! I walked right into that one. *No. Yes. No!* "You're the only one I trust to not think about it every ten seconds whenever you're around me."

He didn't say anything, just brushed my hair. When all the tangles were out, I turned and held my palm out. "Hair tie."

He stretched it until it broke. "Oops. Besides, it looks better down."

Ugh! Why did all men like long hair down? They had no

idea what it's like to have hair whipping around and blowing into your face. I glared at him. He knew I wouldn't be able to make it all the way back to the bathroom to get another tie. Bastard.

"Wait here."

I'd really started to get sick of him ordering me around. He might be able to get away with that with German shepherd, but not me. A couple minutes later he returned, Samantha's hand in his. "Ready to tackle the hall?"

"Yeah," I agreed and asked why he was holding her hand with one word.

"She's your cheerleader."

I smiled. If I could make it down the hall and back for anyone, it would be my daughter. So when she reached for my hand, I didn't hesitate to take it. She beamed at me and tried to drag me out of the room. But Shooter slowed her down.

"Hang on, Sam-I-Am. I'm kinda slow."

Wasn't that just like Shooter? He didn't want Sam to worry about me so he took the bullet.

I shuffled out of my room and into the hallway. As I looked down the long corridor, I might as well be looking into eternity. There was no way I could do what he expected. Why not ask me to stop a speeding train with my tongue?

"Come on, Mom." Sam pulled on my hand. "There's a surprise at the end." She smiled at Shooter and danced her feet. She was so excited I couldn't let her down. The wall at the end of the hall was my goal.

I had to stop several times to rest and Shooter had to remind me to stand up straight, but I put one foot in front of the other. I kept my eye on the end of the hall and forty minutes later I had made it!

"Yay! Can I show her?" Sam begged.

"Of course you can. You're the one who did it," Shooter said.

She turned to the doorway on the right. As far as I knew, it was just another spare bedroom. She opened the door and led me inside. My hand flew to cover my lips when I saw what Sam had done. The walls were covered with pictures of me and the people I loved. Pictures of me, Tyler, and our parents in Oklahoma, high school, my wedding, and Stephan and Sam. I couldn't believe it. She had filled the room with mementos from the past. Not just pictures. My wedding dress hung on one wall, a Strawberry Shortcake lunchbox I used to keep all my treasures in sat on a side table, an antique jewelry box of my mother's rested on the dresser, my grandmother's ice skates hung off the bedpost, every treasured possession from my life had found a home in the room.

"You said you wanted to make a memory book of all your pictures. I started to do that but there were too many. So I made you a memory room. Amanda helped me with the high ones and Shooter said we should put other stuff in here. Like your princess dress and grandma's jewelry box. Do you like it?"

"I love it," I whispered. I couldn't believe it. My five-year-old daughter had done this for me. She would never be able to comprehend what it meant. She gave me a past, a past I could be proud of. I bent to give Samantha a hug. The pain that should have racked my body never came. Pure, unadulterated joy was the world's best pain killer. I held my little girl tight. I never wanted to let her go. She was my angel, my savior. She was the reason I got out of bed every day. She was why I was still alive. And if she grew up to be a good person, the entire purpose for which I was put on the Earth would be met.

I finally released her and stood back up. The pain that had been held at bay rushed back with a vengeance. I put out my arm. Shooter was there to steady me.

"Do you need another break?" he asked.

I shook my headed and just stared at the display. If I cried, I would have been crying. Samantha had given me something amazing.

We started the long arduous trek back to my room. I noticed that, despite the fact I was exhausted, I made it back to my room faster and with fewer breaks. Yay, me.

Just as we reached my door, Edna stopped me. "Mr.

Bonaventure is here to see you, ma'am."

I scowled. "Have him wait in the library. I'll be down in a bit."

Mr. Forrest Bonaventure was one of my least favorite people. He was the CEO of Boudreaux Oil and quite possibly the most difficult person ever born. His life was his job. He had accumulated five years of vacation time since he started at Boudreaux Oil. He had never missed a day of work in his life. He'd sleep under his desk if the insurance would allow it. It made him an excellent employee. It also made him a man who had no family, no life, and no desire to get one. I shuffled into my room, and Shooter followed.

"Who's Mr. Bonaventure?" he asked when we were inside my sitting room.

"You know that saying, only the good die young?"

He nodded.

"Well, if that's the case, Bonaventure will never die. He's evil. Boudreaux Oil takes care of their employees. So what did he try to do the moment he took over? He tried to cut all the employee benefits from employees in underdeveloped countries, and he wanted to cut their pay by fifty percent because we pay more and offer more than the industry standards. He tried to push that through without Stephan's approval. Thank the gods Stephan had allies on the board who told him what Bonaventure was up to so he could stop it. He hates me and treats me like I'm beneath him because I lack his education and breeding. He hates that I am currently in charge of Boudreaux Oil." We reached my closet. "He is an arrogant, self-righteous asshole and the CEO of my company."

I reached for a pair of gray slacks that hung from a rod above my head. When pain rocked through my body, Shooter reached up and pulled them down for me.

"And he intimidates you." It wasn't a question.

"Well, yeah. He thinks he's better than me because he went to Harvard." I pulled a baby blue blouse off a hanger.

Shooter grabbed my chin and turned my face so I looked

him in the eye. "No one can make you feel inferior without your consent."

"Thank you, Mrs. Roosevelt," I said, my voice laced with sarcasm.

"She was a very smart lady, as are you. Will you be okay here for a minute? I have to take care of something."

I nodded and he left.

I changed my clothes, put on a pair of heels, applied mascara and lip gloss, and rolled my hair into a twist secured with a tortoise shell French comb. Just as I finished, Shooter returned.

"Ready?"

I nodded and stood. He blocked my way, and reached around my head to pull the comb from my hair letting it cascade down my back. I opened my mouth to protest but he stopped me.

"There's nothing more intimidating than a beautiful woman." He picked me up and carried me to the door. "Don't worry, he won't see you." He carried me down the stairs, through the house, down the long gallery, and to the closed library door. He set me on my feet and opened the door. All my Marines were in the library with Mr. Bonaventure.

Martinez lounged on a sofa cleaning his nails with a K-Bar. Switch leaned against a floor-to-ceiling bookcase with a menacing glare on his face. Doc and Tyler were talking, one in Arabic, the other in Latin. Every once in a while they would take a pause in their bilingual conversation, turn their heads and shoot threatening smiles to their right. To their right, leaning against my desk with his arms folded across his chest, was Horndog. Mr. Bonaventure sat in front of him in a little chair. Horndog glared at the diminutive man.

I stood at the door for a moment just to take in my Marines. They were an intimidating sight—tall, huge, and you could tell just by looking at them they knew how to kill. I didn't know what to say. The Rat Bastards were there to protect my pride. My heart swelled. No one had ever done anything like that for me. I had to love them.

"I need the room, boys," I said as I stepped into the library.

They got up, shot one last look of death at Mr. Bonaventure, and left.

"We'll be outside if you need anything, Hell Kat," Horndog said as he shut the door. Brotherhood, that's what that was.

I sat behind the desk, ignoring the pain. I didn't bend over, limp, or let Bonaventure know I was disabled in any way. I sat and Shooter resumed his signature stance of strong, silent, and pissed next to me.

Mr. Bonaventure wore a little dark gray suit, little round spectacles, and little black shoes. He straightened in his chair, opened his brief case, and retrieved a thin file. He placed the file on the desk and said, "There was an explosion at an oil refinery in Venezuela. Three men were killed, seven injured." He rattled off the statistics with all the sensitivity of a calculator.

A lead weight dropped into my stomach. To me, my employees were people. To Bonaventure, they were statistics. Whenever an employee was injured on the job, I wanted to make sure they were financially secure for the rest of their life. Bonaventure subscribed to the Ebenezer Scrooge philosophy of management. If they were going to die, they needed to get on with it and decrease the surplus population. "How bad were the injuries?" I asked.

"They range from broken bones, to burns and minor cuts. Nothing to worry about. They'll heal," said the calculator.

"Were the three dead men married?"

"Yes."

"Kids?"

"Yes."

"Increase their benefit by three times and ensure the children's future. Pay for all medical care for the wounded and make sure they have sufficient time off to heal. Pay their full salary while they are unable to work." I showed as little emotion as possible. Emotion can be a weakness.

"Mrs. Boudreaux, I understand your compassion for these workers' families, but don't you think you're projecting your own grief onto them?"

And that's why I had to keep emotion out of it. I could have told him what to do with all the sensitivity of a cyborg, and he would still think my situation in life took place over business. And he was right. I used to pretend that he was wrong and I could run Boudreaux Oil like an automaton, but the simple fact was I couldn't. I cared about the people who worked for me. I was responsible for them. I would take care of them. Even if that meant I had to defy the great and powerful Bonaventure.

"And I want the widows paid three times what a refinery worker would make in the United States, not Venezuela."

He smiled at me as if I were a child. "Ma'am, the industry standard is—"

"I'm sorry, are you questioning me? Because last time I checked, I am in charge of Boudreaux Oil. According to the company bylaws I sit at the head of the board, and my word is all that really matters. So if I tell you to issue a check to each widow in the amount of ten million dollars that's what you do. Am I clear?" I loved making Bonaventure squirm.

"Perfectly clear, but this is simply not fiscally responsible."

Fiscally responsible! He did not just say fiscally responsible. "How much is Boudreaux Oil worth, both liquid and frozen? How much is *my* company worth?"

He folded his hands in his lap. "I don't think that's really here nor there...."

I clasped my hands on the desk and leaned forward. "How much is Boudreaux Oil worth?" I said slowly to make sure his Harvard brain understood the question.

He cleared his throat. "Seventy-two billion and change."

"And roughly how much is triple a refinery worker's salary per year in the US?" I held his gaze. I was in charge of the situation, not him.

"One hundred eight thousand dollars."

It amazed me that he could rattle off these statistics with

such proficiency.

"So multiply that by three and you get three hundred, twenty-four thousand dollars per year. Times that by, let's say, thirty years and we have nine million, seven hundred twenty thousand dollars. Correct? So you're saying that if we never make another dime these women and children will place a one-one hundreths of one percent burden on my company. Am I right?"

His bottom lip started to shake. He was about to pitch a fit. "Yes, but, ma'am...."

I hit the desk. "Why are you still talking? This is my call, not yours. Take care of it, or I'll find someone who will."

Bonaventure's face turned bright red and a vein pulsed in his forehead. "The board will not like this, Mrs. Boudreaux."

"I don't give a damn about the board. I give a damn about my employees. You're not really a board anyway. You're more of a council." I flicked my four fingers the way people do when dismissing an inferior life form.

"Why do you even bother with a board or council? You don't care what we think. Why don't you run the whole damn company yourself?" Bonaventure sputtered. He was about to reach maximum pressure.

"Because if I did that you'd be out of a job, and I know how much you love your job. I would hate to take your only happiness in life away. But trust me, you can be replaced." I had never threatened Bonaventure with his job, but he was beginning to get on my nerves.

He stood up. "At least let us vote. You can't know what you're doing. Boudreaux Oil is a huge, multinational company. You can't handle it on your own. You simply don't have the intelligence to see to the day to day operations." He said this as if he were reading a grocery list.

He'd stunned me stupid. I didn't know what to say. Shooter gave me a chance to gather my thoughts. He leaned down into Bonaventure's face. "Sit. Down." Bonaventure did as ordered.

"I'm sorry, did you just say I'm unintelligent? You are

treading on very thin ice, Mr. Bonaventure." Shooter wasn't the only one with a danger tone.

But, Bonaventure was an idiot. He didn't quit. "You have no idea what it takes to keep Boudreaux Oil running. Frankly, I wouldn't trust you to run a lemonade stand."

Shooter growled low in his chest. I put my hand out to try to keep him from attacking. "Your opinion on this matter is not required. Do as I ask or start looking for a different place to work."

"You can't keep this up. I demand that you transfer power to the board." He moved as though he was going to stand up again but changed his mind when Shooter growled at him.

"You can forget it. That won't ever happen. Would you wrest control of Boudreaux Oil from me? Would you banish me from my own business? Would you lock Stephan's only heir out of a company that is her birthright? Why on Earth would I sign my daughter's future over to you?"

"No, but you would raise her amongst all your gigolos!" His face had turned red and his eyebrows were disappearing into his hairline. I had seen that look before. He would soon have a stuttering seizure and completely block out everything I said.

Shooter stepped forward, and I had to stop him with my arm. My eyes narrowed as I took aim at Forrest Bonaventure. "Did you just accuse me of running a brothel?" My voice was so low I could barely hear it.

"Oh, come on! It's obvious. They all look like they stepped off the cover of a romance novel!"

Shooter pushed against my arm.

"Who is he? Your own personal sex slave, or is he a pimp for the other men you have here?"

That was downright insulting. I would not allow this little weasel to speak of my Rat Bastards that way. I dropped my arm and unleashed Shooter.

Shooter looked down at the man. "No, I'm the garbage man, and right now I'm going to take out the trash." I heard the white hot anger in his voice before he bent down, picked Bonaventure up by his lapels, and carried him out of the library. They were followed by me and the rest of the Rat Bastards. Shooter hauled Mr. Bonaventure through the house and to the front door. He threw—literally threw—Boudreaux Oil's CEO out the door and down the front steps.

I had to smile when Bonaventure stood up. His eyes were as big as hubcaps. It looked like he had summoned every bit of courage he possessed to not piss himself. The man didn't say anything; he just climbed into the backseat of his Town Car and ordered his driver to drive away. Shooter was a handy guy to have around.

Chapter Eleven

*L*ife was good as a Rat Bastard. They had my back no matter what. They were protective, but not in a big brother sort of way. They never made me feel like they were there because I couldn't take care of myself. They were there because I was one of them. They would be by my side at any time, and I would be by theirs. I was so used to being a lone wolf you'd think being part of a pack would be hard. It wasn't. Turns out pack life was nice. *Who knew?*

It had been a week since the unknown man had skewered me. And I had to say I was getting along quite well. The day had arrived for my final test of fitness. Before Shooter would declare me well, I had to walk down three flights of stairs and back up. I was pretty sure I could do it. And the added incentive of getting my life back was well worth the effort. The old Kat would have welcomed that she would no longer need her nurse. But Shooter had grown on me. More than that, he had become important. And not just for his ability to guarantee a restful night's sleep— though that fact alone was enough to grant him god status in my book. He had become a source of strength. He had cheered me on through my recovery. We had stayed awake late into the night just talking about everything and nothing. I had never revealed more of myself to anyone in my life, even to Stephan.

Shooter knew all my hang ups, insecurities, weaknesses, and strengths, and the most important thing, I knew he would never use them against me.

So as I stood at the top of my own personal Everest it comforted me to know Shooter stood behind me. I had tried to keep my endeavor a secret but, apparently, within the Rat Bastards there are no secrets. *Bastards.* They'd joined me at the top of the stairs. If I had any doubts in my ability to climb the stairs, their presence quashed them. There was no way in hell I would fail with all of them watching. It was about pride, and I would like to keep mine, thank you very much.

I attacked the stairs with the same commitment used when killing an opponent. Shooter didn't have to tell me to stand up straight or to stop favoring my right side. On the second floor landing Edna, Sissy, and Ella had stopped their work to watch me conquer the stairs. They all flashed what I thought were encouraging smiles, but as I passed them their expressions changed. They looked like they were up to no good. Forgetting them, I continued down the stairs. Sam waited at the bottom. We slapped a high five when I touched the tile of the entryway.

"Do you need a rest?" Shooter asked. His tone teased me.

"No, I'm fine." I turned to climb back up.

"Are you sure? I could carry you if you like. I don't want you to wear yourself out. There's no shame in admitting your weaknesses."

I rolled my eyes at him and jogged up the first few stairs. Okay, that had been a mistake. It took all my pride and self-respect to not double over in pain. The rest of the stairs were taken at normal speed. The girls weren't there on the second landing. They must be in a room tidying up. At least that's what I thought until I reached the third floor.

My Marines had been joined by Edna, Sissy, Ella, and Yvette.

Yvette hadn't been a regular on my staff. She came in when I needed someone to turn me from a gutter snipe into a proper member of the Southern aristocracy. Yvette could best be described as a Betty Page stripper. She had big boobs, rocket-fire red hair, lots of makeup, and it wouldn't surprise me if she wore a vinyl micro mini to church. I loved her immensely. She was the closest thing I had to a girlfriend. She came to my rescue when Stephan and Madeline presented me to polite society. She got me ready for my wedding. And she turned me into the ravishing widow at my husband's funeral. Yvette was responsible for my public persona. And though we didn't talk often, when we did it was all about men, clothes, and who had what done where. Her skills were in high demand, and she knew everything about everybody. Though I adored her, I made sure to keep anything I didn't want the entire town of Bayou Boudreaux to know, to myself. It's not that she might spill my secrets; it's that she definitely would.

But all that did not explain why she was there. The Rat Bastards had changed back into their fatigues and they all had conspiratorial looks on their faces. Something was up, and that something had to be terrible.

"Hell Kat," Horndog said as they snapped to attention. "You have been selected to join the Rat Bastards. You have accepted this invitation. You are subject to initiation. Do you accept?"

I screwed up my courage and straightened to my full height. "Yes, I accept."

Tyler stepped forward. "In the past three years you have received and refused an invitation to the Jefferson Ball. Your initiation will be to attend. You are required to wear what our advisors tell you to. You will look how our advisors want you to look. And you will be accompanied by anyone we choose."

This is it. This is what the deepest, darkest circle of hell looks like. I almost threw a fit. I could have leapt on my Marines with the intent to throttle every single one of them. But, I contained my extreme displeasure and nodded. Apparently the horror on my face was apparent because they laughed. They were lucky their tongues weren't being served for dinner.

Culinary intentions aside, they parted, and I followed Edna, Sissy, Ella, and Yvette into my bedroom. They continued to laugh as Ella closed the door.

I turned on the *advisors*. "I don't know what you think you're going to do here, but I'm not about to allow a bunch of leathernecks to decide what I wear and how I look."

"Of course not, honey," Yvette said in her Southern drawl and draped a long thin arm around my shoulders. "We get to decide how you'll look and what you'll wear."

Oh, things could not get any worse.

Edna pushed me into the bathroom with strict instructions to wash, shampoo, and shave. As if she thought I actually wouldn't shave. I spent a long time standing under the stream of scalding hot water. I stayed there until I was as wrinkly as a boiled plum and someone pounded on my door.

Edna yelled through the wood. "You're not getting out of this, *cher*. Come on or we'll make this much more painful than necessary."

I stuck my tongue out at the door and turned off the water. I wrapped a thick, white terry cloth robe around my body and went to face the firing squad.

Part of the acreage inside my closet had been set aside as a dressing area. The last time it had been used was when I dressed for Stephan's funeral. Ella led me to my torture. She was the weakest of the quartet my Marines had formed. It wasn't my fault that I pounced on Ella like a dingo on a baby. They really should have thought the situation through a bit more.

"Ella, don't you think I should choose my dress? I am the one being forced to attend this ball. It's really unfair of all of you to do this to me." Insincere tears formed in my eyes. I may not be able to shed real tears of emotion, but I could fake it better than Meryl Streep.

"Save it," Yvette scolded. "We get to do you tonight, and we're gonna do you up right."

Yvette had turned into an eight-year-old princess and made me Malibu Barbie. I had absolutely no allies. She pushed me down into a chair. The mirror atop the vanity had been covered with a towel. Great, they weren't even allowing me to have a look at the progress. Across the vanity table lay an array of makeup that would make Ronald McDonald cringe. There were pots and pans and tubes and jars of stuff in every color of the rainbow. Sissy, my sweet innocent little Sissy, turned on me with a white triangular sponge in her hand.

"Wait." I grabbed her hand. "You don't wear makeup, like, ever. How are you supposed to do my face?"

Edna intervened, "She's an artist. Color is color, paint is paint, and talent is talent. Let her go so she can get to work!"

Sissy was an accomplished painter but did that mean she could wield a mascara wand? No, it did not. But I really had no choice so I released Sissy and the sponge hit my face. My skin seemed to gain weight with every stroke of her sponge. What was she using, spackle? She attacked me with brushes and wands and puffs. When she was done, I was almost positive my face looked like Bozo's cousin. Hopefully she'd plastered my scowl into place.

Next came Yvette. "Ooh," she squealed and danced around. "I've always wanted to roll you up in a set of hot rollers and let your hair down. I could just kiss your brother."

I turned and held up a hand. "Just, please don't make me look like I'm about to be inducted into the Country Music Hall of Fame." In the past, Yvette was only permitted to put my hair up. She had always fantasized about letting it hang down.

She shook her head. "I was told I have complete autonomy. I can do whatever I want. So if I decide to dye you red, chop it off, and call you Reba, I can."

I scowled even more. Every single Rat Bastard had earned a slow, painful death.

"What I don't get," she said as she attacked me with a wide-tooth comb, "is why you don't want to go to the Jefferson Ball. I'd sell my kids to get an invite."

Of course she would. I'm sure she saw herself arriving at the ball in a full ball gown riding in a horse drawn coach that used to be a pumpkin driven by men who used to be mice.

Unfortunately, the Jefferson ball was far less Cinderella and far more Dante's Inferno. The Jefferson Ball was the longest running, most exclusive ball in the state of Louisiana. Everyone who was anyone was invited. The guest list was filled with politicians, celebrities, American aristocracy, socialites, and the simply rich. No one got invited unless they'd appeared in *Star* magazine at least three times, *Time* at least once, could link themselves to the Kennedys in six people or less, or had a bank account of no less than two hundred fifty million dollars. The attendees were the most judgmental, self-centered, self-absorbed group of people ever collected in one place. It was a veritable who's who of the modern debauched society.

Yvette forced me to sit there and let her blow, curl, wrap, roll, mousse, gel, spray, tease, flat iron, and torture my hair into what I was sure would be an exact replica of a bronze Degas dancer. I felt like getting all weepy and thanking my God, my momma, the fans, and the country music community. Or enrolling in Clown College. Edna and Ella made another appearance. They had been lost somewhere in my closet for the last hour and a half. They held my clown costume.

"No," I said. "No, I will not wear that. You can forget it."

They held the red Versace gown out toward me. "Yes, yes you will wear this," Edna ordered. The gown was a stunner. Red, sleeveless, simple draping at the top, to the floor, and like second skin, it would look fantastic on me and that's why I didn't want to wear it. I may collect sexy, form-fitting dresses, but I didn't wear them. I didn't like people looking at me as if I were something on a dessert buffet. It wasn't because I wouldn't be taken seriously. It's that I just didn't like to draw attention. And unfortunately for me, God gave me attributes that drew attention. I hated them.

Ella handed me a lacy, next-to-nothing, Agent Provocateur strapless bra and panties. These were other items I collected and only sometimes wore when I needed to feel pretty. Nothing gave a girl confidence like pretty underwear. I put them on and the team stripped me of my robe and threw the gown over my head. The red clingy fabric hugged every single curve of my body. I would be less exposed if I had remained naked. Sissy came back with the shoes. The black silver studded Louboutins were new and, like the dress, I had never intended to wear them. Sissy had fallen in love with them the moment she saw them. I was going to give them to her. Fat chance of that ever happening. I turned to leave when Edna stopped me.

"Wait, you're not properly frosted."

Edna held a large jewelry box in her hands. She opened it, and inside was the Boudreaux diamond. Eighty-two carats of perfect, white, teardrop diamond surrounded by two rows of two-carat rubies. She hung the hunk of geology around my neck and fastened the necklace. The gem had been mine since I married into the Boudreaux family. But it had never been worn. Just below my neck hung the equivalent of a moderate-sized house, and it made me uneasy. Edna slipped a diamond-encrusted bangle on my wrist and stabbed huge diamond solitaires into my ears. She stood back, assessed my ensemble, and nodded her head. I passed muster.

They grabbed my elbows and dragged me toward the door. I dug in my heels. "I refuse to go anywhere until I see what you've done. I will not enter the viper pit without knowing what I have to defend myself with." That was a bit dramatic, but I had to assess the damage for myself.

They asked and answered questions with their eyes, and finally Edna relented. They took me back into the closet, pulled the sheets off the three mirrors in my dressing area, and let me look.

I hated what I saw. I wasn't ugly or overdone in any way. No, I was—I couldn't believe I was about to use the word—I was stunning. My dress hugged every curve and looked phenomenal. My makeup was subtle but striking. My hair looked perfect. It hung down to the middle of my back in all its natural wavy glory. I had never looked better. I hated every single one of my advisors. A significant portion of my life had been lived in the shadows. At the ball I would stand out like a sore, yet beautiful, thumb. Unless the background was a row of Victoria's Secret models, there would be no hiding.

They led me out of the closet and through my bedroom door.

"Woo-wee, Kat, I'd give my new boobs to go out with one of your Marines," Yvette said as we started down the stairs. She may be a hair miracle worker but that girl was all country.

My Marines waited at the bottom of the stairs. It had completely slipped my mind that I would have a date to hell. Who had the Rat Bastards chosen to accompany me? It kind of made me happy to know that someone else would be in it with me. I just hoped it wasn't someone that smelled bad or spent the entire night leering down my dress.

As I scanned the Bastards, I didn't see the one my gaze usually settled on. Shooter was not among them. Where was he? Just as the thought crossed through my brain, the front doors opened. It was as if I had stepped into a bad eighties romantic movie. He wore a tux and was framed by the setting sun. He was obviously my date. Maybe the evening wouldn't be so bad.

He stepped through the front door. I held my breath. He was gorgeous. Christopher was a genius. Of course, I already knew that. He'd outfitted me for formal affairs, and I shouldn't be surprised that he could work textile magic with menswear, but really he had out done himself. If Shooter looked good in his fatigues and weekend-at-the-Hamptons wear, he looked amazing in a tux. He'd probably look even better out of it. *Katharine Lyn Boudreaux! Put your mind back where it belongs and behave yourself!* I could almost hear my mom's reproachful voice.

Mother's voice be damned, Shooter was a sight to behold. Suddenly the Jefferson Ball didn't seem quite so scary. In fact, I almost started to look forward to it. A whole slew of people would be there who had mistreated me in one way or another. Oh, revenge would be sweet. And I had a bucket load of "take that you nasty bitch" to hand out.

I invoked all the powers of heaven and hell to tear my gaze from Shooter's body. I didn't want to look like a super model in front of an all-you-can-eat-calories-don't-count buffet. When I tore my attention away from his spectacular body to his face, I was surprised. He looked dumbfounded. Calm, cool, nothing-ever-flusters-me Shooter looked horrified. That was the only thing that came to my mind. The look on his face was one of shock and awe, and not in a good way. Great, they had forced him into going out with me, and he knew he would be miserable. Maybe we could just pop into the ball and leave. That should put him at ease.

My confidence shaken, I completed the walk down the stairs and stopped in front of my Marines. I waited for a smartass comment or at least a once over with their eyes. I didn't get any of that. They shot Edna, Sissy, Ella, and Yvette treasonous glances and looked back at me.

"You look good," Tyler whined.

He actually whined as if he had expected me to look terrible. The whole situation was all very strange, and I was about to demand an explanation. But my thoughts were interrupted by the slam of the front door and Shooter disappearing. Yup, just what I thought. He was doing a runner.

Horndog stepped forward. His expression had changed from one of disappointment to one that resembled a situation involving a frat boy, a keg of beer, and a naked *Playboy* model on the pump. Tyler whacked him on the back of the head.

He came back to center and said, "Hell Kat, you will attend the Jefferson Ball. You will stay for at least three hours. You will smile, be cordial, and mingle with the other attendees. You will not change your uniform. You will not attempt to ditch your companion. You will not try to get him to ignore his orders. You will follow the spirit of your initiation and its intended purpose. You will in no way alter, ignore, change, search for loopholes, or disregard these orders. Am I clear?"

"Perfectly."

Tyler had written my instructions. He knew I'd try to

wriggle my way out of the ball. And dammit, he knew me well enough to know I would never go back on my word. He should have been left me in a medically induced coma. He had given me no out. I had to follow the spirit of the order. That basically meant, in Tyler speak, that I had to follow the rules as they were intended. Not as they may or may not be written. He smiled at me because he knew he had me. I could have clawed his face off and used it as mask. But I resisted.

Shooter came back through the door. Oh, I guess his personal pride and honor kicked in, and he would accompany me after all. I wondered how many times he'd need to use the restroom or get another drink. I'd give him fifteen minutes. Fifteen minutes from the time we walked through the doors of the Magnolia Mansion, and he'd be passed out drunk on one of the antique settees. This was going to be fun.

My Marines handed me over to Shooter, and he led me out the front door. Gregory held the door to my new gray Bentley Mulsanne. I slid onto the white calfskin seat. The Mulsanne was not available in the US yet, but Bentley had a great relationship with the Boudreauxs so I was the first to get one. As Shooter slid in, he didn't even look at me. The man who had nursed me back to health, had seen all my scars both physical and emotional, helped me sleep, and had become my closest confident couldn't even look at me. That hurt. I had thought him to be above reproach. He was one of the good guys. It really was just guilt that forced him to care for me. It was only his sense of....

"You look...beautiful." He sounded surprised.

Gregory had pulled away from the house and as I looked over at Shooter, I could see through his window an old rusty jalopy parked on the grass next to the drive.

I wanted to throw a snide remark at him for his earlier "beautiful" comment but was completely lost at the sight of the old 1974 POS in my yard. "What is that?" I asked, maybe a little too loudly.

Shooter turned his head to see. "That was supposed to be

our ride. But, when I saw that Edna had not followed orders, I couldn't let you go to the ball in that. Gregory helped me choose a different car. I hope this is okay?" He pointed to the ceiling and drew a circle in the air indicating his choice in cars.

"It's just fine. What do you mean Edna didn't follow orders?" I knew something had been up. I knew there was more to all this then just a pretty dress and a party.

Shooter rubbed a finger across his forehead. "Edna and the others were supposed to make you look like a drunken trailer park queen." He grimaced and peeked over at me. "They were supposed to do your hair all big and poufy and force you to wear a denim mini skirt thing and a pink halter top that showed off a lot more than it covered."

I laughed hysterically. That should teach my Marines a lesson. Never try to pit my family against me. They would lose.

"I just want you to know," he said, turning his whole body to face me, "that I was against the whole hair, outfit, and ride situation. I told them I wouldn't have anything to do with it if they made you do that. Then they said they'd have Horndog take you, and I couldn't...." He didn't finish his sentence and looked down at his hands.

I had been wrong. Shooter hadn't been horrified by the way I looked because he would be embarrassed. He was horrified because he had taken part in a mean prank. That was it, right? He was horrified at his own actions. Oh please, tell me that was it. I grabbed his chin with my hand and pulled his face up to look at me. "Never look down," I whispered, "it's a sign of weakness."

He held my cheek in his palm, and I leaned my face into his hand. It was a reflexive action. I couldn't have stopped myself if I'd wanted to. And I wasn't saying I wanted to. But, he and I had rules and, just as I was about to get lost in his eyes and start praying for him to kiss me, he moved his hand. But his eyes didn't leave mine. It was as if he looked at me for the last time, and he wanted to memorize every inch of my face. That electrical charge between us ignited into full Chernobyl melt down. I gripped the edge of the seat so I wouldn't jump into his lap.

Control, Kat, control. A few deep breaths steadied my control. I meant to ask him another question but I had forgotten what it was. He pulled his face out of my grip. That action was like someone had cut my soul from my body. His hand slipped into mine and a bit of the panic subsided.

"Horndog give you your final orders?" he asked.

Sometimes his Marine stay-on-task bullshit was really annoying. Maybe he could go from one-twenty to zero in point five seconds but I wasn't that talented.

It took a moment for me to get my libido in check before I could answer. I saluted and said, "Yes, sir."

"Good, then you know there's no way out of this. I'm already breaking the rules by taking you in this and not the rusted out bit of luxury we bought for you, but Edna started it. I'll take my punishment." He paused and licked his lips. He was trying to say something but couldn't get it out. He looked down then back up with a very determined look on his face. "I'm really glad I get to go with you."

I laughed. "You won't think that once we get there. The Jefferson Ball invites all the poisonous serpents of polite society. Just remember the rules of survival. Keep your distance, know that they're all hungry and will strike at any moment, and if one attacks, it's best to grab them by the base of the skull and snap their neck."

He didn't seem amused. "I meant I'm glad I get to go with you. It wouldn't matter if we were going to a state dinner or to the car wash, I'm glad I get to be with you."

A surge of blood rushed through my body. It felt as if my heart hadn't worked in years and all of a sudden it was back to the old lub-dub rhythm. Getting through the night would be hard. Very hard.

Chapter Twelve

The Magnolia Mansion was a New Orleans landmark. Its beautiful white pillars made it look like an antebellum Parthenon. For the ball, the lawn, sidewalk, and part of the street in front of the mansion were lined with photographers and news people. I hated that part. I loathed the entire idea of the ball but the press was the worst part. Shooter gave my hand a squeeze and smiled at me. I knew he'd be with me the entire time but that didn't erase the guilt warring inside me for putting him through all the hoopla. He had faced bullets, bombs, terrorists, insurgents, and knife-wielding maniacs, but nothing could have prepared him for what was about to happen.

As Gregory pulled to a stop outside the manse, the cameras and reporters turned to see which of their prey had arrived. Gregory climbed out to open my door. When I emerged, there was a full two seconds of quiet. No flashes, no talking just quiet. Apparently my absence from the Louisiana social scene had not gone unnoticed. Then an eruption of flashing lights, rapid speech, and "oh my Gods" blew up like a paparazzi IED. When Shooter climbed out of the Bentley, there was another heartbeat of silence. And then a round of "who is he?" and "why is she with him?" assaulted me from all sides. I smiled, nodded and braved my way through the path of photo journalists without stopping for a moment, up the stairs and into the mansion. We were greeted by the upper crust with dazed silence.

Shooter leaned over and whispered in my ear, "Bar?"

Oh God, yes. Yeah, this evening was brought to you by Jack Daniels and Jim Beam. I ordered a shot of whatever was closest and downed it. Shooter handed me a mint julep while he sipped his scotch. Bless that man. I scanned the room for the enemy. I had honed that particular skill over several missions for GSA. It's amazing how quickly things come back to you when you are threatened.

My gaze fell on the first threat, Louise LaLourie. Why her parents had named her Louise with a last name like LaLourie was completely beyond me. Of course she had sported several other last names over the years, but she always returned to LaLourie. At one time she desperately wanted to be known as Louise Boudreaux. But, I was married to my husband at the time, and he had shown her the no trespassing sign right away. Louise held a flute of champagne in her hand; her cunning eyes searched for the next Mr. LaLourie. Her sights fell on me, and she stalked forward. I'm not kidding, she stalked, like a lioness, toward me. I looked over at Shooter. I needed to warn him that the most bedded woman in New Orleans was on the prowl. He was busy at the bar fighting for his constitutional right to get good and shit faced, completely missing my look of caution. Since I knew Louise watched me, I smiled and prayed the words *die, bitch, die* were not tattooed on my forehead.

"Oh my gawd! Are you finally out of mourning?" Her accent was so thick you could cut it with a K-Bar. "I understand grieving but, honey, you can't put yourself in cold storage for the rest of your life. But you are looking great. Look at you. I was afraid you'd locked yourself up in that big ole house and either ate or drank yourself to death. I am so relieved to see you looking as good as ever. Who are you wearing, darlin'? You look positively wonderful."

Of course her compliments were about as real as her boobs, but I smiled back and said, "Versace."

"Donatella?" Louise asked with pity in her voice.

"No, Gianni. It went up for auction at Sotheby's a few years ago, and I just had to have it. Though this is the first time I've worn it."

Edna could look forward to a big, fat Christmas bonus. The envy on Louise's face was priceless. It was worth coming to the damn ho-down, and I mean *ho*-down, just to see her face turn a lovely shade of green. She would have given a lot to own an original Gianni but she didn't and I did. *Take that, you nasty bitch.*

Shooter took that moment to turn around and hand me another cocktail. His eyes went big and he tried to take a step back but the bar was in the way. I hadn't taken in what Louise had on until that moment. She wore a black, too-tight-to-breathe, strapless Dolce and Gabbana that made her boobs spill over the top. Truth be told, I had that same dress in my closet at home. But I would never choose to accessorize it with a purple leopard bra that poked strategically above the neckline. Her lecherous eyes zeroed in on Shooter. She had the sniper in her sights, and he was about to feel the full force of Louise's slut-o-matic up close and personal.

"Well, hello. You must be Kat's brother?"

"No, Louise," I interrupted, "This is my date." I choked on the last word.

She didn't care. She wouldn't care if a man was in bed with his wife on their wedding night, Louise believed all men were available. "And what is your name, gorgeous?"

"Shooter." He smiled and leaned into her gaze, a slight come-and-get-me smile smeared across his face. I seriously wanted to pop his eyes out with a shrimp fork, but I reigned in my rage.

"And what is it that you do, Mr. Shooter?" Translation: Can you afford me? She pressed herself up against his body, shamelessly exposing all her voluptuous assets.

He raised his hand and extended a finger. Shooter pushed the tip of his long, thick finger into the center of her forehead forcing her to take several steps backward. His gaze had gone from playful to deadly. "I kill people." His whisper was sinister. Shooter wrapped an arm around my waist and pulled me up close to his body. In a louder tone he said, "Darling, isn't that the governor? We must stop and say hi." He gently guided me away from Louise.

I wiggled my fingers and blew her a kiss. I won't lie, that was better than a full magazine and a sharp knife.

"Who was that train wreck?" Shooter asked.

"The Madame de Pompadour of New Orleans."

He didn't ask anything else about Louise LaLourie, and I put her from my mind. Not because I had ignore-mean-spirited-bitches super powers, but my mind was quickly filled with the attention of what I like to refer to as *the old guard*. A group of four wizened old widows stood as one from an antique sofa. The old guard were a bunch of old biddies that made everyone's business their own personal problem. They took me and Shooter in with one choreographed toe to top assessment. Their sneer made it clear we were found wanting.

The spokeswoman for the tribal elders extended her hand as if she were a queen and addressed me. "Katharine Boudreaux, I am pleased to see you here. Who is this you are with?"

I clasped her fingers in mine and said, "This is a very dear friend of mine." It suddenly dawned on me that I didn't know his real name. "Shooter."

"Shooter...." They waited for a last name.

"Just Shooter."

"Katharine, I'm surprised you would introduce someone into society when you don't even know his last name. Really, what would your husband say? And Madeline would be horrified. You should be ashamed of yourself." The spokeswoman spoke down her nose at me. It's difficult to speak down your nose. You have to kind of tilt your head back, lower your eyelids, and speak as though you have a lawn gnome stuck up your ass.

Shooter leaned forward as if he wanted to defend my honor. I stepped on his toe to send him the clear signal that I could handle it. "Well, Stephan would say, 'what are you drinking, Shooter?' And Madeline would say, 'it is far kinder to introduce someone with no last name to society than to throw a pregnant, starving young girl on the street because she disgraced you.'"

The old crow recoiled and pulled her hand from my grasp. "Well, I never...."

"Never what? Had an actual beating heart in your chest? Just so you know, her son survived. She didn't. And he's the best damn gardener in Louisiana. That's right, those azaleas you admired last year at my home could have been yours if you hadn't been so damn heartless." I was getting myself all whipped up into a frenzy. Shooter tried to guide me away from the vultures, but I wouldn't let him. "And by the way, Madeline, Etienne, and Stephan all knew it was you who turned her out. Everyone in my household knows it was you."

Shooter tightened his hold on my waist and carried me off. He picked me up off the floor and carried me into a dark hallway to calm down.

"What the hell was that all about?"

He didn't know about Big Joe. "Big Joe's mother worked for that shrew. When she got pregnant, the harpy kicked her out on the street. My mother-in-law took her in. She died giving birth to Joe. I've wanted to let that old hag have it since I learned it was her that had done it. Who does that? Who just tosses someone *who is pregnant* out on the street? I'm going to go back out there and hit her upside her fool head."

Shooter grabbed my arm and trapped my body against the wood paneled hallway. "No, you're not. You're going to stay here and cool down. Only a few people saw you have it out with that woman. Stay here until someone gets drunk and puts a lampshade on their head and your little outburst will be forgotten."

I laughed. Shooter had plastered his body against mine. It took him a moment to realize what he had done. Suddenly we were the only ones in the hall. We stared into each other's eyes. I wanted him to kiss me. I wanted him to drag me out of that hell house, take me home, and take complete advantage of me. I wouldn't be able to stop him. I didn't *want* to stop him. Fire raged through my body. He leaned his head toward me, and I thought for one wonderful glorious split second he would break the rules. He didn't. *Dammit!*

He pressed his forehead against mine and whispered, "Can you behave yourself now?"

No!

I nodded, he moved away from me, grabbed my hand, and led me back into the den of lions.

He dragged me back to the bar. *Oh sweet, alcohol. I hear your siren song, and I am coming.* Before you start sending me pamphlets for The Betty Ford Center let me clear one thing up, I was not an alcoholic. I rarely drank. And I had a rule about drinking to excess. But rules were meant to be broken, especially on an occasion such as the Jefferson Ball. *C'est la vie.* Besides, I most definitely would not be one of the first to overindulge. Some of these people showed up plastered. After a trip to the bar, I ordered a double scotch rocks. No more girly drinks for me. Shooter led me into another room filled with cigar smoke. I guess the men in there didn't get the memo from the Surgeon General about smoking and its annoying tendency to kill you. We were certainly in the men's domain. Cigar and brandy anyone?

Shooter guided me to an empty leather club chair and plopped me down. We had rudely intruded on a conversation in progress.

"Last time I was in Africa, a ridiculous woman tried hunting an elephant, with a bow. Can you believe that? Her guide ended up having to shoot the poor animal after she just pissed the damn thing off." They didn't notice my intrusion until Admiral Nathan T. Beauregard had finished his statement. He wasn't a real admiral. He'd never even been in the Navy. He just owned a slew of yachts stationed around the globe so he insisted everyone call him Admiral. Every single eye in the group of well-bred gentleman rested on me.

"Well, Mrs. Katharine Boudreaux, who on Earth convinced you to grace us with your presence? Was it this young man here? Well, if it was, I must buy you a drink. What's your poison, Mr...."

"Shooter, and I'm good." Shooter shook the Admiral's extended hand.

"Did your mama give you a last name, Shooter?"

"Nope, just Shooter," he said with a cocky grin.

"Well, just Shooter, you may call me Admiral Beauregard, and whilst you are welcome amongst our small circle of compatriots, Mrs. Boudreaux would be more comfortable in a different room."

Aaannnd now we flash back to 1861. War has broken out and all the women folk need to be escorted to safety.

"Are we breaking some kind of rule?" Shooter asked.

"No, not a rule, more of a tradition. I can tell you're a Yankee. We like our traditions down here." The Admiral was direct, but his tone was charming. If he hadn't been quartered with the enemy, I just might have an affection for him.

"Explain this tradition, if you don't mind. As you say, I am a Northerner and this is my first trip to this part of the country." Shooter had an amazing ability to make people like him, or hate him.

The Admiral smiled. "Well, the tradition is that the ladies congregate in a more feminine atmosphere and the men gather in a...different environment. We don't want to offend the ladies' sensibilities. You understand."

I'm sure the Admiral thought the conversation was over but Shooter did not.

"I can assure you, Kat's sensibilities are not an issue. And I have been assigned to be her companion. So either she stays here, or I join all your lovely, lovely wives in a more feminine atmosphere." The threat wasn't spoken but every man in the circle suddenly felt uneasy with the thought of Shooter bringing their wives a drink.

The men looked at each other. The Admiral had a wry smile on his face. "Perhaps a challenge then. If Mrs. Boudreaux can answer a question and complete a physical test of strength, she will be welcomed into our circle. If not, she must go and you must stay, Shooter. Do we have an accord?"

I hated it when people talked about me as if I weren't in the room. Shooter gave the Admiral a nod. If Shooter kept that crap up, I'd be forced to field dress him before the end of the evening. Who was he to "enter into an accord" with someone on my behalf?

The Admiral straightened to his full height and approached me. "Mrs. Boudreaux, you heard me talking about my last hunting trip to Africa. What I would like to know is if you could buy only one hunting rifle, which rifle would that be?"

"Where and what will I be hunting?" I asked. I deliberately put a tone of unease in my voice.

The Admiral smiled and said, "Let's stick to large game of North America."

I looked at Shooter as if I needed his help in answering the Admiral's question. Then I turned to face my inquisitors. With all the Southern charm I do not posses, I said, "Well, Admiral, that would be a thirty-aught-six."

Somewhat shocked he asked, "And why?"

"Because with the right bullet and bullet placement, you can kill any large animal on the North American continent with a thirty-aught-six, including a Kodiak bear."

Shooter chuckled. The Admiral was taken aback by my answer. I didn't tell him that with a thirty-aught-six you can make a target's head explode at a hundred fifty yards. That wasn't part of his question.

"Very, very good, Ms. Boudreaux. Now for a feat of strength." The Admiral turned to Shooter. "As I chose the question, you have the honor of selecting this challenge."

Why am I even freaking doing this?

Shooter nodded. "I will need a volunteer. Admiral, you seem to be the mouthpiece of the group, why not you?"

The other men in the circle patted the Admiral on the back and encouraged his participation. He took his jacket off and put his drink and cigar down on a table.

"Wonderful. You're what, about six-feet-two, one hundred eighty pounds?"

The Admiral nodded.

"Here's the challenge. I want you, to pin Kat to the ground. If she pins you in under five seconds, she wins. If it takes longer than five seconds or you pin her, she loses. Agreed?"

The Admiral nodded with a smile on his face.

"No, no. Absolutely not. I will not participate!" I was done having these chauvinists question me and my right to a chair.

"What's the matter, Mrs. Boudreaux? Are you afraid you'll lose?" The Admiral had the nerve to question me and my abilities. How dare he!

"No." *I'm afraid the temptation to hold your still-beating heart in my hand will be too great to resist.* "You're half drunk. It's not a fair match."

"Darling, I believe you are a bit inebriated as well. It appears to me that we are evenly matched."

The Admiral had no idea how mismatched we truly were. Truth be told, I did hesitate. It hadn't been all that long since I'd been stabbed. I would have rathered not bust open my stitches and have my guts fall out on the Persian rug. I'd fought with much worse injuries, but that was to save my life. This was just to win a stupid seat. I had to decide if it was worse the risk of further injury.

"What's wrong, Mrs. Boudreaux? Afraid to have me on top of you?"

Oh, it was so on.

I kicked off my heels and the men surrounded me and the Admiral. "If I rip this dress, you have to deal with Edna." I pointed at Shooter.

"Right." Shooter winked at me. He held his watch between his thumb and forefinger. "When I say go, the timer starts. Ready, set, go!"

The Admiral made a stupid mistake and lunged for me. I grabbed both of his arms, spun him around, threw him down, and straddled his chest pinning his arms to the ground with my hands. "That would be two seconds flat. You lose, Admiral."

"Oh, I'd take this loss any day." He leered down my dress. I couldn't help myself it happened out of reaction. My fist slammed into his face. His nose erupted in a volcano of blood. I thought he'd be mad. I thought he'd demand security throw me out. But he just laughed.

"Well worth it, Mrs. Boudreaux. Well worth it."

I didn't see Shooter until the Admiral had been pulled by the back of the neck from underneath me. My Marine held the man in place and whispered something in his ear. Whatever he said worked because the Admiral's face paled and he nodded.

When Shooter released him, the Admiral said, "You are welcome to join us, Mrs. Boudreaux." He straightened his bow tie, and another man handed him a handkerchief to clean the blood off his face.

"That is awfully kind, gentlemen. But our presence is required elsewhere." There was no kindness in Shooter's voice. There was only the sound of a trained killer marking his prey.

He pulled me off the floor. I barely had the chance to grab my shoes before he dragged me out. He pulled me through the antique filled rooms and out a set of French doors. He hadn't even paused long enough to let me put my shoes back on. We walked down a set of steps and onto the expansive lawns. The sky had gone dark, studded with twinkling diamonds.

"What did you say to the Admiral?" I asked, breathless.

"What?" He only slightly slowed his retreat.

"What did you say to the Admiral?"

"I explained in great detail how I would torture him to within an inch of his life if he ever looked at you like that again." He stopped dragging me across the yard and pushed me up against a magnolia tree. His face changed in an instant from hard and determined to soft and wanting. We just stared at each other for what seemed like an eternity.

"Why are we fighting this?" he whispered.

"I don't know."

He cupped my cheeks in his palms and angled my face. He let out a sigh, like he wanted to give up. I nearly screamed. I thought he would pull away. His lips lowered and placed a soft, gentle kiss on mine. It had been so long since I had been so close to a man. Once upon a time, not long ago, I thought I'd never have the chance to experience that feeling again. I reached behind him and pulled the leather thong from his hair and threaded my fingers through his long waves. Shooter lifted me up against the tree so my feet dangled a foot above the ground. Our lips, now on the same level, molded and shaped against each other. He pressed his rock-hard body against mine. He licked my lips and I opened for him. His tongue was so different than the rest of him. It was soft, supple. Not hard and unyielding. It dawned on me that I had fantasized about his kiss since almost the moment I saw him, and for some reason I thought his tongue would feel like he could do push-ups with it. It was so nice to be wrong.

I wonder how fast I could get myself out of my dress and Shooter out of his pants. Just a minute, Kat, you are not Louise LaLourie. Sometimes I really wished I could be. If I had courage like hers, I'd wrap my legs around Shooter's waist and.... A hand dropped from my face and feathered down the side of my ribs. A hiss escaped my throat. He trailed his tongue and lips down my neck, nibbling and biting across my collarbone. I wanted the man. I wanted him so bad that if I didn't have him soon it might actually kill me. Could someone die from sexual frustration?

Shooter made his way back to my mouth, kissing me desperately. It was my turn to drive. I pulled his lower lip between my teeth and nibbled up his jaw. I sucked his earlobe, flicking it back and forth with my tongue. He moaned. God, there was nothing better than making a man like Shooter moan. The heat he ignited in and around me, and through me, could have melted titanium. I didn't want it to stop, never wanted to release him. We stayed out there against that tree making out like horny teenagers for five minutes or five hours. I desperately wanted to get home to see what other rules Shooter would be willing to break.

We got to a point where we either had to stop or get naked, so Shooter, with all his damn willpower, stopped. We panted, trying to catch our breath.

"We better go back inside."

I had completely forgotten that we were only yards from the Magnolia Mansion and a hundred and fifty flashing paparazzi cameras. I guess it's a good thing I hadn't acted on my impulse to strip him naked and roll around on the grass.

I nodded and straightened my dress. He picked leaves and bark out of my hair, and I put my shoes back on.

Shooter turned a dial and pushed a button on his watch. "One hour ten minutes."

I gave him a questioning look.

"Until we can leave and get home." The tone in his voice made my heart do a flip flop. If I could manage not to screw it up, Shooter would break all his rules by the end of the night.

It's amazing how a romp in the woods can improve a girl's mood. I smiled, shook hands, told everyone I was fantastic, and didn't draw one more drop of blood. I couldn't say the same for Shooter. While he didn't draw blood, he most definitely was not congenial. When a spoiled socialite made the comment that she never thought Stephan would find contentment with a woman of my background, Shooter told her that he wouldn't think a girl like her would be out in public after infecting half the Quarter with Chlamydia, loud enough for everyone in three parishes to hear. It was my turn to pull him away. Shooter checked his watch every two minutes and with each glance, the spring in the pit of my stomach coiled tighter.

Each time I would smile and ask, "How much longer?" And

whenever an opportunity presented itself, he'd grab me and we'd slip into empty rooms, hallways, and closets to let off a little steam.

I was in the middle of explaining the traditions of the Founder's Day Celebration to a Hamptonite when Shooter's watch alarm went off. He grabbed me by the elbow mid-sentence and pulled me out of the house. He didn't even wait for a parking attendant to summon Gregory. We trotted right over to the mass of parked cars and climbed into the Bentley, startling Gregory from a nap.

"Home," Shooter ordered.

Gregory didn't ask any questions, he just put the car in drive. I tried really hard to conceal my grin. I failed miserably. Shooter looked over at me, and I could tell he was keeping himself in check in front of Gregory.

"How long?"

I liked to be precise. "Sixty-seven minutes."

He set the timer on his watch again. I cocked an eyebrow as if questioning his intentions. But he wasn't stupid. He knew I wanted the same thing he did. I tried desperately to send Gregory a telepathic message to drive faster, but he didn't get it. He followed all the speed limits and traffic laws. There were times when I really wished Bo Duke was my driver.

Chapter Thirteen

When we finally pulled in front of the house, Gregory let us out at the front door. I didn't want to be waylaid by staff or nosy Marines so I dragged Shooter to the back of the house. We clambered through the kitchen door. My head swam with hormones, lust, and fear. I'm not going to lie. It'd been a while since I'd done anything sexual. It had been three years, six months and seventeen days to be exact. But who was counting?

My body screamed for him just to touch me. I'd needed a man to wrap myself around for a long time. But I didn't think there was a man alive who could handle me. Over the years I'd managed to smother that banshee with target practice and beating the shit out of a bag every day. Lately though, the bitch just wouldn't shut up. Her cries made my ears bleed. I was more than happy to give her what she wanted. Shooter was the perfect bedmate. Strong, silent, committed to his work. His body could satisfy my needs then I'd kick him out of my bed and onto the floor. He really was the best kind of man: disposable.

Three flights of stairs—three freaking flights of stairs—later and we fell through my bedroom door in a tangle of arms, legs, and designer evening wear. For a split second I feared Tyler or Edna would be hiding in the shadows ready to catch us. But that was just leftover anxiety from a misspent youth.

We stopped next to my bed. Shooter took a step back. Oh hell no! He would not stop now! He would finish what he'd started in the yard of the Magnolia Mansion even if I had to lash him to my bed for a few days. He was going to break his stupid set of rules. He was going to get naked soon or I would have to break a few federal laws. He asked permission with a look, and I gave it. I wanted him more than you could possibly know. He unzipped the side zipper on my dress and let the gown fall to the ground. And just like that, all my courage and determination flew right out the window.

I knew what he saw. He saw my scarred body. The look of disgust was coming and he'd run for the door. A dragon I'd kept tethered for the past two years suddenly roared to life. I shook uncontrollably. I trembled, and he had to know it wasn't because of anything he was doing.

He wrapped his warm, protective arms around me. "You're okay, Kat. You're safe."

"No, I'm not." Where the hell had that come from? I shoved Shooter away, ran, right for the bathroom, and locked myself in. *Oh yeah, that was sexy.* Why didn't men beat down my bedroom door? I remember now, because I had a chastity belt made from emotional baggage wrapped around my lady parts. What was I supposed to do? Other than be a complete and total idiot, that is.

I sat on that stupid chair that had taken up space in my bathroom since the Civil War waiting to hear my bedroom door open and close. It wasn't the fact that he'd seen my scars that freaked me out. He'd seen them before. He'd touched them. It was that what we were going to do came way too close to how I'd obtained them. I didn't want to be that girl. I didn't want to be the girl who brought trauma to every romantic encounter. I wanted to be the girl who could rock a man's world, not complicate it. A feeling I had never come to terms with flooded every inch of me. Fear.

I wasn't afraid Shooter would post pictures of my

humiliation on Facebook. I feared he would pity me. That every morning for the rest of the summer he'd sit across from me at the breakfast table with that look of syrupy sympathy. I didn't need sympathy, didn't want it. The pain had been dealt with years ago. It had been blown to hell, and that's all there was to it. I had nothing more to work through. Then why was I sitting in the bathroom instead of getting rumpled with the Adonis I'd just abandoned? I hated it when rational thought broke in on my emotional outbursts.

After several long seconds without the sound of oak hitting oak, I started to wonder. *Just what is Shooter doing out there?* Did I really want to know? Oh shit, if he was out there trying on my underwear and heels, he would see a whole new level of pissed. Thinking of him prancing around in my Vicky's Secret and Louboutin's made me smile, a little.

When I heard the soft rap on the bathroom door, I switched from amused to velociraptor. If anything came through that door, I'd shred it to ribbons. Then eat it.

"Kat, I'm not going to ask if you're okay because I know you'll just lie. Here's the deal, I'm not going anywhere. All of this can stop right now. Right now, I'm here as your friend. Tell me what's wrong. You can trust me."

The hell I can. I can't trust anyone with this. Not this. It's humiliating. It shouldn't have happened, not to me. I didn't mean that the same way people say I shouldn't have been audited by the IRS. I meant it in the most literal sense. I'd been trained, I had the skill to defend myself, and I didn't. My will to live had failed me. They hurt me, viciously. I should have done something—anything—to stop them. People like me shouldn't just lie there and take it. *I am strong. I am fierce. I am mean.* Why had I not done anything in the middle of it? Why had I waited? By doing nothing, I had failed my grandfather and every other trainer I'd ever had. That should never have happened. *Not to me.*

"Kat, I'm just going to sit here and wait." It wasn't what he'd said; it was how he'd said it. He was serious. He wouldn't leave until I told him why I'd left him in the middle of my bedroom all hot, bothered, and asking what the hell?

I'm not telling him shit! He has not earned that right. My secret is mine and mine alone. I'm not on some stupid talk show. Barbara Walters couldn't make me tell that story. But the person waiting in my bedroom wasn't Barbara Walters. It was Shooter. He had a way of getting me to admit to things that I normally kept locked up tight. I'd been tortured and interrogated by the best the world had to offer and managed to keep my mouth shut. All Shooter had to do was ask, and I'd tell him anything.

Not this time. I wouldn't share this. I couldn't lay myself bare like that. I refused to give another human being the weapon with which to kill me and paint a target on my chest. No self-respecting person would do that. If I had one thing left, it was my self-respect; I was not letting him have it.

Shooter didn't say anything for a while, but I knew he hadn't left. I could sense him on the other side of the door. He'd meant what he'd said. He wouldn't leave. Well, Edna would have to start serving dinner in the bathroom because as long as he was out there, I wasn't. Then he started to speak.

"When I was twelve, I had this neighbor, Kristy. She was in her thirties, single, pretty as hell. She'd locked herself in her house for about five years. No one really knew why. She worked from home so she didn't really need to leave the house. My mother even used to go to the grocery store for her once a week. On the last day of school my friends and I decided to express our adolescent stupidity and play ball in the street. Part of the end of year euphoria that makes you feel like you're tougher than a speeding pickup truck convinced us that this was a good idea. I whacked a baseball right through her living room window. I'd grown up thinking this lady was a witch, and even though I had passed the age of believing in witches, she still scared me shitless. But I knew what had to be done. I nutted up and knocked on her door. My friends were impressed. Whether they thought I was brave or stupid, I never found out. She opened the front door just enough to see me. I told her it was my ball that had broken her window. She kept telling me she'd take care of it, but I couldn't let her front the cost.

"When the crew showed up to replace her window, they had to get inside to finish the job. I was playing out in the street again. Apparently, I never listened to my mom. I could see her through the window and could tell she was terrified. I ran over to her house and convinced the glass guys to let me try to talk to her so they could get the job done. I did not intend to force my way into Kristy's home. I planned on just talking to her through the door to try to make things a little easier on everybody. I turned to knock, but she'd already opened it. I stepped inside and sat on her sofa until the workmen were done. She'd hidden somewhere in her house while I was there. After that she'd leave cookies and stuff outside on her porch for me and my friends. We never saw her put them out. They'd just kind of appear."

Was he comparing me to a recluse? He better get to the point of his story pretty damn quick.

"Well, one day I was being stupid. I was a twelve-year-old boy and being stupid was part of the job description. My friends and I had been playing Frisbee in my front yard. One of us had thrown the Frisbee, and it had gotten stuck on the roof. Since it was my place, it fell to me to climb up and get it back. The two story house had a really steep pitch. I really should have known better. I climbed up okay and had actually reached the Frisbee before I slipped. I slid down the roof and off the house.

"If the rain gutter hadn't been repaired a couple weeks earlier, I would have made a bloody mess on my dad's front lawn. That tube of metal meant life and I refused to let go for anything. It started to cut into my hand, and I thought I'd fall to my death. Then I heard her. Kristy had been watching us and had run out of her house when she saw me fall. She told me to let go. She said she'd catch me. I tried to see her but she was in an odd place, and I didn't exactly have full range of motion at the time. It came down to trust. Would she catch me? There really was no other choice. So, I let go. And she caught me. She brushed me off, handed me the Frisbee, and returned to her house.

"Kristy and I became friends after that. She let me into her house, and we'd have long talks. Turns out she used to be in the military. Something she'd witnessed had forced her into seclusion. She never told me what actually happened. She didn't need to. It didn't matter. We were friends." He paused. "Let me be your Kristy, Kat. I'll catch you."

I felt the bathroom door under my cheek. At some point in the story I'd wanted to be as close to him as possible without actually leaving my sanctuary. I thought he'd go for the obvious and tell me he'd helped some crazy shut-in, he can help me. But he hadn't. He'd given all the glory to Kristy. He probably didn't even recognize his role in the story. There was one thing you could count on with Shooter: never expect the expected. I'd never told anyone what had happened to me that night. Not the entire story. Tyler and Dr. Wells knew the TV version, but no one knew the whole hairy truth.

"Trust me, Kat. Please come out and tell me," Shooter begged.

"I can't." It came out in a whisper. I don't know if he heard me.

"Please, trust me."

He had no way of knowing how difficult that would be for me. I didn't trust easily, and I'd never trusted someone with all of me.

"Kat, I know this isn't easy for you. It goes against every defense mechanism you have. I know you've never told anyone, but you can tell me. Let me help you carry your burden. I won't say anything. I'll just listen."

Just listen? He'd just listen and not make a comment? Once he heard what had happened, oh he'd comment. He'd do that stupid man thing where they get up and start yelling about a situation that happened years ago and couldn't be changed in any way. That debilitating impotence that made them want to hit walls. No thanks, I couldn't do that to him. Shooter was the most honorable man ever created. I wouldn't torture him with my problems. Of course, if I were to tell someone it would be him. But I wasn't telling anyone so it didn't really matter. He'd be a good person to tell. Did I really want to carry the trauma around all on my own for the rest of my life? I'd done fine with it so far. Okay, that was a lie. I'd let that one thing, that one experience, determine every single action and decision in my life for two years. It would be nice to tell someone. That would require I actually say all that crap out loud. Actually form the words and sentences. I'd have to hear everything that happened to me. Could I do that? I didn't think I could.

All right, what were the pros of telling Shooter? *What? You know I like lists!*

Pros. One, it would probably get rid of the permanent knot in my chest. Two, it would be nice to have one person who understood when I tried to choke a guy out because I didn't hear him sneak up behind me. Three, Shooter would never tell anyone. My secret would be safe with him. Four, he probably wouldn't judge me and tell me how stupid I was. Five, I most definitely wouldn't get laid until I told someone. No one could get close enough to touch me until I told my story.

What were the cons of telling Shooter?

One, he'd know. He'd know that when it really mattered, I'd failed. Two.... *Dammit!*

The pros win. Oh God, was I really going to do it? I couldn't believe I was.

"I...I can't tell you face to face." A bowling ball had lodged in my throat. "I have to stay in here, and you have to stay out there."

"You've got a deal."

I placed my hands on the door and took a deep breath. *What the hell?* "The year after Stephan died I tried to go about life like normal," I said through the door. "I attended all my meetings, all the normal functions. I did what was expected of me. Until February fifth, two years ago. It was Fat Tuesday, and

I had been invited to the single most exclusive Mardi Gras ball in New Orleans. I had just popped in, and my plan had been to get the hell out of there as soon as socially acceptable. That didn't go over well with all in attendance. The vipers pulled me into one group conversation after another. You know how people in the South are. They want you to know they know all your business. My husband, a flesh and blood Boudreaux, had died just over a year prior so they all had hugs, condolences, and cards to drug and alcohol rehabs for me. They were all sure I'd been drinking myself to sleep every night. And to help me with the assumed addiction, they insisted I throw back drink after drink after drink. Before long I could barely stand.

"Gregory had wanted to drive me that night, but I didn't want to have to go through the formality of having a chauffeur. It would have been very stupid to attempt to drive myself home, pickled as I was. I stepped outside to get some fresh air and to call Gregory. Just as I pulled my phone from my purse, someone came up behind me and stabbed a needle into my neck. I woke up in a deserted, destroyed house. My Mardi Gras gown had been stripped off, and I could smell copper in the air. It was the smell of my own blood." My voice shook. I couldn't control it. The emotions of that night stormed me. I was there in that dirty room all over again. It was as real to me as if it was happening all over again.

"I tried to look around, but my head had been tied down to a board. The drug they'd given me had made me very groggy but that didn't stop me from fighting against my binding." I took another deep breath. "I was scared, Shooter. I'd never been afraid for my life. Not once in my years with GSA had I ever been scared. In that moment I was terrified." No one had ever heard me say those words. The force of that sentence nearly knocked me to my knees.

I hung on to the door frame and continued, "My entire body hurt. It was as if I'd had a pelvic exam with a Louisville Slugger. Dammit! I shouldn't have said that. I'm sorry if that was too graphic. I tried to clear my head. That was a stupid move. The more my head cleared the more pain I experienced. Just when I thought I had been abandoned to die, the door creaked open and three men walk into the room.

"I should have fought. I should have tried to get free. But I didn't. I just lay there. I let them hurt me. I let them violate and abuse me. I didn't do anything to stop it. I should have done something, anything. I didn't even flinch. Not an inch. I could have been a corpse for all the struggle I gave them. It would have been better if I'd been a corpse."

I took a moment to steady myself. Was I really going to tell him everything? *Yes.* I could trust him. Above everything else, I knew that for sure. I opened myself up to Shooter. I gave him the very sword with which to slay me.

"They knelt down at my head and said terrible things to me. They made accusations and said I deserved everything they were going to do to me. They said I was responsible for something. I can't really remember what they'd accused me of. I don't think that really mattered at the time.

"The guy in charge had this ratty brown goatee with food stuck in it and dead grey eyes. He pulled out a hunting knife. You know the kind that everybody bought after Crocodile Dundee came out. Apparently they all shopped at the same store because they had matching knives. They cut me. Over and over they cut me. The cold steel slid through my skin, but I didn't feel the pain. I had gone beyond pain. I didn't move. I didn't scream. That just pissed them off. The guy with the goatee told them to stop because he didn't want a piece of dead meat." I cleared my throat. "They took turns, each having a go. They cheered each other on like they were playing for the World Cup.

"I tried to go to a different place. I tried to think of anything that might take me away from that room. It didn't matter where I went, I wound up in the same place. I tried to think of my grandfather. Then I'd think about him training me and how I'd failed him by being captured. I tried to think of my parents but that just made me think of their deaths. I tried to think of my wedding day. Somehow it just seemed wrong to think of that day at that moment. I tried to think of the first time I'd knocked Stephan out. Then I'd think of why we fought the night he'd died. How it had been my fault that he'd gotten in that car. All my happy places had been infested with termites. So, I went blank. I climbed inside a box and huddled in the corner until they were done. Like a child. Like a scared little girl. I wish I could say I waited for the right moment to strike, but I didn't. I waited to die.

"I could smell them. I can still smell them. Sweat, blood, and crank. It permeated the air. I wanted to vomit. I didn't. That would be too human. I was not human then. I probably haven't been human since then. Eventually they got tired or bored or maybe they had run out of meth and needed to make a drug run. They left. I heard them leave the house, get into a car and drive away." I swallowed. This was the part where Shooter would run.

"One stayed behind. He took advantage of the fact that he had no audience. After he raped me over and over, he wanted to humiliate me. He shoved himself into my mouth. Something inside me snapped. It was like I'd been jump started by a bolt of lightning. The thought of him in my mouth forced me to act. I bit down with as much force as I could manage and bit a piece of him off. He screamed, hit me across the face, and passed out on top of me. He had his knife in his hand. With him on top of me I was able to reach it and cut myself free of my bindings. Then I set to work on the bastard left behind. I carved him up like a Christmas turkey. He screamed, a lot, and every single one of his cries was a healing balm on my soul. I bathed in his agony.

"A car pulled up to the house, and I hid in the bathroom. When one went into the kitchen, I followed and bashed his skull in with the lid to the toilet tank. The other one came in to see what had caused the sound of porcelain breaking skull, and I did the same thing to him."

"They deserved it, they deserved every single thing they

got," I heard Shooter say through the door his voice coated with anger.

"I didn't go to the police, and I didn't go to the hospital. I had Dr. Wells stitch me up and I called the chief in Bayou Boudreaux. I gave them enough information to file a report, too little to take any action. It was humiliating, Shooter. That someone could sneak up behind me, drug me, and treat me that way. It's humiliating. I talk a big game, but in the end, I failed. I failed myself. That's worse than failing my boss or my grandfather. You can make good when you fail someone else. When you fail yourself, there's no coming back from that. For the rest of my life I'll doubt my abilities. Every time I move to throw a punch or kick someone in the balls, I hesitate. Self-doubt makes me pause. Hesitation kills. You know that. I might as well walk into the next 'Family Members of the Victims of Kat Boudreaux' meeting and hand them the nails to crucify me. I'm not a fighter anymore."

I waited for Shooter to tell me that shit had just gotten too heavy and run to the safety and comfort of an Iraqi battlefield.

"You are so full of shit!" He actually sounded angry. "A coward did not save my life on the docks a week ago. A coward did not welcome five unknown men into her house. A coward did not make me want to piss my pants when I hit your brother and you threatened to kill me. You are a fighter, Hell Kat. You'll always be a fighter."

No one had ever given me a greater compliment. No one.

"So, are you going to come out of there?"

My body slumped against the door. I couldn't say no. That would make me a petulant child. Shooter hadn't run for cover. He'd listened to the worst of me and stayed. He could handle me. All of me. I straightened my shoulders and gripped the door. I summoned every ounce of courage I had and twisted the knob. It was only after opening the door that I remembered I had next to nothing on. Damn! I'd left my robe in my closet. Shit! I saw Shooter sitting on a chair he'd placed in front of the bathroom door. He looked amazing, naturally. I, on the other hand, was a half-naked, scared, little bird. Not exactly how I'd pictured the evening.

We just stared at each other for the longest time. What is the appropriate social protocol one follows after revealing to a man you'd really like to ride rodeo-style that you're an emotional trash dump? Shooter opened his arms wide, and I jumped. I felt like one of those dirty street urchins you see in Victorian Era movies as he held me against his chest.

The oddest sensation filled my body. It wasn't emotion. I wasn't that lame. There was a strange pricking right behind my eyes. As if out of reflex, my eyes started blinking. My nose stuffed up and my stomach dropped out of my body. Warm moisture seeped from Shooter's shirt. Was he bleeding? How the hell was he bleeding? I hadn't stabbed him with anything. I pulled my head back to inspect his shirt. No blood, just water. What the hell? Shooter gripped my chin between his thumb and forefinger and tilted my face to look up at him. He kissed my cheeks. A sob caught in my throat. I was crying. I was actually crying. What had he done to me?

My body became rigid and went into flight mode. He held me firm. I'd never been so scared in my entire life. Not even in that room two years ago. The only thing I knew how to do was fight, but all the fight had drained out of me. Not in the same way the rapists had drained me. I couldn't fight because I didn't want to. For once in my life I wanted someone else to fight for me.

"It's okay," he said. "I don't mind." He kissed my forehead. That simple gesture took all the prickly bitch out of me.

I didn't relax so much as crumble into a heap of snotty, bawling baby. Shooter gathered me closer and just let me cry. I'd turned into one of those women. You know the ones that ruin every good love scene in every sappy romance novel by turning sex into an emotional act. *Dammit!* I was not one of those women! But I was. I have no idea how long I sat there dehydrating, but it was a long effing time. Shooter would never see me as a sexual being again. *Ever.*

Shit!

Did you know that when you don't cry for more than ten years you build up a tear debt? It's true. I cried four gallons of tears that night. Hard to do when you consider the body only holds one and one quarter gallons of blood. Still, it was at least four gallons of tears. I ruined Shooter's shirt and made a mental note to get him a new one. After I'd stopped the human sprinkler routine and pulled myself together enough not to do that thing you do when you've cried a lot. You know when you breathe and it sounds like your lungs are in a constant state of spasm and you sound like you should be on a ventilator. When I'd stopped all of that, Shooter stood up and placed me on the chair. He wrapped a red fleece blanket around me then just looked at me with his hands on his hips.

What was he doing? Was he deciding just how he could bail without fulfilling the promise he'd made back at the Magnolia Mansion? That had to be it. I had officially made myself untouchable. I should have lied. I should have told him I had a bad case of diarrhea or something. That would have been better than the truth. Why had I said all that crap? Shooter would never look at me the same again. He saw me as weak. I knew he said he didn't but that had to be a lie. Even though I didn't think Shooter had the ability to lie. He still lied.

Just when I thought he'd bolt, he started to unbutton his shirt. One by one he pulled the studs through their holes. What the hell was going on? I had gotten used to the fact that Shooter didn't want me. A trickle of fear and desire started to drip into my stomach. *He's not really going to do this, is he?*

He stripped his shirt from his body. Oh Mary, mother of God. You could sail a ship across that man's chest. He threw the shirt onto the ground. His body could have been carved by Michelangelo. Shooter pointed to a puckered line that ran around his ribcage from the right of his sternum ending two inches from his spine. "I got this one when I wasn't fast enough in Fallujah. The guy had a knife with a curved blade."

"What did you do?"

He didn't answer. He pointed to anther scar across his left, upper bicep. "Grazed by a bullet in Baghdad." Shooter turned around. As he pulled the waistband of his pants down, I saw a huge scar. It was about four inches wide and I had no idea how long it was. "I got this one when an IED went off next to the Hummer I was in." He turned back to face me and pointed to a thin scar on his forehead. "This one is from when I got drunk in Germany and took a header off a park bench."

And just like that I was completely comfortable again.

"We all have battle wounds. Some outside, some in. And who we choose to share them with is our business. Everyone else can go to hell."

I recognized the trust Shooter placed in my hands when he revealed his scars. Force Recon Marines didn't publicize their identifying marks. It's a stupid tactical move. You might as well shave *I am a Force Recon Marine and I've probably killed someone in your family* into the back of your head. Rat Bastards didn't even have tattoos. They stay away from anything that might make them stand out in a crowd.

I stood up from the chair and let the blanket fall to the floor. Lightning flashed in his eyes. He still wanted me. How he could still want all of me was something I couldn't fathom. But he did. I took a step forward so my breasts barely grazed his naked chest. He sucked in and held his breath at our contact.

"I want you," I whispered. That was all it took.

Shooter pressed his lips to mine. The taste of him ignited a fire inside me I'd never known. His tongue, hot and penetrating, was better than silk sheets against a naked body. His hands trailed down my body stopping at my waist.

"You are so beautiful." He sounded out of breath, barely in control.

He tenderly skimmed each and every scar on my breasts with his lips. He kissed his way down my stomach and paused at my scarred abdomen.

Oh, please don't get queasy now.

Shooter traced each scar with his tongue. Moisture and heat

pooled between my legs. If there's a God in heaven at all, Shooter would not stop licking me.

He stood up, lightly brushing his fingertips up my legs, hips, my waist. I expected him to go for the obvious until he stopped just below my bra, wrapping his long tapered fingers around my ribcage. We just looked at each other, locked in a moment. If we crossed the line, there would be no going back.

He brushed my cheek with the back of his hand, leaving a brand down the side of my face. "I love the way you feel. Soft, smooth, but I know a tiger lives inside." He placed both hands on the sides of my neck. "I love the curve of your neck." He smoothed them down to my shoulders. "I love the strength in your shoulders." He moved them back up to my face. "I love the vibrancy in your eyes." He gently kissed each of my eyelids. "I love how your nose turns up just a bit at the end." He brushed his lips over the tip of my nose and across my cheek. "I love the shape of your ear." He sucked my earlobe into his mouth and flicked it with his tongue.

If he wanted to do that a bit more, a bit lower, I wouldn't object.

He released my lobe and trailed light kisses along my jaw. "And I love the taste of your mouth." He claimed my mouth with a passion my pathetic little world had never known. He prodded and probed, and I let him plunder every corner of me.

Then he let go, and pulled back. *What the hell? This had better not be goodnight. This had better not end here.* My body hummed like a piano string about to break, and I was not above hitting him over the head and taking full advantage of his unconscious body. I tried to pull him back to the task at hand but he resisted. Rejection, hurt, misunderstanding must have flashed across my face.

He brushed a thumb across my cheekbone. "If you aren't ready for this, we don't have to," he whispered.

I was a generally selfish person and I always got what I wanted, and in that moment I wanted Shooter. I rose to the tips of my toes and kissed him blind. It had been a long time since I had been the aggressor. I was more than a little bit scared and no, I didn't feel bad admitting that. I'd once been really good at this, but somehow sex was not anything like riding a bike.

A growl that started deep in his chest vibrated through my entire body. Shooter naked was something no woman could ever get used to. He was magnificent but not in a gym rat kind of way. His body had been honed for one purpose—to fight— and that was sexy as hell. The scars on his form only added to the animalistic sexuality he exuded. His stomach looked like a pan of fresh baked biscuits lined up in neat rows. The only hair on his body was a happy little strip that disappeared in the waistband of his pants. I couldn't help myself, a work of art like Shooter deserved to be worshipped. I splayed my hands over his broad chest then trailed them down his sides. He hissed as my fingers crept inside the waistband of his pants. I stopped with my thumbs hooked on the outside. I looked him in the eye and whispered, "I'm ready. I need you. Now."

He bent but before he could claim me, I slid my hands to the front of his pants. He froze. "Slow down there cowgirl or you'll be in for an eight second ride."

I gave him a wicked look then unbuttoned his pants and shucked them to the floor. *Holy shit, not expecting that.* Oh, wait, I meant that in a good way. He'd gone commando, and I'd never been more happy to be disobeyed in my life. He grabbed my waist and spun me around so he ended up sitting on the edge of the bed with me standing between his legs. He reached up to unhook my bra. I inhaled and felt all confidence leave me. I really didn't want him to see the extent of my damage. It wasn't pretty.

He paused just as he gripped the front closure of my bra. "You are beautiful, Kat. Every single inch of you is beautiful."

Yeah, he wouldn't be saying that in about two seconds. He unhooked my bra, and there I was on display for him to see. I could tell he hadn't expected the damage to be as bad as it was. Fire flared behind his eyes and for a brief moment I saw the soldier in him come to life. I didn't want the soldier, I wanted the sex god I knew he must be. In an instant his anger ebbed. He showed me just how beautiful he thought I was as he licked and tortured his way across my marred breasts.

I still wore my pretty girl panties and made the executive decision I had entirely too many clothes on. I pulled away and shimmed out of the black satin and lace. Shooter gripped my hips and threw me onto my back on the bed. Excitement shot straight to my belly, and pulsed there like a second agitated heart. He took his time, stirring and seducing, kindling little fires under my skin, exploiting odd and wondrous points of pleasure. A touch, a taste, a bare whisper of torturous contact pulled sensations from my depths I didn't know I had the capability of creating. I pressed my needy body to his and still he denied me what I knew we both wanted more than air.

Finally, after what seemed like an eternity, he gripped my hips and lifted me to him. I gasped as we connected. I'd never been into foreplay. I'd never understood its purpose. With him, I got it. I saw stars. I actually saw stars dance in front of my eyes. I felt myself starting to reach that ultimate peak. Shooter seemed to know exactly where I was and kept pace with me. And then the world around us shattered into a million little fragments of glass.

He fell on top of me, huffing and puffing. "That was...that was just...."

"Yeah, I know. Wow." I couldn't say anything else. I had to catch my breath. I couldn't think. I could only feel, and what I felt was more exhilarating than a ride in a fighter jet. He moved to roll off of me. I grabbed his shoulders. "No, don't." I liked the weight of him pressing me into the mattress. For the first time in a long, long time, I felt protected.

Sometime later, I lay with my head on Shooter's chest wrapped in his arms. He kissed the top of my head and whispered, "You make me sleep, too."

Somewhere I knew that statement held significance. But he was wrong. He's the one who made me sleep. Slowly the memory of his nightmare came to me.

I propped myself up on my elbows and said, ever so eloquently, "What? How? Why? Huh?"

He kissed the tip of my nose. "You make my nightmares go away, too."

All that time I thought I had been selfishly hoarding all of Shooter's comfort. It felt good to know I did the same thing for him. I smiled and kissed him desperately. I felt a bout of hiccups coming on. Everything had been so perfect, and I refused to start spasming in a completely unsexy way, and ruin the moment. I suppressed the hitches until I knew there was no way in hell I was going to turn into a fish left out of water.

I had lain in his arms for a while when something that had been bugging me all night sprang into my head. The annoyance grew louder and louder until it could not be ignored. I nuzzled his chest and with all my might tried not to sound like a slut. "Shooter, I never thought I would ever be in bed with a man and ask this question, but it's one I need to ask and I need an answer." I could feel his pecs tighten under my head. "Um, what is your name?"

He roared with laughter. I'm glad he found that so funny, but I really did need an answer. I propped myself up and just as I was about to let him have it, he rolled me onto my back and pinned me to the mattress by my arms. I tried to scowl at him but the absurdity that I'd found myself in couldn't be denied. It was funny. Funny in an I-got-drunk-at-Mardi-Gras-and-woke-up-in-a-bed-with-a-hooker-two-frat-boys-and-a-goat kind of way.

"Are you going to tell me?"

He shook his head.

"Shooter, come on. Tell me your name."

He bent down to kiss me and I bit his lip. He would tell me or I would pull it out of him one bloody drop at a time.

"Do you often sleep with men you don't know, Hell Kat?"

I liked the way my Rat Bastard name sounded coming from him. He made it sound like I was a sleek Egyptian cat with the ability to hurt, maim, and kill. Not like a fat tabby whose greatest accomplishment was waddling over to the litter box three times a day. But that would not distract me from my current goal. "No, I don't sleep with men I don't know. I know you. I just don't know your name."

"I'll tell you my name but it's going to cost you."

Oh great, a bargain.

"What do you want?" I hoped his answer would be something I was willing to give.

"Just you." He slid into me and we moved like water, constantly adapting. And when we broke, we did so as one. I'd never felt so connected to another human being in my life. Shooter and I had a bond that seemed stronger than the oath of a soldier or the vow of a marriage. It felt as if we had been meant for each other since the beginning of time and had just been reunited after years apart. Out of breath and spent, I lay next to him. It took me a few minutes to realize he hadn't actually told me his name.

"Aren't you going to tell me?" I asked.

"Tell you what, princess?" He knew exactly what I was talking about. He just wanted to make me suffer. That's fine, two could play that game.

"Fine, I'll go ask Tyler." I pulled away from him and started dragging myself out of bed. He grabbed me around the waist and pulled me back.

"Let's not. I prefer my nuts remain un-cracked."

"Then tell me your name."

And just like that he gave up. "It's Archer. Alexander Archer. I'm named after my great grandpa."

"Alexander Archer. I like it. It suits you."

"You know, I think you're the first person to say my real name in years. Hearing you say it is," he paused, "incredible. But private. I only want to hear you say it when we're alone."

Oh, oh, oh. I had a new weapon and I planned on using it.

I yawned and my eyes drooped. I was exhausted. I hadn't had so much sport in a really long time. Shooter tucked me under his arm against his chest. I think I lasted all of fifteen seconds. Just as I drifted off into nothingness I heard something. I was so close to deep sleep I couldn't tell if it had been real or a dream.

"I love you."

Just three words. Three words that could either raise up or destroy. Those words scared me, and I hoped to hell that I'd imagined them. *Please, please let me have dreamed them.*

Chapter Fourteen

I woke up to Edna pulling the drapes back across my window.

"Now, I've kept the vultures at bay and by vultures I mean the staff, your Marines, your daughter, and your brother. No one has caught you *enflagrante delecto,* and that's all because of me. Shooter is in the shower so you have time to dish. Spill it."

"There's nothing to spill," I lied.

"Oh, okay. I guess it's completely normal to find two *friends* buck naked in a bed. Please, child, this has been building like a tropical storm into a hurricane. And I'm guessing from the scattered clothes, ripped panties, and other discarded items, it made landfall last night. And about damn time. I want to know everything. Was it good or was it gooooood?"

For an octogenarian she could be a little dirty. If I wanted to be honest with myself, there was something I wanted to talk to Edna about. But I seriously didn't think it was the kind of dish she wanted. "Last night."

"Mmm, I like where this is going already."

"No, Edna, be serious. Last night, after the hurricane made landfall, I can't be positive because I was falling asleep, but I think he told me he loved me."

"Oh, please, child. That is old news. I want something new. Something juicy. Something naked."

"What do you mean old news?"

"Oh come now, you had to have seen it for yourself. That man loved you from the first day he walked into this house. Get to the good stuff."

"How could you possibly know he loves me?" The whole idea sounded extremely ridiculous.

She stroked my cheek. "*Cher*, when you've been around as long as I have and you've seen enough people fall in love and screw it up you can see love coming from a mile away. I'm just so happy you've found it again." She stood up from my bed. "Just don't fuck it up." She turned to leave. "I sealed the Club last night. Told your Marines that I'd just waxed the floor and it needed to dry."

Bless that woman. She left the room, and I heard her yell at someone.

"Leave the child alone. You sent her to that party. Are you even a little bit surprised she's nursing a hangover? Don't make me use my voo-doo on you. Get on, get! She'll talk to ya when she's good and ready."

Shooter couldn't love me. We'd only known each other for like a week. And the majority of that time I'd been a bitchy, complaining nag hag. But the more I thought about it, the more I wanted him to love me. It was kind of selfish that I wanted it from him but couldn't return the feeling. I just think that part of my body was ruined. I had loved once. I loved with all my heart, mind, body, and soul. And look where that had gotten me— sentenced to years of hell.

I heard the shower turn off. I inexplicably felt very uncomfortable. Was Shooter going to come out naked and ready to go? Or was he going to come out wearing my robe? After what we'd done the night before, you'd think I'd be comfortable around him. I was so not. Seeing him in the bright light of day seemed much more intimate than what he had done between my legs in the dark. I had a sudden surge of panicked brilliance. I lay down on the bed, pulled the covers up to my ears, and feigned sleep. But he didn't come out as quickly as I had anticipated. He had probably been out of the shower for at least ninety seconds. What was so hard about wrapping a towel around your waist and walking out of a bathroom? Why was he taking so freaking long? I almost got out of bed to sneak over to the bathroom to listen in when the door opened and Shooter came out.

I breathed a deep sigh of relief as I peeked at him through my lashes. He was dressed in clean clothes. God bless Edna! May she be sainted and enshrined at the Vatican or the local crawfish shack, which ever she prefers. Shooter sat carefully on the edge of my bed and brushed my hair from my face. I didn't "wake up." He pressed a kiss to my eyelid. I couldn't stop the smile from spreading across my face.

"Wake up, angel."

He was just so damn sweet! I stretched a fake stretch.

"We need to discuss how I'm getting out of here without incurring the wrath of your brother, daughter, staff, and Edna." Little did he know, he had nothing to worry about with Edna.

"I have a plan," I told him.

He threw my robe at me, and I pulled it over my naked body. Before I was able to secure it in the front, Shooter nuzzled his way past my arms and the terry cloth and laid his head on my chest. I didn't make him move. I didn't want him to. He took a deep breath and pulled away a moment later. I pouted for him, and he chuckled.

"Tell me this brilliant plan of yours," he said as he pulled me to my feet.

"Well, it is brilliant and it's a secret. What I'm about to show you is sacred." I looked at him in all seriousness. "If you tell anyone, I'll have to kill you and that would be a real shame when I take into account your carnal talents."

He slapped my butt and put a mock serious look on his face. "Yes, ma'am."

"I'm serious, Shooter. This is something I didn't even know

until I gained ownership of the house. Got it?"

He dropped the silly face and said, "Got it."

I turned and led him to the corner where the east and north walls came together. I pressed a spot hidden within the decorative molding and the wall slid aside.

"What? This is freaking awesome!"

"Absolute secrecy," I threatened.

He nodded.

I led him through hidden corridors and down a hidden set of stairs.

"So, how many rooms can you get to this way?" he asked.

"All of them."

"No way," he said in awe.

I told him the story about the ancestor with the four mistresses and the wife and about the house's history during prohibition. I told him how the secret was handed down owner to owner. I led him out through the hidden door into the Club. As promised, the doors were shut and the room was empty.

"Now, Edna waxes this floor every Friday. She would have threatened the rest of them within an inch of their life to stay out. You open the door. Wait for Edna to explode. The troops come running and you tell them you've been in here since early this morning. Brilliant. Yes, it's brilliant." I talked really fast and started to ramble. Bad, bad sign. Soon I would be saying exactly the wrong thing and I would destroy whatever we had between us.

Somehow he could sense that I was about to go off the deep end. He pulled me into him and kissed me deeply, forcing me to shut my big fat mouth.

"Go," he said as he released me. "I'll come up and check on you in a few minutes."

I obeyed without hesitation. I knew a panic attack was on its way and I didn't want him to see it. I retreated to the wall and watched through the port hole. Shooter walked over to the door and opened it.

As if Edna had been waiting for the door to open, I heard

her screech instantly. "Shooter! What the hell are you doing on my floor! Boy, I am going to skin you alive and use your hide to make me a new handbag!"

Footsteps ran down the hall. Edna came at Shooter with a broom and started whacking him with it. Switch ran into the fray and pulled Edna off Shooter. He said something so low I couldn't hear. But Edna retreated back to the hall.

"I don't know how you got in here but you have some serious explaining to do." Switch was not happy with Shooter. But then Switch was never happy.

"I came in here early this morning."

"Eeeehhh!" He made a sound like a buzzer on a game show. "Try again. You know those cameras you had me install. You and Hell Kat came in last night through the backstairs and went into her room. From what I saw in the hall you weren't discussing knitting patterns."

Shit, I had completely forgotten about the cameras.

"Who else knows?" Shooter asked.

"Shit, do you really think I'd rat you out like that? No one but me knows and it will stay that way unless you endanger our mission. Am I clear?" Switch was in no mood to be messed around with.

Shooter nodded.

"I already covered you with the rest of the Bastards. They think you're in your room with a hangover. But they're gonna want a report about Hell Kat's initiation. And they're going to want it soon."

Shooter nodded and left the room. I walked through the secret passage back to my room. Shooter had beaten me there and was casually lounging on my bed.

"So now I know how you discovered we were guarding you. Tell me, do you spy on all your guests?"

"No. I mean, I don't know, I don't have many guests. Besides, gathering intel is one of my specialties."

"Your past is your past, Kat. It's something that happened but it doesn't make you who you are."

I guess Shooter would know that more than most. "Why are you here? In my room I mean?"

"I can't want to just spend time with you?"

"No. Yes. Shit, I don't know." Why did he make me so flustered? I really didn't want this to turn into something it wasn't. I didn't want to fight with Shooter. I was afraid for him to tell me he loved me again.

And just as I felt another case of word vomit coming on, he rescued me. "I'm going to gather the Bastards. You get dressed. We'll reconvene in twenty minutes in the library." He got up, kissed me quickly, and left.

Anyone could have seen I was about to lose it, that I was about to say something stupid. I knew Shooter could tell. Good Lord, the man knew absolutely everything about me, almost. But he walked away. Rather than start a stupid, ridiculous fight that I would live to regret later, he walked away. Even Stephan had never done that.

Okay, let's go over how Shooter was the perfect man. He was kind, compassionate, caring, direct, loyal, authoritative, sexy as hell, a great kisser, and he could handle himself behind a Barrett.50 cal, which, let's face it, was one of his sexiest qualities. He understood me. I didn't have to hide things from him. And he wanted me. *Yup, he's my perfect other half.* So why did I feel the overwhelming urge to run from him? Why did I feel like the last holdout on the bayou just as a category five hurricane barreled through my front yard? I didn't care. I was not screwing this up! I had him for a summer, that's it. One single, solitary season, and I would not let my numerous neuroses and insecurities destroy something that I could brag about to the ladies in the old folks' home.

Decision made, I stepped into the shower. The hot stream I usually stood under was too hot. I had to turn it down to a normal human level. I had been completely thrown off my game. I showered quickly, dressed, and sat at the vanity to do my hair. Out of habit I went to pull it up, until I remembered how it felt to have Shooter's hands tangled in it. I left it down.

As I walked from my room, I had a smile on my face, a real honest to goodness smile. I must have looked like a big freaking idiot, but I didn't care. I had to pull myself together when I got closer to the library. The Bastards wanted info on last night and they were expecting me to complain and be a bitch. Bitch. I've had loads of practice with that mask.

I threw open the doors and rushed Tyler who sat in a club chair. My fists clenched, I planned on letting him know how much I hated last night. The party part of last night anyway. Just before I reached him I was lifted off my feet and turned upside down. Or my perception of the room had been turned upside down. Once I regained my perspective, I found that I was staring, upside down, at Shooter's butt. And what a nice view it was, it almost made me forget that I had just been hauled off my feet. Shooter carried me to another chair across the room and plopped me into it. I did not like being treated like a stuffed bear. So, the second my tush hit leather, I stood and headed for Tyler again.

I almost managed to stand fully erect before Shooter pushed me back down.

"Calm down, Hell Kat. We've picked up chatter on your current situation and you need to hear this." He paused to make sure I had calmed myself enough to really listen. For a second I forgot I had been pretending. But as Shooter looked into my eyes, I could have built an ice rink on top of a volcano if he'd asked.

"Switch, tell her what you heard." He didn't take his eyes off me.

Before Switch had a chance to speak, I pointed at Tyler and said, "This isn't over, not by a long freaking shot. You feel me?" Because that's what bitch Kat would have said.

Tyler rolled his eyes and Switch came forward holding something that I guess you could call an iPad, if iPads were made by the Humvee department of General Motors. "I've been monitoring relevant chatter. Anyone says Boudreaux, Bayou Boudreaux, GSA, etc. Anyway, I picked this up early this morning." He played an audio file. The file was of two male voices, one American, one not. They were talking about a Boudreaux and some type of abduction scenario. I'd really love to see someone try to kidnap me. *Bring. It. The. Freak. On.* That will never happen again.

"Where did this come from?" I asked.

They looked at each other like they didn't want to tell me. "It came from New Orleans." Switch was the only one with the balls to tell me.

"Where was the other guy? The one with the accent."

"They were both in New Orleans. From what we can tell, they're planning on attacking within the next week. Do you have any events where it might be easy to grab you?" Shooter had taken control of the conversation.

The next week was a mess. "Yes, it's the Founder's Day Celebration. I have to judge the Miss Bayou Boudreaux contest, I'm in the parade, I have to be at the carnival, and the dinner here at the house. So, yeah it's a tactical nightmare."

"You're going to have to cancel all your prescheduled commitments. We can protect you here, but we can't guarantee your safety elsewhere."

Shooter had not just given me an order! "No, I'm not."

"Kat, you're putting yourself in danger. You need to cancel."

"No, and it won't be the first time I've put myself in danger." Shooter was sweet and all, but I didn't take orders from anyone.

"This is not up for discussion. You will cancel your commitments, and you will not put yourself in more danger than absolutely necessary. Am I clear?"

"And what do you deem absolutely necessary? Is it okay if I shave my legs or am I to stay away from all sharp objects? Can I ride in a car or should I keep clear of all flammable liquids? In fact, why don't you put all my food in a blender so I don't choke on a piece of chicken." I was no longer pretending.

"Kat, I—"

"Yes, Alex...Shooter."

Shooter took a deep breath. If it had been possible to load

his eyes with armor piercing bullets, I would be dead.

"I need the room," he said in a scary calm voice. The Bastards got up and left. I could tell they were expecting him to eat me alive. When the door closed, Shooter and I had the single, most deadly staring contest in the history of the world.

"You were saying," I growled through clenched teeth.

"I will not allow you to put yourself in a position where—"

"And do you think for one minute that if we eliminate their chances to attack me this week, they'll stop? No, no they won't! They'll try again and again." I stood up almost yelling at him. "And you won't be here forever." I could tell I had hurt him. What did he expect? He would be here forever? Eventually he had to return to Iraq or Afghanistan or some other country where people would try to kill him.

"If one of my soldiers spoke to me that way, I would—"

"You'd what? What? What could you do in this specific, unsanctioned, non-military, strictly volunteer situation? What could you do?" I had gone from almost yelling to most definitely yelling.

"I'm here to save your damn life! You could at least do what I say! Are you seriously willing to make your daughter an orphan?"

How dare he? How dare he bring her into this? I slapped him across his face. Well, I almost did. He stopped me before I made contact. "Don't you ever speak of her again. You do not get the privilege to speak of my daughter." I no longer yelled. I spoke in a calm, careful, far more deadly voice. "I will not allow a group of thugs to determine where I go or when. I will protect myself if I have to. If you and your men want to assist in saving my life, I will welcome your aid. But don't ever presume to issue an order to me. Do you understand?"

"I understand that you're biting the hand that's trying to save your life. But I will be here because you are a Rat Bastard and I have an obligation to you."

That hurt.

"I will issue orders to my men. We will attempt to protect

you in multiple positions, situations, and times of day. I will tell them your safety is of the utmost importance. I just hope they follow my orders."

"Just remember I'm not one of your men. I don't follow orders. That's why you're a soldier, and I'm an assassin."

"Oh trust me, no one doubts your ability to take a life! We've all done it, but you're the only one who seems to have no remorse."

I wanted to hit him...again. I wanted to reach down his throat and pull his balls out through his mouth. I wanted him to stop me from turning around and leaving. But he didn't. I turned away from him and sashayed across the room. He needed to know exactly what he'd pissed off. And honey, I could sashay with the best of them. I paused once, safe within the secret passage inside the wall. He left through the double oak doors. Then he was gone. I could act as tough as I wanted, but in the end, as much as I hated to admit it, the fight had been pretty much all my fault. You couldn't attack Shooter. He was too proud to just let you win. You had to come at him with logic. Logic and I were not friends. In fact, we were mortal enemies. So just as predicted, I'd ruined everything.

Sometimes, I really freaking wished I wasn't a girl. If I had been born a guy, I could be more pissed than hurt. Why had he said those things? Yes, yes, I know I threw the first poison arrow but did he have to throw one back? All is fair in war. A weight fell into my stomach. Edna hadn't served lead ingots for breakfast, but she might as well have. My heart had stopped beating. Someone had wrapped their fingers around it and given it a good squeeze. How did Shooter have so much emotional control over me?

I tried to think back to the first fights I'd had with Stephan. Had they been that horrible? The answer was no. Back then my every emotion was regulated. Regret, guilt, and anger could be banished in a second. Or any of those emotions could be pressed into service if it meant getting a job done. The sad fact was, though I had loved Stephan with all my heart, I had never been as emotionally bare with him as I'd been with Shooter. *Damn him! Damn Shooter to hell!* He had completely thrown me off my game and that was unacceptable.

By the time I'd made it to my room, my gut weighed a hundred and fifty pounds and my heart would need a bolt of lightning shot by Zeus himself to restart. Physical distance from Shooter made me weak. And I hated it. A humane person would go downstairs, apologize, and beg his forgiveness. But I just couldn't do it. Pride paralyzed me. Just as I closed the secret passage, Edna stomped into my room and slammed the door.

"What the hell are you doing?" she lectured with her hands on her hips.

I went to tell her to stay out of it, but she held her finger up. That was enough to stop me dead in my tracks.

"What you're doing is throwing away something damn near perfect! You're going to drive him away and, no matter how tough you think you are, you'll never recover. You'll wind up being an old bitter woman. I'm the reigning old bitter woman in this house, and I'm not about to name you my successor."

I fell onto my bed. I knew I had really freaking screwed the pooch. I wanted Shooter. I *liked* Shooter. "What am I doing, Edna?"

"Well for one, you're a stupid stubborn ass." She sat next to me and brushed my hair out of my face with a gentle hand. "The good thing is that he already knows that about you. He's known that for a while and he wanted you anyway. Now, listen to me. I'm going to tell you something I know a lot about. If you take too long to say sorry, the hurt feelings harden and nothing can penetrate them. He loves you. I know he does. And I think you love him. If you do, or if you think maybe one day you might, you need to apologize. Not to mention it's what a decent person would do." She smiled at me and I nodded.

Edna was right of course. But, I had a problem. I had no idea how to apologize. I'd never actually done it before. Seriously, not in grammar school, not with Stephan, never. I had never been in the wrong. My emotional health was in serious need of an evaluation. How did someone live to be thirty-two and never once sincerely say I'm sorry? I'd said the words before but it was always something like, "I'm sorry, were you talking to me?" just before I nailed someone in the jaw. Or "I'm sorry I have to do this," just before I broke a target's neck. It was never real.

If I wanted to issue a sincere apology, I needed to practice. Apologizing to a mirror was just too lame and too Meg Ryan for me. I needed to practice on a something that required oxygen to survive. There had to be someone I could apologize to without making them think I was dying of cancer or a Death Star was about to blow up our planet. I stood up and left my room, went down the hall, and into Samantha's bright pink paradise.

"Can I have a minute?" Amanda nodded and left. "Sam, can I talk to you?" She came over and stood in front of me all big eyed. Damn, had I ever been that innocent? I knelt to look her in the eye. "I need to say sorry for, I mean I want to say sorry for.... What I mean to say is that I'm sorry I maybe haven't been here for you, and I'm sorry about that. I'm really, really sorry."

Sam looked at me like horns had sprouted out of my head. "Okay," she said and hugged me.

This might be a new experience for me, but I was almost positive this wouldn't go as easy with Shooter.

"Can Amanda come back? We were about to have tea."

I nodded and left as her nanny returned.

Maybe a practice lap had been a stupid idea. Maybe I should have just jumped off the apology cliff with Shooter. Dammit, I needed to get it over with. I opened the secret door in my room and went down a different set of stairs and though hallways that took me to Shooter's room. Through the hidden portal I saw Shooter and Horndog.

"I know you're into her, man, but really if she's taken your head to a place it shouldn't be then you need to nip it, like right now." Horndog had made a completely valid point. The fact that I wanted to take his eyelids off with a pair of nail clippers aside, it was a valid point.

Shooter sat on the bed with his head in his hands. "I can't. I...."

What! You what? Please just finish your sentence! But of course he didn't.

Horndog put a hand on his shoulder and nodded as if he and Shooter had communicated telepathically. *Dammit!* Horndog left and I stood behind the secret door, afraid to move, like a scared little bunny rabbit. Yes, the same woman that crept into a harem to slit a warlord's throat in the middle of the day was afraid to walk through a door in her own house. I had no idea how long I stood there. I just watched Shooter. He sat on his bed. He paced the floor then went back to sitting. He stood up and acted as if he would leave. I knew it would be my only chance so I grew a pair and opened the damn door.

As the wall moved away, Shooter turned, pulled a knife from his waistband, and nearly attacked until he saw who it was. The man carried a weapon in his pants when he was alone in an empty room. Could he get any sexier? He dropped his hand with the blade to his side and relaxed his stance. The look on his face was something similar to a drug addict trapped in a rehab pharmacy. He wanted what was in front of him but knew he shouldn't. He moved across the room and sat in one of four blue chintz chairs. I took the one opposite him. He wouldn't say anything. I had hurt his pride. I would have to be the one to start.

"I...I just wanted to say...I mean...." Damn, apologizing was hard. The sentence wouldn't form in my brain. I was going to have to make it as short and sweet as possible. "I'm sorry." And then, just like that, I came down with another case of word vomit. "I'm sorry I said those horrible things. I've put you and your men through hell. I wasn't willing to listen to you. I scoffed at your orders, and I undermined you in front of your men. I'm...I'm just really sorry. If you, well, if you want to change things between us, I'll understand." I'd understand. It would physically kill me, but I'd understand.

My gaze fell to the floor. I preferred not to see the look on his face when he rejected me. He didn't say anything for a while, and I mean a long freaking while. Or it could have been two seconds. I had recently completely lost all time references.

"Kat...."

And that was the part where he told me to get the hell out of his room, right?

"Before you busted through my wall, I was headed out to find you. I wanted to tell you sorry that I tried to force you into a stupid situation. You're right, if we stop them this week, they'll just try again. The smart plan would be to put you out there and let the attack happen. At least then the threat would be eliminated. But I can't do the smart thing. I can't endanger you like that. It goes against every fiber of my being to put you in harm's way." He took a deep breath and paused. "I love you, Kat."

That got my attention. I snapped my head up to look at him.

He stared right at me, no fear. "I think I've loved you from the time you nearly shanked Tongue at the airport. I loved you when you made us go shopping. I loved you when I saw you break that guy's neck. And it nearly killed me to see a knife sticking out of your body. I loved you when you were unconscious, and I loved you when you woke up. I wanted to tell you the first night we both slept uninterrupted for the first time in years. But I couldn't. I couldn't put that out there and have you laugh at it. But I don't care anymore. I love you."

Holy shit, not what I expected. Not what I expected at all.

"Please," he continued, "don't say it back. I don't want you to say it unless you mean it." He didn't move. He just sat there in that chair. You know how when a man tells you he loves you, he has that look of expectation on his face. Shooter didn't have that. His face read confidence. He didn't need to hear it, but he needed to express it. How many men do you know who could pull off that look?

I didn't know what to say. Did I love him? How the hell was I supposed to know? He made me feel safe, loved. And it really pissed me off to think of him unhappy. I melted like a Popsicle in July when he touched me and my body craved him. My skin prickled with the need to touch him.

I slid off the chair and scooted across the floor to kneel in front of him. Without saying anything, I placed my palms on his cheeks and kissed him softly. My kiss spilled life back into him.

He wrapped his arms around me and pulled me onto his lap. I tried to kiss him again, but he put his hand up to stop me. "We'll work this out together. You won't paint a target on your back, and we won't lock you away in a tower. Okay?" He asked, not demanded.

I nodded and kissed him as if I wanted to set the house on fire.

Just when I thought things would get interesting, Tyler, my dear sweet brother with the world's worst timing, busted through the door. The moment it registered that I sat on Shooter's lap, Tyler went ballistic. He looked as if he could take on the entire German army, and win. I, of course, stayed right where I sat. Not because I was shocked or stunned into a paralysis. No, he had challenged my position, and I wouldn't back down. It didn't matter to Tyler that Shooter outranked him or that Shooter had saved his life. He locked into full big brother mode. Shooter had about ten seconds to live. If big brothers had their way, their sisters would remain virgins their entire life and would only have children through Immaculate Conception.

We stared each other down. He was a bull, and I was the matador. He lowered his horns and charged. Tyler pulled me off Shooter's lap and hauled him to his feet. I wanted to dice Tyler up and bake him into a pie, but Shooter didn't even tense his muscles. His forehead remained smooth and his mouth and eyes were relaxed. He wouldn't fight my brother.

"What the hell are you doing with my sister, Shooter?" I could barely hear Tyler.

"Tyler, let him go, now! In case you didn't notice, I wasn't being forced! I kissed him, dammit!"

Shooter still didn't say anything.

"Do you have any idea what she's been through?"

"Yes." Hark, Shooter speaks. "I know what happened to her. But I wouldn't presume to know what she went through and neither should you. I would never force or pressure her into anything. You want to keep her a victim. But at some point you have to give her life back to her. You have to see her for the strong woman she is."

Tyler released Shooter but didn't step away from him. "If you hurt her, if she sheds one tear because of you I'll, I'll...." Tyler had to think for a minute. Then he looked at me with a smile that could only mean he had received divine inspiration. He turned back to Shooter and growled, "If you hurt her, I'll turn her loose on you. You know what she's capable of, and you know I'll be the only person standing between the two of you. If you hurt her, I'll step aside and let her eat your liver for breakfast. You feel me?"

Shooter shook his head. "You don't understand, Tongue, I can't hurt her. It would kill me. Ya see, she's not with me because she needs me. I'm with her because I can't live without her."

Holy wow.

Tyler didn't say anything. He gave Shooter an ocular promise of a slow painful death and left.

Shooter turned his back to me. When the door closed, his shoulders started to bounce up and down. *What the hell?* I thought maybe he might be having a seizure. I ran around to face him and put a hand on his shoulder. "What's wrong?"

He raised his head. He wasn't seizing, he was laughing.

"What's so funny?" I was on the verge of getting pissed again.

"You." He laughed some more, and I wanted to smack him. "You should have seen the look on your face. You looked like someone replaced your milk and corn flakes with broken glass and piss." He laughed until he saw the look I gave him. It clearly relayed the message that if he ever wanted to get lucky again, he'd quit laughing at me.

He pulled himself together and said, "We have to meet with the rest of the Bastards to discuss your security."

I pouted. Sometimes real life just sucked. He grabbed my hand and pulled me out into the hall. The Bastards waited outside, and they all gave me questioning looks. They had to wonder how I'd magically disappeared from the library and then reappeared in Shooter's room. I had no intention of explaining.

And then their eyes scanned down and saw my hand clasped in Shooter's. I tried to pull away but he gripped me tight. Okay, so he wanted the Bastards to know we were sleeping together. Not sure if I did. But he gave me no choice. He dragged me down the hall to the Club. The ruse of the waxed floor had been completely forgotten. The Bastards followed without order or instruction. Maybe surviving life and death situations created a bond that allowed you to read each other's minds. As soon as we got to command central, Tyler pulled a roll of blue prints from a closet and laid them out on the pool table.

"We're going to have to rethink our plan," Shooter said. "We weren't able to retrieve our weapons at the dock so we have to go with what we have on hand." He turned to me. "Do you or any of your staff have any weapons? Hunting rifles, handguns? Anything?"

"Please, who are you talking to?" I scoffed. "I've got you covered." I waited for Shooter to continue with the plan but he just looked at me. "What?"

"Explain." Shooter tried to hide the grin on his face but failed.

"I've got you covered. When you need to be armed, you will be."

My Marines cast wary looks at each other.

"We need to know what we'll have access to so we can make our preparations." Shooter talked to me as if I was still trying to grasp the complex concepts of Sesame Street.

"What he's trying to say is, show us your shit, now." Switch, not the diplomat.

I looked Shooter in the eye. When he nodded, I stepped away from the group to shut and lock the Club's door. The Bastards took it as an invitation to follow. We stopped at a blank wall. I turned to them and said, "I am breaking a very old, very strong Boudreaux family tradition." I pressed the chair rail in a specific spot and the wall moved away. "This hall leads to a secret room that was once used to store liquor during Prohibition. No one is to know this room exists. You are to tell no one, and when you leave here, you will forget you saw it. Am I clear?"

They nodded and we stepped into the wall. I'd crossed line. I knew the moment I decided to show them that room I put all my trust in their hands. That one act galvanized my faith in them. They would never know how serious it was for me. Of course, I didn't tell them the house was infested with secret rooms and passages. They didn't need to know that. I trusted them, but I wasn't stupid.

The room was the most accessible in the house. I could get to it through several passageways. I led them through a zigzagging corridor to a room with a steel door that had a hand scanner next to it. I placed my hand on the device and the door opened. As we entered, they gasped. No one, not even Edna, knew I had an armory in the house. It had been stocked with the most current high tech weaponry on the planet. If you needed an assault rifle, automatic shotgun, hand gun of any flavor, grenade launcher, high powered sniper rifle, machine gun, land mine, any brand of plastic explosive, detonator, hand grenade, ammunition for pretty much anything that fires, or anything that could hold an edge, you could find it there. There was enough fire power in that one room to take on the Louisiana National Guard and have a fighting chance. It was my version of a jewelry box.

"If you would have called to tell me your plans, you wouldn't have needed to trust double-crossing pirates with your stuff."

No one spoke. They had all switched into Marine mode and surveyed the contents of the room. They stroked the weapons with the same tenderness used on newborn babies. I think Horndog may have even cooed at one point.

"How much ammo do you have?" Shooter said, ending the reverent worship.

"Enough to raise Charlton Heston from the grave."

Shooter smiled at me.

"T4? You have T4! Where the hell did you get T4?"

T4 was the most powerful plastic high explosive the military used. Take C4 and shoot it full of anabolic steroids and you'd have T4. "The armory at Quantico." I got all my stuff from the same place my Marines got theirs. I had earned lots of enemies in my past, but I also made quite a few powerful friends along the way.

"Do you have a SOPMOD kit for this?" Martinez asked, holding an M4A1 carbine. He referred to an accessories kit used by the armed forces to make a deadly weapon deadlier and to provide Special Forces with the tools they needed to kill, maim, blow up, and destroy to the best of their ability. It was a stupid question.

"With or without the grenade launcher?" I asked.

Martinez smiled.

"Where. The. Hell. Did you get that?" I turned to see Horndog eyeing a heavy M2 Browning .50 caliber machine gun.

"A Chechen friend of mine." I was kidding but Horndog didn't catch on.

"Some friend. Do you even know how to use the damn thing?"

Was he serious? The man didn't know me at all. "If you think that's impressive, look at this." A large locked cabinet stood against the far wall. I moved to stand in front of it. My Marines huddled around me as though they were senior citizens about to drink from the Fountain of Youth. I unlocked it and opened the door. The room was filled with a chorus of reverent "holy shits." I smiled a bit before moving out of the way.

"Why, for the love of God, do you have a minigun?" I couldn't tell if Switch was impressed or not.

The reason I had the cousin to the Gatling gun that was usually mounted on aircraft was simple: I wanted it. I shrugged my shoulders. "I just picked it up somewhere."

"This isn't a piece of scrap some arms dealer fished out of a military incinerator. This is direct from the factory. All this stuff is practically brand new. You can still smell the lubricant the factory ships them in for hell's sake. Where did you get all this shit?" Horndog had gotten a bit accusatory.

"It was going to be installed in the ceiling of the foyer. If anyone I don't like comes in, I could just push a button, it swings down, and the person is history. Why does it matter? We need it. You need it. It's here. Use it."

Horndog wouldn't back down. "No way! You don't get off that easy. I want to know if I'll have to face state of the art heavy weaponry the next time I'm on patrol."

I rolled my eyes at Horndog who had gotten all huffy with his hands on his hips. "You don't have to worry about that. My supplier is your supplier. I got all this from the US government. Think of them as bonuses for a job well done." I threw him wink to alleviate the tension.

He crossed his arms over his chest and leaned back on his heels. A heartbeat passed where I didn't know if he was going to hit me or kiss me. "Damn. Last time I killed an enemy combatant all I got was a HOOAH! bar."

"Are you sure you killed the right person? HOOAH! bars are the military's way of thinning the herd. Those who can't survive eating one aren't tough enough to be a member of the club."

Horndog laughed and pulled me in for a hug. "You're all right, Hell Kat. You know that? I can see why...." But he didn't finish his sentence.

From the tension in the room I knew Tyler wasn't the only one who didn't approve of me and Shooter. Was I really so wrong for him?

My Marines hauled most of the armory out into the Club.

We spent the rest of the day strategizing, going over security protocols, and visiting the locations where I would be that week. I could completely understand Shooter's concerns. We only had six people to eliminate threats that had multiple opportunities to kill me. They were most worried about the parade. I was most worried about the carnival. Sam would be with me. I wouldn't survive if she got hurt. Well, first I'd hunt down and brutally kill the person who hurt her with my own two hands...then I would die. But we all agreed that to leave her out may let my would-be attackers know we were on to them. I wanted to wrap her in a bomb disposal suit, but Shooter said that would make her stand out in a bad way. I didn't really care. The evening was spent searching the web for child-size body armor.

Chapter Fifteen

$\mathcal{B}$oudreaux House had become an armed fortress. We had fixed gun emplacements on the roof, observation posts around the property line manned by remote operated cameras. We'd changed my regular security protocols and reassigned my private security to make sure they didn't leave any blind spots. We created evacuation procedures in the event of an attack, the entire property was watched over by a grid of motion and infrared sensors, and my Marines and I were armed to the teeth no matter where we went. We had the advantage. We were protecting, not attacking. Our job was to wait for the threat to show up.

I felt fairly safe in my own house. But I wouldn't be in my house every second of every day so we also had to plan security for the parade route, the pageant, and the carnival. It would be a long, stressful week. There really was no reason for them to worry about my safety. I could take care of myself. Everyone else, my staff, the Bastards, Sam, and Shooter were the ones who kept me awake at night with worry. If anything happened to them, I would never be able to forgive myself. I shouldn't have been so naïve as to think my past wouldn't come back to haunt me. But, as my mother-in-law used to say, what's done in the dark always comes to light.

As I lay in bed with Shooter, I wondered who I would lose in the next week. I knew we wouldn't come out unscathed. The sheik's brother was known for being completely ruthless. When he had interrogated his nephew for information, he spent five days inflicting so much pain the poor kid passed out multiple times only to be revived so they could continue. They eventually let him die. But only after they had cut off his nose and ears, electrocuted him, smashed his balls with a sledge hammer, and gave him a thousand cuts deep enough to inflict the most pain without allowing him to bleed to death. They killed him by lowering him very slowly into an industrial plastic shredder, feet first. It was a slow, ugly death that I wouldn't wish on my worst enemy.

"Shooter?"

"Yeah."

"Will you promise me something?"

"Anything."

"If something happens to me, make sure Sam and my staff are taken care of. It's all in my will, but I know there will be people to contest it. I want you to promise you'll do everything in your power to make sure they're all okay." I needed him to agree with me on this.

"I promise I'll help you take care of them. But you're not going to die. I won't let you," he said and kissed the top of my head.

I snuggled against him, and he gave me a reassuring hug.

Neither of us spoke for a while. We didn't want to go to sleep because we didn't know how much time we had with each other. I broke the silence. "Thank you."

He sat up so he could look down at me. "For what?"

"For this, for loving me. I never thought I would ever be able to be with someone again. But I'm safe with you. I know you would never hurt me in any way. I can trust you, and trust is not something I hand out freely."

"To tell you the truth, I didn't think we would ever have this either. After what you told me about your attack, I never thought I would get to have you like this. And I was okay with that, but thank you for trusting me. It means a lot."

"Shooter," I continued, "you don't have to worry about hunting those men down and killing them."

He let out a sigh. "How did you know?"

"It's what I would do if anything ever happened to you. But trust me when I tell you, you don't need to."

"Why?"

"Just because."

"I need to know why, Kat."

"Because they're dead. I wasn't completely honest with you when I told you about my attack. I left out the last bit. After I'd incapacitated them, I tied them up and castrated them. They screamed and bled for every last thing they did to me. I drained their car of gas and poured it all over the house. I tossed in a road flare and let it burn. I could hear their blood curdling screams from the street where I watched. I loved every bit of it."

He didn't have to think of a response, and his rapid reaction to what I'd just told him gave me comfort. "I can't imagine what you must have been feeling. I understand why you weren't honest with the cops. You were ashamed. And not because of what happened to you. You had been trained to defend yourself. It should have been second nature for you to take those bastards out. I get it." He paused and traced his thumb over my collarbone, "How were you able to do it? I know you were pissed and anger can drive a person to do amazing things, but how were you able to hear their screams and not be affected by them?"

I really hoped I'd never have that conversation. Being an assassin was one thing but torture was something most people didn't understand. I really didn't want to tell him that part of me, but I had to. If he was in love with me, he needed to know everything. If I didn't tell him, it would be like I'd committed fraud. *Dammit.*

"I wasn't just an assassin for GSA. I also worked as a contract interrogator." Read: Professional Torture Technician.

They taught me to completely switch off my humanity to get the information I needed. I waited for him to combust. But he didn't. He hugged me tight and kissed the top of my head.

I loved Shooter for that. To him, I wasn't a horrible person. He accepted every part of me. He was perfect in every way shape and form. I was falling in love with him, but I couldn't tell him that. He would be gone as soon as his leave ended, and I didn't want to make that any harder for him.

I couldn't tell him how I felt, but I could show him. In most cases actions speak louder than words, but in the I love you situation that wasn't true. Telling someone you love them was like standing on top of Mount Rushmore with a megaphone that could be heard in Mexico and saying you were going to finish the mountain with a sculpture of the Easter Bunny next to George Washington. A lot was expected when you said something like that.

I crawled up his body, biting my way up his chest and neck. "Are you stalking me, Kat?"

"No, I've already caught you. Now, I'm going to devour you."

"Come and get me, kitten."

Sometime later Shooter said, "You are the most beautiful woman I've ever seen." And for the first time since I had been scarred, I believed I was beautiful. He wasn't the first person to tell my I was easy on the eyes, but he was the first person who made me think he wasn't just saying it to get something out of me. I knew he hadn't referred just to my physical body. He meant my whole person.

In that moment I was struck with a sudden realization. I wasn't falling in love, I was *in* love with Shooter. I had to clamp my mouth shut. My brain had a tendency to wander off and tell my mouth to say things without first consulting me. So I clenched my teeth while the moment passed. There was no logical explanation why I couldn't tell Shooter that I loved him, I just couldn't.

He held me against his chest. I fit him perfectly. My body

had been made for his. After being with him my entire life would change. I was no longer alone. I was no longer missing half of my spirit. Life would be much happier and much sadder than before. Happier because I had Shooter. Sadder because all relationships end with tears. Whether we broke up or were married and lived happily together for the rest of our lives, eventually we would be separated. But until then, I would try to live in the happy time with him.

"My dream is a memory." I hadn't expected Shooter to say anything. I propped myself up on my elbows to look him in the face. "My nightmare is a memory. My spotter and I were sent to eliminate a target, and I accidentally shot a seven-year-old girl. She's why I've volunteered to go back so many times. I have to try to make up for what I've done. I have to make sure she didn't die for nothing."

I kissed his eyelids and forehead. Not many people could understand us. We both couldn't forgive ourselves for something that neither of us were responsible for. Maybe that's why we fell in love so quickly. We were kindred spirits.

I rested my head on his chest. "Does it ever make you mad that people in your own country don't believe in what you're doing?"

He thought for a moment. "No, I don't fight for them. Thanks to me and my men, kids can go to school without worrying about getting shot, parents can go to work and not worry about their house being bombed while they're earning a living, and grandparents can take their grandkids to the park and not have to constantly be on the lookout for suicide bombers. I do it for the people of Iraq and Afghanistan. Everyone has the right to be saved from tyranny. Everyone deserves to live a life without fear. I do it for them."

The US government should really ask Shooter be their spokesperson for the war.

"When do you leave to go back?" I hoped to hell I didn't sound clingy.

"I'm not going back."

"What?" It scared me to death to get my hopes up.

"I'm done. This deployment was my last. I didn't reenlist. I've given the corps fifteen years. I'm retired now." He said this as if it was no big deal. Did he not realize I wanted to spend every waking second with him? How could he not have told me? He could tell me he loved me but he couldn't tell me he was no longer in a committed relationship with the US government. What the hell!

I had to tell myself to not jump up on the bed and do a touchdown dance. I had to keep myself from thinking he would want to stay with me after I was safe. But I had to ask, "What are you going to do?"

"I don't know. I have a cabin in Minnesota. I kind of want to disappear up there for a while." He shrugged. He actually shrugged. If I didn't like them so much, I would have kicked him in the balls.

Don't do it. Don't do it, Kat. He has plans, don't do it. "You could stay here." Dammit, I did it. He didn't answer right away. "You don't have to if you don't want to but if you wanted to you could stay. I mean if you wanted to wait until after winter you could live here, with me. Or you could move in for however long you wanted. It's an open invitation." Crap, I sounded clingy and desperate.

He rolled me over onto my back and looked me in the eye. "Would it make you happy if I stayed here?"

"I know Edna would be happy and Sam would be in heaven."

"Would you be happy?"

Don't say it. You're giving him too much power, you're letting him get too close. Don't say…. Oh, shut up! "It would make me very happy."

He kissed me but didn't speak. He pulled the covers up to my chin and gathered me in his arms. So was that a "yes, I'd love to stay," or an "I'll think about it" or a "hell no?" Dammit! Why did I open my big stupid mouth? He reached over to the bedside lamp and turned it off.

Shooter wrapped himself around me and whispered in my ear, "I'd love to stay with you for as long as you'll have me."

An odd sense of calm washed over me. And that scared the shit out of me. *What*! I'm a woman. I'm allowed to experience two totally different emotions at one time.

ભ

We woke up to streaks of sunlight bleeding through the curtains. A note from Edna waited on the nightstand. It said she had cleared space in my closet and moved Shooter's stuff in. Old Kat would have been pissed that she would have done that without consulting me. But I was new Kat, and she was grateful. Shooter and I climbed out of bed to inspect Edna's work. It was really quite pathetic. While my wardrobe took up a space equal to a middle class home, Shooter's hung on a three foot bar. I would have to change that. I started thinking of all the shopping I could do. And I began drawing up plans to expand my closet.

We showered and got dressed. Then Shooter and I and the rest of the Rat Bastards had to head over to the high school to put security in place. That night was the Miss Bayou Boudreaux pageant. It would be held in the high school theater, and I would be a judge. I had done so for the past ten years and loved it. Not because I thought the girls were pretty, talented, smart, or poised. I loved it because it was every outcast's dream to pass judgment on people who think they're better than they are. I loved to ask the girls questions that made them squirm. One year I asked a contestant what she thought of the current situation in Darfur. She said she loved animals too much to wear fur. It had been an epic fail. It had been beautiful. She won.

As we drove to the high school, my Marines were on high alert. It made sense that the attack against me would be carried out during one of my public appearances, but when did ruthless murderers ever do what made sense? No one talked. We were all too focused on the threat. As we drove past a dead raccoon on the side of the road, I nearly had a freak out thinking it could be a hidden IED. It took a moment to remember that I lived in rural Louisiana, not downtown Baghdad. When we drove into the parking lot of the school, I stayed in the car with Shooter while the rest of the Bastards swept the area for anyone or anything out of place.

When I finally made it into the theater, I found all the girls in the middle of swimsuit rehearsal. The director of the pageant sent them all on a break to speak with me. We made our hellos and how have you beens. After we said goodbye, I turned to find my Marines. They had all been trapped by hordes of barely legal, barely dressed young women. Tyler, Doc, Switch, and Martinez were handling the situation fairly well. Horndog and Shooter were two different stories. Horndog sprayed some girl's bare ass with something from an aerosol can and Shooter had been pinned against a far wall by a group of panting ladies.

I stomped over to Horndog. "What are you doing?"

Horndog jumped away. He didn't think he'd get caught. *Cute.* His hand was glued to the woman's butt cheek, he said, "Uh, Kimberly asked me to spray this adhesive on her so her suit won't ride up."

I cocked an eyebrow at both of them.

"Yeah, right. Well it was nice to meet you, Kimberly. I'll be rooting for you." He handed the can of spray-on swimsuit glue back to Kimberly, removed his hand, and shook hers. She crossed the stage with a scowl on her face that made her look like someone just closed down her favorite strip club.

Shooter needed a rescue. His eyes begged me to save him. I smiled and shook my head. Poor guy, trapped by five young, tight, wannabe swimsuit models. I really felt for him. Was it wrong of me to really enjoy seeing him suffer? It was all fun and games until one of these well-bred young ladies slipped her phone number into his back pocket and didn't remove her hand. I stalked up behind the group like a tigress sneaking up on a sleeping water buffalo and cleared my throat. All of them turned to face me. All of them except the girl with her hand on my Shooter's ass. She was not trying to stake a claim! What she didn't know was that I already bought and paid for that piece of real estate.

"What's your name, honey?"

She jutted out her jaw. "Adrianne."

"Well, Adrianne, I believe you have something of mine. Please take your hand off my man's ass."

She gave Shooter an appraising look. "I don't see your name on him."

Are you kidding me! She dared challenge me? Oh, hell no. I took one step forward so we were inches apart. Shooter tensed as if he thought he might need to stop me from busting open the bitch's eye. I stared at her then turned to face Shooter. I palmed the sides of his face and laid a completely inappropriate, borderline pornographic kiss on him. He wrapped himself around me, and Adrianne huffed away.

"Oh, Adrianne," I called to her. "You left your number in my pocket. I'm not sure if you have it written down anywhere else and I'd hate for you to forget it." I flicked the piece of paper on the floor, draped an arm around Shooter, and pulled him in tighter.

We spent the remainder of the time watching the rehearsal while the rest of my Marines tricked the theater out with security cameras, sensors, and metal detectors. The first few times Adrianne fell into our line of sight, she wiggled her fingers at Shooter. She stopped when Shooter stood up and disarmed, laying all his weapons on the stage. I guess two.45s, four throwing knives, a set of brass knuckles, and a K-Bar would intimidate anybody. She stopped flirting with him.

After rehearsal, we drove home so we could change. I had to wear a formal gown, and my Marines put on their private security gear. Yvette had shown up at the house to do my hair, and I actually asked Sissy to do my makeup. I know. Call me the queen of personal growth. Shooter took his clothes to his old room to let us girls get ready. I didn't fight them that time and when I told Yvette to do my hair like she did it for the ball, she nearly cried.

"So what's up with you and that sexy as hell Marine?" Yvette asked while my hair sat in rollers.

How to answer....? "He's my, well, I guess you could call him my boyfriend."

"Damn, girl, I wish I had your luck! You marry the most eligible bachelor in the country then you hook up with a man that makes GI Joe look like a gay Ken doll. I tell you what though, you can throw any of them my way. Especially Doc. If Doc needs someone to warm his bed, I'll set his sheets on fire."

"How do you know Doc?"

"He came to the house to get me to do your hair for the ball. Oh, he is yummy. He drove me home and while I was here, Hawke, my oldest, wrecked on his skate board. Doc patched him up and showed him how to do the trick he'd been trying to do when he fell. Broke my heart!" She grasped her chest. "But that's me. The way to my heart is through my kids, and Doc went right to my ooey gooey zone."

"I'll tell him." I laughed.

"You better."

"Say, do you know a girl named Adrianne who's in the pageant this year?" Yvette knew everybody.

"Ugh, yes, and she is a first rate bitch. She makes appointments and doesn't keep them, or she shows up an hour late. Then she complains when I don't get her hair exactly the way she pictured it in her head, like I read minds. And that mother of hers, Denise, is a piece of work. She may be married to a city councilman but she's sleeping with everyone in town except him. They're both absolute sluts. I heard that Adrianne and her mom caught gonorrhea from the same guy and they had to go to the clinic together. Can you believe that? The same damn guy."

"You've got to be kidding me." It was probably just small town gossip, but the way that tramp was rubbing up against Shooter, I had to believe at least part of it.

"Nope, my sister works at the clinic. She told me. And if it can be nipped, tucked, sucked, sculpted, enhanced, or lifted, Denise has had it done. I've been called over to their house several times just to wash her hair when she was too sore and doped up to do it herself. And speaking of doped up, Adrianne has been popping Vicodin since she was fourteen. Steals it from her mom, and Lord knows she has tons from her surgeries. You'd think Denise's husband is a complete idiot to not notice his wife is the village bicycle, but the truth is he's having an affair of his own. With Bradford James. They have some sort of arrangement because he'll come in while Denise is getting her hair done, give her a kiss on the cheek, tell her she's beautiful then leave. And guess who comes in five minutes later, her flavor of the moment. Yeah, that whole family is messed up. I might be poor white trash, but at least I have standards."

Adrianne was going to have one memorable pageant. I was going to make her life miserable for the next few hours. I know you're thinking poor little girl she has a rough family life so let's give her a pass in the manners department. And my response would be hell no! She's old enough to make her own decisions. She could have chosen to be a human being and rise above her circumstances, but she didn't. She's made her choices, now she has to suffer the consequences, just like I did, and just like every adult who has ever lived has had to.

I waited back stage for the pageant to start. All the girls were fussing with their hair and makeup and stuffing silicone chicken cutlets into their dresses. I scanned the back stage area for my target. Adrianne stood away from the other girls with her mother, Denise. Adrianne's shoulders and head were slumped and her mother looked as though she was reading her the riot act. I slipped behind a row of curtains to listen in on their conversation.

"You will take this seriously, Adrianne. I was Miss Bayou Boudreaux and you will be Miss Bayou Boudreaux. If you can't win a small town beauty pageant, what can you do?"

"Momma, I know this is important to you, but I really don't care. I never wanted to do this. I don't want to be like you."

Adrianne spoke to the floor.

"What are you talking about? We are important in this town. Everyone wants to be us."

Her head snapped up. "I don't even want to be us! What people see is a lie, and you know it."

Denise grabbed Adrianne with her long red fingernails and shook her. "You listen to me, you ungrateful little tramp. You will win this pageant and you will smile and wave and look beautiful on the float or so help me I'll...."

Adrianne's face pinched with real pain.

"You'll what, Denise?" I wasn't about to let that shit continue. "I think you need to go find your seat." I may not be respected by some people in town, but I still carried the Boudreaux name and that meant a lot.

Denise released Adrianne and left, shooting both of us icy looks. Adrianne fell down on a metal folding chair. I intended to leave her to herself and continue hating her, but when I saw tears running down her face, I got sucked back in. Why, oh why couldn't I be as emotionless as I once was? Why was I handing that wretched girl a tissue? And why was my hand on her shoulder?

"I hate her!" Adrianne mopped her eyes with the tissue.

I didn't know what to say, so I just patted her shoulder as if she were a shih-tzu.

"Do you know she slept with my boyfriend?"

I shook my head, lying.

"Yeah, she did. And she's slept with every male teacher I've ever had. And she thinks I want to be her."

"Moms are complicated." I was seriously uncomfortable with the whole situation. I guess it could be worse. We could be in our pajamas, brushing each other's hair, and eating fat-free brownies. "Sometimes they forget to be a mom. They think they need to be your friend when really they just need to love and protect you."

"She's never protected me. She locked me in the bathroom once so she and her boyfriend could run around the house naked for three days."

Ugh, she actually made me feel bad for her.

"She tried to have sex with your husband. A few months before he passed away she called him over to the house for a 'city council meeting' and when he got there she was all dressed up like she was Alexis Carrington in a satin negligee. But your guy shot her down and walked away. You caught a good one, Mrs. Boudreaux. She's had sex with every other man in this pathetic town."

"I thought she took in more territory than that." I clapped a hand over my mouth. I really hadn't meant to say that out loud. But Adrianne laughed, and I breathed a sigh of relief.

She sniffled into the tissue. "I can't wait to get out of here. My life is not going to begin and end in Bayou Boudreaux."

"I know you won't care but, I grew up in a small town and couldn't wait to leave."

"Did you get out?" she interrupted.

"Yes, but I didn't know what I was getting into. I thought I had found the Emerald City. But the city ended up being infested with flying monkeys and led by a maniacal witch. I'm just saying that when you do get out, and I have no doubt you'll get out, make sure it's for real."

She smiled at me and sniffled into her tissue. "I'm sorry for hitting on your man earlier. When I get stressed, I revert to my upbringing. It's my own messed up coping mechanism. I'm sorry." Dammit, why did I have to be so frigging nice? How was I supposed to judge her unfairly after she apologized? Crap!

I sat behind the judges' table. We had reached the question part of the pageant and Adrianne stood in front of me. As I looked at her, I was faced with a moral quandary. Do I give her the ridiculous question or do I give her the real question? Should I make her fall on her face or should I grant her mother's wish and give her a question she could answer? Adrianne didn't even want to be in the pageant. Her mother made her compete. All right, I guess it's the ridiculous question.

"How did the U.S. involvement in the Soviet Afghan War of

1980 affect the current war, and how can we prevent a similar situation?" She had no hope of giving an intelligent answer.

"The U.S. involvement in the war in 1980 had been covert. While we were able to provide the Afghans with weapons and training, the covert nature of the conflict prevented us from aiding the Afghans in rebuilding their country. The economic and political climate in Afghanistan after the war provided a perfect opportunity for the Taliban to take over. We can prevent this by helping to provide the Afghans with livestock, homes, schools, hospitals, but most importantly, education. If we start teaching young children that there is a much bigger world out there, we can help insure a successful future for Afghanistan."

Okay, that didn't go the way I wanted it to. Note to self, never underestimate a young girl with a single minded purpose. Especially if that purpose is fueled by a horrible mother, bad home life, and an overworked Wonder bra. So when the votes were tallied guess who won? You guessed it, Adrianne, the mother-hating, boyfriend-stealing, STD survivor. She looked less than happy when I pushed the crown on to her head.

As I pulled her in for a hug, I whispered in her ear, "Use this to get out."

She gave me a real actual hug, "Thank you." The winner of the pageant was awarded a ten thousand dollar scholarship, and I knew Adrianne would be off to a college as far from her mother as possible. I wondered if I should send her an application to the University of Alaska.

Chapter Sixteen

*S*o, there I was minding my own damn business talking to Shooter, getting ready for the carnival when Horndog and Martinez burst through my bedroom door. They charged through the sitting room and nearly knocked Shooter to his butt trying to get to me. Based on their determined and focused stride, I knew I'd better give them my attention. I stepped through the door of my closet placing a hand on each side of the frame.

"Hell Kat, how could you? How could you keep something like this from us?"

What was Horndog talking about? A girl was allowed to keep a few secrets. I ran through all the things my Marines didn't know about me. It was a long list. They didn't know that I'd trained and worked as a contract interrogator. They didn't know I had once been called on to pose as a prostitute to eliminate a target in Saudi Arabia. They didn't know I had snuck into North Korea to kill the nuclear physicist responsible for their nuclear weapons program. But something told me they weren't talking about my greatest hits. I cocked an eyebrow urging them to continue.

"We've seen them, Hell Kat. We've seen your collection," Horndog whined.

Again, I needed more information.

"We found your garage. We know what you've been hiding from us. I just can't believe you would do that to us. I thought we were brothers." Horndog actually sounded as if I had committed some deep betrayal.

I turned to Shooter with a *what the hell is going on* expression slapped across my face.

"I sent them to the garage to choose the best car for the carnival. They were supposed to pick one that was fast, handled well, and could be discreet."

I crooked my finger and they followed me out of my room, out of the house, across the lawn, and in to my garage. To call it a garage would be like calling Mother Teresa a nice lady. It's a warehouse-sized outbuilding that housed seventy-five of the most lust-worthy cars ever made. The other fifteen hundred cars in the collection were stored in an actual warehouse in Baton Rouge. Collecting cars had been Stephan's passion. He took automobiles seriously, and I like pretty things so I couldn't help but keep it updated. I know not all men were gear heads but my collection could make anyone with an XY chromosome coupling go weak in the knees. I had everything from a cherry red 2010 Ferrari California to an armored 1920 Cadillac V16 that once belonged to Al Capone.

Horndog and Martinez stopped at and gently stroked a red and black Bugatti Veyron.

"You know, most ladies like you to take them out before you run your hand up their thigh." I couldn't help myself. "I can get you the keys if the three of you would like a little privacy?"

"I would. I would like that very much," Horndog said with reverence.

"We're here to do a job, Horndog." Shooter never let his Marines have any fun.

I threw Horndog a bone. "Maybe he and Martinez should go as an advance team to the carnival." The two Marines looked at me as if I had just told them Santa Claus was real and they would get their Red Ryder BB guns. Shooter looked at me with a slight grin on his face.

"It would make sense that someone should be there to monitor the carnival crew. It would make it easier to pick out employees who shouldn't be there." I had made a perfectly valid argument.

And Shooter knew it. He pressed his lips together trying to hide a smile. "Horndog and Martinez can go to the carnival as an advance team, but they need to blend in. No Bugatti."

Shooter just wanted to be mean. I stepped up to him and, in front of Horndog and Martinez, ran my finger across his jaw and whispered, "Come on, Alexander. Let the kids take the nice car to the prom." His shoulders slumped. I had won. I gripped a set of keys hanging on a peg board and flung them at Horndog. "Be good to her."

He caught the keys and then he and Martinez climbed in as if the car were a real woman. They slid onto her seats with care, as though they didn't want her to feel violated. Then they sat there for a bit to let her get used to them being inside her. They stroked her interior to reassure the car that they wouldn't do anything she wouldn't like and she could say no at any moment. Only after they had gained her approval did they start they engine and the Bugatti roared to life.

"I'll bet they didn't even see the other cars." Shooter was annoyed but relaxed when I threw him a smile.

"I think we should take this one," I said, resting a hip on the hood of a satin black Aston Martin Vanquish. I mentioned that I like pretty things, right?

"That would make you stick out like a sore thumb. I was thinking of this." He pointed to a Mercedes-Benz CLS63 AMG. It wasn't as pretty as mine. "It's fast, handles well, and won't stand out."

"Yeah, because every other person in Bayou Boudreaux drives a hundred thousand dollar car."

"Well, I don't see a Honda in your collection so we're going with the Mercedes."

"We're going with the Mercedes," I said mimicking his no

nonsense tone.

He grabbed me by my arm. "I wish you'd take this seriously. Someone is trying to kill you."

The old Kat would have ripped her arm from his hold and crushed every bone in his thorax with a tire iron. But the new Kat looked into Shooter's eyes and saw concern, love, and desperation. "I am taking this seriously. I just deal with stress in a weird way. I am worried. I am aware of the risks, but I can't hide whenever someone wants me dead. I'd never see the sun." I straightened my shoulders. "And I won't die on my knees." I stroked his face.

He grabbed my hand and pressed it to his lips. I hope he sensed strength from me, not stupidity.

"Let's go see if Sam's ready."

We walked hand in hand back to the house without saying a word. We were both too focused on my impending assassination. As deaths went, it's a great way to go. Dying from a car accident or a lingering illness just lacked a level of commitment. How many people could say they died at the hands of an expert sniper or someone trained in the art of death? Well, I knew of fifty-three, but I was not the average Bayou Boudreaux citizen. The only better way to die would be if a tiger mauled me to death. Since there weren't many tigers stalking the swamps, an assassination it would have to be. I didn't express my opinions to Shooter. Something told me he wouldn't appreciate my views on an honorable death.

We climbed the front steps to find Amanda and Sam waiting in the foyer. My daughter looked perfect, thanks to Amanda, in a pair of dark denim shorts and a red-and-white plaid top.

"Shooter!" she ran to him and he picked her up and swung her onto his shoulders.

I loved to see the two of them together. They had a natural ease, as if they'd known each other forever. He carried her out of the house and into the garage. Shooter buckled my little girl into the back seat of the Mercedes, shut the door, checked his weapon, and climbed into the driver's seat. The rest of my Marines climbed into the Escalade and followed us to the carnival.

Twenty minutes later we pulled into the parking lot of the Boudreaux Family Park. Every public space in Bayou Boudreaux had been named after the family. The Boudreaux public swimming pool, the Boudreaux public gymnasium, the Boudreaux public cemetery. The lawn of the Boudreaux Family Park had been covered with carnival rides, games, and food stalls. The blinking lights from the attractions made everything look like Christmas, Halloween, Easter, Hanukkah, and Mardi Gras vomited all over the place. I grabbed Samantha's hand, hooked my arm around Shooter's elbow, and hitched my "Mrs. Boudreaux" look on my face. You know the look. The one that says, "I'm so happy to talk to every single person on the planet about their simple lives and simple problems. I am genuinely interested in your great Aunt Ethel's gout and your mother's leaky bowel. Please, tell me about every little thing that comes into your mind. I have nowhere else to be and nothing better to do." It's a complete lie, of course. But the town had been good to me, and I intended to be good to them even if it killed me.

"Ooh, Mama, I want to ride that one." Sam pointed at the Ferris Wheel.

Just as I was about to say yes, I was attacked by the oldest woman on the planet. Seriously, I think she was old enough to have bandaged wounded soldiers during the Civil War. A conversation with Mrs. Perry-Hatfield-Adcock-Colton-Snowdon-Riggs-Pierpont-Bartlett had always been an excruciating experience, and I didn't want to put Shooter or Sam through the torture. "Would you take Sam on the Ferris wheel for me?"

"I don't think that's a good idea," he said with a cautiously concerned voice.

I leaned over so only he could hear. "I'm fine. Tyler and Martinez are right behind me. Switch is over there next to the cotton candy vendor. Doc is hanging out by the merry-go-round, and Horndog is watching over me with a sniper rifle on the top of the Junior High across the street. I'm fine."

Shooter looked at me as if I had just discovered he was actually a woman. Apparently I wasn't supposed to know where my guards were stationed. Situational awareness was my middle name so he'd have to just deal with it. "And you can get the lay of the land from up there," I added, hoping to sweeten the pot.

"Don't we need tickets?"

"No, the carnival's free."

He nodded and said, "Come on, Sam-I-Am, it's you, me, and the Ferris wheel." She squealed with delight, and Shooter swung her up into his arms and headed for the giant wheel.

"It looks like you have a new beau," Mrs. Bartlett said with a tone of scandal in her voice.

How in the hell was I supposed to answer that? Was Shooter my new beau? I guess, if he planned to stay with me indefinitely. I just smiled. I didn't want to provide her with any information that might one day be told to a local reporter with an overlarge imagination. "And how are the Daughters of the Confederacy?" I asked. Mrs. Bartlett had been a little sore ever since the Confederacy failed.

"They're just fine, except Mrs. Hicks passed away last month. Had you heard?"

"Yes, I heard."

"How are all the plans for the Founder's Day dinner party?" She asked as if she waited for me to tell her the house burned down and a sinkhole had popped up in my yard.

"Wonderful. But you know as well as I do that I just provide the place. The committee does the planning." Being so saccharine sweet was about to send me into sugar shock.

"And are we going to be in period dress?"

And then I had to burst all her balloons. "No, I think this year the committee decided to go with black tie."

"Hmm, pity. Well, I suppose I'll be the only one proud of my Southern heritage." Translation, she'd be the only one hundred fifty-year-old Scarlett O'Hara. "You know, Nathan Boudreaux and I had a fling once upon a time."

Oh yes, I knew. She told me every time we exchanged more than two words.

"Of course that was before he'd married."

She always made that clarification. The Boudreaux men of the past had a bit of a rakish reputation. Mrs. Bartlett would be horrified if she knew I knew their affair had rekindled about ten years later while his wife lay in bed, pregnant with their only child. "Oh, there's Mr. Hicks. I must go say hi."

Naturally she must. He had recently been widowed, and Mrs. Bartlett was trying to set the world record for most marriages. She'd out lived seven husbands already.

I thought I had sidestepped the social mine field of the Bayou Boudreaux Founder's Day Carnival until I spotted the one town resident who'd love to see me dead. If I didn't know better, I'd swear the man walking toward me had issued my death warrant. He wasn't that tall, sort of skinny, and sported a patchy black goatee. His name was Buck Stokes. But he'd had his name changed when he lived in New York for about a month, to Michael Boudreaux. Yup, that's right, he changed his name to Michael Boudreaux. Apparently his ancestor had been the offspring of a Boudreaux and his mistress. When the Boudreaux died childless, the estate went to his brother. Buck felt he was the rightful owner of my house, my company, and my life. We didn't get along, so naturally he made it a point to sling horrible insults at me every chance he got.

It would be a duel, and I was not about to eat a bullet for the man. "Mr. Stokes, how have you been?" He hated it when people used his real name.

"I'm just fine, Miss Wallace. How are things at the Boudreaux house?" He asked the question as if I was an interloper on his property.

"We're all doing fine. And I haven't been a Wallace in years. You should know that." I smiled sweetly.

Just then Shooter decided to rejoin me with Samantha on

his shoulders.

"Oh, and is this the new man in your life? Will that mean you'll want to move out of the Boudreaux house?"

"Now why would I do that?"

"Well, the house is usually occupied by someone with Boudreaux blood."

"The house is occupied by a Boudreaux. You haven't forgotten Stephan's daughter, have you?" The sweet smile still graced my lips. But I hoped javelins would shoot from my eyeballs and skewer the asshole.

"Samantha's paternity has never been verified. Mine has. Until you validate that she is indeed a Boudreaux, this issue will always be on the table."

I was about to tell Buck to go to hell. I was about to smack him in the face for insulting me, my daughter, and my husband. I was about to pop his head off like a daisy, but I didn't get the chance. Shooter beat me to it.

He stuck out his long thick arm and wrapped his hand around Buck's scrawny little neck. "You will apologize to Mrs. Boudreaux and Miss Samantha. You will never again impugn their character in anyway. You will not even insinuate they are anything less than honorable. Am I clear?"

Shooter relaxed his grip just enough for Buck to answer with a very hoarse, "Yes."

"Run along. Go find someone you can complain to about how horribly you've been treated." Shooter gave Buck a little push that forced him to take several steps backward. I looked around and saw the rest of the Rat Bastards had closed ranks.

Shooter said to no one, "Stand down, Horndog."

Buck really should have given Shooter a big hug. Without him, Horndog would have lodged a hunk of .338 Lapua lead inside his skull. And that would have just ruined his whole damn day. Horndog had no way of knowing Buck was just being a huge pain in my ass. He only saw Shooter's reaction to the little prick and naturally viewed him as a threat. It's probably good that Shooter wouldn't allow him to shoot people just for pissing me off. We wouldn't be able to bury all the bodies.

We carried on through the carnival riding rides, eating popcorn and cotton candy, playing games, and I politely spoke to everyone who came up to me. It was torture. I had leaned down to wipe a spot of caramel off Samantha's face when the head of the giant pink frog I held exploded white polyester fluff all over the two of us. Shooter pulled me and Sam behind a snow cone cart and told us to stay down. Just as I covered Samantha with my body, I heard the unmistakable crack of a high powered rifle coming from the junior high.

"Are you sure?" Shooter asked through his bone conduction earpiece mic. "Where did the target go down? No, no I'll send her and Sam home. We need to keep the authorities off this for as long as possible. Meet me on top of the Piggly Wiggly." He turned to me, held the car keys out, and said, "Take Sam home."

Yeah, like that was going to happen. "No."

"Don't argue, Kat. Go home!"

"Hell no. Tyler can take Sam home. You need me. The police heard that shot and are, right now, looking for the shooter. This isn't New Orleans. This is the bayou. People hunt here. The sheriff and even his most inept deputy will be able to ascertain where that shot came from and where it stopped. You'll need me. I'm a Boudreaux. I can take care of them." The Rat Bastards had gathered around the snow cone cart, and I threw the keys to Tyler.

"Take Sam home, fast!"

He didn't argue. He just scooped her up and hauled ass to the car. Shooter huffed and took off toward the Piggly Wiggly across the park.

We climbed the access ladder on the back wall of the grocery store to the roof. "It's clear. Come on over." Horndog had beaten us. He stood over the body of my would-be assassin.

I charged the body. I wanted to kill him again. But not with a bullet. I wanted to start at his feet and skin him alive. If his shot had been three inches to the left, he would have hit Sam. For that, everyone he ever knew, his family, his friends, everyone he's ever worked with, anyone he'd ever bought a falafel from would all die slow, miserable, painful deaths. Horndog wrapped his arms around my waist stopping me as I ran at the body.

"I'm sorry, Hell Kat. If Shooter had been on the rifle, the bastard wouldn't have gotten a shot off."

I took several deep breaths to calm my anger. "You did just fine, Horndog. I'm glad he missed."

"He didn't miss."

I turned to look at Shooter. I was a bit surprised by his statement.

"Look at his gear. He's packing a military issue M40A5 that's been modified to allow a sound suppressor and Redfield 3-9x40 scope. A man with that kind of hardware usually knows how to use it. He didn't miss. He wanted to send a message."

"Could be a dime store cowboy," Switch offered.

"Could be, but I don't think so."

"Dime store cowboy?" I asked.

"He looks the part but has no real skill. I still say he was sent to deliver a message." The rest of the Rat Bastards all had looks on their faces like they doubted Shooter.

"Shooter's right," I said. "It's what I would've done. If I wanted to get inside someone's head, if I wanted to torture someone with the fear of death, I would have done that."

Switch bent down and rummaged through the sniper's pockets. He wouldn't find anything, and I'm sure he knew that. Snipers, assassins, and terrorists are trained to take absolutely nothing on a mission that would have any identifying information on it. And as suspected, he was empty. I pulled my cell phone from my pocket and dialed.

"Chief, this is Kat Boudreaux. There's a body on the roof of the Piggly Wiggly. Yes, it's as a result of the gunshot that you heard. I'll wait."

Shooter turned on me. "What are you doing? They'll arrest Horndog, and we'll be short a man." He turned to Horndog, "Dog, get out of here." His eyes flared with anger, "Have you lost your ever-loving mind?"

Yes, I've lost my mind and am putting the safety of my child at risk. I put a hand on my hip in a very Bette Davis kind of way and said, "No, Shooter I have not. Would you like the police to find a random body on the roof of the Piggly Wiggly, or would you rather they show up when I can tell them this man took a shot at a Boudreaux and Horndog saved my life."

He didn't speak. His lips pursed and his eyes narrowed to slits so small I'd be surprised if he could see the lamp from an oncoming freight train. He really didn't like that I had more power than he did in that situation.

I tried to smile and said, "They'll probably throw Horndog a parade and erect a statue of him on top of the junior high to commemorate his heroic shot."

Moments later we heard the police sirens. They climbed the ladder. The chief and his officers were taken aback and actually reached for their guns when they saw five huge men, one of whom held a rifle, and me standing around a dead body.

"What's going on, Miss Kat?" Chief Guthrie asked.

I told him about the shot and that Horndog and the rest of the Marines were all part of my personal security. When I added in the fact that the bullet had been three inches from my five-year-old daughter who had real live actual Boudreaux blood running through her veins, they completely relaxed.

The chief approached Horndog and stuck out his hand. "Thank you very much, son. We're all in your debt. If that bastard'd had a chance to take a second or third shot, we could have lost some real good people."

Horndog shook the chief's hand. "Uh, no problem. Glad I could be of service. Do you need me to make a statement or something?"

"Eventually, but for now, why don't you take Miss Kat home? Give her a big ole glass of brandy. I'm sure she's a bit shaken up." He hitched his thumbs inside his belt loops. If Boss Hogg had been likable, he and Chief Guthrie could be twins.

"Thank you, Chief," I said and gave him a hug. *What?* I

could be vulnerable, when it suited my mission. We climbed down the ladder and back to the cars. Tyler had taken Samantha back to the house in the Mercedes so most of us piled into the back of the Escalade. Horndog and Martinez took the Bugatti. Blowing a hole the size of a dinner plate through the back of some dude's head did not diminish their appreciation for old-fashioned heavy metal.

When we got home, I rushed up the stairs to Sam. Tyler stood guard outside her door.

"Everything okay?" he asked.

I nodded and pushed open the door. It had gotten dark by the time we got home, and Sam was in bed for the night. She sat up in bed while Amanda read to her. Amanda stopped and left the room. I picked up the book, snuggled in next to my daughter, and finished the story. Sam handed the photo album to me and we looked through it. I lay right next to her until she fell asleep. I couldn't help but think of a world without her. It would kill me, literally, to lose her. My heart would simply stop beating. Nothing, not my devotion to my staff, my responsibility to the Boudreaux family, or my new found brothers, would save me if Samantha died. For a brief moment I thought about locking her away in her room for the next twenty years or so. But that would just turn Sam into a Miss Havisham, and I didn't want that for her. No, I had to let her live her life. But tomorrow Switch would put GPS trackers in all her shoes and cameras and microphones in her clothes.

I brushed the hair from Sam's face as she slept and then dragged myself from her bed. A horrible feeling nagged at me. She would be leaving me soon. And not to go to boarding school. I knew something would happen that would rip her from my life forever. Of course that was probably my own irrational fear raising its ugly head, but I just couldn't shake it. I left her room surprised to find all the Rat Bastards in the hall. Shooter and Horndog leaned against a wall with their arms crossed over their chests, Doc and Martinez sat on the floor with their heads resting on their knees, Tyler and Switch paced the hall, Switch playing with his switch blade. When I stepped into the corridor, they all jumped to attention. Worry creased their brows and shone from their eyes. They probably thought I'd been afraid for my life, but it wasn't my life that had me worried.

Shooter put his hand on my shoulder. "How're you holding up?"

"I'm fine," I said and shrugged his hand from my shoulder. He followed as I walked down the hallway to my room. "You don't need to stay with me. I'll be fine." Where the hell had that come from? I needed him. But for some unknown reason I had to make him think I didn't.

He looked a bit rejected. "I need to stay with you. I don't care if you need me or not. I need you."

How could anyone be so comfortable with such vulnerability? But then again I had basically fallen apart in front of him and told him I couldn't sleep without him. So I guess vulnerability was all right between us. When I thought about it that way, I kind of felt as if we would always be okay with whatever the other person threw into the soup.

When we stepped into my room, I couldn't handle it. I crumpled like an old newspaper. I wasn't afraid of dying, I was afraid of losing Sam, of losing Shooter. He ran to me and carried me to the bed. He stripped my jeans and T-shirt off and tucked me in then climbed in next to me and gathered me up in his arms. He didn't speak. He didn't need to. He just held me and kissed the top of my head.

Chapter Seventeen

 T he next day would go down in the history books as one of the most neurotic days ever. It started with a meeting that involved the Rat Bastards and the head of my security team. I'd been neglectful of my standard security team. They'd kind of been shuttled to the back burner once the Bastards had arrived. I needed to make them feel appreciated. I needed them to be on their A game. They had been completely left out of the loop on my attempted assassination and security threat. It might seem stupid to not tell them about the threat, but I had my reasons for the black out. It had nothing to do with their competence. It had everything to do with who they knew in the security world. I had always been clear on their duties. Protect my staff. I could take care of myself. I needed them to continue doing their jobs. Jake had been offended. He knew something was up. It was his job to know shit like that. In truth, the only reason Jake had been permitted to sit in on the meeting was because my guests would have to pass through the front gate and him to get to the party. Knowledge of the guest list was necessary. As we went through the list name by name, most of the people were simply passed over as a non-threat. Few deserved comment. The first was Louise LaLourie. Shooter coughed into his hand shocked that Louise had been granted an invitation.

"She may be a bitch, but she's part of society and would make my life hell if I didn't at least extend an invitation."

"And why is Miss LaLourie a bitch?" Switch asked.

"Because she likes to make Kat feel like she's about two inches tall and she's the biggest *pro bono* whore on the planet."

Wow, I guess Shooter really didn't like Miss Louise.

"*Pro bono* whore?"

"She'll sleep with anything that lies still long enough but refuses any type of payment. You know, like charity work."

"Can I get her number?" Of course Horndog would see that as an admirable quality.

Moving on. The next name to merit comment was your friend and mine, Mr. Forrest Bonaventure. "Why is he coming?" Doc, who usually remained quite calm and controlled, was seriously pissed.

"Because I have to deal with him to keep Boudreaux Oil running, and it would be a slap in the face to not invite him."

"Let him come," Switch said. "We didn't have nearly enough fun with him the first time we met."

I almost ordered them to be nice to Mr. Bonaventure, until I thought better of it. I would pay pay-per-view prices to see Mr. Bonaventure made to feel like a fool in front of a bunch of uncouth Marines.

We went down the list, tripping over the names of the old guard and Admiral Beauregard. No name really earned anything more than an eye roll until Buck Stokes. Buck Stokes was another social concession. Surprisingly, my Marines didn't object to his attendance. The looks they shared held promises of payback. I was honestly bummed I'd miss it. The meeting came to an end with Jake feeling less and less part of my household, and the Rat Bastards absolutely delighted with the people on the list they were free to torment for an evening.

For the rest of the day I followed Sam around the house like a little lost dog, pulling Shooter along with me. The event people were there all day to set up for the party. Any other year, you could find me, ass in chair on the back porch with a scowl on my face and a drink in my hand, pissed at the annual intrusion into my life. But not that day. I was too busy looking for unseen snipers through my floor to ceiling windows to be bothered by the people stringing Chinese lanterns across my lawn. Terror gripped me so hard I freaked out whenever Sam or Shooter got too close to a window or walked into a room I hadn't cleared first. The thought that I could possibly lose one or both of them wouldn't leave me alone.

If I could have dragged them into the bathroom with me while I peed, I would have. But that screamed overkill. So I made them stand outside the door until I finished, talking loud enough for me to hear. I know you think I was a bit overprotective and maybe I was, but I've buried a lot of people and the cemetery is not the kind of place you want to spend your weekends, dammit. So yeah, I'd inconvenience as many people in my life as necessary to make sure I kept a couple of them alive. That was not me being dramatic. I came to the conclusion the night before that everyone around me was in mortal danger. That bullet may have been a warning and not intended for my head, but it had been far too close to Samantha. Apart from trapping her inside a bullet-proof box, I would do anything to keep her safe.

Even while I got ready for the party, I made sure Shooter and Sam were right next to me. They sat on the floor of my closet dressed in their party dress and tux while I let Yvette do my hair, Sissy do my makeup, and Edna and Ella dress me. I made them sit there while I tried on five different dresses, thirteen pairs of shoes, and ten different sets of jewels. I ended up choosing a red Valentino off the shoulder with a pair of black and white Alexander McQueen heels. Not those weird ones that look like deformed ballerina slippers—nice ones.

At seven, the three of us stepped out to the back yard. The scene took my breath away. Small tables draped in white cloth topped with hurricane lamps and surrounded by small bamboo chairs scattered the lawn. The only illumination was provided by dozens of Chinese lanterns strung above the tables. In the background a jazz band played *Summertime,* heavy on the clarinet. And all around the periphery were my Rat Bastards. All armed to the teeth with guns, knives, and a killer instinct. It was classic.

I had requested Shooter act as my personal escort and bodyguard to the party. None of the Rat Bastards were jealous. He had to stand next to me, smile politely, and act interested in all the goings on of a small Southern town. It was basically slow torture and violated the Geneva Conventions, but Shooter would hold up. As a Marine, the word *fail* wasn't in his vocabulary.

So we stood side by side in an impromptu receiving line as people paraded past us full of thanks for the invite. The Admiral greeted Shooter like an old friend, and Louise LaLourie tried to hit on him again. He shot her down instantly, which jacked my ego up to an unhealthy level. When Mr. Bonaventure showed up, he had a strange look of triumph on his face. What had he been up to? Had he found some obscure loophole in the company bylaws that would allow him to seize power of my company? Had he finally made enough allies on the board to undermine me? Or maybe there was a sale on those cheap blue ties he always wore? Whatever made him so happy would not bode well for Boudreaux Oil. Or Mr. Bonaventure. Really those ties were hideous.

As he passed by me with that smarmy look on his face, I looked forward to the next person in line. It had to be someone I liked more than Mr. Bonaventure. But no, the fates were not on my side. Right behind Bonaventure was Buck Stokes. If there was a lower circle of hell, I'd hate to see it. Buck had the same self-serving triumphant look on his face that Bonaventure had. Had Bonaventure been using Buck to gain control? Of course he had. Because single celled slimy organisms tended to band together. Those sons of bitches! They were messing with the wrong damn ex-assassin. *They think their lives suck now, they have no idea what suck means. I'd like to see them pull off that cocky attitude when I rip their lips off their faces.* It wasn't just a matter of ownership or personal pride. They were taking choices away from Samantha. I would not stand for that. I wouldn't unleash the more physical talents I possess, but I would definitely start a mind war that would make them want to hide in their panic rooms till the apocalypse was over.

The rest of the evening was spent with me outwardly playing nice Southern hostess while inwardly plotting the mental breakdown of Buck and Forrest. Finally, the receiving line broke up and I could mix and mingle with the party goers. The night just kept getting better and better. Shooter and I collapsed on a pair of golden bamboo chairs that, gratefully, were stronger than they appeared. I picked at the plate of *etouffee*, jambalaya, okra, cornbread, and crawfish. I hadn't had much of an appetite all day and it appeared Shooter didn't either. I think we both feared deep down that all the horrible things we had been anticipating would come to a head over the course of the evening.

"I could really go for a freaking steak." Shooter and I both laughed at his statement. "Seriously, do you all have something against red meat? We've eaten nothing but fish since I got here."

He scooted his chair closer to mine and wrapped his arms around me in a protective embrace. I sighed and let myself hang on him. We waited for the bomb to drop, and the longer it took the more it fried our nerves. Sam ran up to me, holding a teddy bear someone had given her. I assumed it came from one of the society matrons. But when I asked who gave it to her she said it was a gift from one of the waiters. The hair on the back of my neck rose and I looked at the wait staff a bit more critically. "Show me which one gave it to you honey."

She looked around but couldn't find him. Just then Shooter gave orders to thin air.

"Stay there. I'm on my way." He took Sam's bear and turned to me. "Take Samantha and go inside." The look in Shooter's eyes sent ripples of terror through my body

I didn't argue. I grabbed my daughter and carried her into

the kitchen. Amanda and Edna sat at the counter chatting over a cup of coffee. They knew something was up the moment I stepped inside house. A look of horror crossed their faces and as I turned to look behind me, my lights went out.

Someone slapped my face. Why the hell was someone slapping me? My instincts took over and my eyes shot open. I sat up knocking the hand away from my face. I was on. I turned to see what the threat had been, because something told me I was under attack. I jumped to my feet but hadn't anticipated the four-inch heels or the tight red dress and nearly fell on my butt. Why was I wearing such ridiculous clothing? My life was on the line. Who the hell dressed me? I should be in sensible black cargos, an Under Armor top, and a pair of combat boots.

I whirled around to see six men and two women. I knew these people, didn't I? Yes, I did. They worked for me. No, only two of them worked for me, the men were my friends. But why would they have knocked me out? The two women, Amanda and Edna, yes that was their names, they held ice packs to the backs of their heads. A pulsing pain radiated from my skull.

I looked at the men. Yes, they were friends. Two of them were more than friends. One was my brother and the other was my...my, well he was just more than a friend. In a rush all of their names came to me. I remembered the past several hours and then the last several days, weeks, and months. Someone wanted to kill me. *Where's Sam? I brought her in here with me.* "Where is she?" I said out loud.

Shooter, the one that's more than my friend, spoke. "We can't find her. Switch is checking the cameras now."

"I've got her," Switch said looking down at a computer.

"Good. Follow her from that point until she went missing." Shooter handed out orders and Switch obeyed.

I peered over Switch's shoulder watching my little girl on the screen. A man in a waiter's uniform handed her something. A teddy bear. Why had he brought a teddy bear? He was supposed to serve drinks and canapés. The camera followed Samantha across the lawn and to me. I could see the stress and tension on my face. Had Sam seen the same thing? Shooter sat up, obviously alarmed. He ran off, and I took Sam inside. Then the picture turned to snow.

"Where'd the picture go? Get it back." I was frantic, and I didn't care who knew.

"Something is jamming the signal. These are wireless cameras, and a radio frequency jammer could block their signal."

No, no! Switch had to know something. He had to know some magic phrase he could type into the laptop to clear the snow storm on the screen, but he just looked at Shooter as if there was nothing more he could do.

"Where were you going?" I said, unable to hide the panic in my voice.

"What?" They all asked in unison.

"Where were you going, Shooter? When you left us at the table and told us to go inside, where were you going?" I spoke rapidly, my speech fueled by fear. All the training in the world couldn't keep my fear at bay. My little girl had disappeared, and I wanted her back!

"Martinez had found a pile of unconscious bodies on the side of the house. They turned out to be the real catering staff. The ones that worked the party had been imposters."

Dammit! If I had been in my usual spot on the back porch, I could have identified them as fakes, I could have stopped it before it started. I was so busy protecting Sam I failed to see the threat in front of my face. *Dammit!*

"Go back. Go back to the part where that person gave Sam the bear. Follow him back. I want to know everyone he talked to." Switch started to play the recording in reverse. I watched the false waiter carry a tray around offering people flutes of champagne and *amuse bouche*. I watched him talk to the other men who posed as waiters, and I watched as he ducked behind a catering van. He spoke to someone. "Can we see who else is behind that van?"

"No, it's blocking the view."

Damn!

"Stay on the van to see if you can see who went behind it before our waiter did."

As I watched the film, I couldn't believe who walked out from behind that catering van. His life was over. I ran from the kitchen. I knew exactly where to find that son of a bitch. He was dead. He was going to die a slow miserable death. I stomped up to the bar and leaned against it. My target sat right next to me, nursing a whiskey sour.

"Hi, Buck."

He nearly jumped off his stool, his face paling. "Uh, hi, Kat." He clearly thought he wouldn't see me again.

"I was wondering, have you seen my daughter?"

His face blanched and he shook his head.

I knew it. Deep down, Buck Stokes was nothing but a coward. "Would you mind helping me look for her?" He really had no choice. My Marines had formed a half circle around him blocking any escape. "Of course you wouldn't because you're such a good guy."

Shooter leaned down so no one but Buck and the Bastards could hear him. "I suggest you get your ass off that stool and do as the lady asked. Unless you'd like me drag you away by that pathetic display of chin pubes you're sporting."

Buck shook with terror. Without taking his eyes off Shooter, he stood, and we herded him into the house.

We made our way into the kitchen through the side door. My Marines thought I'd stop there but they didn't know anything about the lower levels of the house. Buck seemed to have forgotten Shooter's threat and hesitated in the middle of the black-and-white checkered floor. Before Shooter had the chance, I grabbed Buck by his ratty goatee and dragged the son of a bitch down the basement stairs, through the gym and stopped at what appeared to be a blank wall. The room behind the wall hadn't been changed since the house had been built. Three walls made with old handmade red bricks covered in lichen created a small alcove. I hated the place, but at that moment I couldn't have been more grateful for it. I threw Buck into the room, and he fell on his ass. I closed him inside the room and turned to face my fellow Rat Bastards.

"What I am about to do will be like nothing you have ever seen before. If you want to be present, you have to do as I say. You have to remain quiet. You cannot intercede on his behalf. He cannot think he has an ally in there. Doc, this will be hardest for you. If you," I looked at all of them, "or any of you feel like you can't handle this, you are welcome to stay out."

"We're with you, Hell Kat," Horndog said solemnly.

"All the way," Switch added.

I nodded and, as I had so many time before, turned off the human side of my nature. My face and expression must have physically changed because the Bastards took a step away from me. I didn't blame them. Anyone with a survival instinct would have done the same thing. But they followed me back into the room, and I closed the wall.

The moment the opening disappeared, Switch went ape shit. He picked Buck up and threw him into the far wall. Everyone in the room heard his skull crack against the brick. He slumped on the floor.

Switch stalked toward him with his signature blade in his hand. "You've endangered the life of a child. I will enjoy gutting you." The tone in his voice was deadly serious. I needed Buck alive.

"Switch." He didn't respond. "Switch!" Still no response. The blade hovered over Buck's abdomen. I placed a hand on my deadly friend's shoulder and, in the calmest voice possible, said, "Switch, we need him alive. We need to find Samantha."

He snapped out of his blood rage and nodded.

"Put him in the chair."

Switch lifted Buck up by the neck and threw him into the simple, antique wooden chair in the middle of the room. I filled a bucket with cold water from a spigot sticking out of the brick wall and threw it on him. The icy water pulled him out of his daze.

"You may not recognize this room, Buck. I don't usually include it in the tour. Allow me to enlighten you. This is the South, and this is an old house. This room was once used to punish unruly slaves. I found it when I needed a place to hide my toys. I don't like to share, you see, so I wanted to keep them hidden. This turned out to be the perfect place."

The piquant smell of terror filled the room. It was similar to the smell of roasting pork, and I loved that he feared me.

I turned to the side and removed several bricks from the wall. Behind the brickwork I had hidden the tools of my trade. These weren't the high-tech weapons of an assassin. No, these were the very low-tech implements of torture. I was about to cross a line. If I started in on Buck, I would have to finish. I couldn't have him running to the police. A thrill crept into my belly. I was good at interrogation, and an old, familiar warmth flooded me with calm. I took the bucket I'd used to wake Buck up and placed it on the ground upside down in front of my target. I laid my toys on it, taking my time to make sure he had a chance to look at all the things that would be used on him.

"Strip him bare."

My Marines hesitated for the slightest of moments but followed my command. I reached for a set of chains bolted into the brickwork and used them to secure the chair to the wall. When Buck was naked, I pointed to it, and Switch and Tyler pushed him down into the seat. I handcuffed his arms and legs to the chair. He didn't really bother to struggle. Maybe he had a psychotic death wish. I didn't care. Before our time ended Buck Stokes would beg for death. I was more than happy to grant that request. I gathered my tools and placed them back on the shelf the missing bricks had created. I turned the coal bucket over and filled it again with ice cold water.

"I'm going to give you one chance, Buck. Where is my daughter?"

"I have no idea what you're talking about." He tried to hide the terror in his voice. Men like Buck could never disguise the pitch or tremble. They were cowards, and cowards wore their shame like a flashing neon light.

"Wrong answer." I covered his head with a black hood. Black hoods came in every interrogation starter kit. "Hold his head."

Switch grabbed the hood and wrenched Buck's head back. I poured the bucket of ice cold water over his face. It wasn't water boarding, but it was a close second. "Where's my daughter?" I didn't give him time to catch his breath or answer, I just kept pouring the water over his nose and mouth.

When the bucket ran dry, I pulled the hood off his face. He gasped for air. Before he caught his breath and before I asked another question, I picked up a thick leather strap and whipped him across the face so hard it left a mean slash across his cheek. Buck didn't scream. He didn't have the breath to scream. Tears ran down his cheeks. Tears that had no effect on me. Before I was done with him, he'd shed more than tears.

Some people think physical torture doesn't work, that someone would say anything to stop the pain. But in my experience, if you made the subject think you had absolutely no problem killing them over a period of several days, they tended to say the first thing that came into their head, and that first thing was usually the truth.

"You see, Buck, we have you on video talking to my daughter's abductor. Would you care to revise your statement?"

He jutted his chin out in denial. *Is he serious?*

"Oh, maybe you can't talk because of all the facial pubes in your mouth." I pulled small blade from my bag of toys and gripped his goatee between my fingers. With the knife I sliced off his goatee and a healthy chunk of skin along with it. He screamed like a spoiled-rotten little girl as blood beaded and trickled down his chin.

"Would you like to answer my question now, Mr. Stokes?"

His lip quivered but he refused to speak. Did he honestly think it couldn't get any worse?

"Perhaps you didn't hear me. Maybe I need to get closer to your ear." I reached to my pile of tricks and grabbed a hooked blade. For a fraction of a second, not long enough for anyone to notice, I hesitated. In the past I would have cut off Buck's ear and made him eat it. But something inside me that was completely new and foreign made me second think what I was about to do. Had it really been that long since I'd convinced someone to talk? Was it because I'd vowed to leave that life behind? Was it because I'd become a mother? Or was it Shooter? It didn't really matter. The only thing that mattered was getting Samantha back. I could only do that if Buck believed I was willing to torture him to death. I turned with the blade in my hand, "Maybe you can't hear me. Maybe you need someone to clear your aural cavity. I drew the knife around his ear just enough to draw blood but not so much that he would need to have his ear stitched back to his head if he survived. "Can you hear me now! Where is Samantha?"

Buck swayed on his seat. He was about to pass out. No, he did not get the luxury of losing consciousness. I threw the bucket at Horndog who filled it with ice water. Just as Buck was about to feel the sweet release of all natural anesthesia, I doused him with frigid water. He came back around, gasping for air. "The pain doesn't end until I end it, Buck."

Shooter swayed in his spot. I could tell that he wanted me to stop. He knew what I was capable of. Most normal, healthy people just hope they never have to actually witness it. It took a special kind of constitution to inflict torture, and Shooter just didn't have it. With blood running down the side of his head, Buck shook in his chair.

"You still aren't ready to tell me where my daughter is? You have to be the stupidest man on the planet." I picked up what looked like an iron fireplace poker. I lit a hand held torch and heated the end until it glowed bright orange in the dim room.

I looked to Switch. "Hold his head."

Fear, white hot, sprang to Buck's eyes as I approached him with the poker. I held it as close to his skin as I could without actually touching him. He felt the heat radiate from the poker and I could see his skin turn red. He tried to move, tried to scream, but Switch clamped his jaw shut with his hands. The best Buck could do was an impotent little groan. I could tell Doc hated my tactics. He kept his gaze on the ground and his hands in his pockets. Horndog and Martinez were also more than uncomfortable with the ease to which I applied my torture. But, thankfully, they didn't show it to my victim. It would have ruined any hope of getting any information from him if he thought someone in the room was on his side. Switch and Tyler seemed to have absolutely no problem with my methods.

As I pulled the poker away from Buck's face, I could see his resolve begin to crumble. I thought the man didn't have the constitution to withstand the pain of a paper cut, let alone the agony of what I could do. But he'd held up fairly well. I'd had warlords crumble much sooner.

"You know, Buck, torture hasn't really changed since the Middle Ages. There are only so many ways you can inflict pain on a human body. Take this devise for instance." I held up the poker I had just held near his face. "I made this beauty based on a very old, very common method of torture. It's used to burn the skin, but it also has a much more invasive purpose. The technician—I like to call them technicians. It's much more politically correct than torturer—would heat the tip 'til it glowed white. Then he would ram it up the convict's rectum, tearing and burning the entire way up his colon." I smiled a sadistic grin as terror crossed Buck's face. I threw the keys to Switch and lit my torch. "Unlock him."

Switch smiled, seemingly happy that I was about to sodomize a man with an iron shaft twice as big as his thumb. I didn't really care if he approved or not. Let me make myself perfectly clear. There was nothing I wouldn't do to someone who knew where my daughter was. Nothing. Switch bent down to unshackle Buck, and that's all it took. Buck folded.

"She's here. They never took her from the property. She's here in the house. There's a secret room in the wall of the music room. She's in there."

"Why did they take her?"

"A guy from Iran or somewhere around there wanted to get at you because you killed his brother. He wanted to kill someone you love. He said he wanted you to feel the pain he feels every day." He spoke so quickly, as if he thought speed would save him. It wouldn't. From the moment Shooter had told me someone from my past was after me, I knew I would have to face the brother of the only innocent man I'd ever killed. A twinge of guilt flexed in my stomach. I had enough human emotions to have sympathy for his loss, but not enough to give a rat's ass. He planned on killing my daughter. Any hope he ever had of surviving flew out the window on an F-22.

"What do you have to do with this?"

"He approached Bonaventure for information on you. Bonaventure wants the company, and he knew without a Boudreaux heir he'd be in a prime position to take over. He needed information on the layout of the house. He asked me if I knew my way around. My family has a set of plans that include several hidden rooms so I gave it to him."

"You knew they planned to kill Samantha, didn't you? You hoped you would get the house after her death. You know the house and the company don't belong to me. You know they were left to Samantha. You son of a bitch." I took a moment to contain myself. "Is she still alive?"

"She'll be alive until the Middle Eastern guy gets here. He wanted to do it himself." He had started to feel comfortable as if he might actually survive his trip to Tortureville. A good interrogator would make his victim honestly believe he had a chance. I was an excellent interrogator.

"How is he getting into the house?" I asked with a slightly kinder tone to my voice.

"There's a hidden tunnel with an entrance outside the property."

I knew of the tunnel but had never considered it a threat until now. That had been a huge tactical error on my part. "Where's Bonaventure?"

"With your daughter."

"Unhook him," I ordered. " And wrap him in a blanket. I don't need someone to catch a glimpse of him in all his naked glory."

"Wait! Wait! I told you what you needed. You're going to let me go, aren't you?"

"When did we make that arrangement?" I left the room to get a blanket from a cupboard in the gym. Buck couldn't stay behind. He'd come with us to the secret room, and he'd die right along with the other two.

We left the room, crossed the gym, and walked up the stairs, then climbed the back staircase and into a closet. It looked like a simple linen closet, until you pulled the pile of sheets away from the wall to reveal a safe. I pressed my thumb on the print scanner. Inside were two Sig Sauer P-220.45 caliber handguns. I had taken these two guns on every op I'd ever been on. It felt kind of poetic to use them to save my daughter, kill Bonaventure, and kill the Iranian asshole that started the whole mess. I trekked down the rest of the hall and into the music room. As we crossed the cavernous room, the Rat Bastards pulled out their side arms ready to take down anything or anyone that might cross their path. We faced a blank corner. I turned a wall sconce and a panel slid out of the way to reveal a short, straight hallway.

Chapter Eighteen

"One word, one single solitary sound comes from your mouth, and I'll rip your voice box out of your throat with my bare hands. You got it?"

Buck had learned to trust me.

"Put a muzzle on him just to be sure," I said to Switch, and he took off his bow tie and gagged Buck with it. I raised my guns and stepped into the hall. The room we were about to enter could be barred from the inside. It was basically a late nineteenth-century panic room. I only hoped Bonaventure didn't know that.

Fear flooded me as we reached the door. How would I find Samantha? Would she be healthy and whole or would she be bloody and broken? Would she be terrified? Did she think she was playing a fun game with her Uncle Forrest or did she know the man wanted to kill her? Would I need to put her in therapy afterward or would she bounce back with no problem? Was she conscious? Had he hit her over the head or drugged her? All these questions made my blood boil and nothing would be able to stop me from tearing that door off its hinges to get to her.

I lifted my Alexander McQueen-clad foot and kicked the door in. Bonaventure froze, stunned into paralysis. Samantha sat on a chair, safe and whole. I leveled one of my guns on

Bonaventure.

"Come to Mommy, Sam." She ran to me. I hugged her quickly and shuffled her off to Tyler. "Take her out of here." He picked her up and carried her out of the hidden hall into the music room. I never once took my eye or gun off Bonaventure. "Buck, get up here."

Buck was shoved to the front of the line until I could reach him. I grabbed him by his dirty blond hair and threw him on the ground in front of Bonaventure. The next part of my impromptu plan was a bit more difficult to pull off. These men had to die, but I couldn't implicate my brothers.

I backed toward the door of the room. The Rat Bastards behind me backed away as I did. Switch was right behind me. I needed Switch behind me. If it had been Shooter or anyone else, I'd never get away with what I was about to do. I sent him a look that told him what I had planned. He nodded so slightly that none of my other Marines saw. When they were out of the room and I still in, I grabbed the heavy wooden door and slammed it shut.

I heard Shooter yell, "No!"

But that was all I heard from him. The second the door closed I stepped on the hidden security wedge embedded in the floor. It popped up into place, effectively locking the door. Low-tech but better than a Rottweiler when it came to keeping people out of the room. There was only one other way to get into this room. It was the only way for the sheik to enter my house without having to pass through security. Buck was the only other person on the planet who knew of that entrance and I knew he would have told the sheik.

As I turned to face Buck and Bonaventure, Bonaventure had the bright idea to try to charge me. For his efforts I awarded him with a.45 caliber slug into each of his kneecaps. His dreams of one day walking through a shaded park in his old age had pretty much been blown to hell. The only effect his screams had on me was a warm, fulfilled feeling. Not every Boudreaux had been as honorable as Stephan. Some of them were downright scary. The room had been soundproofed decades ago because the wife of a Boudreaux liked to inflict pain on her servants, a lot. What I was about to do was right and just, and nothing could sway me from my course.

I watched Bonaventure writhe on the floor and a vindictive smile stretched across my face. "I have fourteen more shots in these two wonderful pieces of technology. Now, I'll need to save three, one for each of you and one for the brains behind all this. So that leaves eleven for me to use to keep the two of you in line. I really don't want to leave this room with any ammunition so please, try to take me down again. Your deaths are a foregone conclusion, but I wouldn't mind passing the time turning each of you into a sieve. I do have a couple questions, and talking would be a very wise decision. It could mean the difference between a bullet to the back of the head and a horrible, painful gut wound that'll let you hang on long enough so you can watch yourself bleed out on the floor. So, question one. What made you think the two of you could get away with this?"

I waited several seconds but neither spoke. I zeroed both guns on Bonaventure and his self-preservation kicked in. He gasped and wheezed through the pain in his knees but was able to answer, "It is absolutely ridiculous that Stephan left you in charge of Boudreaux Oil. It's a major international company. You have no idea what it takes to run it. I was supposed to take over the company. It was supposed to be mine, and you and that girl of yours ruined that for me. I won't allow you or that little bitch of a child...."

He wasn't able to finish his sentence, what with the bullet in his shoulder and all. Bonaventure surprised me. He could hold his pain. He grunted when the bullet ripped through his arm, but he didn't scream. Not like Buck had.

His blood splattered onto my face. Just gross. I didn't want any of it to run into my mouth so I ripped the ugly blue tie off his neck and used it to wipe the blood away. "Bonaventure, you really do need to learn some respect. Disrespect will only cause pain." Before I had the chance to ask any more questions I heard heavy footsteps coming up the other passageway. "Could that be our fourth? Wonderful, now we have enough to play bridge!" I waited for the door in the side wall to open just a crack. Before the man on the other side of the door had the chance to register that the woman who had killed his brother stood in front of him in a red evening gown, I grabbed him by the collar and pulled him into the room, throwing him on the floor. He reached for a weapon hidden in his jacket. My reflexes kicked in and I squeezed the trigger in my right hand. A lead slug slammed into his shoulder. He didn't draw down on me. He dropped his gun on the floor. Didn't people know how dangerous it was to lose your weapon? I kicked his gun out of the way.

"I hear you've been looking for me. Did you really think you could take me on and win? Were you seriously that arrogant?"

"You killed my brother," he spat.

"Yes, I did. And he's the one and only kill I've ever regretted. I didn't know he was being killed for financial gain. If I could, I'd take it back. But I can't, and I have to live with that."

He probably thought I'd killed his brother without any thought. His eyes softened for the briefest of moments then went as cold as steel. "It doesn't matter, you still have to be punished. You have tortured my entire family. You must die, and then your daughter will die." He spoke with such hate and anger.

I understood where he was coming from. I couldn't deny that my actions had hurt a lot of faceless victims, but shit, my targets had been the ones trying to commit genocide, most of the time. I would never apologize for my actions. I was good at my job, and I used the sickle of death to maintain peace. I wasn't sorry for anything, except the sheikh.

It totally sucked that I had to kill another member of his family. But all I had to do to remedy that was think about how this man had tried to kill my daughter and I was good to go. The three men cowering on the floor of the hidden room of my house had to realize they would die here. Did they wonder what would happen to their bodies? Were they trying to think of a valid argument to save their lives? Did they think they could take me down and escape? My answer to all those would be the same. I didn't care. Their bodies could rot in that room. I didn't care if their plea for leniency would have swayed the devil, it wouldn't save them. If they tried to attack me, they wouldn't win. I wasn't afraid of my staff or the police finding the remains. It wasn't my first rodeo, and I knew people who specialized in disposing of bodies so I wouldn't have to live with that flesh-rotting-in-the-walls smell.

It was time to bring our lovely little get-together to an end. I wasn't like one of those cartoon super heroes who dished out long, drawn out speeches allowing the hero's sidekick to fly in and save the day. I didn't like to give my targets time to think. I was more humane than that. No one wanted to have to think about their death for a long period of time. Three bullets remained in the gun in my right hand. It was enough. I brought my gun up and zeroed in on Buck. He collapsed as the bullet ripped through his skull. Bonaventure didn't even have time to realize Buck had been shot before a bullet slammed into the back of his head. The last to die was the sheikh's brother. I hesitated for a fraction of a second then fired. The bullet exploded through the side of his head, and he was dead. When the sound from the shots stopped echoing off the walls, the room went silent. It was the most penetrating sound I'd ever heard. It felt as if it would seep into my brain, and I'd never hear another thing for the rest of my life.

I left the bodies behind. I closed the door and walked down the short hall into the music room. I passed a gilded mirror that hung on the wall and caught my reflection. I hadn't seen that woman in a long time. I foolishly thought she'd never appear again. She was hard and unforgiving. And she was splattered with blood. I had planned on running straight up to Samantha's room and covering her with kisses. But that would have to wait. I needed to shower and change. No one wanted their five-year-old princess to see them looking as if they'd just won a fight against Freddy Krueger. So I crossed to the other side of the music room and opened another hidden door that led to my room.

When I reached my destination, I was almost afraid to open the door. I knew Shooter would be waiting. I was positive he hadn't approved of my methods against the men who'd kidnapped Samantha. My stomach got an uneasy feeling, like I'd eaten something bad. It was guilt. I thought I wouldn't feel anything for killing those three men. And I didn't feel remorse for the murders. It was because I'd involved Shooter. I should never have let him see that side of me. I'd never cared what people thought of what I did. Why should I start? I would do anything to preserve those I loved, and Shooter fell into that category so he should be grateful. How many other women did he know who would kill to keep him safe?

I opened the door and prepared myself for the tirade that was certain to follow. I waited inside the wall for something, anything. I wasn't sure if a crystal vase would fly across the room or if a stream of "how could you" and "what were you thinking" would fly from Shooter's mouth. But there was nothing. I took a tentative step out of the passage. With one foot on my carpet and the other inside the hidden hallway, I expected Shooter to appear with a glare in his eye. But he didn't. I put my other foot down on my carpet and still no reaction from him. I stepped away from the hidden door and closed it behind me. I looked around a little annoyed. I couldn't see him anywhere. He was supposed to be there to tell me how pissed he was that I tortured one man and killed three. He was supposed to tell me how horrified he was by my actions. He was supposed to be there, dammit!

But he wasn't. I looked in my office, in the sitting area, in my closet, and in my bathroom. He wasn't there. An inkling of fear crept into my stomach. *He's probably with Sam.* All the Rat Bastards were probably camped on the end of her bed. Of course they were. She'd just been kidnapped. Of course they'd be with her. I rushed to the bathroom and stripped the Valentino gown from my body letting it fall to the ground. I stepped into the shower to rinse the blood and sweat off of me. Ninety seconds in the shower was all I needed. I got dressed and ran down the hall to Sam's room. As I burst through the door and ran to my daughter, relief rushed through me. She was surrounded by the Rat Bastards.

I threw myself on her.

"What's wrong, Mom? You won. You found me. You won."

"Won what, honey?" I said choking back tears.

"The game, the game of hide and seek. Aren't you happy you won?"

"Yes, baby, I'm very happy I won."

I pulled away from her and turned to look at my Marines. I looked around and took a mental roll call. One was missing—Shooter. Where could he be? I went passed slightly annoyed to moderately pissed. He should have been there to make sure Sam was okay. Maybe he was out dealing with the fake waiters? Yes, that must have been it. He was out cracking the skulls of all the serving imposters. He was taking out all his frustration on those penguin-suited liars. I smiled to myself and all my fears were forgotten. It was nice to know he could appreciate the feel of flesh against his fist. Very few people could.

The Rat Bastards didn't say anything. They didn't even look at me. They had been traumatized by my actions. They'd seen some pretty scary shit, but my actions rendered them speechless. In a sick way, I was damn proud of myself. I watched them leave in silence.

I sat beside Sam until she fell asleep. Then I settled in a chair next to her bed until I drifted off. I was pulled from my sleep by a nightmare involving battery acid, Edna, and burned out eye sockets. It had been quite some time since I'd had a bad dream, and right away I knew it was because Shooter wasn't with me. I checked on Sam then left to find him. He should have shown up. I looked in my room but he wasn't there. I took the stairs to the second floor. He wasn't in his room. I searched the bathroom and his closet. His stuff had been moved to my room a few days ago, but it still cut to see it empty. As I was about to leave, I saw an envelope on the top of the nightstand. As I got closer to it, I felt my stomach fall out. I knew that envelope held very, very bad news. No one has ever received good news from an anonymous note left in a vacant room.

I walked over to the table as if I were walking down the Green Mile on my way to the electric chair. I looked over and expected to see John Coffey holding a mouse he magically brought back to life with his golden breath. When I got to the nightstand, I stared at the plain white envelope. I tried to tell my hand to reach out and pick it up but my arm just wouldn't get the message. I kicked my hip out, throwing my arm forward and I grabbed the paper. I sat down on the bed, gathered all my courage, and slid my finger under the seal. As I pulled the letter out, I pleaded with the Lord that the paper would just be a really super-secret grocery list. But my faith wasn't strong enough to truly believe. I opened the tri-folded paper and started to read.

Dear Kat,

I am truly sorry that I don't have the guts to speak to you face to face. I thought I would be able to, but when it came down to it, I found I am much more afraid of your reaction than I thought I'd be. Kat, I knew about your past and I had completely forgiven you for it. I forgave you the second you told me. But I thought that life was over. I never thought it would make an appearance in your present.

I never thought I would be so affected by an act of violence. But I am. I felt every blow Buck suffered. And I saw you change from the beautiful, strong, confident woman I know and love to a cold, ruthless killer. I knew that side of you existed, but I wasn't prepared to see it. Please understand that those men deserved everything they got for taking Samantha. I just didn't want you to have to be the one to hand it out.

I am the biggest hypocrite in the world. I have killed from a distance, I have killed up close, and I have forced people to give me information. I should not be as affected by your actions as I am. I should be able to handle seeing you do what you did. But the fact is, I can't. I can't look at you and not see the tools of your trade. I can't hold you without feeling the pain you delivered. I can't live with you and not see you putting a bullet into someone's head every time you walk into the room.

I will always love you, Kat. I will never get over you. The time we spent together will be a treasured memory. I wish I could just get over myself. I wish I could burn the last hour out of my brain. I wish I could change the way I feel. But I can't.

I love you forever,

Alexander Archer

Shooter's letter fell to the ground. He had left me. He had really left me. My actions caused him to run from me. *I am a horrible person. I am the most pathetic excuse for a human being on the planet.* I didn't think I could feel worse than I did when I came back from being conked on the back of the head to find Sam gone. But somewhere, deep inside, I knew I could get her back. I knew I wouldn't stop until I she was found. And I knew Shooter would be by my side. I knew he would be there to help me through everything. But this, this was something unfixable, and I was all alone. Again.

Chapter Nineteen

*F*or the next two months I pouted and moped and made life miserable for everyone in my house. It wasn't on purpose. I didn't spend my mornings devising ways to make everyone hate me. Everyone knew I had been hurt and tried to shoulder that pain for me. Though I loved them for it, it was totally unnecessary. I couldn't hand that pain off. It was all mine. Lucky freaking me.

The emotions were completely indescribable. You see, I'd never been left before. I had always been the one doing the leaving. My usual relationships went like this. Boy meets girl. Boy likes girl. Girl sees advantage in coupling with boy. Boy takes girl out. Girl exploits boy. Girl leaves boy. Until Stephan I'd never actually allowed myself to like anyone. They had all been strategic decisions made to further my own agenda.

With Shooter, I had given myself to him mind, body, and soul. I had trusted him with my emotions, my insecurities, and my love. And he threw it away. I didn't blame him for tossing all that I'd given to him into the trash. I'd pretty much left him no choice. Who wants to be with a woman who has the moral flexibility to cut your favorite appendage off and stuff it down your throat with no emotion whatsoever? Okay, I'd never actually done that, but I could if I had to. *I am a horrible person, that's all there is to it. I am worse than Saddam Hussein. I'm worse than that sadistic guy in all the Saw movies. I'm worse than the angel of darkness himself. No wonder Shooter abandoned me.*

Losing Shooter hurt so much worse than when Stephan died. When Stephan died, he didn't want to leave. I knew he would have come back, we would have made up, and we would have had a wonderful Christmas. But Shooter ran because he chose to pack his stuff, call a cab, and walk out the front door. He decided he'd be happier alone than with me. And that cut to the bone. I didn't think it could be possible to hurt more than I did when Stephan died. I hadn't considered the excruciating agony of being dropped by choice.

Of course I wasn't alone, alone. I had Samantha, my staff, and some of the Rat Bastards had stayed. Tyler and Martinez had been recalled to Afghanistan three weeks after Shooter left. But Doc, Switch, and Horndog were in the same position Shooter had been in. They'd served their time and were no longer in the Marine Corps. I'd made the mistake once of saying they were no longer Marines. Apparently you are never an ex-Marine. I had invited them to stay with me for as long as they wanted, and they had accepted. It was nice to have them around. We fell into an easy relationship. No pressure, no expectations, no strings. We ate together and lived together. We never talked about Shooter, and we never talked about the night I'd killed three people in my house. The bodies would never be found.

After I'd pulled myself together enough to walk out of Shooter's room that horrible night without melting into a pile of tears and self-loathing, I went back to the hidden room in the wall of the music room. I didn't want to ask any of my Marines for help, but I couldn't dispose of the bodies on my own. So I broke a sacred vow I'd made to myself ten years earlier. I called GSA. They had cleaning crews that took care of situations like that. I called the CEO and owner of GSA, Collin Watkins, at his home in South Carolina. I told him the situation and what I needed. He thought I needed a favor. The smug bastard actually thought I would owe him if he took care of things for me. When I told him I wouldn't owe him anything and that his generosity was just rent for keeping my mouth shut about the whole sheik in Iran debacle, he grudgingly agreed.

The Maids, as they were affectionately called within GSA, arrived about an hour later. They took the bodies away and cleaned the blood from the walls, floor, and ceiling. The way these guys cleaned, all the Luminol and black lights in the world wouldn't be able to bring up any trace that blood had been spilled there. Once they started in on the room I was immensely grateful I had called GSA. The Maids didn't ask any questions, they didn't throw any disparaging looks, they just did their job and left.

Bodies gone, and probably incinerated, I had time to focus on other things. Edna had switched from mild-mannered housekeeper to hostess extraordinaire the moment I went in search of Buck so the party had ended with none of the attendees knowing I had committed mass murder on the property. I find when you add bloody deaths to an event it just creates a negative atmosphere so that's something you want to hide from your guests. The waiters had bolted the second they saw me haul Buck away. But none of my guests noticed. Edna had rallied my staff, and they quickly took the place of the pretend waiters.

After the party had ended, Edna came to find me. I had locked myself in my room. I wanted to be alone with my misery. Unfortunately, she had a key to every room in the house and a need to invade my privacy. I could understand her concern. She had caught me with a gun ready to blow the back of my skull out the last time I had gotten all depressed. But really, sometimes a girl just needed to be alone. You'd think that one request would be respected when you consider I owned the house and I paid her salary, but no, she barreled through my door all pissed off.

"What the hell have you done?"

Well, that is quite the list isn't it? I tortured one man, killed three, disgusted six, and destroyed another.

"He's gone. You do realize he's gone."

Did she think I had turned into an idiot? I had been sitting alone in the dark like a misunderstood teenager so she couldn't really see me. She flipped on the light, and when she caught the look on my face, she softened. Had she really thought I didn't care?

She ran to me and wrapped me in a warm embrace. And I lost it. I bawled like a spoiled child who didn't get a pony for her birthday because that pony had been blown up by a forgotten land mine, splattering the cake with equine blood and guts. Until that night with Shooter, after the Jefferson Ball, I hadn't shed a tear in fifteen years. Ever since the day my grandfather died, I couldn't cry. Since Shooter walked out, I couldn't stop. I wanted to stay in my room for the rest of forever but Edna wouldn't hear of it. She made me get up and carry on with life. After all, I had to appoint a new CEO since I had killed the last one. I needed to make sure Samantha was okay and Amanda hadn't suffered permanent damage from being skull cocked.

So I went on about my business. I kept the house running, I attended to all the Boudreaux Oil business, and every evening I would wander down to the theater where I'd watch a chick flick and eat popcorn with extra butter. I was seriously turning into a girl. I actually had to send Gregory into New Orleans to buy a bunch of Meg Ryan and Julia Roberts DVDs. I didn't own a single one. But when I watched them, they didn't make anything better. They made me feel worse. But I deserved it. I'd earned all the sorrow, guilt, depression, poor movie choices, and calories.

That's basically how I spent the next two months. But it was pointless to reminisce and commiserate. I wasn't able to change the past. I had to get back to the present. I sat in my library waiting for my new CEO, Michael Hatfield. Michael had been on the board for fifteen years. He welcomed me at board meetings and company events. He had been kind, caring, compassionate, and held an MBA from the Harvard Business School. Unlike with Bonaventure, I actually looked forward to my visits with Mr. Hatfield. I really should have killed Bonaventure sooner.

Mr. Hatfield came into the library and greeted me with a warm hug. In the office it was always a handshake but at home it was a hug. "How have you been, Mrs. Boudreaux?"

I smiled. "Fine."

He sat in a sofa directly across from me with a serious look on his face. Great, what had happened? Who was dead? What countries had gone to war? What loss had we taken? "If you don't mind my saying, Mrs. Boudreaux, I don't believe you. You haven't been fine since Bonaventure went missing. I didn't think you were that fond of him. You always seemed to have a troubled relationship."

"I'm fine really. I'm worried about Bonaventure, but I really am happy you're in charge now." Yes, I just told a blatant lie and the absolute truth in one sentence.

"Kat"—he never called me Kat—"you're acting like you've lost someone very close to you. No one has died that I'm aware of, so it wasn't a fatal loss. You know what the only remedy to your melancholy is, don't you?" He paused, then stated, "Go get him back."

Had I really been that obvious? Did everyone know I'd been depressed over a guy? Of course they did. They weren't stupid. My staff knew Shooter had left, and after that I'd fallen into the pits of despair. At least I could count on them to be discreet.

The rest of my meeting with Hatfield went wonderfully. He had implemented new employee incentive programs that had turned out to be a big hit. He was the exact opposite of Bonaventure. He was a blessing. But once he left I didn't have anything left to do for the day, and the crushing weight of loneliness settled on me again. Just as I started to head down to the theater to immerse myself in *You've Got Mail*, Horndog wandered into the library. He plopped himself down into one of the soft couches and draped his arm around the back. He just sat there, piercing me with his eyes. We hadn't had any in-depth discussions, so this was all a bit odd.

"May I help you, Horndog?" I tried really hard to sound as if I were truly interested. Truth was, I couldn't give two shits.

"No, just here to talk. So, how are things?"

"Things are fine."

"And how are things with the new head honcho at Boudreaux Oil?"

"He'll do." That was all fine and dandy, but I really wanted him to get to the point. "Is there a reason you're here?"

He covered his heart with his hand as if he had been wounded by my words. "Can't a guy just come to talk to a pretty lady?"

No, no he can't. He was being weird so I stood up, fully intending to drown myself in a vat of melted butter.

"I talked to Shooter."

I stopped. I hated that his name had such an effect on me.

"We Skyped."

Horndog had actually seen a live image of Shooter! He suddenly had my full, undivided attention. I sat my sad, sorry butt back on the sofa and begged Horndog to continue. Not verbally of course, I wasn't that desperate. I begged with my eyes, perfectly dignified. But, he didn't say anything. He just sat there like a basset hound—all big eyed and innocent. He wanted me to ask. He was *actually* going to make me ask. Damn him to hell for all eternity and may he be strapped to a wheel where a carnivorous bird eats his liver over and over every day.

"And how is our Shooter?" Our Shooter. That was casual and didn't offer any insights into my soul. Right?

"Well, *our* Shooter, is doing great! Just great, you should see him. Yeah, he says everything in the world is just great."

Asshole.

"Really? He's great, huh?" I hated him from the very depths of my soul. I wasn't really sure if it was Shooter or Horndog I hated at that moment but I wasn't selfish. I could hate them both.

"Oh, really great."

Well, that's awesome, just awesome. I wasn't going to sit there while Horndog told me how great Shooter's life was without me, so I got up and walked across the library.

"He's lying, by the way," he said just as I hit the door. I stopped and turned. "Shooter and I have known each other since Parris Island, and I know he's lying his ass off. He's miserable. He's been miserable since he left."

I turned to him with my mouth hanging open and confusion written across my face. Yup, I had to look as if I'd just had a lobotomy.

"He loves you, Kat. I know he freaked out when all that shit went down the night of the party, but I think he just needed a chance to take everything in and process what happened."

"He made it very clear how he felt about what happened that night. He may love me, but he doesn't want me."

"If you believe that, you are an idiot. He wants to come back, has since the second that cab pulled through your gates. He just doesn't know how."

"He knows where I live and how to reach me." I turned to leave.

"And I know where he is and how to reach him." He let that tempting morsel dangle in the air.

I wanted to grab it and devour it like a hot Toll House cookie. But I couldn't. My pride made me walk through the library doors, through the house, and into the theater. I needed brownies to go with abandonment. The theater was modeled after an old 1920s movie palace. It had a ticket booth, concession stand, and over the top Italianate moldings. A batch of Lilly's famous brownies had been stashed behind the candy counter. I carried the treat and two large popcorn buckets into the theater. One of the buckets I filled with popcorn; the other I filled to the brim with rum and Coke. A regular cup just wouldn't cut it.

I sat through *You've Got Mail,* but I still had half a bucket of alcohol, so I needed another movie. I put in one I hadn't seen before. *An Affair to Remember* had been one of my mom's favorites, and I have vague memories of two people on a boat and a tragic accident but that's about it. I settled down to watch the romantic classic and dwell on how alone I was. Good grief, I *had* turned into a girl. The movie was perfect from the beginning. I loved Cary Grant and Deborah Kerr while they were on the boat. I rooted for them during their six months apart. I was heartbroken for them when Deborah was plowed into by that taxi. I got seriously pissed when they ran into each other at the ballet, and they both thought they were still with their original fiancés. And I felt all warm and fuzzy when he finally sucked it up and went to see her on Christmas Eve and found out she had been paralyzed. It was the most cathartic cinematic experience of my life.

I gazed through blurry eyes to the bottom of the empty bucket of liquor. Cary Grant was a real man. He found the woman he loved and went after her. Nothing could keep him from her. Not a fiancé, misunderstanding, or spinal cord injury. I needed to find Cary Grant. I wondered if he was still single. *Is he still alive?* That would show Shooter. I could show up somewhere like the ballet or something, and Shooter would be there with some trollop, and I'd be on the arm of Cary Grant. And Shooter would get insanely jealous, and I would laugh because I would be having a fabulous time. I'd flash my giant engagement ring, and I'd tell Shooter to give me his address so I could send him an invitation. Yes, that would be perfect. I really needed to Google Cary Grant.

I could just see it, "Cary and Kat are pleased to announce their betrothal and will be celebrating their upcoming nuptials at her home in Bayou Boudreaux, Louisiana. Please join them...." Cary and Kat? That didn't sound very romantic. Cary—what kind of people named their son Cary? Had they hoped for a girl? My vision of happiness disintegrated right before my eyes. I couldn't marry a man named Cary. It would be like marrying a girl. *He probably gets all moody and craves chocolate once a month. I'll bet he spends hours getting ready, and when his hair doesn't lay just right he probably throws the brush at the mirror and refuses to leave the bathroom.* Great, perfect. Cary Grant just turned into a sixteen-year-old hormonal cheerleader. Now who was I supposed to marry?

Why haven't I seen any movies where the girl chases after a guy? I'd seen them where the girl is portrayed as a stalker psycho with bad skin and hair who kills every girl that speaks to her boy in a jealous rage. But I've never seen one where the girl goes after a guy and keeps her dignity. Women can chase men. It wasn't the Renaissance. It was the twenty-first century! Women could run companies, lead countries, and bake damn good cakes. There was nothing off limits. I should be able to go after what I wanted and not worry about the consequences. I should be able to track Shooter down, tell him he was being ridiculous, and demand he listen to reason. Horndog did say he was miserable. That he missed me. And Horndog had known him since Parris Island, which meant they were closer than brothers. So, he would know if Shooter had lied or not. Of course I could have been totally wrong and all this could have just been wishful thinking. Horndog could have been teasing me or it could have been his lame attempt at getting me to check back into life. He wouldn't do that. At least, I didn't think he would. He had some morals. Even a completely heartless bastard wouldn't get my hopes up just to flush them down the toilet later. Horndog wouldn't do that.

What would I have to do to get Shooter? What did Cary Grant do? He found her address and went over to see her. Okay, if it worked for Cary and Deborah, it could work for me and Shooter. Horndog knew where he was. I could walk upstairs and ask him for Shooter's location. *That's what I'm going to do. As soon as the ground stops moving, I'm going to walk upstairs and get the info from Horndog. Whoa, a bucket of rum can really mess with a girl's equilibrium. Drunken stupor be damned! I'm going after Shooter!*

I stumbled up the stairs and had to stop several times to get my bearings, but I made it to his room. I didn't bother knocking. It was a very urgent matter which negated every need for social considerations.

"Horndog!" I slurred. "I need to have Shooter. I mean I need to have Shooter's address. You said you had him, I mean it, and I need it."

He bolted up out of his bed. Damn! It was 3:00 in the morning. *Urgent matter, no need for social considerations.*

"Hell Kat," he grumbled, "are you drunk?"

"Very, but I need to find Shooter."

"Why don't we talk about this when you're a bit less pickled?"

"No!" I shouted. "I need him now!"

"Okay, okay. Calm down." He paused as he went to flip the blankets off his body. "Do you mind turning around? I need to get a robe."

I did as he asked and waited for the all-clear sign.

"Okay, come over here. I don't have the address. He's at his cabin. I have latitude and longitude. It's outside Ely, Minnesota. There aren't any roads into it, so you'll have to rent a four-wheeler to get there. But that's where he is." He handed me a slip of paper. I grabbed it and ran for my room. Well, maybe run isn't the right word. Lurched. Yes, lurched is a better word.

I scrambled into my office and made a call to my pilot. He arranged to meet me at the airport. I threw some clothes into a suitcase. Somehow Edna had found out about my plan and appeared to help me.

Gregory arrived at my door the moment I had finished packing and drove me to New Orleans. He didn't complain about being woken up at the ass crack of dawn. He just smiled at me and said, "Go get him."

I tried to apologize to the pilot and crew, but they just said they got a call from Edna and they were thrilled to fly me to Minnesota. I lay down on one of the couches, feeling the after effects of my night of drunken debauchery. One of the attendants put a glass of something green and gloppy into my hand.

"It's an old family hangover remedy. It'll sober you up in no time."

Praise the gods. I drank the goop quickly. It tasted like a cross between chalk and rotten sewage. Just as the plane hurtled down the runway the "remedy" threatened to make an encore appearance. I jumped off the sofa and ran for the head. When I came out, the attendant waited with a smile on her face. "It worked!"

"I was supposed to erupt like Mt. St. Helens?"

"Yup. Now drink this." She handed me a glass of something red. I trusted her so I drank what seemed to be V8 cut with something bitter that I couldn't quite place. "Now go lie down or you'll fall asleep standing up."

"What was in that glass?"

"V8 and Valium." She turned and walked down the length of the cabin. She was right. I nearly fell down on the floor before I reached the couch.

I woke just as the landing gear hit tarmac. I had never been to Minneapolis, Minnesota. And as I looked out my window I suddenly understood why. I had landed in Middle America hell. There was nothing there for me, except Shooter. Then I caught a glimpse of a billboard that said, "Mall of America. The Largest Mall in the United States" Suddenly Minnesota looked very attractive.

As I gathered myself together, it came to my attention that I was quite alert. Wasn't I drunk as a skunk a few hours ago? Yes, I was. Ah, the remedy. It had actually worked. I felt great! I had planned to hire a car to take me to Ely, but now that I had control of my brain and fine motor skills, I decided to rent a car and drive. As long as it had GPS, of course. I told the pilot to stay on standby, and that I'd call him when I knew anything. I strolled up to the Hertz counter and rented an SUV. I saw a whole bunch of them parked outside the airport and you know what they say, when in Rome.... I plugged Ely, Minnesota, into the GPS and found that I had a four hour drive ahead of me. Four hours. Four freaking hours alone in a car in the middle of

Nowhere, USA. It was going to be fun.

Okay, I was wrong. I wasn't in Nowhere, USA. I was in the single most beautiful place in the States. The roads were lined with dark, thick pine trees and the air smelled as if it had just been made. It was so refreshing, so, so pretty. I could see why Shooter chose to escape there. It was the type of place that had no knowledge of real life. People spent their days chasing leprechauns and eating nuts and berries gathered for them by woodland creatures, probably.

I pulled into Ely and suddenly I was transported to another planet, a planet where the headline on the newspaper was about the giant fish caught by Mr. Outdoor in the local lake and the biggest scandal was when Jamie Lyn ran away with Bobby Joe to get married in Vegas. It was a planet I could live on.

I drove through town looking for a place to get a four-wheeler. At the end of Main Street was an outdoor store that had rentals. I rented a four-wheeler, trailer, gear, and bought a handheld GPS unit. I really should have brought mine. The one at home had been military grade and actually illegal for a civilian to own, but I was pretty sure the new one would get me to where I needed to go.

"So where are you headed?" The old man helping hitch the trailer to my SUV asked.

"I'm going to see a friend. He lives in a cabin north of town."

"Oh, what's his name? I might know him."

"Shoot...I mean Alexander Archer."

"Oh, you're going to the Archer cabin. Well you don't need this," he said as he gestured to the four-wheeler. "Archer put in a road about a month ago. It's off the main highway, but he paved the old dirt trail so you can drive right up to it."

There is a God in heaven, and he loves me! "Oh, um, well. I guess I don't need that then." I pointed to the trailer, and the man sighed and went to work unhooking it.

"If you want to come back inside with me, I'll get you a refund."

Go back inside? That might take more than five minutes,

and that's five minutes I could spend with Shooter. "Uh, don't worry about it. Keep it. I made you come out here and hook that up and now I don't need it. So consider it payment for services rendered." He tried to stop me as I climbed into the SUV, peeled out of the store's parking lot, and sped out of town.

I had to put the coordinates into my handheld GPS since the in dash unit wouldn't accept latitude and longitude. I only had a thirty-three minute drive to the cabin. As I got closer, I started to doubt myself. Would he be happy to see me? Would he run to me and kiss me passionately or would he turn his back and leave? Had he forgiven my actions or did he still hate me? Would he run me off his property with a shotgun? Attack me with a pitchfork and try to burn me at the stake?

Just as all these happy doubts settled around me in a comforting quilt made of porcupine quills, I pulled up to the side of Shooter's house. I killed the engine and sat in the seat. My feet had grown roots and entwined themselves around the drive shaft of the SUV. I couldn't move. I had snapped the necks of heads of state, but I couldn't summon the courage to open the damn door. Just as plans to plant a mailbox outside the driver's side door crossed through my mind, somehow my hand reached over and pulled the latch. My legs and feet swung out of the car and, to my surprise, they held my weight and moved me away from the SUV enough so that I could shut the door. I heard footsteps on the wooden stairs at the front of the cabin. Shooter appeared from around the side and when he saw me, he stopped and stared.

Chapter Twenty

Shooter didn't say, "Hello" or, "Get the hell out of here." He didn't run to me and kiss me passionately either. He just stood there, staring. In his defense I didn't say hi or go to him either. I knew why I didn't. Shooter had watched me torture a man. He knew what I was capable of. If he had any self-preservation instinct, he'd fear that I'd attack without warning. I was going to have to treat him like a bear caught in a trap. No swift movements, no unnecessary noise, and exuding an aura of calm.

The aura of calm was definitely not going to happen. Right then I might as well have been a white rat being dangled over a python in a cage. But as it turns out a bear in a trap has more courage than a white rat with lunch written on its forehead.

Shooter, without shifting his gaze, said, "Hi." A two–letter, one-syllable word never sounded so good.

I wanted my mouth to say something eloquent. Did it do as I requested? No, of course not. It said, "Hey." *Hey*! Hi would have been more elegant. "How are you doing," would have been more friendly. Antidisestablishmentarianism would have been better. Anything would have been better than, "hey"!

There was another long pause that seemed to stretch into the eternities.

He rubbed his forehead. "What are you doing here? Is one of the Bastards in trouble?"

He thought I had come on Bastard business. I allowed myself to be offended for a split second, then a plan started to form in my brain. If one of his soldiers was in some kind of trouble, he wouldn't hesitate to go with me. I could tell him Switch had developed a raging heroin habit and needed an intervention. Perfect! *I am a genius!*

But just as I was about to tell that whopper of a lie, I stopped. Sometimes a lie seemed easier than the truth, but it never ended well. I used to be able to mute that pesky little conscience of mine but somewhere along the way that button had stopped working. In truth, a lie could only hurt me. But it would make things so much easier. I compromised.

"I have a meeting with the owner of an oil field in Canada. He has a cabin around here. I was in the neighborhood so I thought I'd stop by." *Okay, yes, I lied! It was a harmless gray lie! Deal with it!*

Shooter's shoulders slumped and he turned, waving his hand. "Come on in."

I scurried after him, grateful he hadn't run me off with a pitchfork. As I rounded the Adirondack-style cabin, I saw how wonderful Shooter's life had become without me. The cabin had been built from rusty red wood with dark green trim. The covered porch stretched across the entire front of the house and had been filled with comfy wooden chairs draped with homemade quilts. He opened the screen door and led me into an open room. The living room, kitchen, and dining room were all in the same area. It was small but cozy. Two wood frame chairs with deep green leather cushions and a matching couch were arranged around a river rock fireplace. A square card table and two metal folding chairs created the dining set. An old desk with a new computer had been shoved under a window on the opposite side of the cabin.

"It's not much...." Shooter began.

"It's perfect," I interrupted.

He sat down on the couch and motioned to the chair next to him. I sat, and the most awkward moment of my life passed. Shooter just stared at me. Why did he have to be the strong, silent type? He didn't give me anything to work with.

"Sam's doing good." I needed something safe to talk about. "She starts first grade in a few weeks. She had a birthday. I got her a Ferris wheel. She's wanted one since you took her for a ride at the carnival."

"You know, most girls get a Barbie when they turn six."

"Doc got her one. Speaking of Doc, I think he has a girlfriend." Shooter raised his eyebrows. "Yeah, he'll just disappear for a few hours, and some nights he doesn't come home. I think I know who it is, but I haven't asked him or her about it yet."

"Who?" It was almost as if we were two friends gossiping.

"Yvette. She drops by all the time with some excuse then asks about Doc. And last week she walked out the front door, but her car stayed in the same parking space all night long."

"You haven't been using your secret tunnels to spy on them?"

I gave him a mock horrified look. "Of course not. The part of the wall in his room that would allow me to spy on him is a little too obvious. He'd catch me. Switch went through his computer and found some very interesting stuff."

"Switch went through Doc's computer?" He had a slightly protective tone in his voice.

"He installed some new security for him and stumbled upon it. Apparently, Doc is going to buy the house Yvette has been renting." We sat in silence for a while. "Horndog has a crush on Sissy. But, I've given him a strict hands-off order. I don't want Sissy to be just another mark on his bed post."

The corners of Shooter's mouth twitched. "You don't need to worry about Sissy's honor. Horndog won't take advantage of her."

"His name is Horndog! And he flirts with everything. Trust me, the way he looks at her, he wants nothing more than to get her naked."

"That may be, but Horndog is a very strict Catholic. He may flirt, and he may talk a big game but he'd never.... Well let's just say he's taken a vow of sorts."

"To, like, God?"

"No, to someone with much more power than God."

That I could not believe. How the hell could Horndog not be a horndog?

"Switch is my official unofficial head of security. He doesn't really get along with Jake, but they've come up with some really good ideas. I'm going to assign a bodyguard to Sam for school. She's young enough that she'll think it's great. I know she'll hate it when she's older. But I can't risk losing her."

"Make sure it's someone you can trust. Bodyguards have been bribed in the past."

"Switch volunteered for the job."

"Switch?" He was sincerely shocked.

"Yeah, he's really changed over the past couple of months. He's nice...to Sam."

"Switch, nice? That's something I'd have to see for myself."

Please, please come and see.

"Tyler and Martinez are in Afghanistan. Apparently their new gunnery sergeant is a pain in the ass, but they're managing. We Skype. Martinez has grown a beard." Shooter cocked an eyebrow at me. "Yup, a full beard. He says it's so he can blend in, but I don't know how he could blend in anywhere. He's built like a freaking rhinoceros." I waited for him to say something. Anything. What had he been up to? Had he spent his days fishing and splitting wood for the winter? Did he sit on the porch at night watching the fire flies? Did he ever think about me?

"I've been doing some renovations on the house," I blurted out trying to fill the dead air. Home improvements were a safe topic among friends, right?

"Really?" His brow was furrowed, and I could tell he had no idea where the conversation was going. The truth was, neither did I.

"Yeah, I filled in that room in my basement with cement. The one where I...well you know what happened there." I twisted my hands in my lap. *This sucked!* "And I sealed off the room where I, uh, took care of those men. And I melted down the tools I used to keep in the basement room. I've been thinking of emptying the armory. Most people don't have an arsenal in their house."

He smiled. I thought I'd never see him smile again. "No, keep that."

I had run out of people and places to discuss. He wasn't offering any suggestions for conversation, and I couldn't think of anything else to talk about. Telling him he took my heart when he left and that I'd really like it back seemed a bit...desperate. I sat on the chair waiting for him to speak. He just stared at his hands.

Come on, Shooter, throw me a bone! You could kiss me, slap me, yell at me, anything. Just give me a reaction I can read! The man would make a great spy. If he didn't want you to know what he was thinking, you didn't. After several minutes of uncomfortable silence I stood. "Well, I guess I better go. I don't want to be late."

Yes, I chickened out! I'd like to see you tell a man like that that you love him and can't live without him.

He stood and followed me to the door and waited on the porch while I walked down the steps. Just as I was about to turn to the side of the cabin to get into my SUV, I turned back. Without any thought, I said, "Shooter, I'll never apologize for what I did to Buck or the other two. I had to save Samantha. As long as they survived, she would never be safe. I had to do what I did. I am sorry for the way it affected you. If I could go back in time, I wouldn't have involved any of you. And not just to keep you from leaving. You have a pure soul, and I am ashamed that I was the one to scar it." I turned, climbed in the rental, and left.

Feeling like a coward, I drove down the road lined with deep green pine trees. The night before, when I had been buoyed up by liquid courage, I thought getting him back would be easy. That I'd have the stones to tell Shooter I couldn't live without him. I wanted to be Cary Grant, and I wanted him to be Deborah Kerr. We should have looked at each other and just known. But guess what? Hollywood lies! The good guy didn't always win, the weird, artsy girl in high school didn't turn into a super model at prom, and no matter how much I may wish for it, I would never be able read someone else's mind. *Dammit!*

I screwed everything up. For one thing, instead of saying "hey," I should have said, "I love you. Can I have your babies?" But why would he want to have kids with me? I was a horrible breeding partner. I was mentally unstable and emotionally retarded. If I lived in the animal kingdom, I would be killed for the benefit of the species. The only reason Samantha was so great was because God took pity on her and gifted her with her father's qualities. In that moment I hated Stephan. He died and forced me into that situation. I never wanted to have to look for a man again! I thought I'd found the person I would bicker with and let myself go for. But did that happen? No, of course not. He'd forced me to—I can't believe I was going to think this—date!

I took a deep breath and cleared my mind. Enough ranting. Ranting wouldn't get Shooter back. At that point I didn't think I could do anything to get him back. I fouled up that meeting so much he'd probably duck behind the broccoli if we were ever in the same grocery store. I needed caffeine and sugar, STAT! I pulled into town and parked in front of a coffee shop. I strolled in with two things in mind. Coffee and apple pie.

I sat at a booth. A cute, perky, little waitress came to take my order. She was nauseating. I bet if I licked her, she'd have tasted like one of those really big lollipops. I ordered and dropped my head onto the table. Exhaustion had caught up with me.

"You from out of town?"

Holy crap, I'd fallen asleep. Miss Saccharine stood over me with my pie and coffee. "Yeah."

"Where are you from?"

No one ever knew where Bayou Boudreaux was so I said, "New Orleans."

"Ooh, I've always wanted to go there! Is it true there's a huge underground vampire community?"

"Let me guess, you've read Anne Rice?" Don't get me wrong, I loved Anne Rice, but her novels and the fact that she wrote them in New Orleans meant that every blood drinker and donor wanted to take up residence in a cemetery in New Orleans.

The waitress actually sat down on the bench across from me. I didn't remember inviting her to join me.

"I love her! Do you know her?"

Yeah, of course I do because every resident of New Orleans is intimately aware of all one point two million of their neighbors. I shook my head.

"Oh, I would just love to visit New Orleans. So what brings you up here?" She bounced on her seat.

"A friend."

"Who is it? Maybe I know her."

Seriously my answers were not meant to encourage conversation. "Alexander Archer."

"Oh, you mean Shooter."

She had my attention.

"I was just up to the cabin yesterday. We dated in high school and stayed friends."

I had to tell my hand not to jam my fork into her eyeball. So that was how Shooter had spent his time, doing waitresses. Fan-freaking-tastic!

"How did you meet Shooter?"

"I saved his life." *Beat that, you syrupy candy coated piece of trash.*

"Whoa, were you in the military?"

"Not really. I was a private contractor," I said nonchalantly.

"What does a private contractor do?"

"I kill people." Shooter had said it at the ball. I could say it at the coffee shop.

"Oh, well it was nice to meet you." She stood up and walked away.

That's right, honey, sugar dissolves in vinegar. Keep walking.

I finished my refreshment and left. I left the sticky-sweet waitress an enormous tip. Killing people was lucrative after all. I wish I could have coated the bills in sarin gas that would make her cough up her own lungs, but I had a plane full of people waiting for me. I stopped at a full service gas station. I found out the attendant also knew Shooter. Apparently they'd spent three nights a week watching baseball games and drinking beer. I really wanted to be a gas station attendant in Ely, Minnesota, right then. Or maybe being Shooter's beer would be a good gig. Yes, I could be Shooter's beer. He could wrap his lips around me and take a long, slow swallow. Stop, stop, *stop*! Thoughts like that lead to a very dangerous place.

I drove to the airport feeling so lonely I seriously considered jerking the wheel into oncoming traffic. But that would just piss Edna off, and I was almost positive she had the power to track me down in Hell and wring my neck. *Great I'm going to have to walk into my house all alone.* The entire estate would have learned of my little trip north, and they would all be anxiously awaiting my return. I was going to have to walk in alone. I could just picture it, me looking like a teenager that just lost prom queen to her arch nemesis, Edna completely disappointed in me, and the rest of the Bastards and staff avoiding me, thinking it was better to feign ignorance than risk incurring my wrath. But first I had to climb onto the airplane alone. Would the pilot say anything or would he just fly the plane? Would the attendant have a broken heart remedy? One that made my heart stop beating so it could be rebooted with a pair of defibrillation paddles?

I pulled into the airport and returned the rental. Even the lady at Hertz looked at me as of she knew I'd completely failed in my mission. I stepped into the restroom. Nope, *dumped* had not been tattooed on my forehead. Maybe I just sent off psychic messages of rejection. I trudged through the airport. Women whispered behind their hands, businessmen scowled, and babies cried when I walked past. The poster for pathetic loser had my face on it.

I dragged my poor, pathetic self across the tarmac for private planes. I saw a mirage of Shooter waiting near the stairs to my jet. But mirages weren't supposed to move, they just shimmered, I thought. Okay it was not a mirage, it was a full on hallucination. Whatever, I'll go with it. The Shooter hallucination stopped in front of me. I didn't. You could walk through a hallucination. So you can imagine my surprise when I slammed right into his very solid chest.

"Whoa, Kat. Are you okay?" He grabbed my elbows to steady me. The hallucination felt and sounded just like the real Shooter. I lifted a very tentative hand and molested his face. I smoothed my palm over his cheek, the stubble of his beard scratchy. It was a very good hallucination. I cranked down on his nose with my thumb and forefinger.

"Ow! What the...."

"You're...you!" That was almost as eloquent as *hey*.

"Who else would I be?"

"No one. I just didn't expect to see you." Graced over that perfectly. He had no idea I'd gone completely nuts.

"I didn't expect to see you this morning, either. But there you were at my house, and I couldn't say what I wanted to say."

Wait, that was my line.

"I wanted to grab you and...." He stopped.

He wanted to grab me and what?! Kiss me, throw me out on my ass, what? A little information please!

He released my arms and looked at his feet. "I should never have left. I understand why you did what you did. I don't like that you had to do it. I should have done it for you."

Didn't expect that.

"Neither of us are pure souls. We've both just seen and done too damn much. But, you are the only one I can ever trust with my...." He placed his hand over his heart. "As stupid as it sounds, you're the only one I can trust with my heart."

I should say something, anything, but apparently I had lost the ability to speak. I'd have even settled for the ever so articulate *hey*.

"You once asked me what the price for knowing my name would be."

Yes, I remember. How could I forget the most amazing night of my life?

"Do you remember my answer?"

Yeah, like I could recall a detail like that right now.

"It's you. I want you."

He leaned down and pressed our foreheads together. Like a complete idiot in one of those stupid chick flicks I'd watched, I started to cry. Why the hell would I cry? I wasn't hurt. I wasn't sad. No reason to cry. But I was. I nodded and whispered, "I love you. I love you, Alexander Archer."

Tears rolled down my face. Shooter's shoulders collapsed with what I hoped was relief. "I've wanted to hear you say that for a long time, kitten."

I can't tell you why I hadn't said it sooner. Dr. Phil would probably say it's because of my fear of rejection, and because I'd built a barrier around my feelings or some equally ridiculous bullshit. What did he know?

Shooter cupped my jaw in his hands. He hesitated as if he wasn't sure I wanted him to kiss me. Screw that! I grabbed the back of his head and kissed him passionately, thoroughly, and deeply.

Epilogue

I sat at my desk in the library looking over a document I had just received over a secure fax line. When Shooter and I returned to Bayou Boudreaux, my staff and Bastards had the good sense to act as if he'd never left. We'd fallen into an easy routine and with no one wanting someone I loved dead, life had become as close to perfect as I could ever have hoped for, which is exactly why I couldn't leave well enough alone.

Shooter bent down and kissed the side of my neck. I hadn't heard him come in. I didn't mind surprises like that.

"What'cha workin' on?" He rubbed my shoulders, and I relaxed into him.

"An idea."

"And what is this brilliant idea?"

I turned to face him, took a deep breath, and stood up. I couldn't put my plan into action without his support. Scared? Hell yes, I was scared! I led him to the couch, grabbing a file off the desk as we passed.

We sat, and I said, "I've been thinking—I know, a scary concept but stay with me. I can't be the only person in my position."

"You are the only person I've met who once had been a ruthless assassin and now runs an international oil conglomerate." Shooter smiled trying to lighten the mood. It helped.

"I meant, I can't be the only person who couldn't count on the police or the government. There has to be a lot of people out there who, for one reason or another, are on their own and basically guaranteed a death sentence. If you hadn't been there, I would have died, Sam would have died." He smiled at my admission. "I want to form a company to help these people." I pulled a piece of paper from the file. The paper had an embossed dark blue drawn bow and arrow and the words "Archer International" underneath it. Shooter took the paper from me and stared at the logo.

"I've put out feelers to the different governments I have good relationships with and have received encouraging responses."

Shooter dropped the paper and kissed me passionately. All thought escaped me. Oh, what the hell. I fell into him, giving him the signal that he could take things as far as he wanted, and I would be okay with that. Much to my extreme displeasure, he broke away from me. *Dammit.*

"You are amazing. You know that, right?"

I was amazing when you were kissing me. I pulled my mind out of Shooter's pants and continued, "I've studied failed operations involving pirates, human smugglers, drug cartels, you know, organizations with less than a five-star rating from the Better Business Bureau. All these missions had the same failure points. They waited too long to attack because of government red tape. They had to follow laws that tell them they can't kill the people who need to be killed. I want to form a company who will go into a situation and do what needs to be done to save someone's life." I took a deep breath. I was just getting to the hard part. "I want the Rat Bastards to be a team." I waited for him to say, *Hell to the no.*

Shooter locked his gaze on mine. "And you would run the company?"

"Yeah, well, I called it Archer International because I want you to be my partner."

"We'd have equal say?" he said hesitantly.

I nodded.

"And we would send teams off around the world and manage them from here."

I nodded.

"All right, since you will be kept safely here, I will allow the Bastards to work for us."

"Wait, wait, I didn't say I'd stay here." Where the hell had he gotten that idea?

"Yes, you did. And that's my stipulation. You can run the entire operation. I'm willing to be a not silent, but quiet partner if you promise never to put yourself in harm's way."

I sat up straight, "Shooter, I can't guarantee I won't be involved in missions. I have skills that are very hard to come by. I may be needed." I would just like to point out how adult I was being by discussing it with him. I could have kicked him in the gut and told him to go to hell, but I didn't.

"I'm sure you know people you can trust with your same skill set. Call them, recruit them. In fact, I'm willing to bet you're not the only person GSA screwed over. You could defend a small nation with the people they've pissed off." He rubbed my arm trying to keep me from flying off the handle.

He had a point, and I started to think of people I'd worked with who had been treated poorly by GSA. Some of them had quit, some of them had escaped into a bottle, and some of them still worked for GSA and would have to be head hunted. But could I really follow his hands-off policy? As I looked into his eyes, I knew I could. I loved him so much I'd do anything for him, including not killing for him. The old me would have told him flat out that I wouldn't stay out of the soup of combat, or I would have told him I wouldn't get involved but have every intention of not keeping that promise. I was amazed at my personal growth.

"Okay, I promise to stay out of the actual fight unless the person we're trying to rescue has a personal connection to me."

"I can deal with that as long as 'a personal connection' doesn't include your high school friend's cousin's half-sister's husband's uncle's sister-in-law's niece. You have to be able to link them to you personally in three people or less."

Damn, he knew me too well. I grudgingly agreed.

"Will our clients be limited to those with the ability to pay for their rescue?" Shooter asked.

"Of course not." *What kind of person does he think I am?* "We will help everyone."

"And how will we make money? You can't be expected to foot the bill for every mission."

"That's the best part. In exchange for our support and out of gratitude for eliminating a national threat, the countries we conduct operations in or for will give us ten percent of the total assets of the group or people we eliminate. I've already entered into negotiations with twenty-three countries."

"So we'll only save people in countries who are willing to pay us." He pulled away from me.

"On paper, yes. In reality, no. No one will be left to rot in a hole somewhere because a country isn't willing to play our game. Those missions will have to be kept very, very quiet, and I will only trust Bastards with those operations."

"You've thought of everything haven't you?"

I smiled. "Now, we need to talk about employee loyalty."

"Employee loyalty?"

"Our organization has to be kept completely secret. I won't have the innocent people I love harmed because of the actions of my company. If an employee betrays AI, they will be terminated."

"Wow, I'm impressed. You're just going to fire someone for treachery." Shooter could be so innocent sometimes.

I placed my hand on his cheek. "No, I meant terminate the way the Marine Corps means terminate."

"You are going to kill people who don't follow your employee handbook." He stood up and started pacing.

"I can't have them putting my other employees at risk and

divulging what we do to the international press. What we do has to be kept quiet."

"What constitutes betrayal? Do they have to actually double cross you or is dropping your name in a bar considered treason?"

Shooter was getting pissed. I could understand why. He took issue with killing people. I loved him for it. "Treason will have to involve aiding and abetting the enemy, killing a fellow team member, or the deliberate death of a protectee either by their own hand or because they refused to act. I won't sentence someone to death because they hurt me. They have to bring harm to my people."

I could tell Shooter liked my terms, but he still couldn't get behind my method for dealing with them. "Who would you send to terminate them? Would you kill them yourself?"

"I could, but I won't," Shooter relaxed a bit more. "I'd send someone they don't know and someone who has nothing to do with AI other than cleaning up after bad operatives."

"And you know someone who would kill because you asked them to? You know someone you can trust to do it right?" He paused to read my face. "Of course you do."

Shooter had not rejoined me on the couch. I stood up and pulled his face into my hands. "I know you think my methods are extreme, and I hope to never have to employ them. You see a death, anyone's death, as something to mourn. That's why I love you and I need you as a partner. I need you to be my conscience. I need you to temper my passion with caution. I won't do this without you."

He relaxed in my hands. "They have to know the consequences the moment they're recruited. I can't believe I'm agreeing to this. And they have to be given the benefit of the doubt, the allegations have to be investigated by both you and me, and the sentence has to be agreed on by both you and me. Can you live with that?"

"Yes, I can accept those terms." I pulled another paper from the file on the couch. "I have received a request from the

Greeks. A young woman attempting to circumnavigate the globe alone in a sailboat has gone missing. They suspect Somali pirates. After looking over the data, I had to agree. I have assets in Africa who have located her." I handed him a stack of reconnaissance photos. "You wanna go get her?" I smiled, knowing he couldn't refuse.

He kissed me. "I'll round up the Bastards."

I watched as the man I was deliriously in love with left the library to gather our brothers. I had no idea what our future would hold. I could dream and imagine, but I didn't want to. I wanted to live in the right now and worry about the future tomorrow. Right now he was making plans to save a defenseless young woman from a fate worse than death. How sexy was that? I pictured him riding in to save the damsel in distress on a white horse. I knew he'd succeed. He'd already done it once. He'd saved me.

Saddle up.

~ABOUT THE AUTHOR~

Katie Harper started writing when two people showed up in her head and wouldn't leave until she told their story. They had a party, invited a few friends over. Now she spends her days doing the bidding of imaginary people. She lives in a city made for sin on the edge of a desert with her daughter, no pets and enough lemon bundt cake to feed a refugee camp.

www.ingramcontent.com/pod-product-compliance
Lightning Source LLC
Chambersburg PA
CBHW071306170626
46809CB00001B/346

* 9 7 8 1 6 1 3 3 3 4 0 9 6 *